MR DERFY BURGER

and the
Law of Common Convergence

KENNETH LOEBER

PublishAmerica
Baltimore

PublishAmerica has allowed this work to remain exactly as the author intended, verbatim, without editorial input.

Hardcover 978-1-4512-5720-5
Softcover 978-1-4512-5721-2
PUBLISHED BY PUBLISHAMERICA, LLLP
www.publishamerica.com
Baltimore

Printed in the United States of America

DEDICATION
(in Serbian)

Mojoj Srpkinji,
da uvek trchi za svojom crvenom loptom pored reke.
(I hope you always chase your ball by the river.)

PRETEXT

It is with unbridled relish, little trepidation, and certainly a naughty if not profligate artistic license that I, William Francis Worster, have recorded the life of one, Eliason Aloicius Nye, for public consumption (and hopefully merriment!), entrusted by the aforementioned to represent the aforementioned as related by the aforementioned to the about-to-be-again mentioned, William Francis Worster. Let it be noted that anecdotes were related vocally, solely, and freely by Mr. Nye to Mr. Worster, over the course of…a pretty long time, whereas and henceforward any/all misrepresentations, perceptions of slander, and/or simple outright lies should be attributed solely to the former. Moreover, due to the author's physical absence in many scenes, prefabrications occur for which the author apologizes to the sensitive reader, but not to the spirit of Mr. Nye. On this I, myself, solemnly swear.

With sincerities,

W. F. Worster, Esq.
13 August 2001

(Mr. Loberg, does this sound official/lawyerly enough as per your request? Oh, and can we try to keep this copy from getting "into the paws" of Mr. Nye, at least until I have done some touch-up work?)

{Willy, I'm your proof-reader, not your lawyer. Please tell me that you wrote like a normal person or I'm not reading this. Oh, I'm afraid

this very copy might have accidentally found its way to Mr. Nye. Sorry...—K. Loberg}

PROLOGUE

"Spain and How Julia Was Kind of Right, 2001...."

"You know baby, the day you finally admitted to yourself that you were in love with me was the day you started losing something that a man should never lose when he falls in love with a woman."

"I can't guess."

"Your fun, kind of. And your irony. But they're coming back slowly."

"I don't know what you mean."

"Of course you don't, so just say 'Julia, you're right.' Go on, repeat after me, 'Julia, you're right.' Say I'm right."

"Okay, you're right."

"You didn't say my name with it."

"You want me to say your name with it?"

"Of course."

"Okay, you were right, Julia."

"That's no good, you didn't sound like you meant it. I think my name has to come at the front. It's more believable I think."

"Like, 'Julia, you were right?'"

"Not I *was* right, I *am* right."

"Good god, okay, you are right. Julia, you are right."

"That's what I thought."

"You *were* right, too, I guess."

"Yep. I changed my mind. Let's get back on the train. Can you grab Veronica?"

"But I just bought these beers." She told me to give them to the couple sitting at the table in the shade. My shins were sweating as we stepped back onto the train to Madrid.

"Julia, can you tell me what you were right about again?"

****

CHAPTER ONE

"The Progression of Decay...or a Dead, Dishrag Cat Kind of Day, 6:43 a.m."

It had been the kind of late October Saturday that you felt, when it was over, the haze of your mind would be lifted. The wind had been blowing non-stop for a week, like it knew something we did not, that it was desperate to blow today into tomorrow, certainly this week into next. A thousand feet down the mountain, northward outside of town, the trees still had their autumn leaves, burning in yellow and gold and red and orange, but after the first whispers of the windstorm, the stronger gusts had stripped all the aspens on the main avenue in town to their bare branches, and the leaves had scrambled along in the dark until a single early morning ice storm had plastered patches of them to the sidewalk. The sun came out at dawn for half an hour, sat atop the mountains on the east edge of town, melted the slush and ironed the leaves to the pavement. The next day the wind kicked up again, swirling the leaves down the streets with the sound of chattering teeth, across the ball fields, through the cemetery, against fences, even up in the air across rooftops and in the cuplike, bouncing hoods of the coats of children as they walked home from school. But on the pavement were stamped the hazy brown impressions of the liberated leaves, the ropey skeletal skeins of some still visible on the sidewalks like the veins on the back of an old lady's hands, hundreds of almost perfect fingerprints of autumn. Then the air would freeze at night and sparkle in the orange streetlights, the floating ice crystals refracting the light and the beams of car headlamps straight up heavenward, and during the day the sky would be deep and purple-blue and clean enough to do it over and over and over again.

"And in November we'll talk not of what we've done or shall do, but whether the snow will ever stop," Julia said, like poetry. "Doesn't July already seem forever ago?"

But that was last Saturday, October 23rd, five days before Julia left me, a week before I found her again. Already it seemed a million years ago.

Saturday the thirtieth of October, 1999, began with a knock on my door. Actually, the day began as do most days, with morning, and *then* a knock on my door. It came from the knuckle of Dave, an alcoholic of the highest order from down the hall. I wish he had a cool name, Wolfgang or Cliff, or that he looked like a movie star, but he didn't— he was just Dave from four doors down. It was 6:46 in the a.m. and I had been awake for only three minutes. I could feel the cold air from the threshold swirling against the tips of my toes and it felt almost liquid, or like something that grows in water, like sea grass rubbing on a fish's belly. I stood and waited. Knock. I stood and waited. kkknock…knock but quietly. I could hear him breathing I thought. kknnock? I rested my whole hand on the knob and slowly tightened my fingers, turning clockwise, half a turn, quietly, holding the knob steady until it stopped, concentrating, my elbow locked and palm facing upward and held like a good guy with a knife in a movie, an American soldier gritting his teeth and feeling almost sorry, poking steel into a bad guy, a Nazi or a redcoat. If I had known then what I would know in twenty-fours hours I never would have opened the door…probably.

"Oh hey Eliason," Dave said, his hair all stuck up. His knock had been gentle and he was practically whispering, like he did not want to wake me. "You sure are quick to come to the door, guy."

I nodded and yawned.

"So what's up, what's going on?" he asked. I wanted to remind him that *he* had knocked on *my* door, but I did not have the strength.

"I'm about to go into work," I told him. He did the crazy caterpillar dance with his eyebrows. "Willy and I are having a meeting with some buyers from Chile," I lied.

"That fascist—on a Saturday?" he said with disingenuous disbelief. I nodded. Someplace or something on his body, a collection of opened sores possibly, smelled like the pungent, gooey residue of three-week old tomato soup at the bottom of an oxidized tin can. "And I bet he's sleeping in," he added.

I shrugged. "Maybe."

"Corporate America, man," he told me.

I stared at him blankly in answer. Willy ran a tiny snowshoe shop in town. I worked for him. Sometimes our town's one homeless guy, Lee, would shovel snow from the walk for a couple of dollars. It was a three-man corporate sweatshop.

"Hey that's nice," he said, tugging on the front of a cherry-red sweater that I had pulled from the floor of my closet. It was a lie of course, a drunk guy's lie, a reflex form of flattery that drunk guys are always saying to others and to themselves, mainly to justify being in a bar at six in the morning watching the sun come up. The sweater patently did not look good on me. It looked good on Willy because he was a bit more filled out, healthier, than I. Willy was fifteen years older than me but he didn't look it, he wore his years well, or that is what various cosmopolitan women told him. Somehow his sweater ended up on my body after a drunken bender at the local brewpub ("local" being thirty miles away). It did nothing for my complexion but it really brought out Willy's eyes.

"Hey guy, does it ever sound like someone is frying bacon in your ear?" I shook my head in answer. Dave looked crushed. He tugged on his earlobe, hung his mouth open and rotated his bottom teeth 360 degrees several times.

Actually, I could picture him twenty years ago, his hairless little chicken legs sticking out from a terry-cloth robe, lounging at the side of a swimming pool somewhere in California, pulling lots of women named Tammy, Jenny and Carol. He had that kind of look, still, even in his fifties despite the red, blotchy cheeks and pocked nose that

11

appeared to have been pecked hourly by a hungry yard bird. He yawned and exhaled thickly right into my face, his breath heavy with the odor of yogurt, of a perpetually fermenting liver.

"Can I have my key now?" he asked.

I turned into my kitchen, only three paces away and grabbed his spare key from my counter. He locked himself out of his apartment at least twice a week so I had put myself in charge of his extra key.

"Go unlock your door and bring the key right back, okay?" I said. I dropped it into his hand but it slid from his palm onto the carpet without him noticing.

"You're a good kid. One of the few from your generation," he informed me, doing the drunk guy wobbly lean-in, as if he were telling me something conspiratorial. I bent down and picked the key up for him because he obviously had no clue.

"Any news on your car?" he asked. I told him "nothing." He shook his head and looked insulted and said, "I just don't know who would do such a thing." He even "tsk"ed three times. I put his key back in his hand, and he looked at me in such grand surprise, as if I had performed the craziest magic trick ever. He even looked at the palm of the other hand, turning it over, staring at his knuckles and wiggling his fingers then, satisfied, gazed with a sway at the key in his other hand. He thanked me with a "That's great."

"Bring it right back," I told him, "and don't get lost on the way." He shuffled about halfway down the hall then turned uncertainly.

"Hey guy (he could never remember my name), some nurse lady from Boulder called last night. What's today? Maybe it was Thursday. Your mom is really, really bad. You're going to go down there, aren't you?"

"Just go let yourself in and bring the key right back."

"Yeah, yeah," he said turning and throwing his hand in the air. I realized for the first time that he had no butt whatsoever, his pants just hung like a wet diaper.

Our apartment building had been a kind of old-age home though anyone could live in it now, especially really poor people, and every room was equipped with panic buttons wired directly to the fire department instead of telephones. The fire department never knew if a pressed button was a *real* emergency from an old loon or just a kid pulling a prank. Just last week they had to fish out of the toilet the dentures of another of my neighbors, Jimbo. I usually did it for him but he had panicked this time and pushed the button so many times it shorted out and threw the breaker for the whole complex and pulled us into early darkness, which took the building maintenance man six hours to figure out, and ruined my microwave dinner. One sad rotary phone wired to the outside world sat lonely downstairs in the TV room, and whether you received your message depended on which fruitcake answered. Dave? Hit or miss. Jimbo? Obsessive-compulsive: one day I came home and there were at least twenty notes taped to my door saying that Willy had called, and it had been only an hour earlier. Old Lady Baltusis? Alzheimer's. Me? I would not answer the thing even if each unanswered ring was a curse of eternal thirst. My mother had stomach cancer and she was dying with every passing minute a hundred and five miles away in Boulder. That was what the call was about.

Dave returned without a shirt on, his chest hair gray on the tips and bushy. Miraculously he had remembered his key. He whisked right by me and put it in its usual resting place.

"Hey that's nice, guy" he lied again, motioning with his ear to my "living room" six steps away. I had put on some classical music right when I woke up in order to ease the early morning buzz of bacon frying in my ear. "You're a real classy guy, real classy," Dave said, but I could not tell if he was making fun. "Going down to the big city I hear, Boulder-town, for some culture. Not enough here in the mountains for the big shot. I bet you wish you could take some of us mountain folk with you." I swear to god I could not tell if the drunk bastard was having a go at me or not.

"Dave, what did the nurse say?" I asked. He looked mildly confused.

"Uh, cirrhosis maybe, with a mild case of delirium tremblings she said."

"No, about my mother. What did she say about my mother?"

"Oh," he said, clacking his tongue on the roof of his mouth and looking offended. He rubbed his chin with his palm. "She said your ma is really bad."

"How bad, Dave?"

"Really bad, guy. Really, really, really bad."

"So she's pretty bad then?" He nodded and tried to look sad. I said "humph."

"If my memory serves me correct," and he exhaled heavy yogurt all over me again, "she kind of doubts that your ma will make it through the weekend. That's what she said, but she told me to put it more delicate-like if I talked to you."

"Oh," I said, surprised by my own surprise, concerned by the concern in my voice. My head buzzed and I noticed for the first time that whomever had hung the wallpaper directly across from my door had not matched up the flower pattern: there was a green leaf sticking right out of the side of a rose and the other half of the rose was floating in a field of white, the stem and petals severed right down the middle. The door of the fire extinguisher case where I sometimes put Dave's key if I was going out of town was bent. The carpet had three cigarette burns that I swear had not been there the day before.

"Hey guy, are you okay?" I heard Dave ask from somewhere.

"Yeah, yeah," I told him and retrieved his key, brushed past him and put it underneath the fire extinguisher, delicately lifting the bent metal on the corner of the door where the red paint had chipped away and then pushing on the glass.

"Do you need to borrow my wheels?" he asked.

"No, I'll get a ride from Willy or somebody," I answered. "Don't forget your key is in here." I felt his hand like an iron anvil on my shoulder.

"It was pretty late when she called, and you weren't here anyways, otherwise I would have told you. Then I sort of got stuck at the gin mill until now, doing what-not, some errands and what-not. And it snowed this morning."

"It's alright, Dave. Don't forget your key," I said, stepping behind my door and pushing it shut quietly. I rested my forehead against it and inhaled shakily like a guy in a movie would do.

"Hey, okay, I'm going down to my place, going to have a little something to eat, take a nap, probably turn on the TV," I heard Dave saying from the other side. "Be careful driving down there. Lots of people dressed up in costumes, ghosts and witches and what-not, and goddamn drunks all over the road." His voice was getting fainter but then I could tell he stopped at his door and turned to face mine: "Wear that sweater, guy. Classy fellows like you always look good in sweaters," then his door opened and slammed.

I went into the bedroom and changed.

The wind was tunneling right past the mountains from the west and lashing me squarely in the back, funneling down the nape of my coat until I hunched up the collar. It was colder than a dog's butt walking backwards in an ice storm. Well, it's not the dog's butt walking backwards but the dog walking backwards, butt first—it was colder than the butt of a butt-first backwards-walking dog in an ice storm. You know what I mean. I was carefully stepping inside someone else's tracks in the thin snow, the first of the season, wondering who other than I could have been up at such an ungodly hour in this godless place. The sky had flipped over gray like the belly of a shark although only the day before it had been the clearest indigo of the cleanest ocean. The footsteps continued onward, past the elementary school to my left, past the library that I still had yet to frequent due to my fear of all things literary or smelling of bindery *[Shut up Willy]* where I swung right and headed up a steep hill. The prints fit my own perfectly and I began to wonder if I had made the walk earlier, that I was already at work, that I had never talked to Dave, that I was now merely trying to catch up with myself. I was vaguely reminded of the fable from The Bible, the one in which Jesus and one of his disciples, Thomas or Robert maybe, are walking along the beach shooting the breeze and after several minutes the disciple looks back in shock and cries out, "Jesus, (not as an exclamation or defamation but merely addressing his walking companion) Jesus, there is only one set of footprints in the sand!" and Jesus, all sweaty and out of breath says, "That's because I'm carrying you." Or something like that.

At the foot of the hill I crossed the street, stepping out of the prints, for to carry onward would have meant confronting Chester. That is what I called him, a dead little cat named Chester. I had been watching the progression of his decay since the end of July. Back then he just appeared to be sleeping; now he looked like a dishrag with teeth, these horrible white fangs like the pointy, sharpened end of a child's sucked-on candy cane, two raggedly black holes where his eyes had been. Horrid. He was interesting three months ago as a sort of science experiment, a biological oddity, but I could not face Chester.

"Toodles, Eliason, toodles."

God help me.

"Toodles!"

It was Betty Livermore. I don't want to bore you but let me tell you quickly about Betty. Her grandmother, as a six-year-old, survived the great cholera epidemic of 1917 by drinking seventeen ounces of goat urine a day ("not quite an English pint!" the old bat would shake a finger at you before she died three years ago due to complications of being an 85-year-old bat). Betty was standing there, a newspaper in its orange bag in one hand, the other waving at me frantically like she had spotted me in a crowded room. She was in her mid-40s, never married, or at least not yet married and losing hope, short-short-short brown hair, glasses, so flat-chested she looked almost painful in her pink bathrobe tied around the middle. When she had bent over to pick up her paper, she did not even bother to splay her fingers across the top of her robe so as not to show herself. Usually I would sneak a peek if such an opportunity arose because I am that kind of guy but with old Betty I just looked away and felt kind of sad. She played violin in the local "orchestra." She was a nice enough gal, old Betty.

"Hi Betty," I said stopping, though my testes were turning over with anger at me due to the cold.

"Oh boy it's nice to get the paper again," she grinned, holding it aloft like a whopper of a fish your uncle would have held for a photo thirty years ago when men still caught fish and took pictures of themselves doing it, "though I guess the world doesn't really exist outside of our little town." She grinned and shrugged slightly. It was true, sadly, and to compound that image, the people who were in charge of delivering our papers from Denver assumed we did not exist and had refused to drive up the mountain for the last six months to bring us our daily news.

"I guess we're important to someone again," I said. "I don't really know who. Didn't they raise the price of the paper by a quarter?"

"Oh if there's money to be made then we'll always be important." She lowered the paper and shook the slush from the bag. She pushed up her glasses and showed a lot of teeth.

"So how are you doing?" I asked.

"Oh, fair to midland I suppose, fair to midland," she said with a little nod, looking at me like I should ask something else. We stared at each other and she gave me another slight nod then another. "Oh yeah, not bad I guess. Wow, winter's coming." She was one of those people who had an uncanny ability to absolutely freeze a conversation. I was just about to say "Okay, gotta move," when she asked how my mother was doing.

"Apparently not too well, Betty. In fact, not well at all."

"Oh dear oh dear oh dear oh dear," she said, making all of these nervous bird movements with her head. "She's down in Boulder, yeah?"

"Yes," I told her. "I'm thinking I'll have to get down there pretty quick, probably today."

"Oh dear, it *is* serious," and she chewed on the side of her pinkie. "Do you need to borrow my car?"

I shook my head. "I'll get a ride from Willy I think, or Dave."

She looked dubious but said, "Aren't those hotshots from Aspen coming to look at your snowshoes today? I know you and Willy have been beavering away," and she hooked her arm with a fist through the air. The news pipeline in this town was breathtaking.

"Yes," I sighed. "Bunch of jerks with their nose hair and expensive suits."

Betty snorted and held the back of her free hand up to her nose, then accidentally snorted again. She stared at me for a bit, a gust of wind almost knocking me over sideways, and I was just on the cusp of saying, "Oh well, gotta run...."

"Do you want to come in, Eliason, for a cup of coffee? It's instant." Now I am not the most Hollywood-looking guy and I have certainly never pulled a girl named Tammy, I might have never been able to break dance in junior high or even pull off a passable robot in the courtyard at lunch, I would definitely never ski off the side of a mountain with a parachute on my back, I had never understood how the stock market worked and I might have been half of Betty's age, but on my best day when my hair was just right and I was wearing pretty big sunglasses, if you saw me through a very dirty window passing by and the light was just right, very dim, and you squinted, and you were wearing very dark sunglasses, I had a vague resemblance to a mongoloid Paul Newman. *[Shut the hell up, Willy.]* You see, I always had a hunch that Betty had a crush on me. I guess I could have gone in, it would have really made the old girl's day, drink some instant coffee, maybe ask her to play some Vivaldi, rosin up the old girl's bow, maybe even read her paper. But the way she asked me, the way she plugged my name right in the middle of the sentence, it was just so awkward.

"Uh, Willy wants me in at seven sharp," I hastened, not exactly a lie, and checked on a wristwatch that was never there. But then I pushed the boundary into egregious fib territory: "We're going to go for a coffee to discuss our business strategems and other, you know, sorts of plans of attack and other ways and means to sort of sell snowshoes and you know, other bits of merchandise. Probably do some errands together, what-not." I expected her, all embarrassed, to jerkily jump through unconnected pockets of space like a swatted-at butterfly and duck inside her house.

"Are you still seeing Julia?" she asked instead from out of nowhere, cutting me with a surgical stare. I squirmed a little. Actually, I squirmed a lot and answered, "Yes of course."

"Well, you know, I haven't seen her in town for a while. Not that it's my bee's wax."

"She's still here, teaching, at the elementary school." I began to sweat a little, which turned into an instant, sheeting layer of ice covering my entire body.

"Well okay then, Eliason, if you say so," and she turned, then revolved just her head to peer once more at me, now looking embarrassed, showing me her back and saying, "I hope your mother's okay. Golly, winter's coming," and just like that she was behind her door. All was quiet again except for the wind. "Winter's coming" was the standard line that the gentle gentry employed as a catch-all greeting or farewell. Locals voiced it as a toddler mimics his/her mother. It was so standard it required no thought, it was simply a response. In actuality, it not only required no thought, it exhausted a thought and made people forget what they were talking about. It was stated without joy to those who loved snow and without malice to those who did not. It could be said as one would reply to a question of whether one took cream in one's coffee—"yes please." The phrase simply was. "It won't be long now" was another standard phrase, though not as common by thrice as "winter's coming." It could drive a person crazy sometimes.

I prayed that I would not run into anyone else and shuffled and huffled and puffled up the final hill into town, not a small order when you already live at 10,000 feet, the air practically frozen and slipping out of the sky to meet the ground with soft tinkles like oxygen Christmas balls, your fingers numb and fat and inflexible. Atop the hill I thought I might keel over from high altitude exertion. I stood, bent over with hands on knees, not quite gasping but thinking that I needed to take up smoking. And there was our little town, Leadville, spread out before me like a ruby under a thin blanket of powdered sugar. It really was a nice little town, one road in, one road out, lined with seven blocks of grand Victorian structures where you could buy an object as infinitely useless as a rubber tomahawk or something as agelessly necessary as a pair of brand new Snow Glider '99 snowshoes made on-site at Weeping Willy's Snowshoe Hut, 602 Harrison Avenue, Leadville, Colorado 80461. Leadville was in a scooped-out valley surrounded by mountains on all sides, perched at 10,153 feet above sea level, and if a mountaintop could be described as being in the middle of nowhere, then that was Leadville: "ten thousand feet up and a thousand miles from nowhere…[or] so it may feel to the uninitiated." (Hufflin, McMullen Map Co., St. Louis, 1963). *(Note to editor: please check this quote; thanks! Worster)* Leadville was so small it did not even have a Derfy Burger. If you wanted a Detroit Drag Chicken Strip Sandwich (and occasionally you do), you had to drive down the mountain to the nearest town, Frisco, thirty-five miles away to get it. The original village of Leadville (not named Leadville at all, naturally, and never really a village but instead a far-flung collection of flinty stones) had sat at the crossroads of two Indian Ute trails under the gaze of Colorado's highest peaks, which you probably would not have known or cared if you were a Ute tribe member because "highest" or "biggest" or "oldest" or "hairiest" are statistics for white people with low self-esteem. But, geography lesson aside, if you have ever wondered what the inside of a hole covered over and thirty feet below the earth's surface would sound like, well that would be Leadville at 6:58 on a Saturday morning in the last year of the twentieth century. No dogs barked, no car engines wheezed down the street; in fact, not a single set of tire tracks disturbed the layer of snow on the main street. Looking up through the patchy clouds of the gray sky I did not see a plane etching itself from one piece of sky to the other, but I heard its fuselage squeaking through the frozen, rarified air like metal on metal. Nothing else moved. Not even the denuded trees agreed to bend in the wind nor did the filaments in the street lamps bother to keep themselves fired up in the bashfully diminishing dawn. You could say that this tiny pocket of the globe was dead. And with some dread and almost panic, I started to believe that I indeed was in some bad movie in which every occupant of the planet had mysteriously died from a swift and incurable disease spread by evil snowflakes and leprechauns, except for me and Betty Livermore and we would have to start a race of flat-chested, oxygen-deprived, nervous children, whom Dave the drunk would attempt to cannibalize and whom I would have to beat to death with a rolled-up newspaper. God I had to get out of this town, quick.

CHAPTER 2

"Black Cowboys and Bleeding Rectums, October, 1994"

I had first visited my mother in Boulder, in 1994, when she told me that she had cancer, stomach cancer, and she had been dealing with it already for a couple of years. I pulled the old "How could you not even tell your own son!" routine when she told me. Truthfully, I would have been a sophomore at a local community college in Virginia at the time, and probably would have been too drunk to answer the phone. When I went off to college, my mother dragged herself to the University of Colorado to teach in the psych department where she could inflict her singular psychoanalytical torture on the innocent, paying youth of America instead of on her only child.

"I know you must be going through the disbelief stage and that's okay," she said to me. "I've already been through the anger and bargaining phases and should soon be evolving into the acceptance stage." Her eyes literally twinkled at me and I realized with some anger that she was too young to have cancer. Cancer was for old farm ladies in Eastern Europe, for people who smoked 8,000 cigarettes a day and had yellow toenails, for people who led unclean, non-Christian lives, and my mother was none of these.

We had been sitting in a coffee shop on Pearl Street, a pedestrianzed strip full of hippy boutiques and natural soap stores, over-priced women's clothing shops and about thirty coffee houses.

The inside of our coffee house was warm and cozy, the windows fogged over with condensation, some white-people jazz coming from the stereo. Some guy with a soul patch was even trying to whistle-scat along to the groovy tunes and I half-forgave him for it because I was in such a good mood, hanging out with my ma for fall break, telling her about school and a nice young lady I had met in French class, how just before my mother had arrived at the coffee house I had read in the Denver Post about a guy who had torched the bottom of his gonads after he had finished cleaning his garage floor with gasoline, in the nude(?!), and decided to admire his work over a cigarette. She laughed softly to herself, smiling, when I told her the paper actually printed "gonads."

"And some high school kid in some mountain town accidentally blew himself up at a gas station a couple of days ago. Killed a lady too."

"Oh dear," she said, not sounding oh-dear-concerned at all, absent-mindedly stirring her coffee. She still had that faint smile lipstuck on her face.

"Obviously people in Colorado are really stupid, or they need to stay away from gasoline," I said. All I got was more lipstick. She had one hand resting on the table, palm up, so I pulled it gently toward me. Her hand was so tiny and cold. She was always complaining about poor circulation. "Look at that love line—it wraps all the way around your wrist. You have a man on the side."

She did not say anything, just smiled, her eyes crinkly in the corners.

"Well it's about time, Mom. What's his name?"

"Stop," she said, forcing herself to laugh a little. "There's no one, really."

I pulled her palm almost to my nose. It was so delicate and pretty, I mean, for my mother's hand. Then I realized that I had never really looked at my mother, really *looked*, like my father would have done when they were sweethearts. If you asked me to draw her nose I would not be able to, or tell you the exact color of her eyes, whether she had hanging or attached earlobes, did she have tiny ankles. I only noticed that the scar under her chin from a childhood Great Dane-riding accident seemed more jagged. Her cheek bones were more pronounced than I recalled, the skin around her eyes a little more taut.

"Have you had cosmetic surgery?" I asked.

"Don't be silly. Why?"

"I don't know, you just look younger. You look great actually, if I may say so. You're thinner or something. You've got a guy obviously."

"I really don't dear. I just don't have time in my life for a man."

"How can you not have time? Come on Mom," I said, releasing her hand. She stared out the window, her mouth pulled back tightly. She looked sad, kind of strained suddenly.

"All the papers I have to grade, Eliason. It's not easy, and I teach all day. Then I have to put in extra time for my dissertation. I'm also doing some volunteer work, nights, at the pet clinic working with strays. They're so pitiful and helpless." She breathed in deeply, unevenly, and wiped away with the fleshy side of her fist some of the wet on the window in a wide circle. She gazed outside and sighed. "It's really pretty with the snow, isn't it?" I told her "Yes it is." The powder blues and smeared whites of dusk had colored the snow all around but were fading into a dull gray. I watched a black guy in blue jeans and a white cowboy hat strolling up and down the mall, plugging in lights hanging like spider webs throughout the trees. He stopped to talk to a young couple pushing a baby carriage, and he scratched his elbow and laughed with the father, clapping him on the back. He seemed like a really nice guy, not the kind of guy who would set his gonads alight without good reason.

"It's rather an early snow for us," I heard my mother say. She sighed again, a big Hollywood sigh, heaving up her shoulders with a smile, trying to look cheerful. "This is my favorite coffee house—something about the feng shui."

I ignored that silly nonsense now. "Does that guy plug in the lights every night? Is that his job?" She told me that it seemed to be. "And do they keep the lights up all year, even in summer?" She said they did. That depressed me a little: Christmas lights in June take the Christmas out of Colorado almost as bad as a hot place like California takes the December out of Christmas.

"When is the last time I saw you, two years ago already? You look good, Mom, trim, fit, thin."

"Put the cookie down," she said, then took both my hands from across the table. In some stretch of time, seconds or hours I do not recall, she told me that she had cancer, not to worry, that she would fight bravely. The guy who worked behind the counter, who took your orders, he was a fat, sweaty guy, about thirty feet away, with sweat above his top lip and on his forehead where some wisps of his black hair were plastered down, a really fat guy, and he was bugging the hell out of me, not because he was a fat sweaty guy but because he would tell every customer to have a great day and when they wished him the same he would say loudly "I'm workin' on it!" and chortle so loudly that conversations would stop, babies in the bookstore next door would do a baby head-pivot toward the sound and begin bawling, birds outside would scatter from trees…and he would say this not to just an occasional customer but to *every* customer, and he would chortle nervously, uproariously, like he just thought of his whippy response off the top of his head and it was hilarious but it was bugging the hell out of me. "I'm workin' on it, I'm workin' on it, I'M WORKIN' ON IT."

"But don't worry dear, I'm following the holistic approach. I'll be taking only herbal remedies. No cold doctors' offices for me. I'm going to conquer this thing on my own terms. I'm saying no to chemo!" my mother said grandly.

"What! Why not just say no to life!" I shouted. A blond woman looked over at me scornfully. She was quite dishy actually.

"Shame on you Eliason," my mother whispered. "The anger phase is not okay in public."

"What about the begging phase, is that a phase?" I asked, way too loudly, my voice embarrassingly shaky. "Can I beg you to do chemo? Can I beg you to take real medicine, not a bunch of vegetable pills or flowers or whatever it is. Please take real medicine, Mom, please."

The blonde cleared her throat. I knew I had given her good reason to trot off to some flower shop later in the day and start moving her chops with the woman behind the counter about the callousness of kids today and they would blah-blah-blah together and tisk-tisk about the sad shape of the world and sleep very soundly that night.

"It *is* real medicine," Veronica Nye, my one and only mother, told me calmly. "But I should be the first to warn you dear, things could get a little worse before they get better. You should know what to expect. I'll be pretty sick, of course, my hair will be pretty coarse and thin, I'll be tired all the time, there may be some bleeding from my rectum."

"Oh good lord! Stop! Stop right there," I pleaded.

"Rectal bleeding, spotting, is a natural result of stomach cancer, sometimes of healing. Can you accept that as a mature adult?"

"Not when the bleeding rectum belongs to my mother!" I shouted, at which even the chortling fat man stopped whisking milk for a latte and looked over at us, and I think I already mentioned a distance of thirty feet. Every table ceased in conversation to stare. The jazzy scat man stopped in mid-whistle, his lips still puckered in a minor C. I was not so out of my gourd to be completely mortified by my actions. A nice sweaty paste arose on my own forehead and I felt a bit gauzy, faint, like I had swallowed a curling iron. Then a hand tugged on my left arm, the fingers gentle, the gentle fingers of a dishy blonde.

"I'm Liz, I'm a breast cancer survivor," she said, and slowly the coffee house wound up to its previous buzz. Full on, she was a straight-up fox. "I'm a living testament to the holistic approach. You should be proud of your mother."

"He will be, he's just in shock," I heard my mother say, but my ears felt full of cotton. My mother introduced herself and the two were instantly old chums, swapping tales of clammy skin, loss of appetite, throwing up in sinks far and wide. In my world however, in point three seconds of Liz touching my arm, I had a fantasy that my mother, too sick to care for herself, would be convalescing at Liz's very clean, very sunny house with a wrap-around deck of redwood, I would come for a visit and after gently infusing my mother with a drip of St. Anthony's Wart tea or something, Liz and I would repair to the kitchen and spontaneously, accidentally, engage in quiet rumpy-pumpy on a three-legged stool in her walk-in pantry, knocking over cereal boxes, bags of couscous, brooms and such.

"He's a very considerate, sensitive, kind young man," I heard my mother proudly tell Liz. "He cries during sad films." What next, that I sometimes wore women's underwear because they are so soft, that I picked flowers as a child?

"Where were you when I was younger?" Liz meowed, the little minx, right in front of my mother. I should mention that she was wearing a black turtleneck, ribbed and tight, and I'm telling you, if some surgeon had done work on her boobies I sure could not see it from where I was. I heard her telling my mother that the doctor had taken a skin graft from her bohiney and done some reconstruction on her left breast—they were talking like there was not a man, me, who might be a little sensitive, sea-sick even, to this issue, sitting right there.

"That's wonderful, you look fabulous," my mother beamed. I picked up my cookie, mouth agape I'm quite sure, as I tucked in, not really tasting anything. I vaguely heard the two hens clucking about "meds," zinc and iron, meditation, medication, vacations, something about a "cancer cruise in the Caribbean."

"Oh fun. Can family members come too?" my mother asked, incredibly.

Liz shook her head. "Just for the sick," she informed us, "and women only." I must have unconsciously huffed because I felt Liz's hand, a molten lava paw, on my arm again. "We can all take a cruise together I think. Who wants to hang around a bunch of sick, crabby old ladies anyhow?"

Now, I had seen enough teenage movies from the 1980s to know something like this *never* happens in real life, but in point one second I was delivering an armful of groceries in brown paper bags to Liz's home in the middle of a hot summer afternoon, Liz in bikini, and within ten minutes of unbagging her bread, we were upstairs lifting each other around in the sack like naked giraffes on the Serengeti. It was a wonderful fantasy. I thought about moving it into another realm, spaceships and sustainable habitats maybe, but my mother broke in.

"You're awfully quiet, kiddo. What are you thinking about?"

The only thing I could think to say, I have no idea why, was "Schindler's List."

My mother looked surprised, then teared up. "We're not even Jewish," she said to Liz. Liz shook her head and said something about me being "*quite* a young man. This film *must* have touched a *deep* nerve."

"The 'Empathy for Mankind Displacement' Syndrome," my mother said immediately, with what seemed a touch of awe, even for her own progeny. "When faced with an individual crisis, the truly sympathetic, or those who want to *appear* sympathetic, displace others' grief onto themselves either through charity work, political activism, orphan adoption, or on a more cerebral level by experiencing character affiliation in tragic films or books. Quite well-documented." My mother gazed lovingly at her despicable, lying son. "But rare in the young and/or spiritually vacant."

Liz said "Wow."

I of course said nothing.

"Yes," my mother continued, shifting in her seat, getting comfortable so as to kill us with some psychobabble. "Years ago as a high school English teacher, I had a student who simply could not read past the first twenty pages of *Wuthering Heights* because her cat Heathcliff had died when we began it. Not so unprecedented when you recall that ninety-nine out of one-hundred people in the early '80s were naming their cats 'Heathcliff' and their dogs 'Odie.'"

Liz nodded.

"Oddly, this girl reversed the plot line of the tragic English novel ("God, I loved that one. So romantic, better than Jane Eyre," Liz interjected): *her* Heathcliff died and she—you know, now that I remember, her name *was* Cathy—she lived. She advanced the illusion with more time, announcing that she was moving to England to live on the moors, speaking quite formally in a British accent, and insisting that her little brother play only with wooden toys." My mother shook her head in remembrance. "She became my first study case, when I decided to expand beyond just teaching. I quit English and went into psychology. Fascinating. It is still the worst case of Survivor Syndrome that I have witnessed for a family pet." I had no idea what the hell she was talking about since my knowledge of English literature came to an abrupt halt at the TV guide *[Shut the hell up Willy]* and I was beginning to think that Liz was beginning to think that she would be a nut herself to continue a friendship with my mother.

"I'm moving to Colorado," I said so suddenly that my mother gasped. Liz clapped her hands once and held them together under her chin as if she were praying.

"Oh Eliason, that would be wonderful," my mother exclaimed, sitting straight-backed in her chair.

"What a treat," Liz purred, lamely I thought, but that ribbed black top begged forgiveness.

"What about school? And your friends? This is very sudden. Are you sure?"

"There's nothing for me back there," I said all hokey but still like the coolest guy you ever saw in the coolest movie ever made. "I can go to school out here, or work."

"Oh Eliason," and she sat back dreaming of the possibilities. "There's tons of cute girls out here with great little figures on them." I gazed over at Liz, who nodded at me with a saucy smile.

"Well, I'm tired of the east coast winters and the class system, and my mother's not very well," I said, at which Liz purred with delight and unfortunately said, "I'll leave you two alone. Veronica, we'll talk." My mother was flushed with excitement and looked so, "cute" is the only word, and damn pleased and young, that I could not go back on my promise, one made instantly, almost exclusively because a middle-aged funbody had shown me attention, known as the "Middle-Aged Funbody Showing Cretinous Young Man Attention" Syndrome. Quite well-documented.

"It's going to be simply grand," my mother said, like a wealthy 80-year-old heiress. "We'll go out to eat, go hiking, go to the pictures."

"What are you talking about—what pictures?"

She sighed. "The movies. Ugh, I hate that word."

"Only old ladies call the movies 'the pictures.' Come on, Veronica, get with it."

She looked scandalized. "As long as we don't go to any weepies. I don't want you blubbering all over my shoulder."

Liz sniggered.

"I don't cry at movies. I merely get grit in my eye or something at certain moments, usually coincidentally at a time when girls in the audience are crying. I don't cry at movies."

"Uh-huh, yeah," my mother said, smiling triumphantly.

Snow began to fall again, Liz even left at some point and the coffee house workers thankfully changed the jazz to pop-lite music, and my mother and I sat there like sweethearts, like kids, like two people who would never get cancer even if they tried and the fat guy quit working on having a good day.

I would move out to Colorado several months later, right before Christmas, 1994. How I ended up in Leadville, one hundred miles away from my mother, and met my boss Willy is another story, maybe later. But I'm quite convinced that 1994, when the internet was hardly known, before cell phones, before robot dogs from Japan, before computers in every home, years before the Complete Retardation of the American Brain, and many, many moments before my mother became really really really ill, was the last innocent year lived by mankind on this planet.

CHAPTER THREE

"Two Murderers and a Jerry Hat-Trick, 7:02 a.m."

Willy immediately jumped out of his favorite chair when I entered the shop to the tinkle of bells hanging over the door that alerted us to the entrance of a customer.

"That is it, little chief, do not even take off that jacket. Just turn right round."

I proceeded to take off my jacket, scarf and gloves and station myself in front of the heater.

"You are allowed to pretend like you did not hear me only when I have asked you to come into work early," he said.

"Will you please let me get warm before you send me out there to get us coffee?" I begged, blowing on my hands.

"On the contrary, you must travel to Boulder with good haste."

I asked him what the heck he was talking about, if Dave had stopped by after finishing his six a.m. "errands" at the bar.

"No, Julia called from Boulder and left a message saying your mother is extremely ill, Eliason, extremely ill. I believe it is urgent. The message appears to have been left Thursday evening, quite late."

"And you're telling me now?"

"I suppose the answering machine was unplugged yesterday morning when I was vacuuming in a lull of customer activity, and I failed to notice thereafter during my day of steady industriousness," he said, digging at me I was sure.

Before I proceed further, let me tell you a little about Willy because I think you'll find him fascinating. William "Snowshoe Willy" Worster had opened his snowshoe shop in Leadville to quiet applause twelve years prior, in 1987. But years before that, he was born a simple child, feet first, of two parents in Stringtown, Colorado; though not even able to afford a Montessori education, he worked his way through kindergarten, junior high and finally, without needlessly drawing much notice to himself, high school. He had always been quite shocked, he told me, that despite his own extraordinary and irascible determination, thousands of his peers were able to accomplish the same. Although he considered himself always a scholar, he applied himself with a similar ungovernable passion to recreational summer camps, except for the summer between eighth and ninth grades when he provided his puritanical drive to summer school, earning high marks in the carpentry/shop class he had failed to pass during the previous school year due to artistic differences with his teacher, the mustachioed and much maligned Coach Sutter, known at the time for his womanizing and de-flowering of single mothers. College beckoned for the humble lad. Seven years later with English degree in hand, he sensed that he was less a pragmatist and more a humanist, and therefore placed more emphasis on his spare time than his work time, becoming "quite a hand" at photography, astronomy, art history, reading the Classics, studying philosophy, improving his memory, finishing countless word puzzles, looking out windows, etcetera and, as the humanities throughout history have proven to be an arduous way to earn a living, he came to consider his folks less as parents and more as dowagers and felt no shame in therefore residing in their residence until his early thirties, which had allowed him the means not only to open his own business but also to explore and not quite complete many unfinished projects, too numerous to be mentioned. He is a proud Capricorn. So....

My mouth went dry. "What is Julia doing with my mother? Why did she call you? What did she say?"

Willy looked at me wearily, twisting one end of his mustache with a thumb and forefinger. "It is not so much that she called *me* as much as she called *here*, as you do not possess a telephone on which people can relay important messages or tell you to come into work, and she left a message. What did she say—that your mother has taken a turn for the worse." Then he hesitated before speaking. "As to why Julia is in Boulder, well that is a matter for the two of you to address I should hazard," and he peered at me despotically, "as boyfriend and girlfriend or even as just casual acquaintances."

"Did she say how bad my mother is? Dave just told me she's really, really bad."

"I would say really, really, *really* bad. And thus I would suggest that the first item beyond debate would be how you are going to transport yourself to Boulder."

"But the Aspen guys. I can't leave today. You can't do this deal all alone." I had always thought Willy beyond the ken of not merely social interaction with women but also of dealing with people on any level, including a business level, despite the fact that he had successfully run his business without my help for some years, even earning a mention in the *Vail Chamber of Commerce Free Skier's Guide*, edition three, Winter 1995, as being the "...new King of Snowshoe Design, [while] bringing innovative ideas and ingenious design...several months ahead of their time to the fledgling leisure activity." He always sneered at this: "It's more a sport than a leisure activity. Mixing chocolate powder and boiling water is a leisure activity. Golf is a leisure activity. Snowshoeing is a cold and dangerous sport." He told me that he could "handle those Aspen fellows. And you must see your mother. A man has two snowshoes, he has only one mother."

"What the hell does that mean?" I asked.

"That means I can handle this alone. Yes, I can do it," and he looked like he wanted to say more but hesitated, and turned his back to me. After about five seconds of such steely fortitude his emotions got the better of him and he whipped back around. "But if I do not 'seal the deal' then, well," and he sucked in heavily, "I will have to sell Weeping Willy's," then he stole all the oxygen in the room with a heaving intake that sent chartered ships off-course thousands of miles away, "and we will have to get real jobs." This of course got my attention like a skillet across the head.

"What do you mean get real jobs? Geez, it's seven in the morning, I haven't had my coffee yet, some drunk guy tells me that my mom is dying and within thirty seconds you're telling me that you have to sell the place and we have to find real jobs. I'm very happy not really working here thank you."

"And you have perfected the art of not really working. Oh Eliason, I did not want to say as much, you have so much 'on your plate' already." He nodded but I just stared at him flatly. "If you have not noticed, corporate America has invaded the snowshoe business and it is time to compare the relative price performance of our brand and decipher whether the money stream is moving upwards at a greater angle than the price. I fear it lags."

I asked if he could please speak English.

"We are hating it, dude." He attached his hands to his hips marmishly and looked down upon me. "You have not been reading the trade journals I brought in for you?"

I shook my head, as if I really had to answer that question. They had not moved from the bathroom. I had used most of the pages for the toilet seat: not for hygienic purposes but to put one more mere later between my skin and the ice of the toilet seat.

"Chieftain, this deal we are talking about today, it is quite a business transaction. We are talking in the ballpark of millions."

I fake gasped. "Millions?" He was full of it. "Come on, Willy. Millions?"

"Big money. I think that is what you kids say. Eliason, if we pull this off today we will never work again. I am not being hyperbolic."

"*You'll* never work again," I corrected him.

"Oh do not you worry, I shall set you up. Invest wisely and your family will never want for a thing."

"What family?" I asked, my mouth drying up again.

"Future family, chieftain. Relax, would you, kindly?"

All of this talk had made me extremely discombobulated, and I leaned for balance on a table with our patented leather-stretching machine and in doing so, sent a pair of Snow Glider '99s sailing to the floor on accident. Willy was strangely unmoved.

"Willy, I knew you were good at snowshoes, but millions? Come on."

He nodded solemnly. "Eliason, I mislead you not. These rich guys, they have the ways and means, the financial backing, the factories and materiel but do they have the—" and he tapped his temple with his pointer finger. "Ho-ho, I think nay. They will pay oodles of boodles for what I possess locked in my cranial loaf and for what you," and he rushed over to me and grabbed my hands, holding them aloft, "for what you have a gift, and that is making snowshoes."

"A gorilla could do my job," I countered.

"A highly-skilled gorilla, maybe, but with such panache? True, a gorilla could make snowshoes twice as fast because he could use his feet, opposable digits and all, but does a gorilla sell snowshoes?"

"If you put a gorilla in the window surrounded by peanuts, you would sell six times as many snowshoes."

"Unethical, little chief." He looked exasperated, picking the Gliders from off the floor with some effort, a hand tucked into the small of his back, and placed them delicately back on the table with a "there, there." He turned to me. "You have a gossamer touch my friend, and also a delicate yet somehow tensile strength. You can make a snowshoe second to none." I had no idea what the hell he meant, but I thanked him anyway. "You are the button and I am the eyelet," he said, kind of creepily. "You are the left," and he held his right hand in the air, gazing at it loftily much like Dave had done when I made his disappearing key magically re-appear in his hand, "and I am the right. You are the hand and I the glove. I am the president and you, Congress." I stared at him dumbly. "That is quite clearly enough," he said, letting his eyeballs travel to the window and at the scene outside. "It is very quiet out there."

I strolled over to the glass, putting my hands backwards on my hips like you see guys in Europe do because I thought it made me look more serious, intelligent. "That's Leadville on a Saturday morning. Everyone is sleeping off their hang-overs."

"But the tourists do not drink like the locals," Willy said. "Come hither and yon with me, to the coffee shop, immediately," and he waddled out the door, knocking my hands off my hips, saying I looked gay. He locked up the shop and we added our prints to the street, the only blemish in the whiteness.

"Millions?" I asked in the middle of the avenue. I still did not know whether to believe him.

"One point eight million, give or take a few shillings," he said.

"You're being serious, Snowshoe?"

He crossed his heart then sniffed his middle finger.

"Jesus, Willy."

The Tabor Grand Coffee House was across the street, only about fifty paces away, located in the most grandiloquent building on the main street, a four-story orange beauty with curlicues around the windows and bulls-eyes around the doorframes. It had fallen into disrepair over the years, housing mainly pigeons, until its back completely collapsed due to either poor architectural planning, the dry air or masonry drunkenness. In one of the government's rare swift moves of the 20th century, the building was declared a cultural landmark (mainly in honor of its benefactor, Horace Tabor, who had become famous for his silver investment and for cheating on his wife) and refurbished it. Two brothers ran the coffee house and were the first to be approached when gauging the pulse of town. Willy flung the door open, his arms spread wide like a blustery aristocrat and puffed, "Thomas, there are no cars on the avenue." Tommy, one of the owners, was a young guy who looked permanently exhausted, a coffee in one hand, doughnut in the other. He was always wearing a butcher's apron and in need of a shave.

"Do you want the fantastic, totally made-up Leadville story or the one that's probably what really happened?" he asked.

Willy answered "The fantastic one of course, silly."

"Well, Shawn (a hot little number who lived upstairs from the coffee house) said that Jeff said he heard from Fritz that some guy from Texas was in the Golden Doubloon last night bragging about shooting some guy to death, so the sheriff ordered the gates of town closed, no one coming or going." {*Editor's note: Interestingly, the Golden Doubloon still resides in the world-record books as the longest continuously running business in American history. Its doors remained open for business, twenty-four hours a day, from August 12, 1884 to July 5, 1956, even through Prohibition. The record (which nobody even realized was a record at the time) was broken when owner Lucy "Goosey" Buttram simply did not feel like covering the morning shift for a sick employee and a lone customer vacated the establishment at around 6:15 a.m., accidentally locking the door behind him upon exiting.*} The gate was a single metal arm that could be pulled down and latched to bar anyone taking the road into town from the south, out of town from the north, or vice versa, depending on which way you were coming. The gate would not impede your grandmother in her Chevy Nova, nor would either deputy at each end with his 9mm pistol, one with his Los Angeles Highway Patrol mustache, the other with his portable oxygen tank {*emphysema—ed.*}.

Tommy leaned against the counter crossing his arms, coffee cup perched halfway on one arm, halfway tucked in his armpit. "The real story is that this snow caught everybody by surprise, especially the snow plow guys, and they haven't been able to clear the roads. That's what the police scanner said. They'll open the gates when they get out of bed, put gas in the snow plows and clear things up. It's not real dangerous but they don't want tourismos sliding off the road and suing the city."

"An escaped murderer right here in our little town," Willy said, clapping gaily. "How exciting."

"And so the rumor grows," Tommy sighed. "Don't ask for whip cream on your latte, Snowshoe Willy, or chocolate sprinkles or skim milk or anything hoity-toity like that. If you want that garbage, go to the coffee machine down at the gas station."

"God bless customer service at the fin d'siecle," Willy sniffed, shuffling over to the counter, fingering one-by-one all the cookies in a basket on the glass. "Burnt, burnt, burnt, burnt. Hey Thomas has your epileptic brother not figured out how to work the oven yet?"

"Shut the hell up, Willy," came a voice from the dish room. I asked Tommy how long he thought the roads would be blocked.

"Who knows Eliason? Maybe til eight or nine. They haven't brought out the snowplows yet this season and they're probably all on empty. Fools."

The back door to the coffee house, the same door that led to the apartments in the building, opened with some effort and Shawn the blonde came shuffling in, an empty espresso cup balanced shakily in her hand. She looked to have fallen three floors down straight out of bed: her eyes were droopy and her feet pointed inward in a pair of violet woolen socks beneath a pair of bell-bottom corduroys. She had on the tightest T-shirt she could wring onto her clothes hanger shoulders, and in between tiny bumps she called her titties (I always hated the word but I liked when she said it) was pressed on a decal of Curious George in a hot-air balloon above Mt. Rushmore. Every time she said "titties" Willy looked like a cartoon steam whistle blowing its lid. I loved it: her titties *and* watching Willy. She and Julia had been in the same graduating high school class in town, the only high school in town, and as they were the only good-looking girls in the same graduating class of 26 students in the only high school in town, they were arch enemies. I, however, secretly always dug Shawn for two reasons: one, she truly was the kind of girl who oozed sex and, even if you were dating Princess Stephanie of Monaco in the early 1980s, you would have still accidentally let your eyes fall on Shawn just a little too long if she entered the room and two, more importantly, she only ever ordered espresso, straight up, no milk, no sugar, and certainly no damned whipped cream—nothing. She sidled up to the counter next to Willy and oozed sex, or at least I thought so. She didn't ooze sex *because* she was next to Willy, however; she just was the kind of girl who oozed sex all the time I suppose. She was the kind of girl who oozed sex *even when* she was next to a guy like Willy, which is saying something.

"Hey buddy," she said to me, putting her hand on my tush without anyone noticing until I almost jumped through the counter. "I didn't think you would be in town." I knitted my eyebrows to denote a nonverbalized question, mainly because I could not quite speak. "Thought you would be in Boulder at least," she said.

I threw my hands in the air. "Jeez, Dave gets around. Does everyone know about everything except me?! Do you know Tom? Does your brother want to know? Do you want to shout it into the police scanner?" The room was silent. "Christ I hate small towns sometimes."

"Temper temper," Shawn cooed, putting her cup on the counter. "One more Tommy. Hey, what's with the flower children out front last night protesting the coffee house at two in the morning? Did they not have anything better to do with their trust funds when the bars closed?"

"I'm going to strangle them all," Tommy growled, staring at some dreadlocked dude on the "locals" couch who was oblivious to all except a string of beads that he was piecing together on a hand-woven hemp (no doubt) necklace that he could sell for eighteen times the price to one of his other hippy buddies. He was concentrating like a surgeon over an open skull. "There's one of the little bastards there," said Tommy.

"You don't have to serve the granola chewers if you don't want to," Shawn said, at which Tommy shrugged and yawned. She turned to me. "They were protesting right below my bedroom window, which you are familiar with," and she grinned with a sly wink, which forced a certain flush to my cheeks and made Willy guffaw several times and readjust his waistband, "just because Tommy kicked out one of their stinky-ass weed buddies for stealing from the tip jar."

Tommy wordlessly brandished a gigantic kitchen knife from behind the counter and slashed it through the air.

"He's too damn nice," came a voice from the dish room over the splashing of water and clanking of silverware. "They should all choke on their own damn veggie burritos."

Willy had fetched his latte, managed to peel himself away from Shawn and had worked his way over to the couch. Hippy boy did not even acknowledge Willy when he placed his considerable girth (which I'm fond of mentioning every day although not all of us are lucky enough to have the metabolism of a hummingbird) on the couch, which heaved and creaked in anger.

"Hey man, you are in the Jerry Hat-Tricks are you not?" Willy asked. Hippy kid snapped to this dimension and offered the standard moronic laugh of the stoned, or in his case, the not-yet-stoned-this-morning.

"You know me?" he said in wonderment, sucking a tubercular-tinged stream of snot through his nostrils.

Willy nodded. "You are the gentlemen who can count themselves among myriad others who play in Grateful Dead cover bands."

Hippy boy nodded and looked serious.

"But it's not so simple," and he paused to ask Willy his name. They shook hands and then each pinched their thumbs and forefingers together in front of their lips, a sign like they were toking to each other, though Willy looked around to make sure no one had noticed. I did of course and later would rip him mercilessly for it. "It's not so simple, Mr. Willy. We're totally different because we play all our songs in threes. Like, some nights we'll kick off with a little JGB, then some Dead, then we'll pause for like thirty seconds then play three more Dead songs. Then we'll, like, play three songs of Grateful Dead cover bands covering the Grateful Dead, so that our songs are always in like, three's, like a hat trick. Get it—the Jerry Hat Tricks? We believe in pushing many boundaries, like the Dead did live." He looked at Willy with his WSG (World's Stupidest Grin) again. "And if you come to our show, we encourage you to tape the proceedings and pass the tapes around amongst your friends."

"Killer, dude," Willy said, looking back furtively. I of course heard that too because I was straining to hear the conversation. Another item for which I could rip Willy at a later date.

"Killer, dude," the hippy said laughing (making fun of Willy, I think) and holding his hand high for a killer high-five. "Right on. It's all good."

Willy cleared his throat and lifted his latte to his mouth. "Hey man, why the protest out front last night?"

The hippy raised his eyebrows and drew back a little, pointing at Willy's upper lip. "You got a little soy cream on your 'tash," he said, then with the back of a dirty sleeve wiped Willy's mustache. Willy drew back in horror.

"Man, this owner is a communist," hippy continued. "He kicked out my buds Trey and Chad yesterday. He said they smell and they need to shower."

Willy had composed himself only slightly, saying, "Perhaps you gentlemen could shower occasionally."

"Bears don't shower," hippy said without missing a beat. Willy asked why they didn't just go to the coffee shop at the other end of town. "They water their coffee *down*, and they don't have free refills. And this place has open mike night on Fridays." Hippy stared at his empty coffee cup for a second. "Kind bud. Hey, you can come to our protest. I think there might be one tonight. It only costs two dollars. Truckin' down to New Orleans, we won't drink your coffee beans, truckin' down to New Orleans, we won't drink your coffee beans." Willy put his finger to his lips and the hippy whispered, "Oh yeah, uncopacetic," then he stared at Willy for a good half-minute then whispered, "Hey, didn't I see you at our protest at the hospital last Saturday?"

Willy nodded and hippy frowned a little.

"But you weren't protesting, you were going inside."

Willy nodded again, turning slightly pink. Hippy said, "Yeah, that was our third protest of the week. The other one was down at, somewhere. We were protesting, I don't remember who, but it was down by a creek where, like, the water is all orange and stuff. They are poisoning our water table, man. Poisoning it!" Willy put his finger to his lips again for hippy boy to whisper. "Oh yeah. But think about your grandkids for just one second, dude, one second, and then try to sleep at night."

"I do not have any kids," Willy said, then hippy boy looked like he was hit by a smoking bong of remembrance.

"I really remember you now man. You were with that cute little Spanish girl at the hospital. Yeah, my bud Quinn said 'What's a big fat turd like him doing with her?'"

"Yes, anyway."

"Oh, sorry. You're not *that* fat I suppose," and a bead dropped into his empty coffee cup. "Hey man, when you're done with your delicious coffee drink, can I utilize your cup for a free refill? I've already had mine and I think this owner guy is getting suspicious."

"I think not." Willy, himself a practicing hippy, sighed, utterly disillusioned. "Why do you have to harass unsuspecting, innocent people just going into the hospital?" he asked.

Hippy reached into his cup, pinching the bead with two fingers but unable to withdraw his hand as his fist expanded and filled the cup. He was dumbstruck with his problem and began to ignore Willy so Willy tapped him on the shoulder.

"Have you read the Aesop's fable about the farmer who puts the long-necked bottle full of grapes outside to catch the monkey who keeps stealing grapes from his trees?" Hippy boy shook his head. "Yes, well, when the monkey reaches into the bottle to grab some grapes, he cannot remove his paw without dropping the grapes, but he refuses to let them go. After so many hours, the farmer returns, catches the stubborn, selfish monkey with his hand in the bottle, scolds the creature for being a selfish monkey and cuts off his head." Hippy jumped back a little. "And eats the rest of him for dinner I think."

"Whoa, violence," hippy breathed, putting the cup down slowly, his hand still inside. Willy nodded wordlessly, seriously, and after about a minute hippy asked, "Why didn't the monkey just keep stealing grapes from the trees?"

"Because they look more enticing in a nice glass bottle."

"But isn't it more natural for a monkey just to climb trees, because that's what monkeys do, and eat the grapes from the trees?"

"The point," Willy inhaled, "is that monkeys should not be putting their paws where they do not belong."

Hippy finally took his hand out of the cup and gazed at Willy for some seconds. Willy nodded with a faint smile and hippy spoke: "I don't really like grapes all that much, dude. I'm kind of a kiwi guy."

"Just stay away from the hospital, please. People going there are having a hard enough time."

"Oh, oh yeah. Kind bud. It wasn't really my idea. I'm kind of new in town. I was just tagging along with this chick Pudenda. Did you see her? She's got one nice rig, man," and he made the Jane Russell hourglass shape with his hands. "She said there are meetings like twice a month at the hospital for girls in the family way, or for girls who don't want to, like, have their kid anymore and stuff. That's messed up, man. I mean, life is soooo precious."

"Yes it is, but just remember what a great Jewish carpenter once said: 'When you remove the splinter from your own eye you may remove the plankton from mine."

Hippy boy stared without expression at his mentor. "I don't know man," then he shifted, trying to do so imperceptibly, a little further away from Willy. "Hey, like, don't grapes grow on like vines and stuff, not trees?"

The front door opened and my best friend Smoky slid into the coffee house. Willy hoisted himself off the couch and met him halfway to the counter. Smoky was a pipe-cleaner in sneakers, a ponytail, always in fleece, running up and down mountains at all hours of the day. He was a good man, Smoky. He introduced me to Julia. The girls loved him because he was a fresh-faced, handsome fellow.

"Snowshoe Willy, these babies are sweet!" he said, foisting a pair of Snow Gossamer 2000s in front of his chest. The Gossamers would not be out for another three months at least but Smoky always received an advance pair. "First snow of the season and I was there, on top of Mt.Elbert. It was like not wearing anything at all."

Willy grabbed the snowshoes and squinted, his eyes trained at the bottom of one shoe. He pulled a sprig of something from between the crampons.

"Bramblebush root," he breathed, cupping it gently in his hand with a mixture of anguish, disgust and predictability, like a toddler looking at his own poo. "A shoer's nemesis," he whispered.

Smoky put a delicate hand on Willy's back. "Not a bramble bush root, Snowshoe—*half* a bramble bush root." After some seconds a smile slowly spread across Willy's face. "That's right, Snowshoe Willy. Your safety quadruple-action blade on the toe cut that root right in half, like it wasn't even there. Sweet. With no danger to the shoer. Pure genius."

"I am good, am I not?" Willy bubbled. Smoky smiled, pulling off his fleece cap and tugging down on his ponytail. He hiked up his fleece pants and strode over to me. "Hey Nye, how's the merit?" he asked. I shrugged and yawned, breathing yogurt all over his face. He was always on this kick about building up your "merit" by being nice to people and taking life as it came, and most importantly, not being a Mr. Jones (a man who is desperately obnoxious due to a lack of sexual contact with women) and still interacting with women as a normal human being. He saw me through some patchy times, before he introduced me to Julia.

"My merit is total pants right now," I told him. "Julia's in Boulder without me," I said under my breath.

"Rockin' town, man. Boulder rules," he nodded. "Merit central. I thought she hated Boulder." I told him she did, that she went shopping "or something."

He looked skeptical. "Julia doesn't shop. Does she?"

"Lingerie," I said under my breath again, between the two of us.

"Oh," Smoky said, reddening a little bit. I saw Shawn's head turn almost imperceptibly my way as she gazed at me in the mirror behind the coffee machine. She asked with a smirk, "Your girlfriend wears underwear?"

"Not after she's been at my place for a couple of minutes," came the voice from the dishroom over more splashing of water.

"Not cool man, not cool," Smoky called to the voice. "Bad merit."

Shawn stood up and brushed her hand against my bottom as she walked by to talk to Willy. I almost fell over sideways.

"Well, you seem kind of down," Smoky said to me. "Keep that chin up, Merit Man. You're out of the single scene so enjoy what you got." I told him that I did, I supposed.

"You suppose, you suppose?! Julia is the nutcracker, the burnin' ring of fire. You got the last of the good ones."

"I know, I know, it's just, I suppose, I don't know, circumstances I guess."

"Everybody's got circumstances, Mr. Jones. I mean, a girl's got to have her time away from her man sometimes, to make him remember what it was like to be a big joneser, before you met her, to make you appreciate her. I won't pretend to understand all of it—I am just a man after all." He thought for a second, stood up, went behind the counter, grabbed a cup and filled it with coffee as though Tommy was not even there.

"Help yourself, Smoky," called the voice sarcastically from the dishroom.

"Hey Nye, what does Julia like the best?" Smoky asked. I sat there for a millennium, thinking. I'll tell you what, the absolute worst (or best I suppose) part about Julia, the nut cracker, the burning ring of fire, was the middle of her upper lip. Her lips were full-flush, like the inside of a split grape, but her upper lip had as many wrinkles as a raisin, which does not sound too damn sexy, but it was. When she frowned the wrinkles seemed to march on order to a central battlefield right in the middle of her lip and then it was war. The tiniest lobe hung down so slightly you would swear to your own personal deity that you would never look at another woman just to kiss it. *[I'll kick your ass Willy.]* Her favorite thing…?

"You don't have to tell me what she likes," I heard Smoky telling my left ear, "but whatever it is, just do more of it. Twice as much of it, three times more of it, and don't ever forget. Merit. Hey, I hear there's a couple of murderers on the loose."

"There's two now?" Tommy asked in surprise.

Smoky stirred cream into his coffee slowly. "Yeah, a young one and an older one, an uncle and nephew or something. Crazy Pete just told me outside the courthouse." Crazy Pete was a guy who had a home but who dressed like a homeless guy mainly because he blew his mind out in the '70s on crystal meth and often forgot that he had a home. Tommy guffawed.

"Come on, Pete's reliable," Smoky said. Pete kind of looked like the bookish chicken with bifocals in cartoons who was always getting blown up right before the second commercial break, his hair always sticking up like crazy, like it had just come unstuck from a pillow minutes before.

"I think we've got to run," I told Smoky, clapping my hand in his. He smiled and nodded with a wink, mouthing "merit." I crept up on Willy and I swear to God, this is what I heard: "I was merely wondering what a young, ravishing lady does in Leadville for Halloween." Oh no, he was chatting up Shawn. "I am sure you would find it galling, what I used to get up to back in my younger days. Oh yes, my high school mates used to call me 'Tricky Bill' back in the age of innocence." Shawn looked like she had been pierced by a needle from a tranquilizer gun. I grabbed Willy's arm.

"Time to head back to the shop, Tricky," I said, pulling him away from any further embarrassment. Because I am too monomaniacal to know it, Willy is quite quietly successful with the ladies, he just does not brag about it. Shawn, the little tart, gave him a sappy, toothy smile, just to tease him or get a free pair of snowshoes out of him. She gave me one of those looks from the sides of her eyes that girls do just to make your knees buckle. Suddenly I had to muster all the powers of every comic book superhero just to leave the coffee house.

"Bye Merit Man," she cooed.

"Oh, goodbye then," Willy said in surprise, his feet looking like they had springs for soles as we stepped outside and into our previous tracks across the street and into the shop. "Keep up boy, chop chop, much work to do," he said all bouncy.

Sometimes I could just strangle him.

CHAPTER FOUR

"Uncle Matthew's Canary-Yellow Camaro, 7:48 a.m."

"please keep Touching In," said the postcard from Japan in the shop window. I thought it was simply the most hilarious thing. You see, even though Willy was so unknown, so drab, so vanilla (I never realized that this was his unconscious plea for anonymous individuality in a world where even a dish of vanilla is made to look fudge ripple) that he would hardly be heralded by locals in our grocery store, he was quite well-known throughout the world for his snowshoes. We had a postcard from Japan to prove it. Well, the postcard was mailed from Denver, but it was mailed by two Japanese girls who had been in the shop several days earlier. This is what it said: "We (blank space) Your store! say Hello Too smoky! please keep Touching In." I filled in the missing verb that they had inexplicably deleted, depending on my mood of the day: We *loved* Your store! We *shat in* Your store! We *hated* Your store! We, *with great joy because you charged us three months' wages for two pairs of crummy snowshoes that we can't even use because we live in Japan nor can we return because we live in Japan, are going to torch with Godzilla-like flames* Your store. Of course they loved Smoky, which burned up Willy. But the best part was the "please keep Touching in" bit instead of "Please keep in touch." I thought it was the greatest, always made me giggle and became my catch-phrase for several months. Willy did not see the humor in it, however. "Do *you* speak Japanese?" he always asked. Do *yoouuuu* speak Japanese? I hated when he did that. Of course I didn't speak Japanese. Who the hell speaks Japanese? You see, on every pair of Weeping Willy's Snowshoes, whether it be the Ice Biter '99, the Gropple Moccasin '93 or the still best-selling and most popular Champagne Pow-Pow Prowler '96 (don't ask, simply don't ask) is attached with brown butcher string (my job) a tag with a glued-on picture (my job) of some good-looking Nordic guy with a cartoonishly-chiseled jaw saying "On our shoes there snow way you can put a foot wrong!" Not one single person, ever, ever, has understood the no way/snow way pun—they think a word is missing or that something is misspelled, when in actuality the problem is not with the tags but with members of the non-reading general public who don't know their butts from a brick, or so Willy said. The worst thing, however, was that directly below the photo appeared "Willy Worster, founder of Weeping Willy's Snowshoes—Leadville, Colorado." So anyone who saw the tag thought Willy was the Nordic Olympian and sent you postcards telling you to please keep touching in, probably assuming that the real-life Willy whom they met in the shop was just the janitor cleaning up that day. It's not that Willy is a bad-looking fellow, not at all, and I have even read in travelogues that in certain parts of the world, Arctic regions, his body type and "look" would be considered quite fetching, but he believes in comfort above fashion, as do most Americans, bless them. I tried to explain to him numerous times that varying shades of warm-up pants and tops do not a wardrobe maketh, that wearing pastel-blue bottoms four days in a row and then switching to pine green on Friday was not a bold fashion move and that the occasional exposure of one's belly or derriere should be left to female pop singers, not overweight middle-aged men with a tire to spare and a dryer whose delicate cycle shrank his cottons with just as much viciousness as his permanent press. Willy would not listen. He had a bushy white-blond mustache which matched his white-blond hair, porky little fingers with these crazy square fingernails that looked as hard and calcified as dinosaur claws and a pair of glasses that turned brown whenever he stepped into bright sunlight, I swear to god, but he was always misplacing them; he usually had a camera worn by a strap around his neck, feathered his hair, and I thought he was kind of pudgy and dorky so I cruelly reminded him of each of his shortcomings almost daily, to try to change him. *[Not change, Willy, update.]* As well, it was beyond my power of believability to think that a song called "Lord of the Thighs" truly existed, and although Willy was always making noise about how he lost his virginity to a high school cheerleader while listening to this undoubtedly awful song, whose release I pinned somewhere around 1976 and was also the year that I cruelly believed was Willy's last to have actually had contact with a woman, I really, really had not meant to hurt his feelings when I told Smoky who told Forearm Bill (a volunteer fireman on our city bowling team *Weeping Willy's Pinheads*) who told Shawn who retold Smoky who told Willy (thinking I had said this about *Jimbo* and not *Willy*—Smoky kind of smokes a lot of pot), that it was a verifiable fact that Willy would never get lucky with a woman, ever, and that any woman, unless she had not a very keen sense of smell, touch, sight, hearing and taste, upon deciding to take the Willy Challenge, was always going to be left sexually frustrated. Just goes to show you I know squat about the birds and the bees because, secretly, ladies really dig Snowshoe Willy.

"It appears that we may be stuck with each other for at least a little while this morning," Willy said as we entered the shop, his face still pink and vibrant after Shawn's attention, "and I believe my next question to you is, appropriately, did you buy the mayonnaise?"

I was silent and dug my hands into my pockets, turning to look out the window.

"Doggone it Eliason," Willy said to my back. "I knew it, I simply knew it. One small task I gave you yesterday only because I believed it needed reiteration after assigning you the task how many months ago? And you have continued to fail me. I just knew it."

"I was a little preoccupied I guess."

"I simply cannot choke down three hundred pounds of tuna without mayonnaise. Okay, I made it through thirty pounds already after two months, suffering through the last ten by adding a touch of mustard and feathering it on some pumpernickel, but I simply cannot do it anymore, I cannot, even if it *is* fancy albacore."

I faced him. "Smoky ended up not even going down to Frisco yesterday so I didn't have a ride anyway."

"Yesterday was the last day for the sale on tubs of mayonnaise."

"I realize that Willy, and I'm sorry. But you know I can't stand going into that DerfMart anyway. There's no windows or oxygen and it's always cold as hell inside and there are always retarded people bothering you when you walk in."

"Mentally handicapped," Willy corrected me, staring at me with pursed lips, his arms crossed, waiting for a suitable excuse from me.

"Willy, I'm no techno genius, but I just don't think this whole Y2K thing is going to pan out," I answered meekly.

"Well ho ho ho, Mr. Nostradamus, suppose it does. This ant has—" and for extra effect he started bending back fingers on his left hand with his right, "two-hundred-seventy cans of tuna, eighty six pounds of various locally-smoked jerkies, six hundred bags of long-grain unstarched brown rice, one thousand liters of mineral water, and a bomb shelter full of other foodstuffs, beans, powdered milk, crackers, Colonel Derfy Wacky Berry Bomb cereal, etcetera, etcetera, yet his grasshopper pal old buddy old friend has been out sawing on his violin instead of buying mayonnaise. And who is going to be the first zombie come January 7th or 8th, year 2000 addo domini, knocking on my hermetically sealed door because he has not eaten in a week and has, with the rest of the populace, resorted to cannibalism? Do I have to answer my own rhetorical question? No."

I had to laugh just a little at Willy. He jabbed a finger in my direction.

"Go ahead, laugh! But let me warn you, too much laughing leads to crying."

I laughed a little again but pretended like I was coughing. "Do you really think all of our computers are going to have trouble figuring out that the year is 2000, not 1900, these machines that do a billion calculations in a second?"

He answered seriously "roger that."

I gave him the dead-eye stare. "Do you really have a bomb shelter?" I asked. He answered "affirmative." I giggled again despite myself.

"Willy, who the hell is going to bomb a town of five thousand people at ten thousand feet in the middle of nowhere, whose main industry is alcoholism? We don't even have a place to buy underwear in town, or shoes or wigs. We don't even have a Derfy Burger. If you want a Detroit Drag Chicken Strip Sandwich, which I know you sometimes do, you have to drive thirty miles down the mountain. Who the hell is going to bomb us and why?"

Willy shook his head at me in disbelief. "Hell-*lo*—Russkies. Has it occurred to you that we are practically sitting atop the North American Radar…" and he sputtered a little bit, "the North American Radiation and…oh whatever the heck NORAD stands for, right inside Pike's Peak, where they launch North American intercontinental ballistic missiles? Have you ever thought that when Y2K hits we will not be able to launch our missiles, computers will be down, no way to defend ourselves, our way of life, our freedom?"

"Uh, won't Russia's computers be down too?"

He looked slightly off-balance. "That is what non-members of the intelligentsia would suppose, wouldn't you? Those crazy Russians will launch their missiles from Cuba with a slingshot if they have to," Willy said, thumbing his lip and leaning heavily on a table. "Don't get me wrong. I like Russians, I really do, tremendous people. Beautiful women. Wonderful gymnasts of both genders. And chess? Whoa-ho. Whip smart, the lot of them. The film version of Dr. Zhivago? Nary a trace of a Russian accent from any of the actors, obviously well-schooled. {*Almost all of the actors, particularly the leads, were English or American—ed.*} I just hope they love their children too."

"Willy, if we ever get attacked by the Russians I'll run up and down Harrison Avenue naked." Willy raised his eyebrows. "I think we need to worry more about what's going on inside our home than what is out there," I said finally, gesturing to "out there," wherever that was.

"Something can *always* happen," he said. I told him "whatever, dude" and mocked him for several more inconsequential minutes until he finally relented with a shrug. "That still does not solve my mayonnaise problem."

"Look, I'll walk down to the store, right here in our little town and buy you some tubs of mayo, okay?"

"But if you went to DerfMart you would save me somewhere between thirteen and sixteen cents per tub. I have crunched the numbers." I asked him how many tubs he needed. "Well, because I already ate thirty pounds, which was approximately two-hundred-ten cans, I will need one less tub, so I will now need, oh twenty, no let's say twenty-five, for good measure. Yes, that should cover it."

I stared at him for some seconds then grabbed a pencil and paper.

"What are you doing there little chief?" he asked but I brushed him aside. "What are you writing there? What is it? Let me see."

After about fifteen seconds of scratching lead into paper I said, "William, I'm going to go high-end here and say you're saving sixteen, not thirteen cents per tub. Correct me if I'm wrong here, but you want me to drive thirty miles down the mountain even though we're paying Moscow prices for gas here in our quaint little town, go to DerfMart, pick up your mayo, drive all the way back and when I return, cruising past our own little grocery store half a mile and one stoplight away from where we currently stand, I will have saved you a whopping—" and I brought the paper up close to my eyeballs for dramatic effect then dropped it back down, "four dollars, even." Willy was silent for a moment.

"Hhmph," he said, crossing his arms and cupping his chin in one hand. "Yes, but you could have bought me a laundry basket too, on sale this week."

A miniature grandfather clock that Willy had made in eighth grade shop class chimed eight o'clock, seven minutes late. He gently slid into his favorite rocking chair, propping his feet up on a foot stool that he had fashioned in same said shop class and soon became immersed in thought, rocking slowly back and forth.

"Little chief, those Aspen guys are going to rip me a new one."

I crossed over to him and sat on a knee-high ledge that ran the length of the front window, pushing a pair of Ice Biters to the side, saying gently, "What do you mean, Willy? I thought you were pretty confident about this whole deal."

"I was, until about ten seconds ago," he sighed. "These guys have lawyers and marketers and good-looking secretaries who wear fashionable bifocals when you walk into their office and cool logos on everything and these big honkin' coffee makers and copy machines and these cool little hand-held label-making machines." He shook his head. "We do not have any of that, Eliason. We are just two dudes trying to get by."

"What do they make labels for?" I asked.

"I do not know, but Tad seemed real proud of his label-maker the last time I was there, in May. He said he was going to make labels with everyone's name on them and stick them on the counter so people would know where to put their coffee mugs."

"That's just stupid. The guy has so much time on his hands that he can make labels for everyone's stupid coffee cups?"

Willy nodded with a frown. "Yes, but they have something like sixty-five employees . It probably took him all day. They do not need us, little chief. Even if they do buy me out they will probably low-ball me like nobody's business." I told Willy that I didn't know what that meant. "It means they will offer me a substantially lower sum than we deserve and I will have to accept it because I am desperate."

I told him that I didn't think they would do such a thing, that the two owners of Rabid Marmot Snowshoes, Tad and Ross, went back a long way with Willy, as friends.

"They are vultures, chieftain, vultures! They will do anything!" Willy cried, ceasing his rocking and burying his head in his hands. "Capitalism and competition make a mockery of friendship."

"Hey Chief Wampum (I always had to resort to Indian monikers when Willy was struggling), pick that chin up. Don't you think Tad and Ross were just two dudes trying to make it at one point too, just like us?"

"Yeah, with rich daddies with condos in Aspen. They could afford to make mistakes, they had the luxury of churning out crappy product." Willy threw his head against the back of the rocker and looked heavenward. "Sweet deity in the cosmos," he heaved.

I pointed at his forehead, thumping it several times, saying "You got what they don't, Chief Wampum: brain power."

Willy began rocking slowly again, very slowly, staring at me without words, rock, creak, rock, stare, creak, rock, stare, creak. He was making me uncomfortable as hell. He just kept staring at me, not saying anything. "What?" I asked. He continued to stare with that intent look that dogs get right before they die. "What?" I asked.

"Uncle Matthew," he breathed.

"Oh no Willy, no. Please don't. It's so early in the morning," I begged.

"Uncle Matthew," he repeated.

I sighed. "It's such a long story, Willy. I mean, can I tell you about Betty Livermore or something? I saw her this morning in her bathrobe."

He shook his head. "Uncle Matthew."

I blew air loudly like a tire stabbed with an ice pick. I knew it was futile to fight. I crossed one knee over the other and leaned forward heavily, pulling in a deep breath and letting it out slowly.

"You know my uncle Matthew pretty well by now. He was born near Colby, Kansas."

"Just south, right?" Willy interrupted. I had told him this story about a hundred times and he always said "just south, right?" because that is what I had said the first time. Willy's mind can be like a steel trap for recalling details, but I got tired of saying "Yes, just south" for the billionth time so I instead just nodded. He smiled self-satisfactorily. I continued. "He was his father's only boy."

"His mother's pride and joy," he beamed. "I love the part about the mule."

"Yes, well don't jump ahead, mind you," I softly scolded. "As a Kansas farm boy, he liked to have fun, getting up on his daddy's shoulders, walking behind their mule under the scorching Midwest sun."

"I love that part," Willy said goofily.

"Yeah, me too." Dramatic pause. "Well, you know life as a farmer can be pretty darn tough, some lean years." He nodded. "And you're really at the mercy of mother nature." He shifted his weight in the chair, which groaned in annoyance, his face ashen. I took an extra long pause. "Anyone with a nice set of encyclopedias knows about the big twister of 1947. Wiped out my Uncle Matthew: his farm, his family, his fields, even his mule. Just took everything," I said with a whoosh, sweeping my hand waist high from left to right, "except for—" and I waited for Willy to chime in. The man did not let me down.

"The family Bible," he breathed.

"That's right," and I bowed my head solemnly. Willy leveled his eyes and offered his own tender nod. "The man's faith was, rock-solid, like a stone."

"Go and tell it to the mountain," Willy said, all fired up, pulling his warm-up pants at the knees then hiking them up at the crotch. Rock, creak, rock, rock.

"Uncle Matthew came to live at the casa del Nye after that."

"Eww, Spanish," Willy said, impressed. "But tell me what that was like?" he insisted eagerly. "I know he eased your father's burden by coming to work the land and that you two became lasting friends, but what was it like having an outside family member living with you?"

I paused and tapped my chin. "Who was it that said when you have guests for breakfast you realize after a couple of days that they start to smell like fish?" Willy looked irritable. "Well, you're the one with the English degree, Wampum Shaker. Anyway, it was a bit rough at first with old Uncle Mattie. He had a pretty bad phlegm problem, all those years of breathing in dust behind that mule I think. And halitosis. But he told me so many stories—"

"Back when you were just a lad, right?"

"In knee britches," I said with a wink. Pause. Creak. "I like to think of him when he had been just a boy himself. I mean, farm life for him was mostly fun when he was a boy, riding up there on my grandpappy's shoulders with that proud mule clomping on ahead." Willy's eyes were getting misty. "I mean, can you picture the beautiful gold of a wheat field and the crisp blue of the Kansas sky?" I stood up quickly, like my britches had caught fire and I tripped over to the heater. The air was frigid by the window. "I would conclude that he was raised on joy, pure and simple." I peeked over the rocking chair and observed Willy wiping his eyes.

"Sometimes I think that *you* are the one in this shop under the tutelage of an English literature degree, not me," Willy croaked. "Sometimes you speak in pure poetry and prose, little chief."

"Well," I said, adding nothing else, because I had nothing to say. I was astounded, as always after an Uncle Matthew tale. Let me explain: you would think—no, GUARANTEE—that any white kid who grew up in Colorado would know *every* John Denver song ever committed to vinyl, maybe even know some of his more obscure tracks when he was still living in California using his real name, John Spangleburger or something {*Deutschendorf*—ed.}. You would think that a Rocky Mountain youngster could whistle note for note the "Winter" portion of Denver's four seasons work on side two of the album *Rocky Mountain High*, or at the very least, just for a gag, have gone to the local T-shirt stenciling store and fashioned on the front of his favorite beige crew neck "Be kind to animals—kiss a beaver," just like John had on his shirt on the gatefold of the same album. Really. You might have even hoped that anyone born in Colorado would stick by John through the icy years, because he was a Colorado boy and Colorado natives needed to stick together in a world full of misplaced Texans, even after he had sold a quadrillion albums, was not considered "cool" anymore and started singing with Kermit the Frog {*Denver was born in Roswell, New Mexico, not a Colorado native at all—editor's note*}. You might have expected a Colorado kid like Willy and now a Colorado adult to get sentimental for at least an afternoon upon hearing about the plane crash that brought about Denver's untimely death in the unforgiving waters of Monterey Bay, California in 1997. But, and this is almost unfathomable, you would almost bet your '76 Camaro that a white kid's parents in the 1970s would have had the album *Back Home Again* which contained classics like "Thank God I'm a Country Boy," "Grandma's Feather Bed," "Annie's Song" (to his wife), and slow burners "Sweet Surrender" and "Eclipse" (my personal favorite), as well as the aforementioned tune "Matthew" about his no-doubt fictional Uncle Matthew from Kansas. Not only that, but you would safely bet your grandmother's dowry that a Colorado kid's mom and dad would have played the album until the needle poked through the other side, thereby cementing any John Denver song from *Back Home Again* into the child's subconscious with a permanence hardly known to man. I know my Ma did, and we weren't even from Colorado. But not Willy. He was too busy getting busy to "Lord of the Thighs." He had had no clue, which was rather embarrassing. You see, when I first started working with Willy, he asked me where I came from, what I did, my family history. So I started in with this malarkey about my Uncle Matthew from Kansas, assuming that he would know the song, being a Colorado kid. I thought he was playing along with me. He was asking a lot of sincere sounding questions that I mistook for sarcasm, but it wasn't until I got to the third verse about my uncle living with us and easing my daddy's burden that I realized that my new boss had no sense of sarcasm, and that he had no idea that I was having fun with him. I mean, I had only known the guy for about three days and I didn't want him to fire me or think I was making a fool out of him; besides, he was too far into the saga of Matthew to turn back, which was a pretty good story anyway. So I had to keep going, and it became this inspirational tale for Willy. I swear I recounted it for him about four months before when he went on a disastrous date with a local lady, Easy Annie, who used to work in one of the molybdenum mines in town. He tried to kiss her behind the Elk's Lodge (or so town rumor has it, falsely) and she told him that she was a lesbian {*a total lie according to her two ex-husbands and about fifty men in town—ed.*}, so he was pretty down on himself, but not after hearing about old Uncle Matthew for the ninety-nine-thousandth time. I wished I had just kept my mouth shut. The worst thing about it was I had not been able to play any John Denver cassettes in the shop out of fear that Willy would find out the truth about my Uncle Matthew. I did, however, spill the beans not long ago because my conscience was tearing me apart. Willy took the news with aplomb. (By the way, he had not really been crying, he had just been discretely and laboriously digging at something unspeakable in his left nostril).

"You know, in all of the hubbub and hullaballoo of the morning, I have not asked how you are, little chief."

Uh, my mother was dying and I had no way to see her, my girlfriend was about fifty towns away, my boss had no fashion sense and I was stuck in this town with two killers on the loose at eight in the morning, Saturday. Willy's eyes bored right through me as I stared at him wordlessly.

"So, how are you little chief, really? No sugar coating."

Crappy, Willy, crapola, crapadelica, crapzilla, supercrapacrapalisticexpicrapadocious.

"It's not right leaving you here with the Aspen guys, without any help," I heard my mouth saying, but I didn't really feel anything. I could have cared less actually, in a way; well, I suppose I cared but I would have cared more on just about any other day.

Willy put his fingertips together and offered me a vaguely Hollywood sigh.

"This is a big deal today, Nye, super huge deal. But if you need to go to Boulder then by god you go to Boulder." And I hated him for it, because by the way the words were falling out of his mouth and assembling themselves, I could not tell if he was having a go at me for leaving or not—the "by god" bit was really killing me.

"You sure it's okay?" I asked milkily, though I didn't know why. My damn mother was dying wasn't she, and no million dollar deal was going to get me down the mountain quicker or keep her alive longer.

"Hey, it is not like Weeping Willy's Snowshoes needs to stay open every day to stave off the taxman. We should all have our days off."

Bastard—the cheap bastard was making me feel guilty as hell whether he intended to or not, which he could not have. He knew my mother was in bad shape, didn't he? I fiddled with a snowshoe, tightening a screw here and pulling on a bit of leather there, refusing to meet Willy's eye. He broke the silence.

"But you have not told me how you *feel*, Eliason. What is going on in your head right now? I have been a little concerned for some months now."

But I couldn't talk to anybody about my mother, not even to Willy, because it made me feel cheap, like I was using her to get sympathy, or using her for better things, like getting out of work. I never trusted those kids in elementary school who took off a day to go to some relative's funeral, maybe even three days if they had to travel out of state. They always seemed so self-satisfied and smug when they came back to class.

"You really want to know, Willy, no sugar coating?" He nodded effetely. "You really want to know? Okay, well, I don't know how I feel, I guess. I guess I'm just fair to midland. That's all—fair to midland."

Willy narrowed his eyes at me and was silent for twenty seconds at least. I felt uncomfortable as hell.

"You know, it is fair to *middling*, not midland," he said, "denoting 'medium'—not bad or not good. Or, I suppose, 'fair.'" Huh? He continued: "Sort of like saying 'six or one half dozen the other.'" Huh?? Creak, creak, rock.

"Yeah, six and a half or a dozen of the other," I said, "like if someone asks you if you want something and they're both just about the same, I don't know, they're six and a half or a dozen of the other."

Willy sighed. Creak, rock, creak, creak, rock. "Well, fair to middling, it means that any way you look at something, it is all the same. Nothing really matters because everything is equal, equally bad or equally good."

"Are you sure? I always thought it meant that you were either fair or to the middle of somewhere, like you're right in the middle of good or bad but just to the good side of fair. Midland. Or something." Truthfully, I had never thought about it at all. It was just a dumb expression and I realized, thanks to Willy and his stupid English degree, that "fair to midland" and many other things I said throughout the day made no sense at all. He plastered on his practiced professorial look, all straight-lipped and blank, so that his face revealed nothing, which usually meant a lecture was on the way.

"Have you ever been to Midland, Texas?" he asked. I shook my head then asked if he ever had.

"Why should I do a thing like that?" he answered, like he was offended. I asked, "Then why the hell did you ask me?"

He shrugged. "Because back in 1986 or so, on some obscure television station, I picked up a high school football game, Midland versus Odessa I believe. Both in West Texas. Eliason, 40,000 people were in attendance, for a high school football game. I always thought it must be the most peculiar place to reside." I didn't know what he wanted me to say so I chuckled lightly. He said the players were like gods in their towns, and asked what would happen to them when they went out into the "real world" and nobody knew who they were.

"They'll get college scholarships and play on national television instead of some crummy channel in Colorado," I answered. "Then millions of people will know who they are."

"Rare is the player who goes on to play college or professional ball," Willy informed me.

"Then they'll go back to Podunk City, Texas and become restaurant managers and sleep with their underage hostesses. Should we really care, Willy?"

"I just think it is cruel to open such a door to a teenager, a young malleable mind, to show them the 'big time,' the bright lights, the glory and power, then yank it away. What message are we trying to relay?" He stood up, crumpled his paper latte cup, waddled about three feet away from the trash can and arched his body forward for a jump shot, missing the trash can completely.

"I think it's better than to never have had it at all, like me or you," I said. He reproached me with his eyes, his eyebrows, even his twitching mustache.

"Sorry, like me," I added. "I keep forgetting that you're big in Japan. I, myself, would love to be adored by 20,000 people for one football season, or even just one night. The quarterback probably gets free shakes at Derfy Burger when his team wins. Not bad."

"Oh there is more to life than just free shakes, little chief. Doing good work for example, doing it honestly, bringing joy to people, performing good deeds, helping the poor, subscribing to alternative magazines, paying your bills." The last thought forced him to pause in the middle of stooping over to put the cup in the trash. He plopped it in with some resignation then straightened up, smoothing out his mustache with a thumb and forefinger, spooning his elbow with the opposite hand then cupping his chin with his free hand. "Tell me that Chaucer-like tale about your car again?" I saw a faint grin etching itself slowly under his mustache and between his pudgy cheeks.

"Absolutely not," I protested. "What is it with people making themselves feel better at hearing about my pain?"

"Schadenfreude it is called, a German word," Willy told me.

"Well that's just perfect isn't it?" I said, stomping over to the wall where I hung my jacket, ripping it from its hook and jousting my arm through one of the holes. "You know Willy, it's perfectly normal for a guy to leave his car running when he's going into the grocery store to pick up a few things when it's about a thousand degrees below zero outside but it's not normal in a small town where you know everybody to steal some guy's car in like, two minutes. That's just not cool." The police never found my car and I had been without automobile for about seven months. I never knew why Willy always made me repeat such an embarrassing episode in my life. It was very un-hippy of him. Was I constantly forcing him to retell the story of how he wandered off to the Grand Canyon some years ago to "learn life the way the Red Man had taught themselves throughout the passage of a thousand summers," how he went to some sweat lodge or teepee or something where you cook yourself silly for four to five days and have visions of what your future holds, how he lasted approximately three hours, went ballistic, had visions of the Indian instructor guy as a huge walking chicken leg like you see in cartoons when two guys are starving on a deserted island and resort to eating their shoelaces like spaghetti and frying up their shoe leather like bacon, how Willy attacked the Indian instructor guy, tried to eat him then broke down in fitful sobs, only to be given his money back after being christened by the Indian instructor guy as "Weeping Bear" and told to leave the sacred grounds before any other unhappiness should befall him before the next passage of the winter solstice? Did I make him tell me that all the time? Did I? No. Of course almost the entire story was completely apocryphal but the previously stated version had become legendary in town despite Willy's efforts to clear not only his good name but his standing with his fellow Native American companions.

"That car was my only financial asset. Now I've got nothing. I'm just a guy borrowing one of your crummy record players and renting an apartment with nothing."

Willy trod over to me and helped my arm through the other hole, asking me gently why I was putting on my coat.

"Because it's frickin' freezing in here!" I spat.

"I know, little chief, I know. But we have to cut back a little." He caressed my back in little circles like a father to a son after losing to Odessa High and watching his free Derfy shakes fly out the window. "You still have Julia, you know."

"Ha, she's hardly a financial asset," I spat again.

"Well, she is a lot warmer than a hunk of metal on four wheels," he said almost angrily. "She is a good woman, your Julia, always looking out for you. Never says a harsh word about anyone. Not a cruel, jealous bone in her body. Strong."

"I know, Snowshoe Willy," I said, feeling miserable as hell, gulping his name. The zipper on my jacket was stuck, and I tugged on it two or three times in frustration. Willy grabbed it with those damn square fingernails and coaxed it upward. "I should have just gone to Boulder with her. Why didn't I Willy? Why didn't I just go?"

Willy looked as despondent as I. "You were scared, chieftain. It is okay." He told me to lift my foot onto his homemade footstool. "Let me tie that boot for you." It was about the sweetest thing another man had ever done for me, even though it took him about five minutes to tie the blasted thing. He pulled his body into a somewhat vertical line, though his belly stayed horizontal, which he offered a loving rub and without looking at me he strayed into the back of the shop, returning some minutes later looking so proud, car keys looped around his pinkie. There was one key on the chain, with a little plastic flashlight that, when squeezed, lit up a pip of light that equaled in magnitude a dying quasar about ten quadrillion light years away. "Spare keys to the Camaro. Take it."

The thing that drove me crazy about Camaro owners was that with them it was never "Do you want to borrow the car?" or "I'm taking off lunch to wash my car"—no, it was always "the Camaro," never "the car" or even "my wheels." Plus, the Camaro was a hideous canary-yellow, and unlike most Camaro-obsessed owners, Willy ignored his car's needs. The inside of it smelled like a dead moose (or that is what I told him last time I was in it) mainly from his unlaundered linens which looked to have exploded all over the back seat. In December, they would always freeze to the floorboards.

"Weeping Bear, your Camaro is still in the shop," I reminded him.

He slapped his forehead dramatically saying, "We sporty types sometimes forget about those mechanical monsters of transportation when we have our trusty bicycle or sturdy foot leather." You see, when Willy had dropped off his jalopy and old Al Fettis the mechanic asked if he needed the car (sorry, the Camaro) in a hurry and Willy casually answered "Alfred, why should anyone who is not predicting the apocalypse ever be in any kind of hurry?" could Willy have known that he had just signed the license for old Al to work at the slowest, most ineffectual, governmental pace? Yes, Willy could have known, should have known, and he should have been ashamed for his lack of foresight. His car had been in the shop for three months. I told him I would hitch-hike, that I would have company at least.

"Peeshaw you will," Willy admonished me with just the right stroke of incredulity. "Hitch-hike! In this day and age? I think not. We shall find you a ride."

He disappeared to the back of the shop like a powder-blue rabbit into its warren. I tugged on my hat, scarf and had on one glove when he returned. He pulled back in surprise. "Why are you under the charge of yet more of your winter gear little man?"

I told him that I was still cold, but really I was feeling the itch to get moving, antsy as hell, wanting to hit the road.

"Let us not exaggerate, aye? And you *are* going to pack heat, in case we cannot procure a ride for you," he said, holding in front of his chest what looked like a harmonica. Then I realized that the harmonica was actually a gun, which he pinched gingerly like a used tissue with his thumb and pointer finger, a gun that if held directly against the eye of an unsuspecting fly and fired would cause the unfortunate insect to have to undergo immediate corneal transplant surgery.

"Are you normal?" I laughed. He insisted that I take it. I asked why, "So if I get into a mess someone can immediately take it from me and shoot me?"

"It is a dangerous world out there and methinks the road you, or we, will travel will be fraught with peril." He held the gun aloft, straight out from his chest, as if it may be leaking radiation.

"Put that silly thing away before someone with really excellent vision walks by the window and sees you holding it."

He put the deadly device on the table and looked at the gun curiously, as if he expected it to sprout tiny, metal legs, hop to the floor and dance out the back door. He then put a freshly printed twenty dollar bill, which practically dwarfed the gun, on the table.

"Nye, with a gun and a twenty dollar bill you can get anything you want in this country," Willy said. "This is your care package. Now I am going down to Fritz's to steal his morning paper," and he bumbled his way over to the front door. He turned around. "I am not really stealing it, he is out of town for two weeks. I just love a good newspaper in the morning, along with a pedicure. Is anything of import going on in the world, you think?"

"Is there ever?" I said, watching him exit to the tinkle of bells. I pulled out a chair and rested my head on the table, feeling so tired all of the sudden that I became a bit nauseated. I instantly fell asleep and dreamt about something weird then awoke with a start, perspiring heavily in my winter garb, asleep only for five minutes. I jumped up, stretched on my other glove, zipped up my jacket to my neck, carefully slid the twenty dollar bill from underneath Willy's iron life extinguisher, left the gun where it lay, stuffed the money into my pants pocket and rushed over to the window. Tire tracks were in the snow on the avenue. I ripped open the door, and sped down the sidewalk, away from Willy, stepping into the street, into the fresh tracks so that he could not trace my footprints, could not follow me as I headed out of town and fat, wet flakes began to float from the darkening sky.

CHAPTER FIVE

"Pudenda and the Dream of Texas, 9:16 a.m."

"I wish it was autumn. Autumn always reminds me of really old country and western songs in my grandparents' house, when my parents and Jimmy and I would drive down to Texas to visit. It was nice during the day when Grandma was cooking and 'the men' were out doing stuff in the barn and my mother was just talking and talking and talking to my grandmother about everything. There never seemed to be a radio on so I don't know where the music was coming from, which is kind of weird. The house kind of creeped me out at night though, because everything was so old and dusty with lots of corners and wardrobes and stuff. During the day it was sunny and it was okay, but at night it always kind of scared me. You could hear crickets in the grass outside and cars going by every now and then way out on the highway, like twenty miles away. It was so flat and quiet you could hear things without ever seeing them. But you know what, it was the shadows that really used to freak me out. At nighttime the shadows in the house weren't like real shadows, they were kind of brown. It was like they got faded or something, like they got bleached out by the sun during the day. So we'd hang out on the big old porch. Jimmy and I would hang out there all night. Sometimes he'd jump right off it and just run like crazy down the road into the dark, just to scare me. The road wasn't even paved, just dirt with stones in it. I always knew there would be a guy with a chainsaw out there just waiting for us. Or there'd be some guy with a missing arm and a shirt with a bunch of holes in it and blood and dirt all over his face from some car crash he'd been in and he'd come stumbling out of the darkness and grab us. One night I dared Jimmy to run to Screaming Bridge, which was, like, ten miles away. Legend has it that a bunch of teenagers in their car were going way over the speed limit and didn't know one of the bridges had been washed away in a storm and they flew over it and crashed way down in the creek and died. People say if you drive by the bridge on certain nights you can hear them screaming. I dared Jimmy one night to run to it and back and he just took off. I was scared to death and crying after about two minutes and ran inside saying that Jimmy had disappeared and somebody had killed him and my mother kept shouting 'Donde esta tu hermano, donde esta tu hermano??' He came back after about five minutes and we got in big trouble. I wouldn't talk to him, even when we went to bed, but he turned on the light when the adults left and said 'Sis, I heard them screaming. I heard them. Look what I took,' and he had a little piece of wood in his hand. He said it came from the bridge. I believed him, although it was way too far for him to run and come back in such a short time. But I believed him. I always did. I still kind of do. He was my big brother. He was crazy. Anyway, sometimes when I hear a song on the radio from back then it still reminds me of being there and watching crickets spit brown stuff on the window when you scare them, and drawers full of rubber bands and chewing gum and stuff." Julia hesitated and pushed a stray strand of hair behind her ear. I loved when she did that. "You don't have any idea what I'm talking about do you? I didn't think so. If a cricket is on the window you can kind of study his belly and his legs and everything tucked up underneath and when you get tired of that, you hit the window and it scares him and he spits brown stuff like an old farmer guy spitting tobacco juice. It's pretty weird." I smiled. "They were always louder at night chirping away at the moon, ugly little things. Chirp chirp chirp, always when Jimmy and I had to go to bed and the adults would be up playing gin rummy and drinking and carrying on when they weren't busy yelling at us, and all I could do was listen to them from bed because I couldn't sleep. They played the music so loud, guys singing about making the world go away, or paper roses and everybody cheating on everybody else. The women always sounded pretty and pink and clean, but the guys, they were just a little creepy—not creeps, just creepy. You don't have any idea what I'm talking about...."

I doubt that my grandparents had ever listened to country and western. I don't know because I don't remember them very well. I don't think they listened to anything. I doubt they even owned a radio. If you mentioned something about Conway Twitty or Loretta Lynn or the Ozark Mountain Banjo Benders, they probably would have looked right through you. They're all dead now—my grandparents, not the Ozark Mountain Banjo Benders.

"I guess it makes you sort of feel like you might be an adult, when it seems like a really long time ago that you were a kid. God Eliason, am I really twenty-three already? Jimmy would be so old now, like twenty-six or so. I mean, don't things seem so hazy and forever ago, like everything that you remember is from someone else's life, maybe. I guess that means you're getting old. Hey baby, you're sleeping on me again."

I forgot to mention that Julia could be depressing as hell.

I could not stop thinking about her as I trudged north out of town, the wind kicking me in the ribs. Every now and then a car would slowly pass, its tires muffled by the embarrassed layer of snow on the road, the snow's arrival not necessarily early but certainly thin and ineffectual. It would be gone by Monday, probably. I didn't care about Monday, I didn't want to see Monday, I wanted to melt by Monday. Julia had held me so tight on Tuesday, a thousand years ago, the Tuesday before the Thursday when she left, the Tuesday before the Wednesday when I quietly fought with her. Another car passed me. I knew no one would ever stop to get me and I felt small underneath the huge, gray sky like a billboard with nothing on it, the snowflakes getting fatter, faster. Five minutes later another car passed and already I was on the edge of the town and the county, which did not really matter since the edge of town was simply the border between a little bit of nothing, Leadville, and a lot more of nothing, mountains, mines and trees. "We love Leadville—you will too," had been painted on the side of a seven foot high wall that had served as the foundation for the north-end railroad station a hundred years earlier, long now disused. The word "love" was represented by a heart, but someone had spray painted from the top to bottom of it a black, jagged crack. I always got a good kick out of that but today it just depressed the hell out of me. The fattest flake landed on my nose and refused to melt, just sitting there. Then a dull green haze stuck in the corner of my eye. A pretty hippy chick had stopped in a, what else, lime-green VW bus, and motioned from the driver's seat for me to get in. She had a smile from here to Montana. I hopped over to the van and opened the door with what I hoped was a fetching, boyish grin.

"Hop in, Buster Keaton," she said. Hippies are so weird. Oh but her smile was so golden, like morning sun on a wheat shaft. She was so pretty I got just a little turned on, despite being a taken man and not allowed to be turned on by women anymore. "You must be freezing your ass off."

"Aw heck, I'm just great," I said, sliding up into the seat like the coolest guy you'd ever seen in the second coolest movie you ever saw. She popped into first gear with a shake and we slowly rolled down the road, through the second stop light in town, past the grocery store where my car was stolen, past a small hotel that inside smelled permanently of cigarettes and wet dog and finally by the gas station where Willy's car was being held hostage. Within thirty seconds we were out of town, out of the county, out of anywhere, buzzing between Douglas firs and aspen stands.

"Funkengruven," I said. The inside of the van was fairly clean, though I was becoming light-headed and overcome by the scent of incense, patchouli and exhaust. On the front of the glove box hippy girl had pasted a bumper sticker that read "Friends don't let friends eat their friends: go veggie!" Another sticker said "Choice of a New Generation—jazz", with this saxophony thing for an exclamation point, or maybe it was a question mark—with jazz, it's all about interpretation. The floor of the van was so old and eaten away I could see actual road passing beneath my boots. Coming from the tape deck was some sort of crummy, twangy, folky, suicide-inducing dreck which sounded suspiciously like the Grateful Dead, or at the very least, the Jerry Hat-Tricks. I had never understood why, when hippy-type people moved to Colorado from Vermont or Wisconsin or North Carolina, the unwritten rule seemed to be to stop showering and start listening to the Grateful Dead. In fact, I was going to take a stand with this chick and not pretend that I liked the Grateful Dead or any of their knock-off minions. It was time to have some personal integrity, spill my guts, lay down the law, roast the chicken, and say I despised them and their two drummers. I was even going to go out on a limb and tell her that I wasn't crazy about that hippy American *{Canadian—ed.}* rock icon Neil Young either. No, I thought I would tell her that I thought he downright stunk and that his song "A Horse with No Name" used to give me diarrhea as a child. {"A Horse with No Name" *hit #1 on the pop charts in March 1972, written and performed by folk-rock trio* America. *It was followed with hits* "I Need You," *which placed #9,* "Ventura Highway," *#8,* "Tin Man," *#4,* "Sister Golden Hair, *#1,* "Lonely People," *#5—ed.}* Heck, I would probably put Eric Carmen's sap-fest "All By Myself," the melody of which he stole from Mozart *{Rachmaninoff—ed.}*, on a mixed tape before any song Neil Young tried to pluck out on his tone-deaf guitar. And you know what, I was even going to risk an injury and tell her just how execrable Bob Dylan truly was. I was tired of pretending, living the lie, acting sweet. In fact, I was going to tell her that if I read one more time how such and such musician owed his/her whole career to Bob Dylan, then I was going to buy every album by Mr. Dylan that I could find, tie them to a monkey and flog the poor beast up and down Harrison Avenue until it died of exhaustion, a martyr for music. Then I would burn the albums. Then I would burn the monkey. And when all was said and done, Bob and I would become quite chummy because I would have been the first person, ever, to tell him just how crummy his voice is. And he would respect me for that. And I would respect him for respecting me for that. And hippy girl would respect me because Bob Dylan knew me. I was going to tell her all of that and more. But I would set the record straight, starting with the Dead.

"You digging the tunes?" she asked, as if reading my mind.

"The Dead? Fantastic. Truckee, Nevada, 1970 I bet." I'm such a cad.

"Could be, I don't know. I'm not into the Dead so much. It's my friend's tape. He got it stuck in the tape deck and it's all I've been able to listen to. When he bought the van there was a cassette by some band called Icicle Works stuck in the tape deck but he took a screwdriver to it and ruined it," she said, kind of gritting her teeth. She was wearing this floppy denim hat, kind of like this hat I'd seen on a woman in a magazine ad for female hair loss and hippy girl had put herself into a thrift store flower print skirt and inexplicably, a pair of brown corduroy pants flipped over about a hundred times above her socks and sandals. The whole get-up looked pretty unflattering but her top half more than made up for what was going on down below: she had on this crazy contraption that looked like she had taken three swatches of carpet from your aunt's mobile home, put a strap through the ends and hung the thing on her shoulders like a mobile. It was the weirdest fashion piece I had ever seen. I could see very clearly her armpit hair and the right side of her breast, of which I kept sneaking peeks because I think I told you before, I'm that kind of guy. Keeping her eyes on the road, she asked my name, to which I replied, "Dirk. Dirk Diggler." She said "right on," kind of rocking her head like a chicken pecking seed from a tin. She turned to me just a second and flashed her baby blues, telling me her name: Pudenda.

"Oh, nothing like Snowdrop or Sunwheat or something?" I asked, giggling like a giddy schoolgirl.

"No, but I live with a girl named Summer and another, Caitlin," and she thought for a second or two before adding, "and another named Kaitlin, but with a 'K' and Justin and Chad and Austin and Quinn, and their dogs Namboo and Tushi and Kenosha and Kenobi and Denali."

"Those are interesting names," I lied. God I hate pandering to beauty—it makes me feel so used.

"They're Quinn's dogs. All I know is that one name means 'black snow' and the other is some sort of grease Eskimos rub on their bodies to stay warm on whale hunts, I think. The other name is a mountain maybe in Wyoming." We sat in silence for some seconds.

"Wow, you must have a pretty big house, you know, all those people and dogs," I said.

She shook her head. "Just a two-bedroom rental. It's our own little self-contained community." She looked over at me straight on and smiled. I smiled. We sat in silence for some seconds.

"Tell me you're going all the way to Boulder," I blurted. I'm such a jerk.

"No way, man. They kill their children there. Haven't those people ever heard of karma?" she said in complete seriousness.

"Nope," I said, a little disappointed. After about ten seconds of nothing I said, "You know what, I had a friend in Boulder who started a company that would clean your karma if you needed it." She said "right on," which I could only translate as approval. I continued: "The only thing is, he just sold a bunch of t-shirts that said 'Karma Kleen' on the front in these puffy, sparkly, iron-on letters and on the back it said 'Have you had your soul scrubbed today?' He sold about a million shirts to guilty Boulder moms."

"Right on. But how would they scrub your karma?"

I could only shrug in disbelief, making crazy things up off the top of my head like a professional. "I was never privy to the actual mechanics of the process. He did try to get a name-brand shoe or clothing company to sponsor him and make more t-shirts, but every single corporate hotshot said that Boulder was no longer profit imperative, that the money stream was moving upwards at a lesser angle than the price"

Pudenda was silent for a moment. "Are you like, some sort of corporate business man?"

I shook my head ferociously, vowing not to look at her right breast again because I was feeling faintly pathetic, but I looked again anyway.

"Man I hate those ad guys," she said, "the big sell, you know. I don't want some old white guy selling me a hamburger on TV with a Motown song or Journey playing in the background. How about some integrity. Hands off my childhood memories." She shook her head at the thought. "Those buttholes don't care what music means." I loved her because she had enough scruples to call someone a butthole...and mean it. This was turning out to be a weird day for sure. She looked at me full on again for a second to make sure I was listening…and probably not looking at her boob. "Where's the Crosby, Stills and Nash, man? Where's the real stuff?" she said. I personally could not stand those whiny old bastards, but who's to say I was listening to the right album? "All for a damn burger. Who do they think we are? Where's the *Crosby, Stills* and *Nash*," she croaked like a dying maiden.

"And don't forget that magician of voice and six strings Neil Young," I added guiltlessly. She reiterated with a "heck yeah" and a broad smile. I was thinking of not going to Boulder at all. I was sure my mother would be okay. There was just an overwhelming sense of sexual, kinetic attraction between the two of us, me and Pudenda. Pudenda looked at me with that Montana smile again, looking right in my eyes.

"Do you eat face?" I heard her ask somewhere from the driver's seat. I felt the bottom of my underwear drop about twenty floors. I must have looked ready to pounce because she quickly added, "Are you vegetarian I mean?"

I answered under my breath, masking the disappointment, "Oh yes, I was raised a vegan baby."

"Right on," she nodded.

"But I was a carnivore from age two and a half to twelve. I thought it should be my choice, being an individual. Then I went back to grass chewing after visiting a Nebraska slaughterhouse on a church outing just before my teens," I said, getting comfortable and putting my feet on the dash. "I wouldn't touch meat again after that. You should see the pus postules they hit on those sides of beef. They'll squirt about five feet, this gangrenous stuff. I still can't eat salami to this day." I think I was a little too graphic because Pudenda gagged outright and lurched slightly. She wiped her nose with the back of her hand, wiped her hand on her corduroys and inhaled deeply.

"Oh man, I haven't gagged like that since I was bulemic," she said, palming the top of her head. I never really liked hearing about a woman's eating disorders on the first date. I was a touch annoyed and stared out the window. Ever-fattening flurries were beginning to fall sideways, rushing in synchronized drifts and swirls across the shallower, shaded, thinly ice-skinned sections of the Arkansas River. The river was narrow here and not very deep, as it started only five miles up the road and would eventually find the Mississippi River and then stumble into the Gulf of Mexico. Last summer, the Weeper decided to go for a boat ride here and tore up the bottom of his canoe because the water was not deep enough to keep his fat butt afloat, or that is what I had led myself to believe, though Willy had actually been testing the durability of his canoe's homemade resin-based wood varnish on the underside of the canoe. I had constantly harped on him that a registered Indian should better understand the buoyancy of his vessel, and made him feel like an idiot, I'm sure.

"Hey, what are you going to Boulder for anyway?" Pude asked, slowing for a curve. I came out of my reverie in an instant.

"My friend and I are laying down tracks for a new record."

"Like a compact disc? That's excellent," she said, beating the top of the steering wheel in, I think, excitement. "What are you called?"

"Well, believe it or not, we have four bands: Tickles Pickles, Pro-Teen, The Bible and Wiggers-Diggler Soft-Drive. Not too many people know that we're the same band, so we're making a kind of greatest hits compilation in which the four different bands guest on each other's songs."

"That's wild," she said. "Are you like, Christian rock—The Bible and all?"

"Oh, we don't like to be labeled," I answered swiftly, like all crummy lead singers say to interviewers, especially when their band falls squarely into one easily-labeled category. "Radio stations don't know where to put us so we find airplay all over the bandwidth, even on amplitude modulation—that's AM to you land lubbers. AM radio put Soft-Drive's song 'My Waistband's Wasteland' into heavy rotation, so to show our appreciation, we exclusively toured in places where listeners could not get FM—Alabama and West Virginia for instance. We had some real barn-stormers."

"That's really great. I'm surprised I haven't heard of any of your bands," she said, bouncing as we hit a rough patch of road that had been plowed and gouged of snow last winter and still had not recovered from its wounds.

"We're not very well-received in Colorado—we're very pro-homosexual."

"Are you gay?"

"Oh no no no no no no no," I cooed, shaking my head. "When Wiggers-Diggler Soft-Drive opened for the Dead in The Congo…"

"Rock *on*," she interrupted, bouncing on more rough road.

"Yes, well, when we opened for the Dead, we were propping open many doors, pushing many boundaries for all-round brotherhood in that country, encouraging people to tape the shows and pass them around amongst their friends. We came back on a high and immediately hit up Utah to some success. We wanted to settle in Colorado because it's kind of the last frontier. Colorado Springs and some remote villages in Burma are really out there, uncivilized, full of missionaries still. Very conservative. We needed to dock in Boulder because it's a safe port of sorts, you know, liberal," I said, winking and smiling at Pudenda, who was smiling with all of her canines and a bicuspid or two. Suddenly we were riding over about a thousand divots. It felt as if the vibration would shake loose every screw and bolt from the pie wagon. There were about ten blurry Pudendas, ten blurry Pudenda boobs wobbling away and ten shaky Pudenda voices, all of them saying something about looking me up in Boulder because she had always wanted to sing.

"I can't speak for my bandmates," I vibrated back to her, "but our main lyricist, Tyler Wiggers—you may have heard of him—he's always wanted to add a female vocalist to his songs. All of his tracks are really from the heart, I mean really personal, and since women are a part of his ying, he'd like a woman to sing the yang. Girls really love him because he's got these droopy, bedroom eyes that just read your soul. If you don't mind really baring your heart to millions of people every night, I can pass your name on to him. But realize the implications: as my granddaddy used to say, with great power comes great power. No messing around in the studio or on stage. You *can*, however, throw televisions and clock radios out of hotel room windows whenever you feel the urge."

"Hell yeah," she said, then, "right on. Rock and roll. Woo-hoo."

"Well, Tyler's working on one of his most important tracks, real romantic, called 'You Make Me Feel Extra-Testicle, Woman (The Mars Testes Overture, Parts One through Three)' and he told me, exclusively, that he wants a female backing vocalist to give the song more of a southern, Georgia kind of flavor, more of a mustard-based barbecue sauce tang to it, as opposed to a tomatoey, ketchup-based feel. He may even need two women, if you don't mind your voice being double-tracked. We could only pay you as one singer unfortunately, but we could cover you food expenses on the road I think," I said all oily, like a record executive would. She was quiet, which unnerved me a little so I continued, "Pro-Teen is our newest venture. We don't play any of the instruments, we leave that up to computers and machines. Nope, it's just our voices dubbed over five times at different speeds so we sound like a bunch of different dudes. As the name implies, we're geared toward the prepubescent female market. We don't like it, but our record company insists on our Pro-Teen singles, or they won't release anything from Tickles Pickles," I said gravely.

"Drag," she said.

"Pro-Teen is rather easy. We have some Swedish Jewish guy who lives in Orlando writing all of our songs. Learning dance steps for our videos is a royal pain in the butt, and appearing live is tricky since we're marketed as a bunch of good-looking studs when there's really just two pretty fair to midland looking fellas: me and Tyler, and sometimes his brother when he's home on leave from the Peace Corps." Pudenda shook her head in befuddlement. "But really, Pudenda, you can feed American teens the biggest pile of doo-doo and they'll gag for more. Kids today are not as discerning as when *we* were budding record buyers, when music meant something."

"I had every Wham! album," she assured me, "except for the first one I think, when they were gangster rappers."

"Wake me up before you go-go," I smiled knowingly. "Anyway, we have found that Germany is a huge market for us. Our singles sell like hotcakes there. And Japan?" I whistled. "Mega huge. Or as they say in Japan, 'kombatanay.'" I saw Pude look off in thought. Surely she didn't speak Japanese? "We do Pro-Teen so that we can pursue our more artistic sides, especially with Tickles Pickles, where we are exploring the usage of live animals on stage. No harm comes to the animal performers, naturally. Bears are fabulous on the marching band bass drum, as you would expect, and the Canadian red-spotted fox has an incredible ear for the xylophone though it has some difficulty holding both mallets in its tiny mouth, unlike its South American cousin. But I digress. As I was saying, sometimes, in order for people to buy more stuff, more quality goods or what have you, you've really got to sell out, as we did knowingly with Pro-Teen. On the other hand, our eighteen-piece band, The Bible, which I think I mentioned earlier, really sells itself without much promotion. We have thus far refused to make music videos for The Bible. Integrity, you know, integrity, integrity, integrity." I was talking so fast a fleck of spittle launched from my mouth and carved out a tiny, bubbly crater in the dust of the dashboard. I quickly moved my foot over it. "But we're trying to take back a little artistic integrity with Pro-Teen. Right now, I'm working on some lyrics that pay homage to all the great lyricists of our time, particularly Rodgers, Hammerstein, Manilow. I want to incorporate all the great songwriters' most thought-out lines and put them all in one song. To wit," and I looked skyward, "I've been waitin'" then I interrupted myself. "Well, first, we'd start with a little acoustic sitar, maybe classical guitar, probably in D-minor, then Tyler would overlay that with some chiming chord progressions on his '48 Rickenbacker. Um, I'm thinking of a sliding descending scale in syncopated seven-sixteenth measure, which is a little tricky, kind of jazzy with a churning, Southern boogie woogie time signature—" and I looked skyward again:

"I've been waitin', just anticipatin',

Like a thief in the night ("That's a little-known Biblical reference actually"),

You're an angel from above,

The one I'm thinking of, the one I dream of, the only one I love

My only love ("That's quadruple rhyme. Rare for a pop song"),
When the mountains crumble into the sea,
May the rain come down and wash me
And my foolish pride ("Why the hell is pride always foolish, never just plain dumb?")

'Cause I'm on a fast train ("It's never a slow train is it?") like a river to the sea

Sha la la hoo yeah la la right on sha la la la la la.

She was painfully quiet, then said, "It kind of sounds like you're mixing some metaphors, Dirk."

You know, that's the problem with the world today: you try to baldly lie to people and the only thing they can say is that you're mixing metaphors, dangling participles, and stuff.

"Possibly, possibly," I said, trying to sound condescending, using a three-second pause with added sigh for effect. "Unfortunately I didn't get to utilize what we in the craft call the 'poetically juxtapositioned prepositional phrase,' which is, well, it's easier to give an example: 'my love has no end, on my love you can depend.' Get it? Instead of saying 'you can depend *on my love*' which is how any ordinary, unpretentious person says it, you switch it around: on my love you can depend. It's all about the rhyme scheme, mainly because 'love' and 'depend' don't rhyme. You also find the most gifted song crafters penning things such as 'I'll be forever true.' Oh no you won't. You'll be *true forever*. It's kind of a sub-branch of the juxtaposed poetic prepositional phrase. Only the craftiest can devise a rhyme for 'forever.' Tyler can but he's a rare bird, the yellow-bellied sap sucker of songwriting you might say."

Pude stifled a yawn behind her hand. "How about 'never?' That rhymes with forever."

"For never?" I guffawed. "A bit linguistically awkward. To change the plot a bit from chasing the muse, I'll tell you about Pro-Teen. I think you might be shocked: Don't go too deep! The kids don't want to hear it. The boys don't listen, and the girls play only one track on your album over and over again, usually the one they hear on the radio. It's kind of infuriating because they never get to track fifty-six entitled 'Paper Sailboat on Walden Pond,' on our eight double-sided album 'Frankly Zappatista.' 'Paper Sailboat on Walden Pond' was my first stab at song writing, when I was a fairly precocious four-year-old. Tyler takes control of most of the lyrics but I had the words, originally as a poem, in a notebook tucked away for years in a desk drawer recently discovered behind a wall in an old guy's attic in Pennsylvania. Back then the words would just flow," I sighed, crossing my arms and looking in the distance. I shook my head as if to clear my thoughts. "But as I was saying, The Bible really kind of sells itself on its own merits as far as shifting units on the shelves of big-box corporations, or finding its way into elementary school classrooms as a teaching device. Let's just say The Bible albums don't sit for too long in the used cassette bins at DerfMart," I chuckled.

"Wow, you know a lot about the biz," Pudenda said with another yawn.

"Flattery will get you some places dame," I smiled, all doe-eyed. "No, I recorded my first song, a capella, at age two, albeit with lyrics provided by my Uncle Matthew, who was quite a famous jug player in his younger days. His jug was always lying around the living room and it was this instrument that I first picked up at age three. He bought me my own jug a year later and we began playing nightclubs in the area before going nationwide. And you know what, it was then that I realized that I wanted to be one of those people who walks into a room and everyone says, 'He's got it, that certain thing that makes someone a star. You can't describe what it is, you just have to have it. And he's got it. When he comes into a room, you can just feel the electricity. He's an amazing talent.' *That's* what I've always wanted, Pudenda."

"And do you have it?"

I puffed my cheeks and exhaled loudly as if I had devoted sleepness nights of exhaustive thought to the idea. "I'm working on it. I'm working on it. The problem is, you don't really know you have it unless someone writes in a magazine about you having it. Usually it comes as a complete shock to the person who has it, who always claims to have been an awkward, ugly duckling in high school and is still just a goofy nerd deep down inside, despite now dating supermodels or, in actuality, *being* a supermodel."

"Hhhhhhmmmm, I don't know if I have it," she said earnestly. I left her alone inside of her brain for half a minute.

"You know, Wiggers-Diggler Soft-Drive is our real vehicle. I think we could use your down-home innocence on track three, side four, 'Thelma and Louise Lived!' Do you know how to play the saw, perchance?"

"I don't think so, but my grandfather used to, I think. Or maybe it was the spoons he played. God, I can't remember now." She foolishly asked what else I played.

"Have you got all day? A little accordion, some violin, piano, Wurlitzer, guitar, flugelhorn, drums, flute, harp, trumpet, Jew's harp, French horn, cello. I'm also self-taught on the—" and I made this clucking sound with my tongue, then made a noise like a brontosaurus choking an alligator, "which is a rare African instrument played by gently hammering a string of giraffe teeth with the femur of a hippopotamus." Now, Pudenda was no dumb blonde, and she began to look incredulous, so I spoke spit-fire again. "But," I said, shrugging and putting my fingers gently on the dash, "it's hard to capture our studio sound live, which is why our album 'LIVE…Outside of Wembley…and down the block a little in someone's back garden….' was one of our weaker sellers. It did quite well in Iceland however."

She slowed down and pulled onto a dirt road. We lurched to a stop and I nearly knocked my teeth on the windshield. "Well Dirk," she sighed, "this is the end of our earthly voyage together. There's my house," she said, pointing to a little rectangular wooden hut across the river and tucked behind some pines in a sage grove. A line of multi-colored Buddhist prayer flags nailed to a porch post whipped in the wind.

"Just like that?" I squeaked.

"Well, I'm thinking that I have to go home and do some homework and you have to head down to Boulder," she said so easily. Already I was feeling morose about never seeing her boob again. I opened my door, followed by a little nod of my head and a very weak "okay then" and slipped out of the seat. The wind almost blew me back into the cab. "See ya, Bogart," she said, struggling with the gears.

"Homework?" I squeaked. "Are you still in high school?"

"Law school, man," she answered. "On-line, if it works out."

"Pudenda, I think I may be in love with you and we need to discuss sex immediately," I said, but only to myself, thank god. I said something really lame like "See you on the dark side, kid," and was about to shut the door, but stood there transfixed. She nodded a couple of times, smiling. I could just sense she wanted some sort of future with me.

"You know Dirk, it was a really amazing ride with you, and interesting," she said, and I was about to slide back into the seat and her existence, "it's just a shame I'm not physically attracted to you."

I hate hippies. I really do. I slammed the door, not out of anger but out of the necessity of always having to slam the door of a VW bus, otherwise it will not latch. I really can't believe I said "See you on the dark side, kid." I can't believe she said she wasn't physically attracted to me. I've never ever said that to anyone, ever. God, you'd really ruin someone's day saying that. I started to give up on everything. She rolled down her window and offered a little hairy armpitted wave. I hate Buddhist prayer flags. And I hate gosh damn hippies.

I trudged back to the side of the road and after a column of wind whipped past me, the world started doing that quiet thing again. Nothing was astir: I heard the actual sound of air freezing around me, crinkling. I heard a Japanese beetle that had burrowed fourteen feet beneath the permafrost last June take a nibble from an aspen leaf that he had pulled over himself for a blanket and then drift off to a beetle sleep. I heard a jet plane at Heathrow airport briefly rev its starboard engine. Pluto revolved with a creak. I heard the liquid in my eyeballs begin to freeze and gather in deposits at the bridge of my nose. The absolute stillness was like the surprised whisper of mortality, that first second of death after the last second of life, of air rushing away, the empty whoosh and echo of life departing a body, for sound is the last sense to leave us as we leave life, just as it is the first to awaken us with a wail to clear the lungs. Simply quiet.

****

"Are you crazy?!" I wailed. "What do you mean Texas would be a good idea?"

"I just thought it would be warm there, and big. I'm tired of being cold."

"Jeez, Julia, do you have no respect for the wisdom of our culture? Haven't you seen *Thelma and Louise*? Thelma refused to go to Texas, though she never says why. I'm sure she was raped or something there. And they give people the electric chair for everything in Texas, for speeding violations, especially during an election year. No way."

"It was Louise."

"Huh—?"

"It was Louise who didn't want to go to Texas."

"Are you sure?"

"Of course I'm sure, Eliason. What, do you think I'm some sort of idiot?"

"No, of course not. I just always thought it was Thelma."

"Well it was Louise." Sometime in August Julia had said something about running away to Texas. "I just thought we could go visit my grandparents or something. You know they'll take us in. We could stay for a little while at least and, you know, see what they do all day."

I told her that I already knew what they did all day: her grandma boiled chicken for their seven cats and her grandpa fed the birds. And they would sweat, all day, on furniture covered in plastic, in Texas, and at night the shadows would turn brown.

"Well, it just seemed like a good idea," she pouted and said angrily at the same time somehow, and her eyes got all damn sexy. For a second I thought about going to Texas, then my senses got the better of me. You see, a recurring nightmare of mine, not one that I actually have ever dreamt but one that I liked to imagine myself dreaming just to make me appreciate where I was at the time and not in a place like Texas, involved driving through Texas. I would be on the fringes of it, or maybe somewhere worse, like the middle of it, thinking that I could drive a full day and still be in Texas, or maybe I had been there a full lifetime and never been able to get out. It would be summer. The heat would shimmer like waves of water across my hood. There would be nothing but fences and dirt. An old country song would play on the AM radio and remind me of a hot summer night at Grandma's house. My shins would be sweating. The air-conditioner was a goner days ago and just spewed out hot air with grit that shot right into my eyes, yet I would keep it on for circulation. Oil derricks, long ago abandoned, were scattered like gigantic crickets that spit brown stuff across the western wasteland, and a rest stop, composed of triangular shapes of concrete and rod-iron bars, considered very useful and stylish in the 1960s, would offer no shade or reason for even a passing glance. Then my car would start to sputter and die. I never thought of death like driving, however, my hell would be driving an old station wagon down an interminable stretch of Texas highway with one of the red lights on the console coming on, then blinking off, then slowly fading on again, slowly fading off, so you did not know if there was really a problem with the car, or whether the light bulb was just burning out. It was pure unending anxiety, pure unending hell.

"You shouldn't knock it, Eliason. There's a majesty about Texas, a mystery. You can drive forever and never get anywhere. And the wind blows so hard sometimes you can taste the dirt in it. And you know that smell on the street when the rain just starts to fall, the hot dust?" Julia said. She was so sweet I could just eat her up. "People always go to Texas when they're running away, you know, kind of how people always go to New York to make something of themselves. Texas is where you go when you're hiding out from something. The sky is bigger there than anywhere I've ever been and you can just hide under it. It sort of marches down on you if you lie on the ground and look up. It almost has sound, it's so big, like drumbeats that get louder and louder. It just stretches from one horizon to the other. It's real easy to get lost in Texas."

I thought about that for a second. "The only problem is, even if we go to a place as big as Texas, I still have to bring me along. As hard as

I try, I can't ever get away from me," I explained to her. "There's not a car that can drive fast enough to get me away from me."

"I love you Eliason Aloicius Nye," she said very softly to me. "You can bring yourself along anywhere you want us to go." I wanted so badly to say that I loved her too.

And then a ferociously yellow Camaro pulled up. "Hey little chief, hop in."

CHAPTER SIX

"Spring Back, Fall Forward, 9:49 a.m."

"I couldn't just leave you out here, Eliason Aloicius Nye," Willy said, looking across the steering wheel after I propped open the Camaro door. People who actually knew it loved saying my whole name. My name was one of those brilliant ideas that parents sometimes get of creating their unsuspecting child's first name from the last name of his maternal grandmother: Eliason. I always had to repeat my name three times to people. They asked how it was spelled. They knitted their brows. They scratched themselves where they normally would not. It had strange effects on people. Even I would admit, out of a special degree of modesty, that it was a weird name. I might even make fun of my name if it was stuck on somebody else. Eliason Nye. Thank god I never had a sibling, who would have received and been forced to endure my father's mother's name: Teagarden. Imagine prancing around your whole life being called Teagarden Nye. My god. I mean, I always wanted a brother, but not under such circumstances.

"Well hop in, little chief, we have far-flung lands to conquer, damsels to distress, booty to procure through means of buying, borrowing or most commonly in your case, stealing," Willy announced. The thing I liked about Snowshoe Willy was that with him, everything was within the realm of impossibility. One of those impossibilities was the Camaro keeping itself together all the way to

Boulder, however there was Willy in his magic chariot because he could not stand to think of his "little buddy" hitch-hiking over a hundred miles with the possibility of getting picked up by a mass murderer, a psycho or a Republican. I decided that, despite the evils of the world today and the horrific way that one single man could dress himself, the Weeper was not such a bad fellow. The aspens all around us were aflame in ambers and orange, smeared with yellows and in some patches, masses of luminous green held on to unexpired life. "I simply love the fall. What a splendid time to be alive. The sky so rich, the dirt so brown, the fauna—"

"I thought the Camaro was in the shop," I interrupted

"Keys were still in the ignish—just had to trot over and drive her away. Well, actually, Fritz gave me a lift on his handlebars. In fact, he is still in town. I am still feeling the ripple effects of our joyride," he said, lifting his bottom from the seat slightly and caressing his right cheek then his left. "Yessir, I have not ridden gunner on someone's handlebars since junior high, back when Peter Frick—"

"Willy, who's watching the store?" I asked abruptly.

"I thought you might inquire as such," he answered and shrugged. "Door is locked, dude."

I stared at him in disbelief. "Maybe it sounds silly, but did you forget that you have a million dollar deal going down this very morning, a deal of which I'm sure requires your presence?"

"Let me tell you about my grandpapa, little chief," Willy said, twisting his mustache and peering ahead through the snow which was falling with some haste now. I told him that I did not want to hear about his stupid grandpapa and that he needed to turn right around and go back to the shop before it was too late. He completely ignored me.

"I was able to speak quite extensively with my grandpapa during the several months before he died and do you know what he said was his biggest regret in life?"

"Buying the Ice Biter '98 Special Edition, which proved inferior a mere one year later when the Snow Glider '99 was released?" Obviously he was not going to turn around so I figured at least I could humor him.

"My grandfather did not snowshoe," Willy answered, easing the Camaro, which groaned and wheezed petulantly, around a curve. "His biggest regret was that he read too much."

"As opposed to not watching enough television? Finally someone is being truthful about all of this reading nonsense."

"He didn't watch television either, and if somebody would refrain from offering his cute quips I might finish this story before Y2K strikes." I scowled at him as he continued. "The point is, chieftain, my grandpapa wasted much of his life reading, at the dinner table, in bed, at the office, on the weekends. When he had only days to live, he told me that he should have spent more time with family and friends, that a person's life is much more interesting than some old book, and what he would have done to get it all back. The usual lament I suppose."

"But aren't books just stories about people's lives? Don't snap at me."

Willy sighed and coaxed the Camaro around another corner. "You are my friend, little chief, not those Aspen guys. They are of no import to me. You are a part of my life and that is what counts. You are the story of Eliason Nye, and that is what is going on right now. I do not want to miss it."

"Are you trying to make me break down in tears, you bastard?" I asked.

Willy shook his head seriously and rotated a finger violently in his earhole then studied scientifically what lurked underneath the nail.

"But I can't pay your bills Willy, and if *you* can't pay your bills *I* won't have a job and then *I* can't pay *my* bills. Then what are we going to do? Turn the car around please. Drop me off here."

"We will make do, little chief. Do not clutter your head with trivialities."

"Willy, please turn the car around. I can find my own way to Boulder."

"Release yourself from guilt, little chief."

"First of all, shut the hell up. Second of all, drop me off right now. Third of all, shut the hell up. I can make it to Boulder myself, okay? Maybe I *want* to go alone. Stop the car."

85

"You need a friend, Eliason. Trust me."

"Stop the car and let me out Willy. I'm serious. Just leave me alone." Willy kept on driving, not slowing down except for another curve, not listening. I demanded that he stop the car or I would jump out. He kept right on moving, twisting that damn mustache.

"You need me more than you know, young fellow."

"What the hell do I need you for?!" I exploded. Willy jumped a little. I had never really yelled at him before. I think I had never really yelled at anybody before. I yelled, "Huh? Tell me exactly what I need you for?" He eased the car over to the side of the road and turned off the windshield wipers, but kept the engine running. I reached for the door handle.

"Do not get out," he said firmly. Surprisingly I listened. I turned to look at him, not feeling as resentful as I thought I should have. I noticed for the first time that he was wearing a bright-red knitted winter cap, the kind with a beanie on top. Worse, he had sewn a "Farto" patch on the front—you know, Farto is that antacid product that a sizable population of poor flatulent-suffering souls sprinkle on their food to keep from getting gas. The patch had a picture of a bean, that ever musical fruit, with a wisp of gas swirling out from the top. "What the heck do you need me for? I would say that you need a pretty darned good friend right now. At risk of overstepping my boundaries, I might even say that you need someone who would be like a father to you. And as a subset to that thought, you need someone with a car."

I won't tell you much about my father, like what kind of pants he wore or if he owned a pair of pink cowboy boots or if he stirred the milk in his coffee with the handle of the spoon instead of the spoon part of the spoon (if he *took* milk in his coffee) because I frankly don't remember. My father died in a plane crash when I was ten—not a big plane crash with a bunch of screaming, praying passengers like you or me, but a little twin-prop Cessna. He went down with two of his business associates and the pilot somewhere outside of Las Vegas. I always thought it would be an awful place to spend your last second on earth. He was a stoic guy, I think, so it probably didn't bother him, knowing that he was going to die, but I bet it really killed him that he had to die just outside of a crummy, depressing place like Las Vegas. I have little kid memories of him I suppose: going to the zoo with him when he was "in between jobs," going to the park with the twisty slide sticking out of this useless concoction that was supposed to look like a rocket, him picking me up after school with the radio on, having his dad smell of Old Spice and Juicy Fruit gum, his sweet windbreaker collection. I was quite shocked recently when I smelt his breath coming out of my mouth while I was brushing my teeth really close to the mirror, only it was my breath—it wasn't bad breath, it was just an older guy's breath, my dad's breath, coming from my mouth. It was horrifying and comforting. My memories of him are gauzy now, beige in some of the corners, with a dream-like pallor, and every year they get fuzzier; only the photos of us together have the weight of remembrance, probably because I have looked at them so much. They seem more real, more tenable. I remember when my mother was around him she was all angular lines and motion and smiles. She was never the same again after he died. My poor mother. I think the worst thing for her was thinking of him piling into that faceless ground, as if the bleached-out sun and rocks and burning sand would trap his soul. I had always hoped it did not.

There had been quite a long silence between Willy and me after he finally put the Camaro in motion again.

"Oh bother, we change our clocks tonight, do we not little chief?" he asked. I nodded looking at my wrist for a watch that still wasn't there. Willy said, "I never remember what to do, all of this falling forward and springing back nonsense, all because of western society's fear and misappropriation of the number zero many centuries past." I didn't say anything because I had no idea what the hell he was talking about. "So at midnight we set the clocks to one in the a.m. because it gets darker earlier around Halloween time so we want the dark to get here faster, right? Or do we, hold on, if it was seven o'clock at night and dusk, and then we changed the clocks to eight p.m. when it was already dark, we would thus be making it dark earlier by changing from eight to seven, correct? Wait—"

I interrupted. "Snowshoe, tonight, when your watch hits midnight, you will turn those little hands in a counter-clockwise rotation thus making it eleven o'clock, thereby gaining an extra hour of sleep if you're so inclined."

I really used to love October, the smell of it, the dead leaves and the rich shadows, the clean chill of the air and the long twilights. I was pretty excited about gaining an hour. I was excited every year about that hour. I liked the feeling of gaining an hour. It suited me. It should be a national holiday.

"Oh I am so inclined to be reclined for an extra hour!" Willy hooted. "I love getting that extra hour of William time, catching up on the finances, reading a magazine of my choosing, taking a bower (this allegedly is when Willy royally reclines in his tub with the shower head raining down upon him and the drain plugged: bath+shower=bower), maybe even going for a shoe in the cemetery. Hot diggity dog, I am a gain-an-hour kind of guy. Are you quite sure you are correct about this procedure?"

I think my mother had been beautiful once, especially when my father was alive, and she was still pretty in a mom way, always wearing a headband like a 1950s housewife, and I'm not stumbling into that trap that people always fall into headlong when a woman is dying and everyone around her says 'Oh she was *so-oh-oh-oh* beautiful. You should have known her when…blah blah blah blah blah.' And then you see a picture of the so-called Miss America and she was an absolute rattler. Women, when they are dying, suddenly become beautiful, and men, even if they used the bones of orphaned children to floss their teeth, are magically transformed into *the kindest, gentlest man you'd ever meet.* You know what it reminds me of—when some big fat liar says they either "love someone to death" or love someone "dearly." If you ever hear these words beginning to leak out of someone's mouth then just tell them straight away to shut the hell up, they're full of crap and to go to hell. Por ejemplo:

"I told you about my sister, didn't I? The one who got 1.6 million dollars in her palimony suit and is spending everything on herself? Don't get me wrong, I love my sister to death, but she should really think about me and the rest of her blah blah blah blah blah...." Or even better:

"My friend Carlyle is a bit of a loser, I know. I mean, I love him dearly, but I'm not sure why I'm even friends with blah blah blah...."

You know ten times out of ten, if someone says they love someone to death or love so-and-so dearly then they may well be the lyingest, filthiest, most execrable person on the planet and they don't deserve such a good friend as you. I mean it.

"Willy, why the hell do you always say in *the* a.m. but never in *the* p.m.? You know Oklahoma Bob down at the bank? He does the same thing. He never says, 'Today is Friday so your transaction will be processed Monday.' No, it's always 'Today is Fri*dee* so your transaction will be processed Mon*dee*.' I mean, he doesn't say, 'To*dee* is Fri*dee*,' does he?" Willy looked astonished. "And you know he damn well knows it's pronounced Fri*day*, but he pronounces it wrong just to bug the hell out of you and remind you that he's from Oklahoma, and you can't say anything because he has your money 'tied up in frozen assets, inactivated accounts' and other phrases that make no sense. Bastard."

Willy reached over and patted me on the knee. I jumped like a surprised cat. He told me, "Your crankiness will not deter me from my mission, nor is your sour disposition going to distract me from having a killer extra hour sometime today. I cannot wait. And try to keep your feet on the mat," he ordered, passing a disapproving glance at my boots. The "mat" was so threadbare it was just a collection of sinewy strings with a couple of rubber pieces thrown in for effect.

"Snowshoe, you know we're getting ripped off?" He looked at me from the corners of his eyes. "That' right. Think about that hour we gain in the fall. We are given an hour every year, right? Now let's say your average white male, you or me, lives to be eighty. From birth, that's eighty hours given to us for nothing. We don't have to pay for them or anything, we just have to survive. That means, and check my math here though I know it's not your strong suit and the only reason you have an English lit degree is because you didn't want to take math classes in college, but those eighty hours add up to over three extra days of living." Willy strangled the steering wheel in what I could tell was deep thought. "Three extra days!" I reiterated. The Weep was thinking, I knew, because I saw his shoulders slouch a bit and his body relax.

"That is right, Eliason. You are absolutely right," he whispered.

"You bet I'm absolutely right. And guess what else, Willy?" I paused for just a moment after he could not guess, though I gave him credit for wasting two whole minutes of those three theoretical days trying to guess what else. "Those fascists take our three days away from us every spring." I felt the Camaro decelerate. Willy was one of those guys who could generally only uni-task, I suppose because he was responsible enough to devote all his attention and energy to the most important matter at hand, which had been driving, but soon we would be going in reverse with all of his brain-draining.

"Dadgummit, Eliason, do you have to ruin everybody's day?" he said, followed by yet another kind of crappy Hollywood sigh.

"I'm just thinking of our economy—six bucks an hour, 270 million people in the U.S., eight hours a day times three days equals twenty-four multiplied by six bucks times 270 million people every year. That's a lot of money not going to Weeping Willy's Snowshoes." I really would have loved to have done the hard numbers but, come on. "All because there are spring forward people in this world."

Willy did not say anything, his foot like a feather on the gas pedal as he fell deeper into thought. He jutted his finger in the air when he finally spoke. "Eliason, you may well be an alarmist."

"I beg your pardon."

"It is not so esoteric, this losing and gaining of hours ritual. It's just a less than perfect system we inherited from our less than perfect Copernican ancestors. I suppose you have a deep-seeded almost Freudian problem with the leap year as well?"

"Well, Willy, as a matter of discussion, does it not seem odd to you that a leap year is every four years? Why not give us the extra day for three years and take one day off the fourth year? Why not do that for us and our struggling economy? Do I have to do the math for you again? Don't be so naïve, chief," I said. I swear to god, I couldn't tell if this was a serious conversation or not.

"Think of all the children we could feed in Cambodia if we had that extra day for a little more work," Willy said, bless him.

"Cambodia was for starving kids when *you* were a youngster. All the starving children have moved to Ethiopia now," I informed him. "Think about it though, Willy—we could get rid of poverty just by getting rid of the leap year. Sometimes the simplest change makes the biggest difference." I swear to god I could not tell if we were being serious or not.

"We could call it the Great Leap Year Forward or something to that effect," Willy said, then pushed a hearty "humph" my way. Being born in mid-February meant that Willy was an Aquarius, which entitled him to come up with the slogans for the Big Ideas without actually doing any of the work for them—that was up to the Aries of the world. He was instantly lost in alliteration and assonance, I'm quite sure, and other measures for how to feed the hungry when all he really had to do was become a famous actor. Suddenly we were gaining in altitude, reaching a part of our little corner of the mountains that had been sliced, diced and completely gouged for apparently an invaluable substance that, when accidentally leeched into water (such as our drinking supply), kills almost instantly and, we're told from people who "have nothing to gain from the mining business," practically painlessly.

"What about groundhog day, grumpy butt? Do you have any Communist manifestos against that particular holiday?" Willy asked rather tetchily after what seemed fifteen minutes. I had already lost the thread of that conversation so of course I did not have to answer how ridiculous that day was, and instead watched the watercolor world blur by my window.

"You know who picked me up?" I asked Willy after several minutes had passed. He could not guess, though he spent another two minutes of our short lives trying to guess, again. "This pretty cute hippy chick wearing a hat from a hair-loss commercial. Her name was," and I realized that I had completely forgotten her name already. "Plutanda or Pudanja or Plutonium or something weird like that. She lives with a girl called Snowwheat, some extra-stinky hippy dudes and like a hundred dogs. They have prayer flags on their porch."

"Extraordinary," Willy said. "Did you know her already?" I shook my head. Willy said, "See, not all hippies are bad? She gave a complete stranger a lift," he said triumphantly. "'When a brother is in his hour of need call on the hippiest of hippies indeed.' What did you kids talk about?"

"Oh, rock and roll and stuff, you know, Neil Young and Bob Dylan and stuff."

Willy glanced over at me in disbelief. "Why, every time I try to put on one of their long plays in the store you start fake retching and calling them whiny old hippy bastards. I had just about given up on you ever appreciating *real* music. I'm so proud of you, Eliason," then he narrowed his eyes at me. "Did she offer to partake in a sex act if you listened?"

"Please," I huffed.

"Was she the brunette we saw down by the creek, remember when we drove by the group of protesters last week, and her breasts were hanging out of her top?"

"No, I don't think so. I didn't notice," I answered, turning a little red. Willy shot me another skeptical look. "She did say she wasn't physically attracted to me. Can you believe that?"

He looked a little perplexed. "How does a woman go about saying that she is not physically attracted to a fellow, just out of the blue?"

"She was dropping me off and said something like, 'Okay Dirk, this is where our planetary voyage ends' or something like that, then she said 'It's such a shame that I'm not physically attracted to you.' How uncool is that?" I felt miserable all over again.

"I will not ever claim that I always understand women, Eliason, but mayhaps she was picking up on some pheromones that you were exuding and they did not agree necessarily with her particular body chemistry. Why did she call you 'Dirk'?"

"It's a long story," I said dolefully. "I bet if I was rich or in a movie or something she would have extended our earthly voyage. I hate hippies."

"If you *were* rich or in a movie. Now, now," Willy scolded. "At least she gave you a ride. And besides, why do you have to worry if girls are attracted to you or not? You have Julia and she is all you need."

I shrugged. "A man wants to know if he's still got it, no matter his circumstances."

"I suggest you start concentrating on what you already have before you lose it instead of wasting energy on what you will, and should, never procure."

"When did you turn into such a preachy old bastard?" I said, and immediately I felt bad for saying it, but it was the kind of thing that, after being said, could not be immediately apologized for, nor could Willy have granted forgiveness had I asked for it, without the whole scenario smacking of Hollywood hypocrisy. We both knew it, and we both allowed ourselves to act out our prescribed emotions: me residually angry and Willy lingeringly offended. The minutes dripped by.

"Hey Willy?" I said after a while.

"Yes, Eliason?" he answered, prickly picking out each syllable, the vowels and "-esses" like ice dropped into a glass of scotch by a guy trying to kick the habit.

"Do you see that idiot on the bicycle just up ahead, all decked out in his spandex like it's summer and he's in the Tour de France?" Willy extended his neck slightly, looked over to the shoulder and told me he saw the biker well up ahead. "And do you see the car coming down the mountain towards us, way up the road up there?" Willy stretched his neck more but said he could not see so far even on a clear day with no snow, and that his glasses were completely fogged up anyway, which was very reassuring from a passenger's perspective. "Well, a car is coming our way. I can see its headlights and I think something interesting is going to happen."

"Like what?" Willy asked, politely stifling a yawn.

"Just don't slow down, whatever you do," I said, feeling the car immediately pull back as if he had activated a parachute from the rear. "I said don't slow down, give it gas—but don't speed up! Not so fast now. You're killing me Willy."

"What is it?!" Willy asked in a slight panic.

"Just drive natural, like I didn't say anything," I instructed.

"Well how can I act naturally now that you have introduced these artificial parameters? Shall I maintain a constant velocity or nay?"

"There's no parameters, just drive as if I wasn't here."

"You *were not* here."

"Very well," I said, grinning, thinking that Willy was doing that little act when someone says "Forget I even said that," and the other person says "Said what?" as if he had already forgotten or never heard, but with Willy he usually started explaining again what he had said when someone asked "Said what?" because he was quite literal. Albert Einstein was the same way and could never remember his own street address *{phone number—ed.}*. "Okay, I was never here."

"You *were* never here," Willy repeated.

I said "Oooookay," assuming that Willy had begun to lose his metaphysical mind.

"You *were* never here, not you *was* never here. Conditional," he said, tapping his right nostril. "If I were a rich man, if I were a poor man," he sang under his breath.

"Oh, oh yeah," I said, staring blankly through the windshield, watching the oncoming car get closer as it sped toward us, the biker looming larger on the right. "I think you're slowing down," I said, which was (were?) the Pavlovian conditional response for Willy to immediately remove his foot from the gas pedal. "Snowshoe, don't slow down!" at which he immediately crushed the pedal like a cockroach with the pad of his foot, at which I was thrown to the back of the seat under the sudden G-force. "Jeez, just act natural, dammit."

"Naturally," he corrected, even in his state of mild panic. "What is happening? Why are you doing this? And there is no profanity in the Camaro."

"Ease up on the gas, and just keep doing what you were doing before, you're doing fine, just fine," I said, like a kind dentist to a kid getting a filling.

"But what am I doing?" Willy begged. "Oh Eliason, what is about to happen?"

"Just hold steady," I said soothingly. "Oh my gosh, there's one of those big portable orange signs for loose gravel up ahead." Willy immediately decelerated. "Don't slow down!" I commanded. He immediately sped up. "Don't speed up!" He slowed down.

"Oh little chief, please tell me what is happening. I beg of you," Willy said. It took all my will power not to burst out laughing, it really did.

"Just hold steady, you're doing good," I told him. "Almost there Willy, almost there. Don't fail me now. Here it comes, here it comes." I glanced at Willy who had his eyes trained, unblinking, on the road ahead. "Almost there. Watch carefully. Ahh, wait for it. Heeeerrre…itttt…is!" I exploded, and precisely at that moment, the oncoming car, the bicyclist, the street sign and the Camaro were perfectly in line, passing each other at the same time. "Did you see it?" I breathed.

"You are doing *well!*" Willy erupted. "You are doing well!! And what the hell did I miss?!" I noticed little beads of perspiration between the first fold of his cap and his bushy blond eyebrows that, many times I had told him before, could have used a friendly trim.

"The law of common convergence, obviously," I said, folding my arms tightly against my chest. "And there is no cursing in the Camaro."

Willy looked at me, wide-eyed and speechless through his glasses, then spat out, "And what is the law of com and convergence?" He was annoyed. I asked if he was annoyed.

"No I'm not annoyed!" he snapped.

I told him softly "Com*mon* convergence, not com *and* convergence. It's a little theory I've been dragging around for some years now. You just witnessed a little nugget of science, in real time." He looked ready to strangle me so I did not hesitate: "Didn't you see how we all passed each other at the same time—the cars, the bicyclist, the street sign, on this desolate patch of road at what time is it? What are the chances? That's the law of common convergence."

Willy looked at me angrily. "Do you want to feel how my heart is pounding? Do you?"

"Keep your heart to yourself, boy," I told him but he began to puff up his cheeks in agitation. I cut him off. "The question is, of course, were you meant to slow down or is there a psychological impulse to want to slow down or speed up, how much did I affect your speed and decision-making, would we have been further up the mountain if your

car actually had the power to go uphill faster than a prairie schooner—
" he looked defensive—"is it gravitational pull that brings all the
objects together at the same time, a bending of the thread of attraction,
a cupping in the fabric of space and time though none of the objects are
massive enough to have such an effect on their surroundings or other
bodies, or is it just luck?" Willy looked slightly more contemplative. "It
happens so often, Bear. I just can't write it off as luck. I mean, how
many times have you backed out of your driveway and you always have
to stop and wait for someone to drive by, even though only about four
people live on your little country road. And three of them don't even
drive."

"It is just chance, chieftain," Willy said, still trying to sound miffed
and dismissive, but I knew his wheels were turning.

"No such thing as chance. It seems almost pre-ordained."

"Fate then," he offered. I shook my head. "Fate's too big. It's too
dreamy, too God-like, too fake. This is something more scientific."

"I think maybe it is just random, little chief."

"So the universe tends to fall into disarray?" He looked at me
worriedly. "Or is it ordered randomness?"

"Okay Mr. Metaphysical. Ho-hum, ho-hum, tired old idea," he
smiled to himself smugly. "What you must deal with, unfortunately my
little scientist, is the uncertainty principle, as applied to the quantum
world in quite a departure from the realm of classical thinking and
given life by the German physicist Werner Hindenburg {*Heisenberg—
ed.}*. In a nutshell, he states that the more we try to study something,
more pointedly, the *closer* we attempt to mark its surrounding and
movement, the more *impact* we have on its natural state, obviously.
The more you try to grab a bouncing molecule, not unlike a woman, the
more it tries to slip away." Sometimes Willy was a pretty smart guy.

"Well, I mean, it *has* to have a human there to witness it and record
it, otherwise it doesn't really happen does it? Well, it happens but who
cares that it happened if no one says anything about it. You know, a
deer doesn't look up from chewing some grass and think 'Whoa, those
cars almost hit each other.' To a deer it's just cars driving by, but you
know, if a human is there and, and *thinks* about it—" but the smarmy

bastard had made me lose my thread. "If the two cars hit each other and knock over the guy on the bike then it's just an accident really, not the law of common convergence. But if they *don't* hit and someone was there and thinks 'Whoa that was close, if I had left my house two seconds earlier I would have hit that dude' then it's kind of like the law of common convergence, I guess. I don't know. Just shut it."

"The more Eliason Nye attempts to find out why two cars keep passing each other at the same time, the more they slide away. I am sorry, chieftain. I do like the way it sounds though, the alliteration," and he repeated three times "the Law of Common Convergence," putting stress on different syllables, saying that it might need another hard "kuh" sound to be more commonly accepted.

"Well, you work on the aural mechanics of this generation's next greatest scientific breakthrough while I—" and there was a horrific explosion underneath the car. KaBOOM!!

CHAPTER SEVEN

"All Froze Up,
10:02 a.m. "

KaBOOM!! Actually it was more like a terrific slipping pop, the sound of the splitting ligaments in a 45-year-old guy's knee during a game of touch football in the front yard on an icy Christmas Eve.

"Oh dear!" Willy cried out, the front of the hood now veering across the opposite lane and pointing toward a 600-foot drop, and certain death. Three dudes had driven off the very same spot last winter, only going downhill—corpses.

"We are going over, young brave!" Willy called. "And we do not have on our safety belts!"

The sound of a thousand strangled geese was screaming from under the hood. In his panic, Willy stuck his foot to the brake with such force I almost swallowed my tongue. The car skidded an undramatic five inches and settled into inertia. Willy looked over at me, his glasses all fogged up.

"Run for it chieftain!" and he threw his door open, kicked it shut and instantly disappeared. The car was belting out a steady "rar-rar-ree-rar, rar-ree-ree-rar," so loud and piercing. The entire frame trembled, so I reached over and turned the key because that is what cool guys in movies always do. If I had been standing outside the Camaro gazing into its headlight eyes it would have looked at me like your miserable, dying dog does when you finally tell him that he will be going to that farm where all doggies go when it is that time. "Thank you," the Camaro said with watery headlight eyes, shuddered in a wave from tailpipe to grille and went "ping." Then silence. We were dead center sideways, straddling both lanes. I peered through the driver's side window to see Willy lifting himself off the street, delicately picking his way around the back of the car and brushing off his chest and butt. I propped myself up and leaned over in order to see out his window: the fattest, most perfect snow angel was standing out in asphalt grey from the snow. There was a whump-whump at my window made from the side of Willy's mittened hand. "Is everything okay in there?" he asked through the glass.

"It's not bad," I answered.

"You did not run for it."

"We're pretty far from going over the cliff," I informed him. "In fact, we're kind of sitting right in the middle of the road."

"Expertly deduced," Willy said, smoke pouring from his mouth, flakes collecting on the top of his cap. He stood outside, scanning from the front of the car to the back, then over to both shoulders of the road, up and down the hill. "Well, I have made an area risk-management assessment and concluded that it is safe to return to this vehicle," he shouted through the glass, and I watched him prance once more around the back of the car, crank open the door and wedge himself back into the driver's seat. "I think you killed the 'Maro, dude," he said lowly.

Offended, I asked how *I* had killed the Camaro.

"All of that incessant slowing down and speeding up and slowing down and attempting to maintain a constant velocity. It was too much for the old girl, too confusing."

"When is the last time the old girl has had a tune-up?"

"Moot point. You are a killer of cars," Willy said, wiping the sweat from his brow with the back of his mitten, "and now we are two of those people you always see stranded on the side of the road about whom you always think 'But if there by the grace of God go I.'"

"Well at least we're not dead," I said, nodding toward the cliff. Willy said "pff" to the windshield. "And, and we still have each other." He shot me a quizzical look then returned to staring straight out the windshield again, his shoulders high, like you would see a husband do when he was lost and his wife suggested consulting a map, at which the husband would stop the car in a huff and spray, "Do you want to drive—do you?!"

"Snowshoe, I'm no mechanic, but I think we have a problem." And for the first time that I had known Willy, possibly for the first time since his teepee session, he looked like he was going to start acting like a verifiable man: maybe he would call me a moron, he could toss a cuss word my way I hoped, he may mock me in a high-pitched voice, he may just tell me to "shut the hell up, I'm thinking."

"Could be anything," he said instead, softly. "I have not taken her out in some time. She is probably all frozen up under the hood." I loved that Willy called his car "she" and that he said vaguely mechanical things like "under the hood."

"Sounded like a blown fuel gasket," I suggested, having no idea what I was talking about.

"Do ya think so?" he said without a twitch of a facial muscle. I had to admit that Willy, just by the tone in his voice and the near catatonia in his expression, could always make a guy wonder if he was being completely mocked or if he was being taken seriously.

"I don't know though, I mean it could be your clutch or something. Like I said, I'm no mechanic." No response. "Or it could be something bad like a universal joint." No response. "Heck, it could just be that your washer fluid is low."

He just sat there looking dully out the windshield. At least he wasn't the kind of jerk that would tell me to go to hell and go look under the hood. All he said was "Just a minute, Eliason," heaved open his door and labored to the front of the car where he proceeded to scamper about like a scientist jumping from one fizzing test tube to another. He reached underneath the grill, then beat the nose of the hood once with the underside of his mitten, then hunched down, completely disappearing for a full minute, though not because he had slipped like before, and he remained supine in temporary paralysis while I offered no assistance. He popped back up, mitten-less, wiping his palms on his chest like he had accomplished something terrific, opened the door and slid into the seat.

"Hummpphhh. How's about reaching into the glove box and passing over the owner's manual?" he said, pointing to the glove box as if, just because he could not figure out how to pop open the hood, I must be a bigger wing-nut unable to locate the glove box at my knees. I asked how long he had owned the Camaro.

"Twenty-six and a half years," he proudly replied.

"And you still don't know how to pop open the hood?" I said, passing him the thin booklet in its faux leather pouch.

"I believe she is all froze up, General Washington. Now shush." He flipped through the brown, dusty manual that is placed in every car and singularly designed by auto experts to tell you absolutely nothing in an effort to make you feel like a complete tit. I gathered from the wrinkled circles embossed on the front of Willy's manual that its main use since about the year 1978 was as a coffee cup coaster. "This damn thing doesn't say anything!" he erupted after about twenty seconds of perusal, after which he nevertheless leaned over and placed the useless artifact back to its resting place as gingerly as he would have a ruby on a bejeweled pillow. "Maybe you could give it a turn," he offered meekly.

I did not say anything, only pushed a Hollywood sigh his way and opened my door, the wind piercing me instantly with a shock to all of my involuntary bodily functions. Surely I would die in seconds of hypothermia but, mustering strength, I trudged to the hood, pounded with both fists on it five or six times like you see a tough guy in a movie do to his buddy's chest just after he has been dragged from drowning out of the ocean, and then the drowner miraculously starts spewing a cookie-dough mixture of sand, water and crabs from his mouth and everyone crowded around starts crying and laughing in relief. Miraculously the hood sprang open and almost knocked me on the underside of the chin. I found a ribbed length of frayed rubber lying atop the engine, grabbed it and returned to the sanctity and steadily diminishing warmth of the car.

"What the hay?" Willy instantly said after I jumped into the car.

"Do you think this is important?" I asked, holding up the rubber piece where it hung over my hand in a slightly rigid C-shape.

"What is it?" he asked, slightly aghast.

"A piece of rubber something," I answered smartly.

"Well I can see that, dummy, but what is its function?"

"Obviously, it's a very important piece of rubber because it has these ridges in it," I said professionally, running a finger down the side. Willy eagerly shifted in closer, lifting his glasses and squinting his eyes at the mysterious object, "and you can see here, no just down here Willy, see where it is split and all burnt up? Yep, there's the problem."

Willy dropped his glasses back onto the bridge of his nose and stared at me a little cross-eyed. "Hey, that is pretty good, Eliason."

I could see that he was impressed. I shrugged a little and smiled.

"It looks like a giant rubber band almost," Willy breathed, "or a belt of some sort."

"Yeppo, that's the prob," I said, wagging the rubber snake in my hand. "Don't think we're going to be finding any of these on the side of the road or even at any of our local garages. These things are probably not very easy to come by, not very common, and not cheap. You'll probably have to special-order one from Europe or Japan or something."

"Well dadgum," Willy said, gazing out of the windshield again, his eyes fixed on the abyss over the opposite shoulder. "We were a good twenty, fifty meters from going over the side I would wager."

"A fairly close call," I responded though in fact it never was.

"And yet you stayed with the Camaro," Willy said, almost tearing up I thought. "I thought she was going to blow."

"She's the mother ship," I told him, then added, "I've already lost one car this year, I'm *not* losing another."

He gazed upon me with complete gratitude.

"I am a wretched car owner," he lamented.

"There there," I said, not sure if we were being serious, but I think we were.

"What does that say about me, that I bailed on the Camaro so quickly?" I stared at him with raised eyebrows. He was being serious.

"Eliason, what if I desert my friends with such haste when I am called upon during a time of action? What if I am not there for them? What if, what if I 'chicken out?'"

"Do I have to remind a certain Pawnee—who shut down his shop just to drive his buddy all the way to Boulder? Who laughed at a million-dollar deal and said 'Some other day, Cochise.' Who didn't think twice about braving the season's first and nastiest storm just to help a pale-face out?"

Willy beamed. "I guess that would be me." I gave him my biggest Eliason smile.

"Though I am in fact descended from a branch of the Pueblo, a very peace loving, sedentary tribe," he said.

"Naturally," I replied.

Willy twisted his mustache, still grinning and beaming. "Hey Eliason?" to which I said, "Yes, my sedentary, peace-loving friend."

"Um, due to the fact that we are currently sprawled across two lanes of traffic, and a car barreling downhill may have trouble seeing us and coming to a halt in these icy conditions, do you think it would be a capital idea to push the Camaro to the shoulder?"

"Yeah, pretty capital," I said, and in not so many seconds I found myself, alone, grunting and attempting to manhandle the Camaro to a safe resting place on the shoulder.

"Well, *someone* has to steer," Willy reasoned. After so many minutes in which I pulled a right hamstring, scrunched the entire left inner sole of my boot into the toe compartment of my left boot and practiced grunting some curse words that Willy had probably never heard, the Camaro was resting safely on the shoulder of the road, although facing the wrong way. I stood next to Willy's door with hands on knees, panting. He slowly rolled down his window.

"Eliason, it just occurred to me that we are facing the wrong way."

"Is that so?" I said, an entire icy sheet, formerly sweat, for the second time in not so many hours now encasing my body underneath my many layers. "William, this car is from the era when cars were actually made of steel, not fiberglass and plastic. Plus, it contains your 275-pound butt, so all in all, it's quite heavy." A halo of smoke encircled my head, thick mist leaking from my mouth, some vapors twirling directly from my scalp, like I was in some mentho-lyptus throat lozenge commercial.

"Two-hundred-thirty-three pound bottom" he said, hastily rolling up his window. I waited for some minutes then let myself into the car. I knew he was agitated.

"Willy, we'll put a little orange flag on the antenna and the cops will know that something is wrong with the car and not mess with it."

"Why is my weight such an issue with you?" Oh gawd. "Maybe I have a thyroid problem. And why do you always have to do things backwards just to be different, pushing the car the wrong way just to get back at me? You could do well to think about others sometimes." His cheeks were all rosy and blotchy, his hands resting on the steering wheel like he was still driving.

"I was really just letting gravity do the work, Willy. You did the steering. I can try and turn the car around for you." He was silent again, twiddling his mittens like a little kid.

"Maybe my ancestors were mountain-dwellers, the cold climate type, and were predisposed to collect fat in the body. You should count yourself lucky, you," he said, hands still on the wheel. "One afternoon of snowshoeing and you come back looking like Adonis."

"I'm sorry, Willy, I was just joking around. Your weight is not an issue with me." This completely disarmed him. "And you know I'm quite far from ever being Adonis."

"I have been trying to lose weight, little chief, but it is such an aggressive endeavor. It is not just a past-time for the leisure class."

"I know that."

"It is a relentless task, chip chip chipping away, twenty-four hours a day. And it hurts! But I have been doing my best, Eliason, my best by golly."

"That's all we can ask for," I assured him. We sat there quietly looking downhill on the wrong side of the road, like two idiots in the first roller coaster car cresting the first big hump. The snow was beginning to collect on the hood and already our tire tracks were invisible. You could not hear a sound save for Willy's breathing.

"Believe you me, I want to be just as desirable as the next guy," Willy said.

"Don't we all," I told him. He looked over at me like he was going to say something, but decided against it and just stared at me, like he was trying to decipher some sort of look on my face. I thought I noted a vague smile awakening on his face, but after several moments he returned his gaze to the windshield and we sat in silence.

"Do you believe in epiphanies?" he asked after some minutes, almost to himself it seemed.

"Like tooth fairies and pixie dust and stuff?"

"No," he said, shifting his body to face me. "An epiphany is a moment of striking personal realization or insight."

"Oh," I said, thinking. "Well, it's always happening to guys in movies. You know, the part where they snap their fingers and say 'I got an idea and it just might work.'"

"No no no," Willy corrected me. "You are thinking of the Hollywood Farcical Flash of Ingenuity. An epiphany is something that changes a person's life forever."

"Oh," I said again, thinking again. "Like losing your arm?"

"No, that's a tragic accident. An epiphany happens here," he said, pointing a fat mitten at my heart. "And then here," he said, pointing the same fat mitten at my head. I felt like I was having a Hollywood False Flash of Phoniness.

"That never happens in real life," I told him. "That kind of stuff only happens to people on TV or in movies. It's so stupid and fake."

Willy placed a big actor's sigh right on the seat next to me. Siigghh. "Eliason (siigghh), what is the last *book* you read, and when?"

Well I had to think real long about that one. The snow even stopped for a period while I thought, then started up again.

"I suppose it was 'Beloved,' or 'The Beloved' maybe, about the kid who dies."

Willy looked astonished, then instantly skeptical.

"Okay, what was the last book you *chose* to read, not one you were *forced* to read in English 102 class?"

"What does it matter whether I *chose* to read it or I was *forced* to read it, I still read it didn't I?"

"As you like, little chief," he said, staring without blinking at me.

"What?" I asked, somewhat annoyed.

"Well, what did you think about it?"

"About what?" I said, deflated.

"The book," he said, "the book!"

I gazed out the windshield, desperately trying to find that little pocket of my brain where I stored my book reading memories. I failed. "I guess I didn't really get it."

Willy guffawed and started clucking wildly like a chicken on a runaway Guatamalan mountainside bus.

"Nobody in class knew what the hell he was talking about, not even the professor," I said defensively, lying. I'm sure everyone knew what it was about, I just couldn't *remember* if everyone knew.

Willy asked "He who?" his clucking turning into residual chuckling.

"The black guy that wrote it. At least I wasn't sitting around reading a bunch of dead white guys all semester was I? I was pushing my many personal boundaries. You should be proud of me for that at least."

Willy became deathly silent.

"What now?" I whined.

"Eliason, Toni Morrison was the author."

I said, "You know better than me. Yeah, that's right. Right?"

He looked at me so sadly. "Eliason, that's Toni with an 'i.'"

I shrugged. "Okay."

"Eliason, Toni Morrison is a woman."

I felt as if I had been run over by a slow-moving rickshaw then was trampled on by the coolie pulling it. "Well I'll be," I said. "Are you sure?" He nodded wordlessly. "Well that puts a different spin on things doesn't it?"

He nodded again excitedly I think, saying, "A perfect experiment to re-read said text and extrapolate how differently you perceive feelings, mood, denouement, etcetera, knowing that the author is a woman, and should a writer's gender have any kind of impact on the reader's approach to and understanding of the book? Very interesting." He crossed his arms over his belly and looked so pleased.

"You want me to read it again?" I asked incredulously. "That book took me like eight months to read."

He ignored me. "The child was a ghost, chieftain, the ephemeral personification of the narrator's past demons, the embodiment of her guilt and ultimately, the spirit of her salvation."

"Oh yeah, now I remember," I lied. Willy's disbelieving silence filled the car. "I swear my professor said it was a black dude," I protested. He shook his head and told me that I should instead re-read "The Outsiders," which he knew was my favorite book of all time. And what a movie, chock full of unknowns ready to shine, from Patrick Swayze to Tom Cruz *{Cruise—ed.}* to Charlie Sheen *{his brother Emilio Estevez—ed.}* to the Karate Kid kid. I was inside my head for some seconds, wondering why I should re-read "The Outsiders," which didn't take me as long to read. I could definitely do that. Then, an epiphany!

"That was *not* a girl! The author was not a girl. No woman could write "The Outsiders." No way."

Willy nodded his head solemnly, touched the side of his nose, and gave me such a big smile his mustache pushed up through his nostrils.

"How heavy it is to see the gravity of enlightenment," he said, all hippy-like.

"Man, Willy, are you sure?" I said, crushed. The man was killing every flower that ever budded in my soul. I mean, I didn't know why it mattered whether S.E. Hinton was a man or a woman, but it was going to change the whole way I thought about the book. Willy had to go and ruin everything for everyone. I mean, the greasy kids were always cool and tough—*tuff* actually—with their knives and leather jackets and greasy shoes. Now I was always going to sense an underlying degree of homoeroticism in the story, how they were always barging in to each others' houses without knocking and instantly wrestling around on the floor, there were never adults around, Johnny was always kind of nervous around Darry, how they all kind of looked like something from a Toto music video.

"What are you thinking about Ponyboy?" Willy asked me. I almost slugged him.

"Nothing," I said, miserably. "Nothing gold can stay," I said, feeling like crying.

"Stay gold Ponyboy," he said to me. We were silent for some minutes. "Chieftain, I think we are about to enter the phase of your story when it graduates from being a melodrama and turns into a fantastic buddy road movie, like Butch Cassidy and the Marlboro Kid. Hopefully we will get to ride bicycles and wear vests."

"That doesn't sound right," I said, still miserable. "It's Butch Cassidy and some other kind of kid but now I can't think of it because you have the Marlboro man stuck in my brain. *{The Sundance Kid, you blithering fools, the Sundance Kid! My god—ed.}* I'll think of it later when I'm not thinking about it."

I stared down the length of my nose, down the hood of the Camaro, down the slope of the mountain, off into the snow, and thought about Julia. Why did I not just go with her on Thursday? Maybe because I like to leave but not arrive, because as long as you are still moving you have a goal, and you don't have to face certain realities. Just keep driving. Julia loves to drive. It's an American bloodline thing, as undeniable in all of us as the San Andreas Fault tearing underneath California and itching for release. And I know there's a psychological connection between traveling and not wanting to arrive—it doesn't take someone dressed up as Sigmund Freud to tell me I'm running from something, and I'm too childish to want to get somewhere and therefore get on with life. But I hate self-analysis because I'm told by Willy that it leads to Abraham Maslow's fourth tier of self-actualization, and I don't know what that means. *[Shut the hell up Willy.]* What I do know, is that if Julia and I alone could drive forever and never ran out of gas and never had to stop to eat and never ran out of money and it would be just about past noon so the heaviness of morning had worn off but the fears of night were not even close to being within poking range, if the day was just within a hairs-breadth of turning the shadows eastward, but they would never stretch further than a perfect summer song that would never end on the radio, well then I could be with Julia forever and love her forever.

"It appears that we are hitching, dude," I heard Willy say, his breath now a mist hanging inside the car. "Shall we establish an m.o. (which I later learned meant 'modus operandi') or simply 'wing it?' I think we should have a plan."

Shortly thereafter, Willy lost a mean game of rock-scissors-paper for the privilege of stepping outside the Camaro with his thumb hitched heavenward, which he would do for the next five cars. If no one stopped then I had to hitch for five cars, then Willy for five, and if nobody had picked us up by then, we would each nibble a cyanide pill. "That's some tough luck, Chilly Willy, but look, with the car pointed this way we can see someone coming for miles," I said merrily.

"Understand this however, I will not always allow 'dynamite' to be used as a legitimate throw in rock-paper-scissors, but I know you have experienced a morning of some tribulation," Willy said to my toothy grin.

"Warm up that thumb, boy, I see someone coming," and sure enough, sifting through the flakes was a big rumbling and rusting Dodge truck which needed about three hundred and sixty seconds to crest the hill we were on and about three seconds to blow right by Willy without a sniff of acknowledgement. Willy jumped into the Camaro and blew on his mittens. "Remind me to buy a Ford the next time I am in the market for a junky old truck," he said bitterly. After about ten minutes he had to launch himself back out in the frigid air in order to inspire two red sports cars, obviously following each other, to zip right past him with a friendly toot. "Gosh do you think they thought I was on the side of the road selling snow cones? Blue raspberry, pina colada, tutti frutti, bubble gum anyone?! They must sleep better at night knowing that their horns work so grandly." At that point I was legitimately beginning to freeze, my toes starting to feel rubbery, my fingers non-operational, my knees like ice. After many minutes Willy was witness to yet another act of random human kindness when a huge Expedition or Exposition or something big enough to fit me, Willy and the population of North Dakota inside, chugged right on by him, leaving eddies of flakes in its wake that spun and danced as Willy climbed back into the Camaro. He looked on the verge of panicking.

"I do not know how many more instances of unkindness I can pretend did not happen," he said. "Do you think it is me?"

And then a humbling, horrible yet undeniable conclusion hit me: no one with a brain, even if he or she had just the tiniest stem still attached after a freakish playground accident, would pick up a paunchy man wearing lime-green sweat pants, an ill-fitting sky-blue button-down poking out from his overstuffed black jacket and a red beanie cap with an orange fuzzy pompom on top and, sewn across the front, a Farto patch with an expiring, flatulent, little supine bean with a curlicue of vapor swirling over it. Images are contrived, consciously or not, to enforce opinions and we do live in a society based on image, but occasionally you unearth someone like Willy, a Shakespeare play trapped in a romance novel cover…but not on the side of a mountain in the middle of a blizzard.

"Maybe I should take the next car," I suggested with a catfish-wide yawn.

"Preposterous, a deal is a deal, and I think you will be happy with our next selection," Willy said like a disc jockey on the radio, touching his right nostril twice with his pointer finger. "Fifth time is a charm, according to the hitchhiker creed."

"The hitchhiker's creed? I've never heard of that." Another yawn and my molars sang out in the cold. I dug my hands between my thighs for warmth. "Man I'm tired, Sodapop."

"You just shush now and gather your strength as we still have a long day ahead of us. All of this sleepiness you have been mentioning lately is a lack of iron, possibly potassium, leading to a fundamental breakdown in your electron transport chain and therefore your inability to convert protein into your critical thirty-two ATPs of energy *(note to ed., please check this figure! Cheers, Worster)*. Have you been taking the herbal supplements I prescribed for you?"

"Of course I have," I lied. Everybody knows herbal supplements don't do anything except make hippies feel better about taking medication. "I *am* just going to put my head back for a bit," and I was out, because the next thing I knew, Willy was excitedly scattering things across the front and back seat in attempts to collect them.

"How long was I out?" I yawned. I was pretty sure the tip of my nose had frozen and fallen off.

"Not long, but our savior is here little buddy so wakey-wakey and make like a snakey for goodness sakey."

I began zipping zippers, buttoning buttons, tying laces. I had nothing to bring. "Please tell me it's as warm as a Turkish sauna in his car," I said hopefully.

"Warm enough to roast a doner kebab," Willy said. He then explained to me, because I didn't know that a world existed outside of hamburgers, soda and cup o' noodles *[You're pushing it Willy]* that a doner kebab was a sort of Turkish delicacy consisting of mystery meat in the shape of a traffic cone that revolved slowly on a heater, and the chef sheared off layers of meat which he stuffed in a warmed pita with lettuce or cabbage, onion, tomato, yogurt sauce and red pepper if desired.

"Now that I've gotten my lesson on delicacies from the eastern world, can you please tell me that the car is driven by an exceedingly hot brunette," I said, reaching for the freezing door handle.

"Oh not at all," Willy huffed as he fumbled with a bag in the back seat, his body folded at waist level and the blood rushing to his head. "The driver is a wonderful man with a fetching British accent, and the passenger his son. He hopped in the back seat so you can have shotgun if you prefer."

"Are you crazy?" I said, slowly drawing my hand back from the handle. "No way am I getting in that car." Willy looked up at me, stunned. I asked him, "Do you recall that there are two mass murderers on a sight-seeing tour of Leadville who perfectly fit that description? No way Chief Wampum."

"Oh," Willy said, pulling the front seat back with a click and looking at me perplexed through his fogged-up spectacles. He twisted his mustache for some seconds. "Yes, but I don't think the killers had English accents." I gazed at him skeptically, looking in the rearview mirror to get a glimpse of the car, but our windows had been too fogged up, the condensation now a thin layer of ice on the back window. "Not to put too fine a point on it, Mr. Nye, but if they were murderers they would not very well be picking up hitch-hikers."

"Those are precisely the people who are murderers!" I exclaimed. "People are always picking up hitch-hikers and killing them and the corpses are discovered like twenty years later with their bones all wrapped up in vines and newspapers and plastic grocery bags in a creek somewhere in Mississippi. No way."

Willy had quit his mustache-twisting and advanced to drumming on his lower lip with his pinky. "Gosh, I was always under the impression that the *hitch-hiker* was always getting picked up and murdering the *driver*. But who can correctly say? In the interim, however, I must bow to your wishes. I did promise him our company however."

I sat there stonily, watching the snow falling faster. "Chief?"

"Yes dear?" he replied.

"Is it really warm inside the car."

"Deliciously warm, like a Reykjavik thermal hot spring."

"Is it a nice car?" I asked hopefully.

"Extremely," he replied. "Cherry red with wood paneling I think, tan interior."

"God Willy, is it a station wagon?" I said in desperation.

"No, I believe it is a Cutlass of some sort," he said thoughtfully, turning to look out the door and over his shoulder. "My bad, I believe it says Monte Carlo, and alas, there is no wood paneling." He returned his skull to the Camaro. "Whether it is an El Camino or a red Barchetta or a Carmen Ghia, we really have not much of a choice if we mean to see your mother pronto."

"Willy?"

"Yes?" he replied impatiently.

"They don't seem like mass murderers, do they?"

"As I previously stated, the driver seems like a really wonderful man, and the son has stationed himself in the back seat so you can sit up front. Now get."

Willy was correct of course, about the necessity of having to skedaddle, though if you ask me, only male fashion designers should ever be allowed to describe another man as "really wonderful" and warmth as "delicious." I wavered on the precipice of life or getting chopped up into thousands of itsy pieces and deposited in trash bags and put to the curb next Tuesday morning. I did not choose life. I pulled the door handle, inhaling deeply, casting the frigid safety of the Camaro one last longing look.

"Splendid, let us motor," Willy exclaimed, grabbing his backpack, slinging it over one shoulder and pushing his door shut with his rear end. "I think you are really going to take a liking to these chaps. Did you lock your door? Oh this is going to be such good fun. I do hope they can carry us further than Frisco. Now Eliason, do be polite, do not be purposely difficult, do not say too much or give away too much information and watch my back at all times. Oh bother, did I turn off all the burners on my stove when I left my homestead this morning?" he asked as we made our way around the back of the car to the passenger side.

"I'm sure you did—oh, and Willy," I said, taking his shoulder, his smile stretching across his entire face as he reached out for the door handle, "if you ever call me 'dear' again I'll thump you."

I inhaled deeply, cracked open the door and looked murder right in the eye.

CHAPTER EIGHT

"Ding Dong Bell and the Little Dinger, 11:17 a.m."

"But it's not murder is it?"

"God Eliason, no, it's not murder. I'm a girl even, and I would say 'You did the right thing' I guess. I don't know. Who cares, unless you're running for president."

"Look, it's starting to rain again."

"Just quit worrying so much—you're not going to burn in hell."

"Do you know tomorrow is the first day of September? That means it rained every single day in August. That's like seventy inches for 1999. I'm getting a little tired of it."

"I know baby. I am too, but we really need it."

****

How would you describe our so-called savior other than as a black man, mid-40s with tight, curly black hair graying at the temples, a pencil-thin mustache, swollen, rather blood-shot eyes and sunken cheeks with a smattering of black guy freckles, a tight little salt-and-pepper beard with semi-detached soul patch, big loops of earrings in both his lobes, this crazy Greek fisherman's cap atop his skull, the slight squint of a person who usually wears glasses to read, then forgets that he is not reading but driving, but still squints anyway, slightly stooped shoulders, dressed like a professor in browns, grays and dull mustards, certainly stylish, but best of all, had this nutty English accent. I guess that is how you would describe him. His son, considerably larger, rounder, darker and noticeably more sullen, with thick, curly eyelashes and a big, black puffy jacket, in his early twenties, was on a cell phone in the back seat. He didn't even look over at us. The car was not new but it was not old, it was not junky but it was a bit rough—it was a car that a person would have just before he started making some good money at his job but did not know it yet. I pulled the door closed quietly, thinking that if the driver did not hear me, he may not notice me and therefore not kill me.

"The name is Teddy Bell, but you can call me Ding Dong, as in a bell."

That was the first thing he said to me, sticking out his hand, which was about the size of a frying pan. I shook his frying pan wearily as I held the seat forward for Willy to shoehorn himself into the back, and introduced myself which surprisingly elicited no looks of confusion. I quietly thanked him for the ride. Man, I was nervous as hell, not because they were a couple of black dudes in the mountains on a cold, snowy October Saturday. I suppose I just had hitcher's angst. Even if Ding Dong and his kid had been two nuns in a 1964 four-door pink Tempest I still would have been nervous as hell. But I was the nervous sort. I got nervous going for a haircut. I got nervous just deciding if I *wanted* to go for a haircut. That was my nature.

"Where are you gentlemen headed?" he asked in that cozy British accent.

"Places," Willy shot back, reaching up and squeezing my shoulder slightly after I lowered myself into the front sea, choking on my own panic.

"Riiiiiigghht," Ding Dong said, drawing out the word for about five seconds, all croaky like the front door of a haunted house in a scary movie. "Well, now that we know each other, how about closing that door and we'll be on our way."

"Oh yes, jolly good, give it a good tug Eliason," Willy answered with a giggle. It was going to be a long day if he was going to keep up with that fake British accent stuff. At some point I *would* smack him if necessary. "And where are *you* blokes going?" he asked.

"Places," Ding Dong answered, gazing at him in the rearview mirror, not smiling or anything, just staring. God, we were dead. The morning's latte was percolating in my stomach like a bouncing sack of pure acid heartburn.

"This is a nice car," I lied, trying to flatter him, possibly trying to distract him long enough from killing us, then maybe he would forget that he wanted to kill us. "Where are you from?" I asked, trying to sound casual.

"Where are we from? All over I suppose," he half-answered. Dead we were.

"Oh let me guess, should I hazard, I think I shall," Willy said excitedly, pushing up to the edge of his seat, "slight Welsh inflection but certainly not Liverpudlian, so it could be Midlands, not sing-songy enough to be Geordie, but I detect a working-class, industrial brogue. Could I guess the outskirts of Manchester, possibly Stockport or Burnley even?" That slap I mentioned earlier, it was about to come. Teddy Bell looked pleasantly surprised however.

"Actually Hull, northeast, Humberside," he answered. "You certainly know your English geography, William."

"Literature mainly: the Brontes, Austen, Hardy," Willy said, touching his finger to the side of his nose, "not to mention Longfellow, Keats, Yeats and some Morrissey for good measure." I had no earthly idea what or who the hell Willy was talking about. Could these have been writers for the English version of TV guide? *[Willy, you're an idiot. Oh by the way, shut the hell up.]*

"So you live in Colorado?" I asked, nervous as hell.

Teddy pulled down slightly on the brim of his cap and looked at me like I was his mentally handicapped little brother, and answered, "Of course we live in Colorado—a bit early in the season for skiing, a bit late for fishing for us to be tourists, wouldn't you say?" He hated me. I knew that Ding Dong hated me. Everybody always hated me when they met me. And then the thought struck me: we were already dead. Everything suddenly seemed like a curious delusion to me, an illusory diversionary tactic trying to camouflage the inevitable, the scarcely mattered and the obviously known: that we were already dead, the four of us. When we got out of bed that morning—wherever the Bells slept, wherever Willy's little rolled-up Indian mat was, my mattress on the floor—we should have realized that we would bring about each others' demise. No one, not us or anyone outside of Ding Dong's car, would have been surprised by the mass illusion, and so few people knew who we were that only a handful could really have cared. I wasn't sure if *I* really cared. Did the Big Dipper scudding across the night sky ever take notice of any of us, an ant underfoot ever move out of our way, did the speed of light give a damn, gravity, infinity, God? I knew that Willy's memories of childhood, of tattered plastic kites and balsa wood airplanes with rubber band propellers and the smell of chlorine in his swim suit and the heat on his forehead of winter fires at November carnivals, of his first kiss behind the mining museum and his last ever math test, of walking home alone in the dead leaves of autumn twilight, were now illusory enough to have never existed, and that my recollections were slipping away themselves, were yellowing and turning beige at the corners. I had no siblings, father, soon no mother, no grandparents, no aunts, uncles, cousins—nothing. And everything would dissolve with me. I had Julia only, kind of, but I wasn't going to survive this trip.

"I love the T-tops," I heard Willy say from another universe. "Wow, I have not seen them in years. Who needs a lowly sunroof when you can tan the top of your pate in style. Did you install them yourself, Theodore?"

"They came with the package. Not so water-tight though. The car was like a swamp in August with all that bloody rain, and the smell of mildew—" Ding Dong said waving his hand in front of his nose. "That's TJ in the back seat with you, if he ever gets off that phone. Theodore Junior. Sometimes we call him Little Ding, but mainly TJ, since he's not so little anymore."

"Oh splendid," Willy clapped. "I always wanted initials for a name, like PJ or RC for example. Alas, 'WW' is a bit of a mouthful."

Ding Dong chuckled to himself and said "Indeed."

Willy practically frothed in excitement. "So, a father and son out on the road, yes? And Mrs. Bell, she is at home attending to the needs of the kitchen, securing the family burner, stirring the oats?" he asked merrily. If silence could ever said to be stony, then the Rock of Gibraltar had taken up residence in the car. And the seconds felt like birthdays to an elderly widow with dementia.

"She's no longer with us," Ding Dong finally said, not to the rear view mirror but to the windshield, "but thank you for asking."

"I am so sorry, Theodore, so regretfully sorry," Willy said, and the way he said it, the sincerity and the words and the delivery, it actually sounded like he was always meant to ask it, and that Ding Dong's wife was always meant to be dead and that Willy was always designed to offer his condolences. I noticed TJ had ceased talking for a few moments, then resumed with his conversation. Ding Dong skillfully segued into another subject.

"It's rather rude, these cell phone conversations when other people are trying to live in real time," he said. I looked over my shoulder at TJ, unaware of the three of us.

"Oh they will never 'catch on,'" Willy said. "I believe people like to sit in their homes and speak, to see that cord snaking out of the wall, a physical representation of our tenuous connection to one another, our 'connectedness' so to speak." He slouched back in his seat and gazed nonchalantly at TJ. "Nay, cell phones will prove to be just a passing fad. I believe, if we let them run amok, they would expose our inability to plan more than one step ahead into the future, and that would prove fatal in a fast-moving modern world run by the Chinese."

Willy, as was quite common, was putting me into a relaxed state of somnolence. I was nervous as hell, I wanted to remain at a level of heightened awareness in case Ding Dong tried anything tricky, though I did have the able and lethal hands of William Worster within jujitsu distance, but I could not keep my head from bobbing, my eyes from crossing, my temples from throbbing and then I was out.

****

"Eliason baby, try to stay awake when I'm talking to you. I said that you should really address your fear of dying sometime. I mean, everyone is afraid of dying but you should honestly address it."

"I don't know what you're talking about."

"I know you lost your father at a difficult age, and your mother is not doing too great either but, I mean, I lost Jimmy. I don't mean to say that I have the answers but, I think it's a control thing sometimes."

"I'm just a little sleepy. I promise I was listening. Really. I just don't know what you mean."

"I know you were listening," Julia said, lying on her bed and resting her chin on her hand atop her bedroom window sill, while looking out her apartment window at the sunset. We were four stories up and had a commanding view of tiny Leadville spread beneath us. It had been the late Saturday that I told you about earlier, when the wind finally stopped blowing and Julia said we'd talk not of what we've done or shall do, but whether the snow would ever stop, and didn't July already seem forever ago.

Indeed it did, when the buildings on Harrison Avenue pulsed in their paint, orange and bright red and pastel blue and olive green. The sunlight hurrying through the thin mountain air could make you blind in summer. Where the rest of the west would be baked in humid heat, we would get seared. Noon could make the most cancerous of men feel like one of Paul Bunyan's lackeys in the story where they grease his gargantuan, sizzling skillet, the perimeter of a large pond, by strapping massive strips of bacon to their feet and skating across the surface. Only, in Leadville, *you* were the bacon.

"You know this will all be a pile of rubble one day?" Julia told me. I lovingly gazed at my dear, radiant girlfriend. "It's true. Vines will grow up four floors through this apartment window and trees will sprout up right in the middle of Harrison Avenue, and the sidewalks will all be cracked and the telephone poles all bent over. Then the sand will blow through and cover everything up."

"Where the heck is the sand going to come from, the Sahara desert?"

She shrugged. "I don't know where it comes from, but sand always covers a town and a thousand years later people come along and discover it twenty feet down. I hope they find us lying side by side." It was a grim thought but romantic somehow. I kissed her lightly. She asked, "I think we need to go to Boulder maybe on Thursday. Maybe we can visit your mom or something? When is the last time you talked to her?"

I reddened slightly—Julia was always ribbing me about not visiting my mother enough.

"Oh gosh I talked to her last weekend," I lied. "She was moaning about her students and having to grade tests. She said she's feeling a lot better though, says it's the mountain air or the groovy hippy vibe in Boulder. She's gone totally herbal."

"Let's go," she repeated. "I'm starting to feel really isolated here. I just need to get out for a long weekend."

Julia was born and raised in Leadville after her parents hopped the border from Mexico and ended up in the area, first picking vegetables in New Mexico, then her father worked in the mines in Colorado, and finally graduated to folding rich people's linens and fixing their heaters in the nearby ski resort hotels of Vail and Breckenridge. Her father worked in a hotel in Vail—maintenance. Her mother worked in Vail—laundry. Her uncle Lupe and his wife Cheryl worked at Copper Mountain—landscaping and dishwashing, respectively. All of her cousins worked in Breckenridge. Her brother Jimmy had worked in Vail—night auditor—but plummeted off the side of the mountain just past Red Cliff during a blizzard while driving to work at ten in the evening three years ago. He died from massive head injuries. The police never recovered one of Jimmy's shoes, his shirt, his wallet and believe it or not, the steering wheel to the car. A year ago some famous movie star filmed a scene for an action movie only twenty yards from where Jimmy's car came to rest, only a few feet from where Jimmy landed after he went through the windshield after hitting a tree. The director had the bruised, leaning tree and Jimmy's wooden cross removed, but not of out spite or lack of respect; they just didn't fit the scene. The movie went straight to video. You've probably never seen it.

"I want to see the world, Eliason. I want to go somewhere romantic like Venice and listen to a woman play the harp in a ballroom and then I want to have dinner by candlelight in Paris and go to sleep that night in Berlin and wake up the next morning in Moscow." I was about to tell her of the logistical nightmare of such an undertaking but she relented. "But if I can't have that, I'll just go to Boulder instead. I want to go where nobody knows me."

"Maybe Jimbo will let me borrow his El Camino." She looked instantly tragic. "Come on, that El Camino is cool and kind of rustic," I reasoned.

"More like 'rusty.' That old cheese grater won't even make it to Frisco, and it's all downhill from here."

I ignored her. "Jimbo's son just replaced the eight-track player with a regular cassette player. Dave said it's pretty nice. So at least we'll have music."

"Eliason, dear, the last cassette I bought and owned was the 'Goonies' soundtrack," then she thought for a second, "or the 'Gremlins' maybe. What's the movie with David Bowie?"

I pulled into my vast storage of useless pop knowledge. "I think 'Never-Ending Story,'" I said. *{Willow—ed.}* "Is that the movie where he has one brown eye and one blue eye?"

Julia shrugged. "I don't think so. Anyway, I haven't seen that cassette in about ten years. Nobody listens to cassettes anymore. Nobody *wants* to listen to cassettes anymore—they're done, obsolete, inconvenient. Who has time to fast forward anymore? What?"

"Was it 'Dune'? Wasn't David Bowie in that?" *{Sting—ed.}*

"Definitely not. Just listen to me carefully," and she pulled my face to hers and looked straight into my eyes then said aaawwlllllll sexy, her big dark Mexican-American eyes the richest brown of my favorite chocolate, the pupils the deepest black of my favorite licorice, "I will make it worth your while for us to have a little romantic weekend away."

I gulped heavily, my mind stalled, even after three years of knowing this girl quite well, in a Biblical way. "Okay, I'll get on the phone straight away and tell Willy I might be gone from work for a couple of days. Start thinking of what you want to wear. We can leave within the hour probably," I hastened. "I'll go to my apartment and get my cassette collection."

Julia was silent for a second. "You're not going to play that song about Uncle Matthew the whole way there?" she purred, nay, suggested.

"Hey, did the David Bowie movie have a munchkin or something in it?"

"Baby, everyone else has forgotten what movie it was and what songs were in it and who starred in it. They probably remember the ads and the trailer with the dancing popcorn and soda better. Here, put your head in my lap and take a little snooze."

"But I want to leave for our romantic getaway. I need to get the El Camino."

"I know you do baby," but Julia's lap was so warm and soft and I could hear the steady thump of her heart all the way down in her stomach. She was humming something pretty.

****

"Really, it is quite remarkable. He *is* under some stress which tends to tire a young fellow out," I heard Willy saying from way in the back of my ears. I woke up with a start to find Ding Dong staring at me, then he moved his eyes back to the road as the car bumped along. On the other side of the windshield the snow had stopped falling, if only momentarily.

CHAPTER NINE

"Limping to the Finish Line of an Already-Lost Race, 11:35 a.m."

We had just zoomed by Copper Mountain ski resort and merged onto Interstate 70, which meant that I had been zonked out for about ten minutes, ten blissful minutes in which I was not worrying about how my demise would occur, in fire or ice, hastily, slowly, painfully or hardly noticed.

"Do you feel refreshed, little chief?" I heard Willy ask from the back seat. I turned in surprise, like someone who had been walking down what he thought was a deserted street and suddenly heard a rustle of papers, a misstep, a whisper in the ear.

"Yeah, I think so," I yawned. Actually I did feel pretty good, better than I ever had in the morning after seven hours of sleep. The snow had stopped but as we entered Officer's Gulch, a carved out pass between jagged, not particularly tall but treeless peaks on both sides of the highway, between mountains that draped the interstate in shade all day, the wind barreled at us and practically punched the car backwards. Yellow, red, and blue floaters on power lines overhead bobbed back in forth in a blur of primary colors. The highway was uncommonly empty.

"Now TJ, as I was saying, Jeffrey Osborne was more comfortable in the adult contemporary pop, soft soul genre as typified by his prominence on the 'We Are the World' single despite his patchy appearances on the Top 40 charts and relative anonymity to the general public. But Al Jarreau was a scatologist through and through. Quincy Jones was a genius to include an old school scat singer if only for one line in the song."

I looked over my shoulder to the back seat. I was tempted to drift off into slumber once again if all I had missed was a discussion of the merits of 1970s pop/soul singers. Is that what I had to look forward to for the rest of the day, the rest of my life? I felt desperate, dumber, like I was sprinting to the finish line of an already-lost race.

"I don't know who any of those people are that you're talking about, except Michael Jackson. Anyway, you can't say this Al Jarreau guy was the first rapper just because you think scat is a more intelligible and earlier form of rap or whatever it was you said. Does *anybody* even know who these people are anymore? That was like ten years ago. Ancient history. Rap is all that matters now."

Willy sighed deeply. "Mornin' mister radio, mornin' mister cheerio, everything's fine in mah mind," he sang, snapping his fingers and doing this sort of bongo thing with his lips, thinning them out and tucking his top lip under his teeth so he looked to have nothing but mustache under his nose. "Boo-dee-dee-dahh-dah-do, some walk by night, some fly by day." Willy finished "scat singing" and nodded expectantly at Little Ding, whose face betrayed a sudden case of food poisoning. Willy sighed with a defeated shrug. "Okay, I realize that 'USA for Africa' was a paltry, dare I say cynical, attempt to 'one up' the British for originating an idea to feed Africans through Western guilt, but it really typified that feel-good era."

"When I was a child celebrating the holidays, I often stopped and wondered about Africans, 'Do they know it's Christmas time at all?'" Ding Dong said sarcastically.

"Gosh, Theodore, though the icon of jolly old St. Nick is world-famous and recognized throughout the globe as embodying the Western tradition of gift-giving and offering peace to all mankind, I doubt the continent of Africa, mostly non-Christian, does realize when it is Christmas," Willy said.

"You're exactly right, Willy," Ding Dong said, glancing my way with what I thought was a smirk.

Willy babbled on shamelessly. "In fact I just recently read that Santa's merry visage is in the top five of the most recognized around the world, including Jesus, who is really just another holiday version of Santa without the red suit and reindeer and toys isn't he, umm, Buddha and, who were the others," Willy said, tapping his temple with a finger still wrapped in mitten. "Well, King Fred was one of course but I can't recall the other."

"King Fred!" Ding Dong exclaimed. "How did he make the list?"

"Oh the Derfy franchise is the biggest in the world of course, everybody knows that. As far as production and profit margins, it simply dwarfs the second-placed global business, which is some oil company in the Middle East," Willy told us with a shrug. "In fact, I just read that Derfy's has gone extra-terrestrial. They put a hamburger, fries and drink in a hermetically sealed, temperature-controlled rocket, along with a photo of King Fred and his zany cast of characters, as well as a recorded message of peace to any Martians or Venusians or Plutonians in whose backyard the rocket might one day crash."

"So if some space dude finds this rocket a billion years from now, they're going to think we all look like King Fred and Chief Buff Burger?" Little Ding asked.

"Actually, Chief Buff Burger had not been invented before the picture was taken, but all the other guilty players are there, Private Pickle, Happy Hindoo et al."

"That's just sick," Little Ding said, shaking his head. I noticed that Teddy Bell's face had turned crimson, his eyelids pulled back so that his eyeballs appeared ready to pop right out of their sockets but when he spoke his voice was controlled: "How do you know so much about Derfy Burger?" he asked Willy

"Oh, I read postboxfuls of magazines, particularly science magazines, and this particular article covered the unwavering human interest in time capsules, how we are so much more fascinated by our own pasts, family trees, etcetera, than we are about the future. But there are some of us, notably capitalists and/or the mega-wealthy like the folks at Derfy Burger, who have more of an interest in the future. Oh, add politicians seeking re-election and science fiction writers to that list. Apart from them there is the kooky fringe, you know, people who freeze themselves or try to reincarnate their souls before they are even dead into some of our longer-living fellow inhabitants of the planet, elephants or alligators or sequoia trees for instance, which can live for hundreds of years. The magazine article reasoned that the majority of us are quite content spending our lives just trying to be remembered by our fellow earthlings, those living around us at the time, as well as by our own future generations, mainly through near self-replication—you know, making babies," Willy clarified, at which Teddy dutifully nodded. "While most of us are happy if our grandchildren remember us, or even more radically, if our great-grandchildren can name us in a photo, the kooky fringe want to be *discovered* in the future instead of merely being remembered, even if it means only being discovered by space aliens who do not even know what they are seeing." I felt myself nodding off into near oblivion again.

"All of that was in an article about shooting a burger into space?" TJ asked in disbelief.

"Oh yes. There was also a fascinating article on how mitochondria might be linked to the feminist movement, and that how left-handed people may actually be the mirror images of themselves in alternate universes. I found that article a dreadful sludge of pseudo-science. The whole alternate universe idea is quite silly."

"What do you think about Derfy Burger though?" Ding Dong asked, looking at Willy in the rearview mirror.

"You mean before or after they added bacon rashers to the Tennessee Bourbon-Soaked Wild Squirrel Sandwich?" Willy asked with glee, clapping. "It's a taste sensation. I know I know I know, Derfy Burger is not good for me but it is so yummy and comforting."

I was starting to get a headache. Gawd, Willy was talking so much. I just wanted him to shut up so I could concentrate on survival and getting out of that car as soon as possible. I was beginning to feel that my whole life was just a Snowshoe Willy monologue. Then Ding Dong turned those throbbing eyeballs to me.

"What about you? What do you think about Derfy Burger?"

I was about to shrug and say that it was just another crummy fast-food place like all the others when Willy butted in: "Eliason, hah. He is not very fond of Derfy Burger or DerfMart or anything derfy," he said, somewhere between disbelief and exhilaration, like a kid who just discovered that he had a loose tooth and wanted to tell an uncaring world his secret.

"I don't really care where anybody shops," I said quietly, "it's just easier for me to go to the grocery store in Leadville. It's thirty miles closer. I'll spend the extra two cents on tampons and save gas."

Willy patted me on the shoulder. "He hates these big modern shopping complexes without windows, filled with artificial air. Eliason's campaign is to have every town in America filled with little mom and pop shops, where you drink soda out of green glass bottles and eat ice cream sandwiches in waxed paper," I heard Willy saying. It was true in a way, though I wouldn't call it a campaign—I wouldn't campaign for anything. In fact, I was beginning to realize that I may never fully support anything that required commitment. But I was about to punch Willy nonetheless. The worst thing about him saying all that stuff to Ding Dong and Little Ding however was that he wasn't being snide or anything. I mean, if you're going to tell someone's pathetic dreams to total strangers, at least be an ass while doing it so the other guy can get defensive and deny everything and tell you to shut the hell up.

"Eliason would love it if wherever he went, a classical music soundtrack followed him, or one with a sort of twangy slide guitar," the Weeper continued. "And the wind would always be blowing." I wished that Ding's Monte Carlo had been a fighter plane instead of a car because I would have instantly ejected Willy from our existence.

"I don't know, William, it sounds pretty enticing to me," Teddy said. I turned around and stuck my tongue out at Willy.

"Really mature, Nye," he said crossly, "real classy." He pushed himself further into his seat and crossed his arms. Little Ding's phone rang and once again we lost him to the electromagnetic world of telecommunication. Suddenly Willy stiffened his arms and pulled his girth to the edge of his seat again.

"Ho-ho, Theodore, could we swing by DerfMart? I was hoping to pick up a laundry basket and a watch band. This one makes my wrist turn green," he chirped, thrusting his round wrist into our space and turning the band with the fat, square fingernails of his right hand. The color was the pukey shade of green that you see on the walls of some mind-numbingly ugly Department of Motor Vehicles office in some godawful building from the 1950s.

"Next exit, Theodore," Willy directed, pointing ahead with the fat, square fingernail that had just spun his watchband. "According to some people in the know," he said, tapping his right nostril three times, "a brand spanking new SupaDerfMart is going in just up the street from DerfMart. Oh do not miss it!" Willy cried, signaling the exit to Ding Dong, though it was quite clear to everyone in the car and probably to drivers five miles back that the hood of the Monte Carlo was distinctly pointing toward the exit. "I wanted to price some lawn mowers as well if time permits, the kind you can ride."

"And what good is a lawn mower in your town? You can't very well mow snow now can you?" Ding chuckled to himself.

"Oh Theodore, for the three weeks of Leadville summer we have the most luxuriant, mowable grass," Willy assured him. "Right, Eliason?"

"You don't have a lawn, Willy," I croaked, my voice still a little unused to conversation.

"You know, details bog us all down, little chief."

I noticed that Ding Dong kept glancing over at me, like he was completely taken aback that there was someone camped out next to him in the car, as if the headrest had suddenly begun speaking. I had started having this Invisibility Effect on people lately, which had been okay with me because I had really just wanted people to leave me alone. Willy asked if I needed anything, "Perhaps a 200-sheet count of college-ruled notebook paper, maybe some nine-volt batteries or medicated foot powder?"

"That's quite an eclectic grocery list," Ding Dong noted.

"I am an insatiable coupon clipper," Willy said proudly, lifting his pack of supplies from the floor and shaking it heartily, signaling that his coupons were floating somewhere inside like weightless astronauts in a space capsule. "Tubs of mayonnaise *were* on sale last week," he sneered, glaring I'm sure, at the back of my skull.

"I think I'm okay with my necessities," I told him. "I still have some notebook paper left over from an eleventh grade book report."

Ding Dong chuckled lightly. He exited the highway, took a sharp turn right and half a mile down the street a huge DerfMart sign loomed on the skyline. For several minutes we drove on in silence, except for Little Ding's occasional utterance into his phone's mouthpiece.

"What a beauty," Willy said of the building as we pulled near. "Maybe not so architecturally challenging, as it is merely a very large rectangle with no windows or other masonry frills, but what a symbol of the working man's only way to save a buck. Lord knows the government is not going to do it for him." He tapped Ding Dong on the shoulder. "I shall not be too long, Teddy, and then I hope young Eliason and I can carry on apace with you and your son."

Teddy nodded affirmatively, silently, though his eyeballs again looked as though they may drop from their sockets.

"Jolly good then," Willy clapped and sunk back into his seat with a smile. "Jolly good."

CHAPTER TEN

"Monte Carlo, Religion, Race, Politics, 11:45 a.m."

I had this habit, or a custom, Willy might even call it a character flaw, of always assuming that people didn't like me right from the start, that somehow they knew something that I was trying to hide: that I might be a befuddled hooligan or a ham-fisted molester or just a phony hypocrite. It took me forever to call Julia on the phone, even after Smoky introduced us and kept bugging me to call her: tomorrow, I thought, after breakfast, no, after lunch, no, after dinner, right at seven, no, seems a little anal retentive to call right on the hour, eight fifteen would be better, not too early, not too late, nine o'clock maybe is a little better, quieter, nine twenty is even quieter, nine thirty-three is too late now, nine forty-six is definitely too late, maybe tomorrow after breakfast. "If you're not real busy and you want to have coffee sometime, maybe within the next couple of days even, I mean you don't have to if you've got other stuff to do but if you want to...." I'm sure I said something exactly like that. It's a wonder she agreed. Maybe she said yes out of pity. [*Willy, do I have to repeat myself? Shut the hell up.*] I knew Ding Dong hated me, I could just tell by his tone of voice, the way he didn't answer me straight away, the way he looked at me. I was sure Little Ding hated me too. That is why I said, "I think I'll stay in the car while you guys go in," when the Monte Carlo came to a rest between two yellow stripes in the parking lot in front of DerfMart, the ground slick with melted snow but the sky still a dark gray.

"Oh who would turn down a perfectly pleasant opportunity to visit his/her local friendly DerfMart?" Willy asked in disbelief. He had pushed up to the edge of his seat again and I could feel his warm breath on the back of my neck. "I believe potting soil is half price."

I ignored him. Little Ding quickly turned off his cell phone.

"Don't leave this fool alone with the car, Dad."

Mr. Bell shot him a remonstrative look in the rear view mirror. He hunkered down a little.

"I'm just saying, we don't know him at all."

Teddy turned to me. "Though rude, he is quite right. You seem like an honest, upstanding young man, but who would leave a stranger alone with his car?"

"Yes, Eliason. Who would leave his car completely alone with the keys in the ignition?" Willy asked through a clearly visible grin.

"You can take the keys," I said, though I really would have liked to have listened to the radio while they were gone, with the heat cranked on HIGH. Ding pulled on his little mustache with his tongue and upper teeth and said, "No, I fancy staying here."

And that was that. I was stuck. Then, any opportunity of escape from two suspected killers or any chance of eluding the nervous drudgery of entertaining a single complete stranger fizzled when Willy popped open his door and said, "Right then, Theodore Junior, let us enjoy the fruits of capitalism!" and hopped outside with all the abandon of a pirate leaping to shore after being lost at sea for thirty years. He duck-walked through the dozens of parked cars and disappeared so quickly into the vortex of the DerfMart that the automatic door slid closed between him and a hapless TJ. He was also thrust into the void after so many seconds. I watched where their fuzzy forms had been and wished I was in the Seychelles islands. I stared out the window, motionless, and felt a hot, nervous sweat moisten my forehead, the prick of a billion tiny, hot needles in my stomach.

"You alright then?" I heard Ding Dong ask. "You look a little flushed."

"Oh," and I instinctively felt my cheek with the back of my hand. "I think I'm okay," I said, feeling a trickle of sweat roll down my spine and into my shorts. I desperately tried to think of anything to say, but the more effort I put into it, the more my brain failed me. The only thing I could think to talk about was mayonnaise, and that was inappropriate.

"Maybe you should take off your coat. Perhaps you're overheating," Ding suggested.

"Yeah," I said, but I just sat there fidgeting, forgetting to take off my coat. After about ten seconds Ding said, "Here, I'll bump down the heat a little."

I was feeling kind of queasy. That latte was killing me. I thought that maybe I was having stationary car sickness or the delayed queasies or some other nonsense like that. He rolled down his window halfway. After about three decades of silence he asked if he could roll up his window, that he was getting a "trifle chilled." I said "Yes, I'm sorry, of course." It was probably the first time I had apologized for anything in years, but I didn't mean it. We sat in silence again for several more years. Ding seemed like the kind of fellow who didn't mind embarrassing pauses though, and he was humming some kind of Winnie-the-Pooh tune to himself. I was going silently insane.

"You don't really sound very English," I said from out of nowhere, "you know, when you talk."

He looked surprised, putting his hand over his mouth, the ridge of his topmost knuckle resting just under his nose, then he slowly pulled his hand down and scratched the in-grown hair bumps on his neck. His fingernails roughing against the tiny mounds was like a tooth against the chipped edge of a ceramic mug. I tried to swallow silently.

"Well I've been gone for twenty, twenty-five years now," he said, swiveling those painful eyeballs my way. Nothing else.

"Oh," I said, and after several months of dead silence he went back to his Winnie-the-Pooh thing. I checked the watch that never existed on my wrist and watched an enormous man and a spaghetti-thin woman go into the store, and wanted to yell out the window that they were all wrong, that the man is always thin and his wife large beyond measure. Potting soil *was* on sale. Another sign in the window urged me to "Join the Derfiest Team In Colorado—Apply Inside!" before the holiday season began. A suburban assault vehicle the size of Canada pulled up next to us and cut its diesel engine with a snort like a Rottweiler settling down for a nap, but nobody got out. I felt the driver was looking at me but I could not be certain. I could feel his stare from up high in his cab.

"I think the English accent is kind of nice," I said.

"Yes, it's a little less clamorous on the eardrum than the American accent isn't it?" Ding said looking straight ahead through the windshield. I nodded, probably imperceptibly. Winnie-the-Pooh. SUV man staring. Eliason getting very nervous. Stomach churning.

"And you and your son, you're just going down the mountain a ways?" I asked, trying to sound gently quizzical. He slowly rolled those shark eyes my way; I was surprised they didn't turn over all white as he bit into me, my blood fountaining all over the windows, slickening the seats in crimson.

"Just heading down to Denver for the weekend," he said.

I added, "That's always a nice time," and was inches away from inquiring, "So, lived in Texas recently? MURDERED anyone lately?" when he suggested listening to the radio. He clicked it on before I could consent, which I happily did about four seconds after he turned the knob and started twisting it. Static, then National Public Radio came in quite clear.

"Tremendous," Ding Dong said with a smile for the first time, which was shocking, because he hated me. I would have preferred to listen to music, some '70s pop/soul singers, but as long as the people did not discuss religion, race or politics then I could relax. The announcer said the time was exactly noon.

"Today we celebrate the resurrection of the world's ghouls, goblins and ghosts and scores of the unliving." Gawd. "It's Halloween and you're listening to 'Hardly Anything Matters' on National Public Radio. On today's program: he's the trickiest boy of them all. Find out why religious fundamentalists in Kansas have a problem with the spell-binding, magical young wizard from Britain and why they want the three children's books, currently placed number one through three on the American Library Association List of Most Challenged Books, banned entirely from their state (RELIGION). Then we go to California and ask, "What scary effects is west coast gangster rap having on white suburban youth in the state (RACE). But first, gearing up for what should be a scary campaign season: it's McCain versus Bush gearing up for next year's presidential elections so will it be either of the two Republicans or Al Gore scaring his way and into the Oval Office a little over a year from now?" (POLITICS).

"What, no Y2K?" Ding asked the radio sarcastically but suddenly the car rocked like someone had placed a bomb right beneath us and the radio immediately cut to static.

"Bollocks!" Ding said, twiddling the knob again to no effect. "Bloody wind," he said, still playing with the knob but giving up after a couple of jogs up and down the dial. "Look at it howl," he said. American flags on every lamppost nipped anxiously at their poles, the blue fields and stars closest in shifted only vertically but the red and white, further from their mooring, blended into a pastiche of flapping pink. Then the scene turned white with fat flakes.

"Damn the luck," Ding Dong said and removed his fisherman's cap, tossed it next to him on the seat and scratched the top of his head, back and forth, slowly, as if he were trying to coax his brain into action by pure physical stimulation since neither the radio nor I could provide mental calisthenics. "I really wanted to hear the bit about banning Harry Potter from the entire Midwest," he told me. I admitted that I didn't know who he was.

"He's a character in a book naturally. There's nothing like a Midwest Protestant, or a fundamentalist more like, to bring misery and boredom to your life. Mercy, they take all the fun out of life."

I didn't say anything, as my modus operandi was dictating.

"You're not a fundamentalist, are you, or your parents?" he asked.

I gave him a damp shrug. "My mom, I don't know what she is. A hippy I suppose so I guess she doesn't believe in anything. I don't really know what my dad was."

Ding Dong raised his eyebrows. "What he *was*? Did he walk out on you and your mum when you were young?"

"Actually, he died…when I was ten." I sat there.

"Oh. How did he die then?"

"He drowned," I said, without really thinking, sitting there some more. "It was in the local paper where we used to live, but it was just a tiny little article."

"I've read it's a nice way to go, drowning. Quite peaceful I've heard," and he stared at me for a little bit. "But how would anybody know really?"

I nodded and shrugged at him. Most people would say that it was a rude, callous thing to say but it didn't seem so with Ding. It just felt natural. He glanced at me and put his cap back on. "That's a tough age for a boy to lose his father. No age is easy, but that's a tough age. You've just begun to know him."

I nodded, again looking out the window. "Yeah. I don't remember much about him. I'm not even sure what he did, sold stuff maybe, for some big corporation. But I don't think he liked it much." I stopped and pictured my mother on one particular Christmas Eve (well, I pictured a picture I had of her and me on that Christmas Eve) when she was much younger, curlers in her hair, just me and her. She was wearing these huge sunglasses that covered up her eyes, her eyebrows and most of her cheeks and she had on this crazy kind of full-body, one-piece pink dress and top thing that puffed out at the knees and elbows, with bonus shoulder pads and extra-wide belt, as well as this nutty Bananarama sweatband with jaggedy neon pink and green and blue triangles that wrapped around her forehead and made her hair stick straight up. It was like the worst pharmaceutical drug trip you could ever imagine. It was hot. I was wearing a very faded E.T. long-sleeved t-shirt and pretty tight red pajama bottoms with elastic cuffs around the ankles, and mismatched socks, also pretty hot. I don't remember why my father was not there that year. I do know that he wasn't taking the picture—that was probably our drunk neighbor Mr. Ray who popped over to wish us a merry Christmas, check out my mom and make himself a Harvey Wallbanger at our built-in bar. I looked very serious in the picture, which I would only have done if a neighbor was visiting. My mother's hand was resting delicately on my shoulder. I don't remember why my father wasn't there. Maybe he was already dead.

"He died during a business trip," I heard myself telling Ding Dong. "At least he went while he was working, which I guess is a more honest way for a guy to go, maybe. I don't know."

Ding nodded and looked pensive. "You know what I don't understand? These nutters who hike to 16,000 feet to go snowboarding and get buried in an avalanche, then you have to send half the bloody army looking for their corpses."

I nodded along with him.

"Imagine dying during a leisure activity?" he said, whistling some air between his teeth. "People always say 'Well at least he died doing something he loved.' Piss off. I don't want to expire doing something I love, I want to *enjoy* doing something I love." He looked at me. I gave him a wry smile. "Shoot me in a parking lot somewhere or when I'm edging my driveway. You know, get me while I'm doing something I hate."

I didn't know what to say and picked at the knee of my jeans, making sure he was finished. "So, I'm not really anything, I suppose, not any kind of religion."

He did not answer at first, relaxing a little further into his seat and watching the snow, even putting his fingers to the driver's side window to watch the little misty fingerprints spread around the tips then slowly disappear when he removed them.

"Well, everyone should be something in the absence of having a moral compass or in the presence of a catastrophe, when the weak-willed need something to put their blame or their hopes on." I didn't know what he meant but I nodded anyway. "You know mate, there are two things I never trust: a born-again Christian and a starving dog. Either of them will bite at you at the slightest provocation." He shook his head, bending a leg up onto the seat toward me and resting his elbow on his knee, getting comfortable. A comfortable man rarely murders another man so I was beginning to feel a little better, but vigilant still, ready for any shenanigans. "But at least a hungry dog has a good reason to bite you. He deserves to be suffering because he's hungry." He glanced at me for some sort of affirmation I think. I was about to tell him that I was a major dog-lover, but he continued. "But a born-again Christian? No one suffers, and repents, quite like them. Flagrantly and conspicuously, publicly, just in case you missed it." He stopped and stared at me, though surprisingly his eyes were not burning red; they were just black, like his pupils had swallowed the irises. I glanced out my window. SUV man was still inside, the windows lightly fogged but in that instant I saw his beady little eyes, his green baseball cap with the white brim, his stubble. Ding infringed upon my attention again.

"Christ, no one loves to suffer like a Christian. Actually, it doesn't matter: Baptists or Catholics or Buddhists, Islam or Anglican, Jew. They all think they have the lock on suffering. They all love to suffer. They think it makes them stronger. 'It wasn't until I hit the absolute bottom, the worst time in my life, that I was able to pull myself up, find God and become the preachiest son of a bitch you ever met.'"

I didn't say anything.

Teddy said, "If I had my druthers I would walk this planet as the happiest man living. Hey, today I won the lottery. Tremendous! Teddy, I'm glad to say you are the father of a beautiful boy. Why, thank you doctor! Or, I don't know, it looks like we'll have a gorgeous sunset. What a beauty. Goodness, look, I woke up this morning. Wonderful, just grand!" He paused, reached out to turn down the heat and let his arm linger in the air, outstretched, for some time. He finally dropped it, then reached up to remove his cap again, absently scratching at the short afro.

"I suppose most people would call those things blessings," I said.

"Bah! Aren't blessings just tiny pardons from their angry God? To hell with their angry gods. These people seem less glad to *have* that blessing and happier that God actually *gave* it to them."

I was just so tired. Tired. And Ding Dong sure was jawing a lot. We both gazed out the windshield at the flakes that drifted down from heaven, pinned themselves on the warm glass and moved haltingly, geometrically down the surface like pinochle balls looking for their holes, only to dissolve into insignificant squiggles of wet.

"If I can be so bold to ask you and Willy's reason for going to Boulder may I?"

"Oh that," I said, my brain whirring. "We're going to Willy's Alcoholic's Anonymous meeting."

Ding looked completely shocked. "He doesn't look the type," he said.

I nodded solemnly. "Firewater," I stated. "It's been devastating to his people. I go to support him, you know, through the twelve-step process. He hasn't gotten past step one, where he admits to everybody but himself that he has a problem." It was kind of fun to make fun of Willy, but it wasn't as fun to lie to Ding Dong as it had been to lie to the hippy girl.

"Blimey. He told us while you were napping that the two of you were going to visit your mum, that she's quite ill."

"Oh," I said, startled. Wonderful—Willy had been busy blowing our cover all morning while another guy was busy getting some shut-eye. "Well, there's that too," I scoffed. "She's not so bad as Willy might make it sound. He can be very dramatic. He has an English literature degree."

"Indeed," Ding said, looking perplexed. "But the two of you live in Leadville?"

"Yes, Willy for much longer than me. He runs a snowshoe shop and in his limited spare time is a Meals on Wheels driver, you know, a person who takes food to old people, and he's also a volunteer fireman, a ham radio operator, an amateur astrologist and an emergency medical technician." The last was kind of a lie of course. Though Willy took several classes of combat life support at the local college, he had to quit to devote himself to full-time snowshoe production. But if you were ever in need of expeditious and expert aid, you would do well to get hurt on Willy's shift. I naturally assumed that Willy could not administer a band-aid to a child but that just shows you how much I know about the practice of medicine.

"Boulder is quite far to go to an Alcoholic's Anonymous meeting," Ding said.

I chuckled to myself. "Willy goes mainly to meet women. The pickings are pretty good there, from hippies to hotel clerks. Lots of merit in that town."

"Right," Ding Dong said. To my ears he distinctly gave the odor of digging at something, which in turn was giving me the distinct odor of nervousness. Then I remembered that he was a homicidal madman.

"And where do you work?" he asked.

I was tired of answering questions that might get me killed somehow. Though an innocent such as I didn't always know it (unless I read the newspapers or stepped into the hallways of a high school as a substitute teacher) the planet was peopled by unsavory characters bent on my destruction. I said, "I work with Willy," then quickly added, "Mr. Bell, could you see what the person next to us is doing? He hasn't gotten out of his car the whole time and it's making me really nervous. I think he's watching us. But don't be too obvious."

"Oh, okay," he said in surprise and leaned across his seat, throwing his right arm over the back and sticking his face right past me, his nose practically touching the glass, his mouth closer to my right ear than my own mouth. I became paralyzed.

"That guy?" he said. "He appears to be having a conversation with himself. The world's full of nutters, mate." He gracefully pulled back his torso. My entire body had become petrified at the near proximity of another man and I jumped like a pinprick when he laughed at me. "You need to take a break, mate, relax a little."

I sucked in a deep breath and looked at Ding Dong. He stared back at me.

"Ding Dong," I started, "uh, I kind of lied a little. My dad didn't really drown." Ding looked ready to kill me, or so I thought, so I quickly corrected myself. "I mean, he died, when I was ten, but in a small plane crash with a couple of other guys, near Las Vegas." I looked at Ding Dong fearfully but he was just staring at me. "But everything else I said was true, I swear it." Then I remembered that I had called Willy an alcoholic. "Except for the part about Willy," I swallowed. "I mean, everything I said about him is true, about him being an amateur astronomist but he's not really an alcoholic. He's, he's not anything at all really," I struggled. "I mean, we're not going to an Alcoholic's Anonymous meeting or anything."

Ding Dong pulled on his mustache with his tongue and teeth. "So why are you going to Boulder, or are you even going to Boulder at all?" He didn't sound too mad really.

"Well, for that, um, we really are going to see my mom. She's in the hospital, she's pretty bad." Ding didn't say anything. "She has stomach cancer."

"You shouldn't make fun of something like that Eliason," he said seriously.

I pursed my lips together, nodding, about to burst into tears. It was worse than any scolding I had ever received in elementary school, and I felt exactly like a child.

"I'm trying not to lie so much," I admitted. "I don't tell big lies. I do it just, I don't know, for fun sometimes." I don't know why I sometimes lied for no reason. It just seemed to make life a little funnier, a little more interesting, to see if I could get away with it. "I won't lie to you again, Ding. I swear it."

"That's a good idea," he said, his voice deep.

Seconds later Willy's visage appeared from around the redneck truck, his eyebrows holding snow like two hedges, smoke pouring from his mouth, his Farto cap already collecting an inch of snow on the beanie peak. I could have kissed him. Hitched to his side was a laundry basket with something inside. TJ also stepped over to my side of the car, so Willy pulled in his paunch to allow him to pass, hoisting the basket onto his right hip. TJ looked so frigid that his eyes were halfway shut, his fingers shaking as he reached for the handle and yanked open the door. "H-h-h-heat," he trembled, pushing the seat forward with a shove and complete disregard to my eating the dashboard, and then inched his body across the seat behind his father. I removed my teeth from the dashboard and lifted myself outside with a grunt.

"Hey asswipe, watch the door," I heard a wood timbered voice warn. Mr. SUV had rolled down his window—I noticed a cell phone attached to his sideburn—to threaten Willy, who stretched his eyeballs down to where the door had just barely licked the other.

"And a twiddle-pip to you, fine sir," Willy said, grinning like a lawyer after hearing that his wealthiest client has been having some marital problems. Thankfully the man went back to his phone with a shake of his head and a "Damn foreigners. Go back to Australia." Willy twirled the laundry basket into the car next to TJ and shoehorned himself in, saying "Theodore, your son is an absolute Corinthian, indulging in everything: the finest Dutch Edam in aisle five, a lovely boxed Montepulciano in aisle sixteen, even the bulk malted balls in aisle two, shame on you TJ."

Ding Dong projected his strained eye socket toward his son.

"I didn't really eat this morning," he said meekly, "and he was trying everything first."

I pushed the seat back into place before SUV guy decided to mix my eyeballs, nose and teeth all around, and sealed the door against the outside world.

"I see you re-stocked your wardrobe," I told Willy, peeking into the laundry basket at two new pairs of sweat pants, one traditional grey and the other shocking red. He also had a box of ninety-nine cent extra crunchy peanut twister nut bars.

"What a sublime excursion," Willy exhaled, his cheeks pink with satisfaction. "And a lovely check-out lady of Thai descent at the handicapped checkout."

Teddy cranked on the Monte Carlo and we began to roll gently forward when suddenly SUV dude jumped out of his truck and slammed his door, scooted over to the front of the Monte Carlo and stopped.

"Jiminy cricket," Willy exclaimed, "what in the name of all that is holy?"

The man seemed to be paying us little regard, his attention somewhere off in the near distance, then a leggy blonde jumping between snowflakes in super, super, super, super tight acid-washed jeans and big, black puffy sneakers entered the left field of the windshield.

"Yowsers," Willy said. She was pretty in that feathered hair, bony, bulemic, washed-out, I pick my nose in private, green eye shadow, trailer park kind of way, preserved beyond all logic by a steady diet of cigarettes and booze. I knew she was the kind of lady who, when laughing, sounded like the gluey phlegm that secured her lungs to her ribcage was dislodging with painful rips. She was wearing an extremely thin green sweat top with the hood off but the strings tied around her neck, the handle of a white comb sticking out of her back jeans pocket. She must have been freezing.

"It's like a time warp to thirty years ago. She's got Abba playing on her eight-track, no doubt," Ding said to himself. Her ear was stuck to a cell phone when she walked over to the knuckle head, her slightly bucked teeth tumbling over her bottom lip in a grin.

"Well you can goddam hang up now that I'm right in front of you!" we heard the SUV man yell. He had a phone pasted to his ear so they had obviously been talking to each other, probably trying to find each other. He was wearing one of those shiny, pro football jackets, but it was a Derfy employee jacket for guys who unloaded stuff all day in the cold. He was about six hundred feet tall and eight thousand pounds, absolutely massive, especially compared to the woman. Still grinning like a little girl, she sheepishly began to take the phone from her ear when he strode up to her and slapped it, smacking her ear and hand and cheek all at the same time. The phone exploded into three pieces as it smacked against the asphalt.

"Well Jesus," Ding exclaimed, "was that necessary?"

She put her hand up to her scarlet cheek then instinctively began to stoop over to pick up the pieces of her phone. SUV grabbed her wrist, lifted his boot high and clamped the biggest piece of phone between his foot and the earth, grinding it into the parking lot. He suddenly jerked her by the arm and, though small, she did not seem to move as she might have. Like a tornado trying to whip a straw of hay through the air, the force of the great violent motion seemed to have lesser of an impact than had she been a stouter woman. When he next pushed her, however, his mass plus force sent her splaying to the wet asphalt. Still she looked more surprised than hurt.

"My god, what should we do?" I asked the others. No one spoke. I started to go for the door handle but Willy put his hand on my shoulder and pushed down.

"Get in the truck!" SUV man yelled, turning our way and glaring through the window before wedging in between his truck and the Monte Carlo. "Get in the goddam truck!" he screamed, his phone ringing once more. "Hello!" he said, his butt cheeks in his tight cowboy blue jeans almost plastered up against my window. I could have reached out and made a pencil rubbing of the Wrangler tag just below his belt loop without him even knowing. "Yes, I'm still on my lunch break. What do you want? No, what you've forgotten is that *I'm* the boss and you're the new guy—" and he slammed himself inside the vehicle. The girl had been on the ground for some time, her legs bent and pulled to the side as if she were simply at a picnic on a blanket, watching her children playing down by the brook as she unwrapped the potato salad and waited patiently, just waiting, when in fact she was broken. She was on the ground long enough for TJ to insist that he was going out to help her, "let me out Dad." Idiot man honked long and loud until she was back on her feet, her jeans wet at the knees and butt. She had her hand up to her boxed ear and absently dried the other palm on the front of her wet jeans, looking unsure of where to go. The moron gave his horn another long honk and she nudged her sad being over to the passenger side.

"There's nothing for it now," Ding said brokenly and rolled the car slowly forward again, turning on the windshield wipers as the snow began to collect on the glass and obscure the world outside.

I heard Willy suck in unevenly, almost sob. "I feel like openly weeping," he said, his peanut twister bar half-eaten. "I feel so useless," he whispered. "He is simply too big for her, and too big also for one such as I, otherwise I would have shown him what for."

"Dad," TJ said meekly, "they've got Derfy Burgers in DerfMarts now. There's one inside."

Ding Dong rolled his head sideways on the headrest as if he were Joan of Arc *(Marie Antoinette—ed.)* waiting for the ax *(guillotine— ed.)*, his Adam's apple stretched so tightly the skin glistened over the knot as it bobbed up and down: "Bloody hell, son. Bloody hell."

CHAPTER ELEVEN

"Burning Pearls in a Dying Sky of White Elephants, 12:12 p.m."

"The moon is really yellow tonight."

I suddenly felt a little whoozy and clammy, the inside of my stomach a fiery red and searing yellow, phlegmy green around the lining, burning rotten as nicotine and battery acid, gritty like old coffee grounds as we lurched back onto the highway. The inside of the car had become strangely dully electric, silent, with a tinny odor of tragedy about things, a quiet clamor in our brains like a song for a dying princess, something steely and cold and untouchable, an icicle lying in the snow.

"It's kind of dirty yellow, isn't it, like sand in the ocean," Julia said.

Worse than anything, I felt like Ding Dong thought that Willy and I were up to something. Worse than that, I felt that Ding Dong felt that I knew that he felt that Willy and I were up to something. I probably should not have lied to him about Willy.

I told Julia that, indeed, the moon did look more yellow than pale. It was a scupper resting atop the mountains, a hair bigger than the sliver of a fingernail clipping, lying on the curvature of its back.

Several minutes down the highway the snow began to blow in unfurling gusts of white sweeping over our militant automobile in waves of attack. Ding Dong peered through the windshield, some of the flakes escorted by the wind in whirls over the blades, while other flakes reached out to the warmth of the glass only to be pushed aside and mashed into a gray slush like soldiers massacred in a column. We headed cautiously down a steep incline of the highway, eighteen wheelers desperately trying to grab onto any bit of asphalt to avoid a death slide, and Ding Dong's attention snapped to the right, down into the valley, into the armpit strip malls of Silverthorne.

"There's no turning back now, gentlemen," he said, just as abruptly pulling into the exit lane, pointing the hood of the car toward oblivion. If I had known then what was ahead, I might not have gone forward. But I couldn't know of course. My tiny universe was about to spin out of control.

"Oh don't say that Eliason. Don't tell me that we can't do anything now. It sounds so tragic, like we have no control over anything. God," Julia said to me, biting with one top tooth, one bottom on a pinky cuticle. I knew it would bleed the next day, a raw pink patch of flesh on the otherwise brown edge of her fingernail.

"Don't do that," I said, gently pulling her hand away. She let the finger and her attention rest on her lap, her bangs caught atop her eyebrows, the hair jumping up then down with each thought flashing by, with each pulling together of her lips for words.

"Something can be done you know—an operation," she said. Did I mention I was freezing? She had dragged my butt and a blanket out to Turquoise Lake sometime at the beginning of August to watch a meteor shower she had read about in a tiny corner of the newspaper. And it was colder than a cat's nads walking backward in an ice storm, or something like that, sitting outside. August at ten thousand feet was just a short prelude to winter leaping its way, our way, right past autumn.

"It'll all be okay," she said, picking up her chin, her eyes sweeping the heavens just in time for a sudden burst. Her face was illuminated in the blue-white light of a falling star that had slid like a firework into our atmosphere. It was bright enough to light everything around us in the color of winter's dusk on snow, the tall, thin shadows of the pines behind us pulling back then scattering forward as the star threw its light at us and began reeling it back again in its descent toward the horizon. It sliced through the blackness in a greenish arc and left a faint L-shaped scar in the sky minutes after it fizzled out. A loud pop then crinkling sound rained down on us, loud enough to cause Julia to cry out and bury her face in my shoulder. It was as if the sky was the back of a woman's black dress, unzipped or ripped open. I would not have been at all shocked to have seen a huge shoulder blade come poking through the newly-etched seam, the cluster of stars in the Milky Way spilling out to reveal itself as a spinal column.

"My god, I've never *heard* a shooting star before," I said, scared as hell but trying to look unfazed. "Look, you can still see the trail. It's incredible."

Julia tilted her face back to the sky where I pointed out the gash, the faint trail of cooked dust hot enough to throb and seethe like the edge of an ember. "I thought it was going to fall right on us," she whispered.

"I did too," I admitted. "That was pretty freaky. I wonder if something like that has ever happened before." I pulled her in close and smelled her hair. Roses and something else in her fruity shampoo—it was wonderful. And I thought about the best smell in the world: autumn, with that candy corn, vanilla scent that floats just on top of the wet dead leaves, so faint, before the acrid smothering of a chimney fire overwhelms everything else. It's the best smell in the world. Well, second best, just behind the smell of the back of a woman's neck in winter.

"What are you thinking about?" Julia asked as a less spectacular object unpeeled itself from the universe, fell and sacrificed itself to billions of other ions. I paused a little too long and felt her body sag anxiously into me as it often did when I became trapped in the spirit of "the universal reticent maleness" as she said. I was picking the words in my head, arranging them like a little kid's red and green and yellow and green magnetic letters on the fridge, just as clumsily and slowly.

I said, "It's just, it's more like a surgery I guess than an operation. I mean, a surgery always seems to take out something but an operation is to improve something."

Julia rocked forward and wrapped her arms around her knees, shutting me out with the curvature of her back. "Well god, if you want to look at it *that* way, like some kind of scientist."

"No, I mean, my mother had ovarian cancer and they just went snip snip down there. It's simple I guess. It's kind of the same thing, sort of, isn't it? I don't know. I don't know anyone who's ever had it done."

"Well it's a little different with me isn't it?" she said, annoyed. I traced the depressions of her spine with my finger but she pulled away. I put my hand on her shoulder but she scrunched herself up even tighter. Oh boy. I couldn't say anything, my mouth dry as a cracked river in hell. Anything more that I said would only get me in more trouble. So for once in my life I did the smart thing and kept my yap shut tight.

"Surgery, operation, whatever. They're the same thing, Eliason." She sounded so cold, clinical, sticking my name right in there like Betty Livermore. "Sometimes you're so—" but she did not finish, thank goodness. We sat saying nothing for several minutes, me being so something, watching more stars slip from the sky.

"I can do it if you love me."

I was relieved to hear her speak. "It's up to you."

"I can do it if you don't love me also."

"But I do love you so that's that."

"Everything is going to be okay," she said. But was it? God knew. At least she didn't tell me to "Just drop it." Man, if a guy ever hears "Just drop it" from a woman he can reassure his poor doomed carcass that he will re-visit the "dropped" subject two days later, sometimes four weeks later, maybe nine months later, possibly even two and a half years later. Maybe ninety years later if he was extraordinarily unlucky. Doomed. But Julia didn't tell me to drop it; she did however say, "You're just so—" again, not telling me what I was just so, which is worse than hearing, "You're just so...shallow...idiotic...immature...stupid...or something...sometimes," because then you are quite clear about what you are. We sat silently for minutes again.

"It's so dark," she said as a kind of reconciliation. She was really lovely, my Julia.

"I didn't really mean—" I said, but she turned, put a finger to my lips and told me to shush. I shushed. She rested her head against my chest. I could tell that she was looking at the reflection of the stars in the water, picturing the whole universe upside-down, that the stars in the lake were real and the ones in the sky a reflection, whizzing by the snow-limned peaks that rocked ghost-like in the tiny waves like white elephants in repose. I could imagine all the stars floating in the water, rippling in the silent troughs and washing up on the shore, elbowing each other in their piles until Julia bent over and threw them back in. I saw her almost translucently, glowing, picking up a red pulsing star and resting it on one of her palms, giving the thing a flick with a thumb and forefinger, watching its flight like a real, falling, dying star burning itself from the material to the chemical.

"The last time I spoke to my mother she asked what I was going to do with my life," I said. "Why would a mother do that to her poor kid?"

Julia was quiet for a long time and then said, rather softly, "Well, what do you kind of think you'll do?"

I shifted uneasily on the blanket. I thought that maybe there was a piece of drift wood or a half-burned log up my butt. I was feeling really uncomfortable.

"You mean with my life?" I felt her head nod slightly against my chest. Why did I do this to myself. "Well, chumps get rich all the time today, without really doing anything, certainly for not doing anything really good, which I could be good at."

"I hope you're not planning on doing anything bad."

"Oh no, I'm not planning on doing anything bad." I sniffed her hair silently. "I'm not planning on doing anything particularly good either."

"So in other words, you plan on not doing anything for the rest of your life." I felt her start to pull away from me.

"No, I do. I mean, it will be something, kind of like doing something." I didn't know what the hell I was going on about. When I was a kid I wanted to be a veterinarian. "I'm going to market myself as the non-man, the man no one knows. I think it's a good idea, an original kind of marketable idea."

"Eliason baby, what exactly does non-man do that is worth marketing?"

"Absolutely nothing," I said. I had thought all about this one day in the shop when I should have been sharpening the grommets on a pair of Mountain Flattener '92s or possibly some Summit Seeker '90s. "I will be Non-Man, the man no one knows."

"You're a disaster."

"I'll appear on TV and write a book for eight million dollars on, I don't know, how it takes a village to raise a Non-Man and after I become famous for being Non-Man, which I will because there are tons of stupid people out there who will want to meet Non-Man, I'll write a book on how it feels to be a non-Non-Man. I can moan and whimper about how horrible it is to walk down the street unrecognized, and how I never asked for any of this, that I just wanted to be Non-Man and live in peace. I'll bust up some hotel rooms too. Maybe I'll make a movie. It will be about Non-Man, but I won't actually appear in it. And I'll record an album about how hard life is on the road touring as Non-Man, and how I miss my girl and how every town looks the same."

I thought I heard Julia snoring softly. "Are you being serious?" she asked. Zip went another star, then zip, zip.

"I don't know," I answered. "But doesn't it sound interesting?" I felt her head shake once more against my chest. "Not even the album part?" Shake, shake. She lay down fully, putting her cheek and ear on my knee to face me.

"Let's just go to Texas," she sighed. Oh Jesus!

"I wish you wouldn't talk scary to Non-Man. Texas is too far away."

Zip, zip, zzziipppp. She rolled over. I couldn't resist weaving my fingers through her hair. I sang softly, or at least tried to sing, "The moon that lingered over Leadville town, poor puzzled moon, he wore a frown. How could he know we two were so in love, the whole darned world seemed upside-down."

She giggled lightly—a delightful sound—and flipped back over to face me. "Why are you singing that?"

"I don't know. I sang it to you when we were driving back from Denver that time. Remember, when we got the flat tire?" I think it was the last time I really impressed her, that I could change a tire. I put my hand on her cheek; it was warmer than the night air would have suggested. I saw her eyes trace another dying star. Zzzipp. She turned back over and we sat quietly looking into the dark.

"It's just sand," Julia said after some length.

"I know," I answered. "Actually it's dirt. And ugly as anything."

"What's so ugly about it," she asked defensively, flipping back over to face me.

"It's dirty and hot and big and full of cowboys."

"What is?"

"Texas!"

She pulled her face from the crease of my legs and said, "I meant the shooting stars. They're not really stars at all. They're just grains of sand." She tucked an arm under the back of my knees. "It's just speed and heat and sand."

"Speed and heat and sand?"

"How can you take something that's so small, like the sleep in the corner of your eye, and make it go so fast that it can explode and make its own light?"

I shrugged, naturally. I had received a D—in remedial life science. *[D+. Shut the hell up Willy.]*

She said, "They're just like oysters, only opposite." Before I had time to offer a double-huh she said softly, "But they're more about time, aren't they? Sand and time." I felt her forehead—it was a little warm. I think she was coming down with something. "Poor little oyster. He's just minding his own business, doing what oysters do, which I think is just laying around not bothering anybody and then a piece of sand gets stuck in his mouth." I briefly wondered if clams really had mouths. "They don't have any way of getting it out so what do they do?" She didn't wait for me to answer, probably realizing that I had no clue anyway. "They kind of spit on it to coat it, over and over and over and so on and so on and after a really long time, what do you get?"

"A pearl?" I ventured.

"You get a pearl, all because this piece of sand was bothering this poor little oyster inside his little shell. It's beautiful. Something beautiful comes from something kind of annoying." With the fingers of her free hand she dusted her neck where she had seen pearls hang on rich women in magazines. "All of that goes on inside some little shell as long as you don't try to pry it open too early."

I asked how people knew if a pearl was inside.

"They don't," she smiled. "It's like a little gift from heaven. It's just chance."

"Why don't we collect all the oysters on the beach and x-ray them. Then we'll know if there's a pearl inside. We could make a million bucks."

She punctured the dark with a drippy Hollywood sigh. "You're such a guy," she said, all depressed. "You want to add speed and heat to everything so that everything is destroyed. You want to take the chance and romance out of everything with some stupid answer." She dropped a couple more Hollywood sighs into my lap.

"I was just trying to be funny," I said, kind of mewled. "But if it worked it would be a good idea, kind of, I think."

"If every stupid thing worked then every stupid idea would be a good one," she said.

Well she didn't have to get ugly about it. Zzip, zip. Her eyes were closed. I could practically hear her eyelashes rubbing against each other like the crunch of shoes on pine needles. She bit back a sigh and I felt her chest fill with the air. I felt desperate.

"The moon dropped into the sea, and the sea into the sand, and all of the buildings into the land...." Julia was reciting poetry now. Things had become worse than I had imagined. Oh gawd. "At last he kissed her hand, and there was not a soul to see the last of the boy turn into a man...." God I hoped that was the end.

"The buildings were righted, the moon was relighted and there was one wandering, lost girl, a girl with two souls...." I felt I was about to be slighted.

"…There was one wandering, lost girl, who was for once in this world excited."

I waited several interludes so that I knew she was finished and said, "Did you make that up? It was nice."

"It wasn't supposed to be," she said.

I was in trouble. She was mad. I wanted to wrap her up and take her somewhere far away, under the rainbow, through the moon, outside the universe, or crawl into my shell and hope nobody cracked me open until I made a shiny silver pearl.

"Let's go skinny dipping," I heard from somewhere near my loins.

"Excuse me?" I said, shocked.

"Let's just hop in, just for a bit," she said, standing up and tugging on my hand. I anchored myself to the blanket.

"You know this lake is fed by mountain streams?" I said. She nodded. "And those mountain streams are fed by melted snow?" She nodded again excitedly, those bangs jumping up and down so sexy on her eyebrows. "Which means sub-sub-*sub*-zero water temperatures." She shrugged, pulling on my hand still. I stood slowly with a bleat, my knees cracking more than the stars that popped and fizzed into our universe. "And you are fully aware of what cold water does to a man's ego?" She nodded slowly, pulling me toward the shore. Lord have mercy.

"Just dive in," she said, stripping fully naked in about two seconds, which was really nice, then suddenly she dived through the air headfirst and slipped silently into the wet blackness like a devil's mermaid.

CHAPTER TWELVE

"Hate the Pickle, Not the Process,
12:21 p.m."

"From the bottom of my soul, as I've already stated, I refuse to put in even a toe," Snowshoe said to me. "I will not compromise my beliefs, but Eliason, I am dying for a Derfy Burger. Please, please, please."

Ding Dong had pulled the Monte C off the highway to a little nothing town called Silverthorne, and he drove straight to the next Derfy Burger, which was only about two and a half miles down the road from the Derfy Burger inside the DerfMart. He nudged the fender up to the parking lot curb and spun the key backwards in the ignition, the car wracking itself under some sort of automotive asthma then shuddering to death as if it may never start again.

"I just have to spend a penny," Ding Dong told us. TJ informed us that he meant "go to the bathroom."

"Derfy Burger," I heard Willy say, tapping lightly on my shoulder.

Back in a very brief idyllic time, 1947, somewhere in central California, Freddy "Derfy" Gerbroni and his younger brother "Daffy" Larry (don't ask) began an empire. They packaged burgers in little sheets of crisp waxed paper, they sold french fried potatoes in tinfoil tubes, they put malt in their shakes, so much that the consumer would inadvertently choke on malt powder with just the slightest intake of air through the straw suctioning the bottom of the cup. Those days are gone. Waxed paper? Gone. Tinfoil tubes. No more. Malt in a shake?

Give me a break. That's why they are called shakes and not malteds. A child today would not know a malted even if you tied one to the front of a train and ran him over with it. Sad. Hell, *I'm* not even sure *I* know what a malted is, but that's not the point. The Gerbroni Brothers own the planet. That's the point, sort of.

Today, no child in the USofA, Canadian provinces and most member states of the Commonwealth can call his friend or siblings "derf," even in jest, without first getting express written consent from the Derfy Burger franchise (and oddly, the National Football League) because the Derfy Brothers own the word "derf." They are currently in a legal battle to own the word "burger" and soon, no doubt, "the." There is a Derfy Burger in every country in the world, even Anarctica, despite the deaths some years back of its three employees who succumbed to a severe case of hypothermia (most sitcoms or TV dramas show unlucky people getting locked in the walk-in freezer and almost freezing to death? These employees got locked *outside* the freezer and froze.) Children by the age of two consume more ounces of Derfy Drink (an almost blinding concoction of milk, coffee, chocolate powder, some sort of orange soda and nicotine I think) than they do their own mother's milk. By age three, children react more cognitively to the visage of King Fred than they do their own father's. By age eight, seventy-seven percent of children have spent more time in Derfy Burger restaurants than at their grandparents' homes. By age ten, they will have eaten well over their own body weight in Derfy product. By age sixteen, globally, more kids have worked in a Derfy Burger than attended school. Ten years ago, there were more old farts (aged 65-80) working in Derfy Burgers in the South than there were old farts living in old-age homes (excluding Florida). In a 1997 national survey, one out of every three Americans claimed they were "more likely to understand and/or have had a positive interaction" with a mentally-handicapped person because of their exposure to them as employees at Derfy Burger restaurants (unfortunately, nobody surveyed the mentally handicapped employees' experiences with the mentally-challenged customers). There are no statistics on how many citizens die prematurely from a life of Derfy consumption, but one fellow in Tennessee by the name of Alston Crance, Jr. was buried in a replica of a Daffy Derfy Dinner box, which usually includes a Derfy burger, bag of Daffy fries, a Derfy shake and a prize; he was buried with the first three in his coffin—we must presume that he considered himself the prize. He was 82. It was Freddy Gerbroni's dream, or at least he told the world on TV that it was, to outlive Alston Crance Junior, as a tribute. Freddy G. is 79.

"Please, please, please, Eliason," I heard Willy begging from the back seat like some worn-out Smiths song, tapping me on the shoulder. He was killing me. I turned to him, trying to ignore his big soupy grin and batting eyelashes. "I mean, as long as we are here, Eliason, littlest chieftain of all chiefs."

"So what you're saying to me," I said in disbelief, staring hard at him, "is that you will drive thirty miles to shop at DerfMart, the single biggest factor in the destruction of America's downtowns and mom 'n pop stores and the biggest reason we all buy the same plastic crap all over the country without even thinking about it, but you won't go into a Derfy Burger because it, and I quote, 'supports fascist regimes in South Africa'?"

He managed to look smug and embarrassed at the same time. "Little chief moneymaker, I realize your grasp of economics is less than tenable, but you are comparing a haddock with a pike—both have fins, gills, a predilection for water, same phylum, i tako dalje, but my friend, such a different taste when cooked. To wit: One part of the Derfy family owns Derfy Burger and another part owns DerfMart, and hardly the twain ever meet over the Thanksgiving Day table. The burger side does some very shady business 'round the globe."

"But it's all the same," I insisted. "It all goes into the same pocket that keeps handing us the same crap that we buy, made by, and I quote again, 'our little brown brethren in Middle Eastern militia puppet states who are paid five cents a week.'"

He played tiddlywinks with his fingers and even hid a yawn behind his hand. "Did I say that? I believe I was mentioning MonstaBurger in that particular conversation. Correct me if I need correction." I ignored him, wishing he would spontaneously combust and leave a little pile of white dust and mustache on the back seat.

"Oh Eliason," he said patting me on the shoulder like a mother to a child whose balloon had just slipped from his fingers and was weaving its way to the stratosphere, "I know it is a rough-hewn road being an idealist in these stable times, but we *do* live in a capitalist society. If we choose to buy poorly crafted bits of baublery then it is our choice. And whoever makes and sells the most product to us while retaining the most profit, wins. It is called business, my son. Lambs are eaten by lions every day."

I sat without moving, saying nothing, not facing him, torturing the hungry man.

"The man makes sense to me," Little Ding said in the hanging silence. I turned in surprise. "I mean, why pay more for a pair of shoes than I have to? I don't care who made them or if he had to eat the nickle they gave him for a week's work just to survive. My boy Snowshoe is a good man, he just wants his burger," Little Ding said, shaking his phone at me and his father. Snowshoe nodded in accord. "A man's got to eat like a dog's got to bark," Little Ding said. The Weeper nodded once with a smile, patting Dinger's knee. "If only to survive."

Teddy Bell pulled those eyelids back on those rolling red eyeballs, the tendons in his neck stretching and roiling, wriggling like an unearthed worm, his voice box pulled tight so that his words were higher pitched than usual. "I would say that he needs less to survive, and is more a slave, a weakened lump to his taste buds, which have been bombarded with sugars and fats and salt and beef tallow since he was a boy. Lord, deliver the weak man from his weaknesses." He sounded kind of like a preacher.

"I say, deliver the strong man from his weaknesses, for in those weaknesses lie something that is stronger than strength," Little Ding countered, sounding even more like some crazy preacher than his father.

"Oh I like that one. I have to remember it. And nothing upon which to write. Drat!" Willy said, poking around for a pen inside the abyss of his jacket. I slowly turned to him, to see him soaking up all the twisted wordplay and turns of phrase with a huge, delighted smile. Little Ding was in a staring contest with his father. My latte was beginning to churn again.

"May I butt in?" Willy asked meekly. Both father and son nodded silently. "Gentlemen of the jury, I confess, I am a weak man, a study of contradictions, a dichotomy of modern mankind. I am the self-destructor of my own body and mind. I am the fellow in the check-out line who sees the beautiful women on the magazine covers and I want one, so desperately, though one will never have me." He choked back what sounded like a sob. I noticed Teddy's face slacken just a little. "I want to own the beautiful as opposed to earning the real, the less than perfect." He heaved a massive sigh our way.

"That's right Willy," TJ said tenderly, patting his knee this time. Willy pulled off his Farto! cap and fingered the patch absently, picking at a dried food product on it with a square fingernail. His thin hair was all stuck up like cotton candy, his mustache slightly moist, his window triple-fogged from the body heat he was exuding and I thought instantly, cruelly, beyond my ability not to think it, "This dude is never going to score a babe." But then I felt bad all over, like watching a dog get hit by a car.

"I want to spice myself with the nicest cologne, eat the richest food, attend the most vibrant art festivals and be seated with an eloquent, exotic woman who gazes at me with…adoration. Is it so much to ask?" We all sat quietly as, yes, it was all so much to ask. "But instead, every day, I sit back and give in to my cheap and belittling temptations, the false riches, to the plasticity of our time." He strangled back another sob with a full glottal stop of some impressiveness. "It is becoming harder and harder to forgive myself for being a weak, weak man."

Dang, the inside of that car was quiet, so oppressive that I thought it might double in on itself and start sucking Silverthorne into its vortex, like a black hole, scooping up the Derfy Burger and all the shoebox-shaped businesses and suburban assault vehicles that would desperately try to scurry away but would be pulled over the lip into nothingness and then cast to damnation. Damn, Willy.

"We're living among the godless, soul brother," Ding Dong said. I almost gasped aloud, it was so great, just like something a real black dude would have said in a distant past, before everything had turned to plastic.

"And living among the godless obscures our ability to forgive," Little Ding said. Little Ding said pretty smart stuff…when he talked in real-time, and not on his phone. I noticed Ding Dong pull on that little mustache of his with his tongue and teeth. He looked beyond angry at his son, who was staring out the window like a little boy, his fingers folded in his lap. Willy stared at the back of TJ's head, twisting his blond mustache with thumb and forefinger. I sort of wished that I had a mustache of my own to do something with.

"It's our own pity, and our blind introspection," Teddy said, finally releasing the steering wheel to wring his hands and crack his knuckles, "that deceive us into thinking that we're rising above the mundane. It makes me ill."

I kept my eyes on Willy but watched Ding Dong with a sideways gaze.

"Soooo," I said gently, opening my eyes wide then rolling the irises to the sides, toward the passenger window, to signal to Willy to get out of the car with me, "uh, Willy, you need those burgers?" I even tilted my head once or twice toward the door.

"Oh jolly good yes!" he cried, reaching around to his fat butt, caressing out his wallet and fishing from it two one dollar bills. He balanced them on my shoulder. "Do you have something in your eye, chieftain or a kink in your neck that needs attention?" I could have killed him on the spot.

"Let's get out of the car, TJ," Ding Dong said, immediately propping open his door.

"Okay Dad," he said, almost a challenge, then I heard him say as he ducked his head outside, "Gawldang, it's snowing like crazy," the blowing flakes inviting themselves into the car like you would imagine they would if you owned a cabin in the middle of Siberia and nudged the door open one morning to check if it was snowing for the thousandth straight day with the wind screeching like a ghoul. He slammed the door so that my eardrums almost burst.

"Three burgers, dude," Willy said, holding up three little sausage fingers (I always made fun of his working-man fingers, calloused, slightly swollen always from twisting and stretching and pulling metal and fabric, heroic almost). His nails were beginning to collect dirt I noticed.

"Jeez, Snowshoe, these guys are freaking me out. We need to make a run for it," I said. I looked over his shoulder at the Bells, who had collected themselves at the trunk and were having a guarded discussion about something, probably about whether the trunk was big enough to stuff both of our bodies into. "They're like preachers or something."

"Did you become discombobulated by that little session of verbal backgammon?" Willy said, chuckling to himself. "They *are* very eloquent and well-spoken, those two. TJ must have been schooled in Britain. I think it is wonderful to be accompanied by two such erudite men."

"Well they're scaring the hell out of me. Come on, Willy. Let's get another ride from a little old lady or something."

Willy folded his hands over his belly and studied my face with a frown.

"What?"

"I am simply shocked, Eliason, that you are skeptical of these men because you, like your fellow American brethren, are innately petrified of men of color."

"Oh shut the hell up. That's not it at all and you know it." He pursed his lips and stared out his window. "The guy calls himself Ding Dong for Christ sake. And he goes into a kind of frenzy over weird little things, like when you were talking about Derfy Burger shooting that stuff into space. What the hell were you talking about anyway?" He shrugged, not taking his eyes from the window. "Come on Willy. We'll go inside, get warm, watch the snow, you can have all the ketchup you want, I'll buy you a sundae, heavy on the nuts."

"You know I am allergic to nuts," he sulked. I stared at him for several moments but he kept his eyes pasted to the window, pretending to watch the snow.

"Willy, how is it you can eat peanut butter but not peanuts."

"Something in the process, dude," and he dragged his sad eyes back forward. I had never seen a man look so forlorn. "There is something in the squashing and the processing of the nuts, so to speak, that grants me tolerance."

"Come on Willy," I begged. "Look at the nice people going in and coming out, happy looking people, safe looking people."

Willy looked past me through the front windshield. "Well, maybe if—" and once again our tiny little automobile world was rocked by another boom. Willy almost jumped through the seat into my lap. "Chieftain!" he cried out.

"It's okay," I reassured him. "It was only Ding Dong slamming the trunk." Willy looked like he may collect into a puddle on the seat and quiver away down the crack to join the loose change, bobby pins and old French fries.

"I am afraid that my little speech before, about my belittling temptations, has simply left me incapacitated, Eliason. I just do not possess the energy or catalyst to change my inertia into motion. I am merely a slave to Copernicus' [*Newton's—ed.*] law. I'm just so, thirsty, and hungry."

I twisted around and watched the Bells enter the Derfy Burger together. Something inside, instinctual, told me not to go in.

"You better protect me the rest of this damn day," I addressed Willy, gazing at the bills on my shoulder. I grabbed them and began to push the door open into the wind.

"Three Derfy burgers please," he bleated, instantly lighting up.

"For two bucks? What century are you living in boy?"

"You may have to spot me twenty cents, for tax," he said with a wave of his right hand and such condescension I really could have kicked him in the teeth. I heaved open my door, gave it a push shut and glared at him all snug in the back seat. He didn't look at me, like he was embarrassed, as if I was the guy in a spy movie who was taking a bullet for him when the details of our mission fell into the enemy's hands because Willy had left them on his Derfy Burger tray and had accidentally thrown them away with his cheeseburger wrappers and his retainer. I started to head inside but turned, tapping on Willy's window instead. He didn't even roll the damn thing down, he just mouthed "What?" through the snow-stuck glass.

"Do you want hamburgers or cheeseburgers?" I asked.

He mouthed "What?" again.

"Do you want hamburgers or cheeseburgers?" I yelled.

It was first-monkey-in-space time as he jerked his head from side to side, heaving a shoulder into the seat so that it flipped forward, his hand pivoting here and there grasping for the knob to roll down the window. After about thirty seconds, the window cracked a millimeter.

"I cannot quite hear you, little chief," he said, lifting his butt crack marginally off the seat with his ear to the window crack.

"Do you want hamburgers or cheeseburgers?" I sighed.

"Eliason, honey, if I had wanted *cheese* on my Derfy burger I would have asked for a Ger*broni* Burger." Jesus, how dim of me. "Without pickles."

"You'll have to pick the pickles off yourself otherwise I'm going to be in there for fifteen hours waiting for your special order."

He frowned.

"Hey Willy, why is it that you like cucumbers but hate pickles?"

He shrugged. "I guess it's the process," and he quickly rolled up the window through its millimeter of space.

I turned to see a busload of what must have been high school basketball players getting off a yellow bus. They were all tall, gangly, awkward, not quite fitting into their bodies and they all had the same televangelist haircut as the old guy with the pock-marked face who must have been their coach. If I hurried I could beat them inside.

"Eliason! Eliason!" I heard just as I got to the front of the car, the words thin and wavering as if they had been forced through a tiny space. Willy sounded urgent so I rushed over to the window, thinking that he may be asphyxiating on his own carbon dioxide. The window was open about a centimeter now. Willy stretched his mouth to the crack.

"I thought if you hurried, you could beat those young men to the line, otherwise it may take forever."

"Thanks, Willy," I said, looking up to see the first kid reach the door and hold it open for his fifteen vulture buddies who would pick the grill clean of all once-living matter. I bent down to the window. "And if you ever call me 'honey' again I'll thump you."

I shuffled in after the jocks and joined the back of the queue.

I don't mind standing in lines, usually because I don't have anything urgent to attend to in my sad, miserable life [*Shut the hell up, Willy*], but remember, my mother was dying. And there I was standing in line for three damn hamburgers for a guy who didn't have the guts to support fascist regimes in South Africa like the rest of us. I forgot how I hated the smell of post-pubescent boys: they've lost that sickening sugar cereal smell that pre-teens have from chewing too much gum, snarfing too much candy and downing too much soda, and have moved on to a scent completely unlabeled by anthropologists. But it's kind of a chemically, powdery, musty armpit underwear smell. And the dudes were all pimply on their foreheads, some on their cheeks, the backs of their necks, all with backwards baseball caps and drooping pants so you could see their boxers, some with their shirts tucked into their undies like crazy old German men. And the shoes? I'll never understand them: all kinds of rubber and zippers and things to push, blocky enough to anchor Frankenstein's monster. I jammed my hands into my coat pockets, checking the place out. I had not been into a Derfy Burger in years. I noted with some alarm that the place was wall to wall TVs, all with the volume turned up to eleven. Most of the tables were filled with satisfied diners: a couple of numb-nut skiers in one corner with their knit caps and chapped faces. Some little twirp must have been having a birthday party because about ten kids were gathered around a huge pink cake and practically molesting the French Friar, a round-cheeked, squat guy with a monk's ring of baldness fringed with stringy brown hair, his bright pink monk's robes tied around the middle by a sash that was supposed to be a french fry (the French Friar was one of King Fred's underlings), around his neck a huge cross of what was meant to be two interspliced French fries I think. Peter Potato, who was this moldy brown-green potato-shaped thing with about a hundred eyes all over its body, but no mouth or nose, and should have scared the bejeezus out of kids but didn't for some reason, was trotting about, twirling in circles like a fat ballerina. I directed my attention to another little twirp who had just started heading my way after receiving his order, his mother in tow. He dived into his Daffy Derfy Meal box, eyes all aglow with the sweet innocence of a child. Then he started doing some sort of voodoo ritual with his face, twitching facial muscles that I never knew could twitch individually, then scrunching his eyes closed, then drawing out his face, as if he was trying to pull it back into shape. He held something made of plastic wrapped in plastic from his Daffy Derfy box and planted his feet.

"This is the hundred and fourth piece!" he screamed. The chattering basketball players stopped, turning. The whole restaurant became deathly quiet.

"Darling," the mother said, putting her hand on his shoulder. He shrugged it off violently.

"This is the hundred and fourth piece! I need the hundred and fifth piece!" he wailed.

"That *is* the one-hundred-fifth piece," cooed his mother.

"This is the hundred and fourth piece! I already have this one!" He did a little more voodoo and kind of spun round on his heels like a demented court jester. "*I need the* HUNDRED AND FIFTH PIECE!" he hollered, grunting, the tendons tensing in a neck that could so easily be snapped under the right adult supervision.

"Darling, by my count that is the one-hundred-fifth Daffy Derfy Meal that I have bought you in three weeks. Undoubtedly it is the one-hundred-fifth piece," the mother said, pleased with herself. She was pretty good-looking.

"Do you think I'm some sort of a idiot?!" the kid yelled. I just loved that. I loved when little kids said adult things that you didn't expect, like "Do you think I'm some sort of a idiot!" About a foot away from me, a man in dark shades and a suit began talking urgently to himself, under his breath, into his shoulder. It was nut day at the Silverthorne Derfy Burger and I was there. But it was priceless entertainment.

"Mommy does not think you are a bad child, Brandon dear, but what you are doing is a bad thing. This is not okay. This is totally not okay, okay?, and there are several reasons why it is not okay," the mother said, crouching to his level, bending back a couple of left-hand fingers with a couple on her right hand, ready to tally the reasons.

"Actually, ma'am, that is the hundred and fourth piece," said one of the basketball players to the mother. She looked up at him in open-mouthed horror. He blushed fiercely. He was short and very dumpy— he must have been the manager. "I have all the pieces myself, except for the last one."

"These people are crooks! This place is a fraud!" the boy screamed. I chuckled despite myself. I really loved that—I had to get this Brandon kid's full name for future parties or something, for entertainment. Keep touching in. A girl, another manager I guessed because she was equally as dumpy and probably taped the players' ankles and called herself the "trainer," slapped the manager-ball boy kid in the shoulder.

"Be quiet, Augustus. Now he'll never shut up."

Augustus slouched, frowning, rubbing his shoulder.

"Geez Violet, I was only trying to help."

Before they could say anything else, Peter Potato peeled away from the birthday party, pirouetted through the crowd, engulfed the little brat in his spindly arms and they disappeared out a side door, the kid's legs kicking like a dying cockroach's. The man in the suit and sunglasses trailed closely behind, looking serious, blabbing away into his chest. Happy Hindoo! There was Happy Hindoo, another of King Fred's minions, one of my favorites, magically on the scene. He was a Gandhi look-alike, dressed in neon blue robes and a shocking yellow turban about eight feet high and two-foot-high golden sandals, an ever-present box of Derfy chicken drumsticks in one hand, in the other a cane shaped like a snake that he would sometimes pretend to mesmerize with this weird flute thing in commercials. This snake had a tiny hand-carved wooden burger between its fangs. It was pretty neat. He shifted the cane expertly and took the mother by the hand and led her through the same side door. It was a vaguely violent, creepy scene.

The tension eased and everyone started clamoring away excitedly. Augustus had become a mini-celebrity to the team. Despite old Violet's admonitions, the guy who had previously been around only to supply balls and towels had suddenly become the center of attention, the star, as if he had bagged a last-second jump shot against Doofus High. I heard words like "cool" and "mack" and "da man" peppering the warm-up crowd, and old Augustus was soaking it all up, blushing a little despite himself. I felt good for old Augustus, that for once in his life he was being noticed, that he had a little slice of fame that he could take away with him. I hoped he wasn't the kind of fellow who would say "Hey guys, remember at Derfy's three weeks ago, when I told that lady her kid actually *did* have the hundred and fourth piece? Remember? Remember?" And everyone would start to hate him again because it wasn't *that* funny after the fact and they had just lost to Idiot High so shut up Augustus, and his little bit of self-esteem would vanish after such a short shelf-life, and they would go back to calling him "fatty" and pick on him and mess up his hair and tell him to sit down and shut up, and the coach would smile to what he feigned was himself but was really for all his players to see. And a month later fat old Augustus would go to school and shoot them all with a gun he stole from his uncle or bought at DerfMart because that is what kids do today when they have had enough. Or so I've read.

Then again, none of it would happen, because once the kids filed onto the bus and sat in their seats with Violet and Augustus at the very front behind the driver, he would be just Augustus the Fat Manager again. And that is all he would ever be, just like I would only ever be The Guy Buying his Boss Three Damn Hamburgers because our boy Willy had to eat "like a dog's got to bark." And I stood in line thinking that I'd never heard a black guy, ever, ever say "gawldang." Then, my goodness, you wouldn't believe what I saw as I finally stepped up to the counter.

CHAPTER THIRTEEN

"The Coronation of Mr. Derfy Burger, 12:55 p.m."

You wouldn't expect to encounter the most beautiful woman you've ever seen working behind the counter of Derfy Burger. I mean, you see some cute girls and some awfully good-looking ones of course, just as you would see at clothing stores and behind the perfume counters at department stores in the most backwards Midwest towns, but you don't expect to see the most beautiful girl you've *ever* seen. You only see the most beautiful girl you've ever seen sitting on an airplane one aisle away from you next to some lucky bastard who couldn't possibly be cooler than you by half but just happened to get seated next to her because God is an unkind God to everybody but lucky bastards like him. Or you see her in a magazine, and for all you know, she is completely computer-generated. Or you see her in traffic in the passenger seat of some knobbo's very expensive car, or you see her through an office window or walking through a park with her attractive gray-haired middle-aged mother, the pavement slick with autumn mist and an occasional yellow leaf fluttering to the grass, covering the whole scene in a golden sheen. But you never really expect to see her working at a Derfy Burger. And that is what I saw when I stepped up to order. Her name tag said "Leigh." I had always loved that name: straight-forward, non-gender specific, ageless but not age-bound (like a Joyce or Myrtle would be), cute in all its curvaceous loops and circles, beautiful in its crisp cleanliness.

"Hello," she said with this toothpaste white smile.

"Well hi," I replied, super smooth. She asked how I was today. "I'm good, really good. Yeah," I answered smartly. Now I'll admit, I'm not always the sexiest guy west of the Mississippi, but the exchange was the most surreal, hormonally-charged order I had ever given in a fast-food restaurant, and I sensed it within seconds. I guessed that Derfy Burger had dispensed with the cue-card "Welcome to Derfy's. Is that for here or to go? Would you like a swift kick in the balls with that apple pie?" spiel that I had grown accustomed to hearing when I was a beef tallow-addicted kid. My, how the world had changed for the better! The bonus was that the most beautiful girl a guy had ever seen gave me the juiciest smile you could ever see. I stole a look at my hair in the reflection of the spotless metal on the back of the cash register. I must have been looking good.

"How has your day been?" she asked, her teeth as white as if they had been carved by the expert hands of the finest African artisan from the purest white elephant tusk.

"Wonderful, great, a real gem," I said. I usually wasn't so effusive about even the best days of my life—my sixth birthday for instance when I received not one of those crummy balsa wood airplanes with the little silver clip on its nose that enables the plane to fly half a foot before executing a kamikaze dive into the ground but instead I was gifted one that had a rubber band-powered propeller hand-made by my very own grandfather—however the most beautiful woman I had ever seen had never asked me before how an even okay day of my life had been.

"Well, welcome to Derfy Burger. I'm glad you picked us today," she smiled, eyes all a'sparkle.

"Leigh, I have not always been a big fan of the Gerbroni brothers, but today I'm here, you're here and—" but what else could a guy say. She smiled and nodded. "My boss dressed as Private Pickle for Halloween last year though," said a voice impersonating my own coming from my mouth. I really didn't know what had come over me. They were undoubtedly the rantings of a mad man. Private Pickle was another of King Fred's staff, a life-sized piece of food like Peter Potato, except Private Pickle was a kosher dressed in an army uniform with all

167

kinds of medals on his chest and stripes on his shoulders (though he didn't really *have* shoulders because he was a pickle), a sword, a stovepipe hat, knee-high riding boots and this French-looking little mustache. He looked quite gay actually, and he was a bit of a camp figure in every junior high school across the country and had been for generations. Leigh handled my crazy ramblings with style, tucking her long blond hair behind a single ear and blushing like she meant it. She was a kind of California perfect, the kind of girl you thought about when you were a boy and just beginning to like girls, the kind of girl who lived in a low-roofed, rectangular house with a perfect lawn with lots of oversized potted plants inside on the floor and little windows too high to see out of, the garage door always halfway up at night up and the haze of a single light bulb escaping from it orchestrated by the sound of crickets and late night sawing, the kind of girl you could meet only in California, who could live only in California, like the sand was part of her skin, the smell of coconut lotion always a layer of air around her limbs if you were ever lucky enough to get your nose close enough to sniff it in the air-conditioning of her bedroom, her whole body scrubbed so squeaky clean by the water and brine that she would taste of cellophane, and then subtly you would pick up the flavors of avocado and orange and lemon that you were sure were all over California and must have sprinkled her very genes as she rode her bicycle through the trees when the highways had still been orchards.

"May I take your order?" she asked. The girl next to Leigh, I noted, was also pretty but not as pretty, and I caught her stealing a glance our way. For one split second her order-taking countenance dropped and I saw not hatred or jealousy but exhaustion, a loathing aspiration. Leigh was beyond her. And it was almost sad. Almost.

"Three hamburgers please," I said, leaning onto the counter.

"Would you like cheese?" Leigh asked, shifting her weight ever so slightly to lean closer to me. Soon I would be gasping for breath, I knew it, just to smell her.

"Leigh, if I wanted *cheese* on my Derfy Burgers I would have ordered Ger*broni* Burgers," I said, offering the cheesiest smile so that she knew I was joking.

"Right you are," she said with a slightly incredulous laugh and fixing my eyes with hers, the kind of stare that a woman gives a man to let him know, so that he doesn't have to doubt, that she means business. Then she moved her gaze over my shoulder to a fixed point in the near distance, and looked long enough to make me a little agitated, like I was about to be ambushed. I stole a few furtive glances around and noticed the place was even more crowded with people, especially with men in suits, which must have meant that some cheapo boss had brought the saps from his business convention to Derfy's instead of the hotel buffet room. Most of the basketball players had shuffled to the sides of the lines while they awaited their food, obviously upset that they had not made the kind of time I had with Leigh, the most beautiful woman you'd ever seen. Happy Hindoo was back with his box of chicken, Peter Potato reappeared and by golly, there was Chief Buff Burger, the newest member in the particularly zany cavalcade of collectable characters that the Gerbroni marketing machine had dreamt up. He had been invented several years ago when buffalo burgers ("Put an arrow through fat, not your heart") were introduced to the menu as only a slightly less fatty burger. He was an absolutely massive Indian with a set of bow and arrows about ten feet high, an always serious face ready for battle and war-painted, a suggestive loincloth, and comfortable moccasins. He was Willy's least favorite character ("How dare they exploit the already exploited," he sniffed, but, just to annoy him, at the shop I had glued onto one of the tabletops the Chief Buff Burger action figure some kid had received in a Daffy Derfy meal box and accidentally dropped on the floor). I swear to God I even saw King Fred himself putter through the kitchen, quick as a cat, and out the side door that employees use to sneak off to the bathroom and sneak back in after not washing their hands. And I could swear that all the employees behind the counter were edging ever closer to me and Leigh, migrating, as if they too were magnetized by our raw animal connection. But I could have just been seeing things.

Leigh punched in the burgers, bink bink bink. She looked up at me, one piece of hair escaping from behind her ear, falling delicately across her left ear, the curled tip resting in a C-curve against the middle of her lips like a fisherman's uncouth hook taunting a mermaid. It drove me daffy, derfy, batty. I noticed her shirt was spotless: no trails of dried ketchup or mustard caught on her not large but certainly pert bosom. I loved her cleanliness, her Godliness.

"Anything else—fries, orange soda, or a Derfo shake?" she smiled.

"I think that's about it, Leigh."

"Great. That's four dollars and twenty-one cents," she beamed.

"Pardon me," I said.

"Um, four dollars and twenty-one cents," she repeated, squinting at the cash register's read-out to make sure she had seen it correctly, then straightened herself and looked at me with crinkled eyes. "I know," she apologized, and I loved her even more for it.

"Wow," I said, thinking how much I hated living in or near ski resorts where Derfy's could charge NASA prices for a crummy hamburger and billions of rich people would still gladly pay. I felt Willy's two dollars, which I had been crushing so tightly in my hand they had practically become a part of my chemical make-up, and wrapped the same hand past my waist to my wallet, dug it out and, already knowing my folly, slowly peeled the folds apart, empty, where it practically opened and shut, opened and shut, opened and shut of its own accord, painfully, like a wide-mouth bass slung up on a dock and desperately snatching at all the oxygen it could not convert into life. It was not the first time in my life that I didn't have enough money to buy something.

"Heh-heh, well all right," I fake chuckled, stalling for time. Leigh lowered her eyebrows into a concerned, unspoken "What?"

"I'm a little short on that sort of cash. I guess you're going to have to erase that order. I mean, I can go to the car and get more money I guess, but it's probably going to mess up your drawer."

"I wouldn't do that," she said quickly. "I would not walk away right now," she practically whispered.

"Okay," I said, to ease her mind. Man, she seemed really attached to me. I didn't mind. In fact, you could say I was a little flattered. It was a novel feeling, like everything I'd ever seen in the movies, only far better, because it was happening to me instead of some good-looking guy with stylish hair. I was about to tell her that I'd never walk away, no matter how much someone in line wanted to thrash me for taking ten minutes to order.

"Do you want your life to change forever?" she asked. Man. I looked around a little nervously. I asked if I was in some sort of danger. "No," she said with some seriousness. The basketball kids were still milling about and I heard the first "Let's move it, pal" from behind me, probably from some hippy goathead.

"Are you alluding to us spending the rest of our lives together?" and if it was "yes" I would have bounded over the counter, folded her in my arms and run like a triathlete to the furthest corner of the globe, Sebastopol maybe.

"Not exactly," she said, and it was *that* about beautiful women: they can tell you "not exactly" until the day you die, and you will always pray that some day they will leave the "not" part out.

"I will tell you right now, if you walk away and go to your car for money and stand in line all over just so you can talk to me again, you will hate yourself forever."

She could see right through me. "Leigh, I've made a jerk of myself over beautiful women before, and I only hated myself for about six months afterwards," I said, chuckling daintily. Instinctively I tucked my hands into my pants pockets to offer a full-on, straight-armed shrug and felt something foreign nuzzle against my fingers. I pulled it out, unfolding the twenty dollar bill with an unconcealed bark of glee.

"Heh, I'm always finding these things in my pockets. Ring it up lady, and go ahead and put an orange soda on that order for yourself."

Leigh smiled with a "That's okay," then her countenance completely changed. She frowned and looked disturbed for the first time, upset. It was an expression I had dealt with many times upon chatting up the female species *[Willy, just cork it]*.

"You can have grape-raspberry if you want. It doesn't have to be orange," I said. She leaned forward, speaking barely above a whisper, so that I had to pull in close, close enough to smell the shampoo in her hair. It was intoxicating. A hot-oil treatment had been used in the last twenty-four hours, I was sure of it.

"Do you want the whole planet to know you and to win like a million dollars? Can you handle something like that without going totally crazy insane?"

"You're kidding right?"

She shook her head seriously.

"I think I could handle that, Leigh."

She bit her lip coyly. "Well, here goes," she said, hunching up her shoulders and plastering on an Aphrodite smile. Her finger rose in mid-air, slow motion and it mashed another button which coughed up an interminable beep.

BEEeeeeEeeEEEeEEEPPpPPPPPPppPPPPP.... In less than an instant, I felt her hand behind the back of my head, pulling me close, kissing me straight on the mouth. I think I really would have enjoyed it if not for a couple of blinding flashes and than an explosion of noise that gave the whole scene a whooshing weightless feeling. There was a horrific bang and my legs went numb, my body went numb and I felt the blood in every vessel leaking out of what must have been a gaping hole somewhere in my body. I had been shot, I just knew it. I knew at that moment as Willy and Ding Dong and TJ waited for me in the car, I was dying. The roof exploded and down came a million pieces of confetti, filling my eyes and filtering through my consciousness as what surely were the tiniest remnants of my life flashing before my eyes, memories that people always say they have just before dying (except that they don't actually die I suppose), but it would have been nice if they could have glued themselves into a coherent picture or two. A band filed through the side entrance and began bleating this kind of brassy, anthemic dirge that bounced and returned off the sterile walls and tables in a million directions. As the confetti sifted down, what seemed to be hundreds of yellow and red and white balloons escaped from somewhere underfoot and writhed to the ceiling, lolling against the panels, some with painted-on faces of King Fred looking down, gagging, gawping. Leigh's face shimmered about a million miles away from my retinas, and soon I knew her colors would fade to pastel, then monochrome then gray then black and finally a second of blinding white and I would cease to exist.

"Congratulations," I heard Leigh say, her voice all weirded-out, deep and backwards, like the devil always sounds in movies, "you are the billioneth-served Derfy Burger customer. You're Mr. Derfy Burger." And I had a vague recollection of seeing shock on her face, of her reaching out to grab me as I swooned backwards and passed out into blackness.

CHAPTER FOURTEEN

"A Target the Size of Texas, 1:02 p.m."

I awoke with a start. "Eliason, baby, you fell asleep again. You were dreaming something weird," I heard in the semi-darkness. It was Julia. I rolled my head in a lap of the softest, most iridescent blue, silky. Looking up, I saw the blurry visage of Gandhi with about a fifteen-foot-high snake-charming turban staring down at me.

"Jesus bro, are you alright? Just relax, and rest a minute."

"Don't let me fall asleep!" I started with alarm. I felt a delicate hand on my forehead, pushing me back down in the warm, twilight-shaded room.

"I won't baby. I'm here," Julia said. Her skin was warm and radiated the smell of fruity soap. I knew if I fell asleep again I would dream of tornadoes driving soda straws through telephone poles, of swirling, doorless shacks floating a thousand feet in the sky, of having to ford rivers that would be wholly lifted from their beds into the air, of legs like sand as I ran, of the funnel cloud ripping through open fields, twisting and swirling my way with its evil power. Then I would wake up sweating, then fall back to dreams of nuclear bombs ripping people's bones right out of their flesh, the sky all tipped over in bruised purple and orange. Then I would wake up sweating and roll over and dream of losing my teeth, spitting blood and flints of enamel. Then I would dream of losing my hair. Then I would wake up, losing my mind. I couldn't think straight. My thoughts were misfiring all over the place. Attached to nothing, dead weight.

"What happened?" I croaked.

"We were laying down here in bed, just talking, and you just sort of passed out, right in the middle of the conversation." Julia leaned her head on her propped up arm, lying next to me length-wise and looking at me with concern, pity? She was wearing only a towel, with another swabbed around her hair like a Hershey's kiss. "I got up and took a bath. Do you remember what we were talking about."

"Yes, yes, of course. I'm sorry, I just, it's like I'm drugged or something."

"It's okay," she said, resting her cheek on my shoulder. Her eyes were open so I knew she was thinking about something.

"God it's hot," I said, my thoughts still whirling, sinking and pooling somewhere around my feet, so far away from my brain. My apartment had been soaking up the western rays of the day for hours, the walls practically caked with the heat of residual sunshine, and the air nudging up against it and outward was stuffy, but the sun had slipped behind the mountains and twilight had settled in for its slow fade.

"Smoky said it's been the hottest two days for the middle of September ever recorded in Leadville. This year has been kind of weird," Julia said. She had just shaved her legs, which felt as smooth and pliable as the skin of a citrus, and I pictured one leg sheathed in the rind of a lemon, the other in a lime, my little 7-Up Girl. I felt her try to stifle a sigh, unsuccessfully.

"Yeah, it's been pretty weird," I said, turning my head to look out the window. I could see the tops of the mountains off in the distance and heard two or three kids playing baseball on the field two stories beneath my window, though it was already quite dark. My senses seemed sharpened somehow although my brain was clicking mechanically, sorting, cocking, misfeeding my thoughts, jamming the barrel with something resembling feelings or emotions or nerves. I didn't know which. I knew Julia could feel how fidgety I was, and I needed to say how much I loved her, but I was fighting with every fiber, tendon, nerve and tissue to appear placid. I lay there stupidly, silently, with a thousand misfired thoughts of nothing and I couldn't even hit a target the size of Texas. "You feel hot," I said to Julia instead.

"It's okay, it's because I just got out of the bath," she said, rolling over onto her back as if to fan out her body and release some warmth. After only a matter of seconds, she delicately rolled on to her side again, carefully touching her stomach against my hip. She put an arm across my chest.

"Eliason, baby, don't worry so much. Everything will be okay. Really. Girls get pregnant every day."

Her cheek was against my arm and within minutes I felt the steady rhythm of her sleep. I too fell asleep soon thereafter, waking in the middle of the night to find Julia gone, the room dark except for the light over the kitchen stove, her little jacket hanging on the back of the bedroom doorknob, and I pictured her walking the streets back to her apartment in her short sleeves, cold, then I fell asleep again.

****

"I don't think anyone's going to let you sleep for a long time, bro. I think you fainted."

"Why is my head in your lap?"

"You passed out and I caught you just in time. You've been out for about ten seconds, that's all." Gandhi smiled down benevolently upon me. The deep-blue folds of his dress practically swallowed my entire head.

"Am I dreaming? Who are you?"

"I'm Happy Hindoo, of course. Who are you, other than Mr. Derfy Burger?"

"Hey Happy—you're one of my favorite characters," I said all loose-jawed, like I had been to the dentist and had gotten a doppel draught of Novocain. He beamed and tried to prop me up. I rubbed the top of my head. All around us was white noise, commotion, chaos, madness. The noise was deafening. "My name is Eliason, Eliason Nye."

"Well, you're Mr. Derfy Burger now, bro."

"My god Gerald, what happened to him?"

"Just fainted, boss. Everything's okay," answered Gandhi, who was slowly straightening himself up and gently pulling me up by the armpit with him.

"Of all the millions of people out there we had to get a fainter," The Boss grumbled, glaring at me.

"I thought you said you were Happy Hindoo," I said weakly, looking unsteadily upon Gandhi. "Who's Gerald?"

"That's my real name bro. I'm Happy Hindoo but my real name is Gerald." I looked at him in total confusion, and he returned it with an expression of utter pity. "That's just a character. I just *play* Happy Hindoo." I noticed him shoot a worried look to his boss.

"You do?" I warbled. I must have really hit my head hard. The boss, who looked like a 1960s NASA croney with government-issued black specs, jug ears and plastered-down hair stepped in and by the crook of the arm grabbed a guy who was filming the whole episode.

"Mikey, you don't have to film this. In fact, edit it, chop it out, lose it. And we just need to quickly re-film the part right after the blonde gives him a kiss and, I think he made it until the balloons came out yeah, so just film him at the counter and splice it in. We can't go beaming all over the place this guy fainting" and he yanked me over to the counter and told me to spin to the right and say in shock "My goodness what happened?", okay good, good now Happy you jump in, "As the pretty lady told you, you're Mr. Derfy Burger!", perfect Gerald, perfect and everyone quickly rush in and crowd around, hurry, hurry, okay that should do it, Mikey go splice that in, nobody will be the wiser.

"Where's Leigh?" I asked no one in particular.

"Gerald, what did this guy say his name was? We're losing lots of time here."

"I didn't get it boss, Allie something. Hey, what's your name again bro?" Happy asked me, very soothingly, nicely, unlike the boss, who I was about to impale with one of Chief Buff Burger's arrows.

"Eliason Nye," I told him. I was a little scared. He looked at me for some seconds then turned to his boss and shrugged.

"I think he hit his head," I heard him whisper.

"Look read this," jug ears said and thrust what appeared to be a non-bound phone directory for the city of New York at me, I could barely hold it with both hands, "and sign the last page at the bottom. Quickly now, that's good."

I propped the thing on one knee, turned about a million pages and signed it, having no idea that I could have just written off one of my testicles or first-born children to the Derfy Empire. Jug ears lifted up his glasses and squinted at the signature. "Okay, so it's e-l-l-i-s-o-n and then n-y-e?" he asked, cramming a pen between his teeth and balancing the tome on his forearm.

"Actually, it's one 'l' and an 'a,'" I corrected. "Tell him Happy."

Happy shrugged.

"Roger that," jug ears said, yanking the pen from his teeth and scratching something onto another sheet of paper. "So it's a-l-i-s-o-n and then n-y-e? Not that it's Derfy Burger's business, but isn't that a girl's name?"

"Yes, 'Alison' is a girl's name. My name is El*i*ason," and I spelled it slowly, letter by letter. He looked skeptical. He asked if I ever went by 'Eli' or 'Elijah' or 'Big E.' Absolutely not, and my mother would bottle him if I came out in the local paper named Eli Nye. He chuckled robotically under his breath, saying something about "local newspaper. Yeah right, kid. Social security number please." I looked at him suspiciously and he fanned his hand in front of his chest in a "C'mon, c'mon, let's hurry up" gesture. I turned to Hindoo who reassured me: "It's okay bro. Trust me," and jug ears took my information and handed it off to some other guy in a suit who went springing off through the crowd. "And tell Ralph at data base he's got half a minute, no, thirty seconds to come up with the info, pronto, skip the background check," he shouted after him. Then he faced me and turned into some sort of auctioneer, cramming about a trillion words into a ten-second span, saying something about me winning a million dollars and filming Derfy Burger commercials "all over the world, in every country, whether it be free, under communist rule or run by fascists, such as in South Africa." In a daze I signed away wherever he pointed his chewed-up pen. I wasn't really listening to a word he was saying.

"Leigh doesn't like me at all, does she?" I said to jug ears and a sympathetic Happy Hindoo. "She's just a gorgeous prop for the promotion of your newest Derfy Burger in Silverthorne." As was I, only I wasn't gorgeous. "Umm, exactly what day is this coming out in the local paper so I can get a couple of copies? Will it have my picture?"

I mean, Derfy's was really blowing this whole thing out of proportion. Our local newspaper The Herald Democrat did the same thing several years prior when it held a photo contest to celebrate its 125th birthday and promised a super sweet digital camera to the winner. After the contest, and I do stress *after*, they revoked their own rules and made the prize a 24-exposure disposable camera and free access to the newspaper's dark room for two weeks, the bastards. Not that I won first place or anything but let's just say in theory, only in theory, that a guy wins third place and he's promised a dinner for two with two free drinks at the local swanky steak joint and a guy has already invited a nice lady for said dinner, don't go changing the acknowledged prize and giving the guy a five dollar coupon to the local barber shop instead and telling the guy there were only three entries to the contest anyway, as an example. *[Get over it already, Willy. Move on.]*

"Mr Nye?" the jug-eared fellow addressed me. "We won't be putting a period in the 'Mr.' in Mr Derfy Burger. I hope you don't mind. Our accountants figured that leaving it out would save the company annually around eight hundred thousand dollars in ink, advertising space, etcetera." He looked at me hopefully. "Then again, it doesn't really matter because you don't really have any say-so in the matter," he chirped.

"I wasn't really listening before, I'm sorry. Is this just a promo for the Derfy's here or are you lying to me about going all over the world?"

He looked solemn. "Derfy Incorporated doesn't lie, most of the time. You truly are getting a million dollars, well, before taxes, and you will travel the Derfy globe. Look around you," he said, hunkering back down into the million page contract. I looked around me. Indeed. There was Peter Potato doing his pirouette thing with Private Pickle for a guy with a camera the size of a bazooka. Happy Hindoo had weaned himself away from me and was passing out free chicken drumettes to the basketball team, the kids at the birthday party were gathered around at least twenty television cameras, the little party-goers jabbering on without pause. There was a guy about ten feet away from me who appeared to be interviewing himself, but he showed up on a TV monitor as speaking to this cowboy guy with a dangling cigarette, a popular Derfy figure from the 1950s black and white days but who had been phased out about four decades ago. It was a pretty swell trick I thought. Suddenly I felt really alone and missed Julia like hell.

"You will be allowed one guest to travel with you throughout the Derfy globe," jug ears said, pulling his snivelly little snout from the contract agreement and squinting at me apprehensively. "Are you gay?"

"Not yet," I answered. He wrote down something feverishly, though he seemed relieved. I looked around, wondering just what the hell I was supposed to do or why they had picked me as Mr Derfy Burger. A million dollars? What was the catch? I was the man of the hour yet everyone seemed to be completely ignoring me. The whole restaurant, in about twenty seconds, had become absolutely stuffed with people: men with microphones and lots of product in their hair, FBI men in suits (turns out the one-hundred and fourth piece kid was whisked away by such an agent so as not to spoil Derfy's, and the world's, moment), women with big boobs and green mascara, some old people with walkers, a handful of professional athletes, the members of the biggest rock back in the US whom I couldn't stand because they were whiny 34-year-old bastards who sang about being in high school, and they wore knee pants. I mentally noted that in the most aggressive politically correct way there were representatives of just about every nationality: some dude with a fez and a really droopy mustache, some black guy who looked like a Zulu all dressed in tribal garb and carrying what appeared to be an impala-skin shield (he was cuddled up to the heat of the deep-fat fryer and looking miserable), a woman in a sombrero, a samurai, an Eskimo couple (they would rub noses for the cameras in a matter of minutes), an aborigine with matted hair, a Viking. I swear to god I saw the vice president of the United States of America. The whole world was there! After some more annoying, quick questions (shoe size, any visible tattoos/piercings/STDs, would I be interested in donating thirty percent of my winnings, tax-free, to the D.erfy E.vangelical R.evivalist F.und?), jug ears pulled me over to a podium where King Fred was smiling from his crown to his boots. King Fred was easily as strange as all of the other characters combined. He wore this fancy ketchup-red hat that I think was supposed to be a French fry container, narrow and curved on the bottom just above the area where his eyebrows should have been, and widening at the top. He kind of looked like a Catholic bishop. His head was shaved clean beneath his hat; in fact, he had no eyebrows or hair of any kind. Now that I thought about it, he was extremely creepy. He wore a shiny silver shirt with all kinds of fringe, a bright mustard-yellow cape, a fat red belt with a hamburger buckle, flared-out emerald-green pants and knee pads that looked like pickle slices (a holdover from the '80s when he was briefly a break dancer), a scepter shaped like a French fry and these pointy ruby-red high heeled boots that even kids who dressed like him for Halloween refused to wear. And shovelfuls of make-up. His face cracked when he smiled so that he looked like the old lady with the eighteen cats who lived down at the end of the cul d'sac and scared the heck out of you when she drove by, frowning at you from her Cadillac. King Fred was camp as hell, way more camp even than Private Pickle. ("He desperately needs a make-over," Willy told me last year in Buena Vista when we accidentally got stuck in the downtown Derfy Day parade on our way to the local hot springs. "What perchance do they do with all the cash with which they must surely endow their marketing men?! And Chief Buff Burger?! As if Happy Hindoo weren't bad enough! What's next, a gruff Russian general, an efficient Japanese office worker, a Middle Eastern arms smuggler? How insensitive! Why did they not just sally forth with their highly effective, tried and true campaign of using life-sized vegetables as human representatives?!" Of course, I had already dozed off at this point.)

"Well *there* you are," said a barrel-chested man with a shock of white hair and rabbit-like teeth, all forearms, squeezing me in a brief bear hug and wedging himself between the king and me. He looked like a very large rabbit, and also like our perpetually red-faced fire chief in

Leadville. "I'm Ray and we're going live on air in eight seconds. No cursing please, no cursing. Let me do most of the talking and we'll get through this just fine, just fine. Four seconds now, don't be nervous, no need to be nervous, no siree bob," and I immediately felt that I may spray brown paste in the back of my shorts.

"You mean live, for real live?" I hastened.

"Oh yes, all over the world. We're on," and he stuccoed on the most expert smile I had ever seen. Even I believed it and I was standing right next to the guy and knew he was a phony. "Hello world!" he bellowed, and on cue the entire restaurant cheered back, as if answering for an absent but captivated planet. "What a wonderfully Derfy day!" he proclaimed, and the restaurant exploded again. I had to admit, he had these playful, sparkly blue eyes that put me at ease. He started jawing to about fifty cameras about being in the ski resort town of Silverthorne, Colorado, and in one hand he was dangling a burger to the cameras as if to a starving dog. He put his other arm around me. "And by simply ordering this one little hamburger," and he held it chest-high, at which point a little fellow in a suit jumped up and clasped the sacred object, slid it into a plastic bag, sealed it professionally, and scampered off through the crowd, "Mr. Eliason Nye has entered the annals of history. Tell me son—no, tell the world and every nation on this planet right now how it feels to be Mr Derfy Burger."

With my famous poise and practiced grammar gymnastics, I said, "Uuhhhhhhhhhh."

"My goodness, cat's got his tongue in all this excitement," rabbit man said. "By being the billioneth-served customer in Derfy Burger's long and illustrious goal of bringing good food to good people, Mr. Eliason Nye of Leadville, Colorado has earned himself a ticket around the world, feasting on healthy Derfy Burger fare wherever he goes. I bet you feel pretty good about that."

I looked up at him with only a slight pause this time. "A man's got to eat," I puffed, slightly breathless from nerves, but I couldn't squeeze in the part about the dog having to bark.

"Spoken like a true Mr Derfy Burger," big rabbit said. "And what is your favorite item here at the world's favorite restaurant: the wholesome burgers, chicken drumettes, our world-famous hand-cut French fries?" he asked, cramming the microphone practically inside my mouth. I hesitated almost too long, thinking that no French fry had been hand-cut in this country since about 1952, unless it was by some little Vietnamese lady in the basement of a factory somewhere in Idaho.

"I think I like the Spicy Derfy Rack o'Ribs the most," I stuttered, and tacked on a smile because I knew the world would appreciate it.

"The Spicy Derfy Rack o'Ribs," Ray said triumphantly. "Wow. Mr. Nye obviously has fond memories from his childhood of a product that was discontinued at Derfy Burger thirteen years ago, but as our ribs really stuck to your ribs in the good old days, obviously the Rack o'Ribs sandwich has stuck in Mr. Nye's memory all of these years."

"Actually, I had one in Toronto three years ago," I piped in, and in case six billion people were not sure where Toronto was, or at least for our American viewers, I appended, "in Canada."

"Oh ho, a world traveler. Ladies and gentlemen, we have a world traveler," and the place erupted again. "Well, you'll be seeing lots of the world as Mr Derfy Burger I can assure you." I nodded at him innocently. "Tell us Mr. Nye, other than the obvious, which is that Derfy Burger is the most popular, most trusted way to delight yourself in the culinary arts, what brought you to Derfy Burger today?"

"A car," I said smartly.

Rabbit man looked surprised then lifted his microphone to the crowd, which exploded with hoots and cheers.

"We have a comedian," he said, poking me in my Derfy rack o'ribs, and everyone started clapping and hollering again (I didn't know what I had said that was so "funny" until about a year later when Julia replayed for me on video my first nudge of fame, but anyway...). "No, ya silly goose, how did you happen upon Derfy Burger today?" rabbit asked.

"Oh. Well, they're kind of hard to miss, aren't they, since there's one in just about every town. Except where I live."

"So," rabbit interrupted quickly before I said anything else funny, "you traveled thirty-five miles just to satisfy your culinary needs? That's wonderful. Real commitment." Microphone up, hoot hoot, holler, cheer. Mistakenly, he bobbed the microphone in front of my teeth again so I was forced to say something, anything.

"Actually it was my boss' idea. He loves Derfy Burger," I said slyly. "He's been to just about every one in South Africa. He's waiting in the car."

"Ahh, is he?" rabbit said, I thought, joylessly. "Taking a day off from making snowshoes are we? Well maybe you can scoot along and get him, to double the fun. Meanwhile we'll pass the mike over to King Fred," and he held the microphone up high again—hoot hoot wooh wooh clap holler—before enfolding it into King Fred's effeminate hand, the nails of which were painted lime green. King Fred started moving his jaws about "the magnificent brothers Gerbroni" and "great Derfy workers bringing great food to average folks" or something. Rabbit sighed and turned to me, putting a hand on my shoulder. On the back of his hand and around his wrist he had straggly white hair that looked to have been combed and groomed for the camera.

"Okay, you've got about a minute to collect yourself, relax, and then we'll go back live. But you have to start telling the world how much you love Derfy Burger."

"But I don't love Derfy's. In fact, I don't even *like* Derfy's," I told him. He quickly sh-sh-sh-shushed me, looking around furtively then patted me on the cheek and squeezed it gently like you see a mafia guy in the movies do to a guy he is about to make eat lead through his temple.

"You might want to start," he said, but nicely, like your favorite uncle. "For a million bucks, you should be able to love anything."

"You know, I was kind of wondering about that actually," I said above the noise, but low enough in case anyone was eavesdropping. "If someone is the billioneth-served customer at Derfy Burger, wouldn't it make more sense to give him a *billion* dollars, not a million?"

"Well, a billion's a bit much, don't you think?"

Jug ears came bounding over, hopping up and down like his shoes were on fire.

"Jesus Ray, you're killing me. We've only got a three-second delay on this kid. We haven't been able to splice anything in. We got zilcho good copy from that whole exchange. No 'I love Derfy's.' No 'I eat Derfy's five days a week.' No 'I wish King Fred would adopt me.' Nothing. You're killing me Ray. We brought you in all the way from Des Moines on reputation alone."

"Well it's not exactly stealing candy from a baby, is it?" Ray said, noticeably annoyed with jug ears. King Fred must have said something inspirational because the crowd behind us exploded with a cheer, then started doing the wave. I jumped about a foot. Rabbit patted me on the shoulder.

"It's okay Eliason. Try not to be so nervous. We still have a couple of minutes—problem with the feed from London. Why don't you run out and get Mr. Worster since he's such a big Derfy's fan and we'll get the two of you up here. Oops, just a second," and he fiddled with an earpiece, communicating to someone somewhere in England. "Clive, Clive, are you there?" he said, putting his hand to his ear like you see rock stars do in the recording studio when they're about to concentrate on belting out a note they have no business attempting to belt out. Ray waved a couple of fingers in the air and the high school band inside the restaurant began playing "God Save the Queen" (which their band leader had told them was "My Country 'tis of Thee").

"Quickly Eliason, quickly," Ray instructed so I hopped from the little podium, still feeling vaguely shunned despite being the man of the hour. Jug ears grabbed me by the forearm. Oh, him.

"Two words, Ray—results. Results," he shouted above the music.

"Not a problem, Mr. Gerbroni," rabbit said, clenching his teeth. Juggy began pulling me through the people. Some of them grabbed at me, jostling to see me—that made me feel a little better, that the madness was truly designed for me, that attention was on me. Now, before we carry on with Mr. Gerbroni ("Grandson on my father's side," he said tersely when I inquired. He really was very unlikeable), let us ponder a little bit about life and the Law of Common Convergence. I would never feel sorry for the dude who tried to climb Mt. Everest and died in a sudden storm somewhere between Base Camp Certain Death and Camp I Wish I Had Stayed Home On The Couch, and I definitely would not make him out as some hero who expired testing the extremes of the human body and nature. I sided with Ding Dong on this one and would tend to think he was really dumb for dying doing a fun-filled recreational activity instead of going out normally, naturally, like being shot in the parking lot of a supermarket, dying the way an American is meant to die, intentionally, often at the hands of one's fellow countryman, during the course of a normal day. I also had no time for these cry babies who spent their entire lives trying to become famous, appearing in diaper commercials, taking singing and dancing lessons, auditioning for every kiddie movie out there where the hero-kid (inevitably named "Max") befriends one of God's larger creatures and rides it, arms in the air. Then they become teen stars, then adult stars, and when they had become fat and full of drugs, all we hear is how they never asked for this kind of fame. Non-Man! Bastards. In other words, I had no time for the frantically famous then the regretful wordly-known. In a split second, I realized that I was probably going to be very famous, even if for a very short time, and I was going to love every single gosh darned minute of it. I deserved it more than anyone else. I was smart, I was funny and I had watched a lot of TV.

"I love you Mr Derfy Burger!" a teen red-headed slimbody with a faceful of braces shouted at me as jug ears and I made our way to the exit. I turned to her to check her out, give her a nod and a wink, maybe slip her a backstage pass for after the show, and my eardrums rattled with the pain of about a hundred young girls screeching in unison, in ecstasy.

"Keep walking, eyes forward, too young," Jug Ears Gerbroni instructed. A throng of security men had been posted on both sides of our path to keep back the surging crowd. A woman with helmet hair managed to push her way through and zonked me over the head with a microphone.

"Hey!" I cried out, and a man jammed a bazooka camera in my path.

"Gerbroni, it's Janine from CNN. We've got to interview Mr. Nye now."

"Very busy Janine, very busy, got to be back on in London in 045 seconds."

"Do I need to remind you that CNN is sponsoring the one to one o' five time slot and is guaranteed an interview? Mr. Nye, how does it feel to be Mr Derfy Burger?"

"Well—" I said but Juggy yanked me by the front of the shirt so hard I swallowed the words that were about to come out, which were going to be "Pretty sweet as soon as I get my million buckaroos."

"Read your contract a little closer Janine. If your bosses have any problem they can contact my brother Larry Jr. at legal affairs. They have his number."

"You promised this spot six months ago to me. You gave your word," the lady protested, furious.

"Situations change Janine, you know that. News moves. Come along Mr Derfy Burger," and he scrunched my shirt into a wad even tighter, pulling the few chest hairs that I owned, and that I had so proudly nourished into existence *[Shut up Willy]* right out with one tug. I howled in pain. Juggy ignored me, looking wearily at the thousands of microphones poking over security men's shoulders, under their armpits, some through their legs, cameras whirring and flashes going off like lightning.

"Stop," I demanded, "you're pulling out all of my manhood," and I slapped his hand away from my chest, which finalized the ripping of all my hair from its firmament, my chest. He looked at me in shock. "And while I have your attention, just how did Ray know my name and where I live and where I work and what my boss' name is and whatever else?"

He looked at me, shaking his head with an incredulous laugh. "The internet, Nye. We don't have time for this," and he began to tug at me again but I remained rooted. He looked weary.

"Name, social security number, hometown, whatever. It's powerful, Nye. We already know just about everything about you, as we could anyone in this room if they had been the one to step up to the counter at the right time. Now let's move along." This time he didn't grab me so I followed as obediently as a dog. Just as we reached the door I heard the sexiest Voice ever endowed to Womankind by a benevolent Being smarter than us.

"Hehlo Mr Darfee Burger."

Even Juggy stopped and got all wiggly in the knees.

"It's Zica Dunga," he breathed aloud, and he pulled her way ever so slightly, as if magnetized.

"It's Zica Dunga," I whispered, the blood rushing from my brain to certain nether regions involuntarily, as if every corpuscle had a testicular life of its own. I saw Juggy nod almost imperceptibly. Zica Dunga was a Brazilian supermodel, reckoned the most beautiful woman in seven generations, with skin of cocoa, smooth as a placid lake, legs from here to somewhere else, the roundest, most feminine bottom, eyes that could turn a man to quick-drying cement, the Nefertiti of the 20th century. She had her bright-yellow and green shirt cinched up and tied around the middle, her saucer-like, heavenly hips spilling out of both sides of white hip-hugging jeans, her breasts defying scientifically-proven laws of gravity, her belly button like the unforgiving eye of Cyclops. Just two nights before I had been flipping through a magazine and saw her in a perfume ad and thought, in my small and fantastic little universe, if only I could, just once, if by some odd juxtaposition of the stars, simply meet her in real life, I would...do exactly as I did in real life: said "Uhhhhhhhh."

"I hhawp to see zhu in Brasil soon," she purred and instantly, any material want I had ever desired, any wish for bodily sustenance through food or water or shelter, the necessity of oxygen, the absurdity of religion or philosophy, the instinct to survive into elderliness, simply vanished as her hand came into contact with my butt. I practically fell through the door outside to the pavement, where Juggy and I found ourselves, shot out of the crowd like a cork from a shaken bottle. He turned to me and smiled for the first, and only, time. It was snowing like mad, and windy, and quiet.

"That was Zica Dunga," I said. He nodded breathlessly. "There's the car," I told him. I knew I was glowing after being touched by the hand of the Goddess, the snow melting in my aura before it even came near me.

"You've got about thirty seconds to find your boss and get him in here," he said, arms akimbo in limbo between the safety of Derfy

Burger and Ding Dong's car, to which I slinked over, stealing a glance or two backwards at Juggy. I propped open the passenger door. I poked my head in and surveyed my three no-name compadres.

"Did they run out of hamburgers?" Willy asked, crestfallen.

"What in the name of all that is sacred is going on in there?" Ding Dong asked in what sounded like panic. Just at that point, three jets cut through the sky, trailing some sort of red, white and blue dust. Two more jets followed, wing tip to tip, leaking yellow and red smoke, the mustard and ketchup bleeding into Old Glory.

"I'm not sure what's going on," I spewed excitedly, saliva parachuting from my mouth. "I went to the counter and ordered Willy's burgers and the place went nuts. They said I'm the billioneth-served customer and that I'm Mr Derfy Burger and that I get a million dollars and this guy who looks like the fire chief interviewed me and we're supposed to talk to some guy in London in like, thirty seconds but they wanted me to grab you guys." I stopped to catch my breath. "And that crazy hot model I was telling you about yesterday Willy, the one from Brazil, Zica Dunga? She pinched my butt!" I could actually feel electricity within me, I could feel it pulsing from my skin.

"Right mate, I think you need to slow down and start making sense," Ding Dong said. I noticed for the first time that he was sporting this weird fake beard that hung down way past his Adam's apple. It kind of suited him, though it looked like some sort of faux spider web stuff your grandma puts in the front hallway and outside in the bushes for Halloween.

"What's with the beard?" I asked him.

"Halloween costume. Now, what is going on?"

"I'm the billioneth-served customer," I said, my excitement returning. "You should see it. King Fred's in there. All kinds of famous people are in there. It's nutty. I think I have to eat burgers all over the world as a kind of spokesman and they're going to give me a million dollars." Then my excitement reached fever pitch: "Zica Dunga pinched my butt!!"

"Man, she's hot," Little Ding said.

"Shouldn't they give you a *billion* dollars?" Willy asked.

"Well, a billion's a bit much, don't you think?" I told him sternly.
"That's superb," Ding Dong said rather stiffly. "A million dollars."

At that moment, three army tanks came rumbling through the wide-open empty parking lot of the strip mall stripped of all cars, people and businesses after the SupaDerfMart moved in right up the street and put everything else out of business. The tanks had Derfy Burger flags hanging from their turrets, and three of many King Fred stand-ins, waving gaily at no one, were spread Playboy-style atop each tank.

"That's right," I said, though the din of the approaching tanks was becoming slightly deafening. "And they want you guys to be on TV with me. Isn't that cool?" I glanced over at Juggy Gerbroni, who was pointing manically at this watch, snow collecting on his head and his crossed arms.

"Hell yeah," Little Ding said, jumping in his seat and flashing me some kind of gangster signs in approval. He was wearing a huge pair of shades though there was no sun and a bandana across his mouth plus a huge LA Lakers baseball cap. Crazy costume.

"Come again," Ding Dong said, cupping his ear and looking annoyed in the rear view mirror at the approaching tanks.

"I said you guys all get to be on TV with me," I yelled, just as the tanks rolled into the Derfy Burger section of the parking lot. Ding Dong motioned for me to sit in the passenger seat so I swung myself inside and sealed the door.

"Thank goodness," I sighed, as the noise outside decreased slightly. "We don't have a lot of time. See the guy with the big ears?" I nodded in his direction. He was looking more menacing, his body shaking out of anger or the shock of the cold, blustery air. "He wants us to go inside and do some interviews. Then I guess they'll give me my million dollars and then I can leave. I'm not sure."

I watched the top of Ding Dong's hand, the color of butcher's paper spattered with grease stains, shoot across my chest and punch the door lock down. With the same speedy hand, as if in slow-motion, he popped the car into reverse, his head swiveling backwards, and with remarkable skill and speed, he flossed the Monte Carlo between two tanks, fish-tailed forward and into drive, then zoomed away through the parking lot.

"You just kidnapped Mr Derfy Burger!" Willy squealed, and the car raced through the parking lot, bumped out onto the street and through a stoplight, cut off a couple of unsuspecting cars, then bounced onto the entrance ramp and back onto the highway.

CHAPTER FIFTEEN

"Willy von Morgansteen,
Just Ten Feet Between,
1:36 p.m."

I knew I must have been paler than the palest pale-face Willy had ever had nightmares about in his Indian teepee dreams. I couldn't even speak, my mouth was so dry.

"Dad, what are you doing?!" TJ asked in a panic through the bandana over his mouth, his voice about eight octaves higher than a nine-year-old castrato at a winter retreat. "They're going to catch us for sure now. They're going to know we did it."

"I'm saving this young man's life, son. Now just be quiet a minute and let your dad think."

"Think about what? About going back to jail?" He ripped off his silly bandana and put a hand up to his forehead, throwing his head back and rolling it from side to side against the back of the seat. "I knew we shouldn't have picked them up, Dad. I knew it. Just pull over now and kick them out of the car and we'll keep driving."

"Jail!" I thought to myself, in some panic.

Ding looked at his son thoughtfully in the rearview mirror. "It's rather cold outside, TJ, and it's snowing like mad," he said somewhat rationally.

"Dad, there's about a thousand cars going by—someone will pick them up. This guy just won a billion dollars. *Someone* will pick him up."

"A million," Ding Dong corrected him, maddeningly calm.

"A million, a billion, who cares?" TJ said, his panic increasing. "We've got to drop these honkey fools off. No one is going to be afraid to pick them up, look at them. Come on Dad. Listen to me." The car started pulling back as the elevation suddenly increased.

"I'm listening," Ding Dong said, a touch annoyed, twisting his head slightly to try to look to the back seat. He was silent, thinking to himself, pulling on that dang mustache with his tongue and teeth and turning the hoop earring in his ear. Somehow I found my own voice, though it was only about half an octave lower than TJ's.

"Mr. Bell, maybe you should let us go. I can send you some of the money somehow, if that's what it's about." I still heard the word "jail" reverberating in my head.

"Oh I don't care about the money—I'm saving you," he said, and the way he said it, even though he didn't look at me, it just sounded like he meant it, almost, like he wasn't quite a preacher saving my soul, but a real guy instead, a guy who actually cared.

"Why don't you save him by letting him go back and get his dough," TJ insisted. I thought it was a fabulous idea. Little Ding made some kind of distress noise but his father ignored him as he rubbed his hands on top of his knees. I thought he might start a fire on his kneecaps. Ding said we would turn around "very soon."

"We're on the highway now," TJ persisted in a very slightly lessened panic. "You can't turn around on the highway unless you use the emergency turn-around, and that's against the law. Oh man."

Ding Dong just kept those bloodshot eyes aimed forward and drove.

"Zinca Dunga pinched his butt, Dad," he said, tapping his father on the shoulder.

"That's been established," Ding said, "as if that was the most important event today."

I wasn't sure if I believed that we would turn around. The two of them could still be mass murderers, but it was going to be astronomically harder to make Mr Derfy Burger disappear than the former Eliason Nye, though No Name Willy hadn't a chance.

"Right now I think everyone needs to remain silent."

And we did—we all sat quietly while the car tried to catch its breath after each successive upward foot. Teddy took his cap off and rubbed his short hair back and forth, then angled his fingers so his nails raked the little rows of tight curly hair. I stared out the front window and wished that I was just about anywhere else in the world, except going through Turkish customs with bricks of marijuana strapped to my waist. Willy was way too quiet in the back seat, though I was afraid to turn around, to even look at him; I began to wonder if he had accidentally leaned on his door a little too hard and had fallen out five minutes ago without anyone noticing.

"Ding Dong, are you a complete psychopath all the time or just on Saturdays?" I asked. Not really, but I wanted to, I was about to, when he said, "Hey Eliason, could you do us a favor and try to find NPR again?"

Now some people call it being obsequious, some call it kissin' ass, whilst others call it the Stockport *{Stockholm—ed.}* Syndrome, where a captive begins to feel he owes his life to his captor, but if Ding had asked me to put my hand in a flaming hammerhead shark's mouth to find NPR, I would have, I jerked that hand out so fast. His radio must have been one of the first ever built for a car, maybe one of the first built ever: it had no digital read-out, only a crummy kind of panel that glowed a sort of dull brown-orange, the silhouette of a dead fly, trapped as if in amber for hundreds of years, was splay-legged in front of the numbers to the far right, and when I delicately twisted one of the two knobs on either side of the panel a little paper clip-looking piece of metal quivered, almost hesitantly, from right to left. Nothing but static. Just below the panel were six or seven square buttons that stuck out like they were being ejected from a Pez dispenser. I forgot myself for several seconds and started mashing them, watching the little paper clip jerk back and forth like a gazelle trying to elude a leopard.

"Gently mate, gently," I heard Ding Dong say soothingly through my fog. "Try to the left of the dial, that's where the good things always are."

"Oh yeah," I said, coaxing the paper clip toward Ding's side of the radio, then like a professional safecracker in a movie, I leaned in close, training my ear, buffing the tips of my nails on my chest, softly turning the dial with the tips, just the tips, of all five fingers including pinky, because that's how guys in the movies always did it. Slowly, nope. Ah there's, nope. Hup, some strains of what sounded like Hank Williams actually being broadcast from 1952 but just now making it to the Monte Carlo's speakers, but then gone. Hey, there's some...static. Static, then a high pitched whine and then what sounded like extraterrestrial voices from another universe began to filter into the car. Ding leaned close to the radio.

"It sounds like," and he peered at the panel. "Mate, you have it on AM. You'll not find anything but right-wing nutters there." He pushed a button and the clean, fresh taste of FM, also known to Pudenda and you land lubbers out there as frequency modulation, filled the car. "Go on then," he directed and I began safecracking the dial again, a slight sweat greasing up my palms. "...ing to 'Nothing Considered.' I'm Terri Dolan—"

"That's it!" Ding shouted as if he had won the lottery. The radio continued, a male's voice now, "—and I'm Phillip Pinder. Fighting continued in the Middle East...." Then I faded off into my frequent ether, the comfort zone, but I found that I could not release myself completely. I was still pretty excited (even if I was in the process of getting kidnapped) about being on tv and having all those girls yell at me and standing next to King Fred and of course, there had been Zica Dunga. I had a desperately weighty feeling somewhere just behind my belly button, like the anticipation a guy gets before doing the lambada sin garderoba with his girl, a slight nausea I remember having at kindergarten show 'n tell when I was supposed to bring something interesting but forgot and instead just brought myself. It was that split-second flutey feeling when you see someone famous on the street, maybe even talk to him or her, and then you want to tell all your relatives about it, as if some fairy dust from the superstar may have wiped off on you and made you a better and perhaps more exciting person. I wondered if Ding Dong and Little Ding and Snowshoe had the same feeling sitting next to me, not that I was anything special, but I was suddenly special in an unwarranted way, which is almost as special today as being special for something deserved, like saving a dog from a mine shaft or something. I knew I would have felt pretty cool if Snowshoe had gone in for his own damn hamburgers and had become Mr Derfy Burger instead, and I was just the jerk sitting in front of him in a Monte Carlo getting kidnapped. Ding Dong sighed next to me, absently stroking his fake beard, probably thinking about how he could have been a millionaire if he hadn't gone to the bathroom instead. I was really starting to hope that he would turn the car around because a million bucks can go a long way for a guy like me. For instance, I always wanted to take Julia to Aruba, even if I could not find it on a large-sized map *[Shut the hell up Willy]*. I began to doze and vaguely, just vaguely, I wondered what exactly Teddy and TJ were doing anyway, where they were going, what—

"Bloody hell!!" Ding Dong exploded, his hand darting to the volume knob on the radio, his eyes as large and round as timpani drums. He nudged me on the shoulder and my cloud instantly dissipated. From the speakers I heard fireworks popping, what sounded like a high school band and then the sound of tanks murdering concrete under their chain wheels, all edited in that seamless way that NPR does, so that it sounded like a high school pep rally was taking place on the war-soaked streets of some tiny Balkan country.

A man's voice began: "Today is being billed by the world's largest corporation, Derfy's, as a global celebration of its billioneth-served Derfy Burger customer. Here we are in Colorado, an hour west of the state capitol Denver, in a mountain hamlet plagued by the biggest business conglomerates the U.S. has to offer and strip malls that appear to have slipped into town overnight and settled at the base of the mountain like a neon avalanche. Typically the big news on a normal day here in Silverthorne revolves around how much snow fell the night before and whether employees in the service industry, typically ski bums and snowboarding miscreants, will even bother punching the clock that day."

There was a buzz of a roomful of voices and clanging dishes, like the reporter had magically stepped into the kitchen of some cruddy brewpub and was going to interview the first moron he could find. Indeed he did.

"Yeah man, it's like cool and all that you, like, I don't know, have to work for The Man but I don't know. Like, when the snow gods smile down on you and offer you many inches of powder on those majestic, beautiful mountains…" and the dude gave the Official Moron Laugh of Colorado (OMLC) that designates that he's a stoner, tripped-out and working not for The Man but for a ski pass, "…like, you better ride it because who knows, man, I mean you may, like, I don't know, like, die tomorrow." More clanging of silverware and dishes and the drone of dining room conversation. "Dude, I doubt if anyone even, like, notices if I'm here anyway. It's like, if they do notice then I'm real surprised [OMLC inserted] and if they care, I must be doing something wrong," and it was a voice that could have belonged to any of the thousands of hippies, wastoids, boarders, skiers and general OMLCers that crawl on the mountains.

The NPR talking head resumed: "One man who may never have to work again in his life, or spend another penny on a meal for that matter, is a twenty-four-year-old gentleman from nearby Leadville, Colorado, who was earlier crowned Mr Derfy Burger. The Virginia native and snowshoe factory employee, a Mr. Eliason Nye, now resides in a town that rose and fell on the whims of the silver industry one hundred years ago…."

"My sweet Lord," Ding Dong breathed, staring at me with unhinged jaw. But as if looking at my aura hurt his eyes, he glanced back at the radio, then out the windshield, then at the radio, then out the window in a sort of perpetual motion. TJ's phone rang but he hit a button to silence it then edged to the front seat. Willy, also mouth agape, was blowing like a hair dryer on the back of my neck but uncustomarily was without words.

"…stakes its claim as the highest incorporated town in the United States. Here of course you'll find the highest high school, highest laundromat, highest hospital and the local judge, who claims to be of the highest court in the land. But you get the feeling that the town's soon-to-be globally recognized Mr. Nye will be the biggest thing to emerge from the cozy mountain hideaway in a hundred years. Interestingly enough, Leadville, in the record book with only a handful of other towns on the planet, has no Derfy Burger of its own."

"Welcome to Derfy Burger. I'm glad you picked us today," said a voice out of the car speakers, the voice formerly owned by Leigh but now being translated into billions of bits across the globe and out into space. "May I take your order?"

"Three hamburgers, please" said another voice that I believe had once belonged to me. Little Ding let loose with a sort of surprised schoolgirl shriek. Snowshoe let out some weird sound like he had been stabbed with a knitting needle. Ding Dong said nothing, he just kept staring at me with those timpani drums, then peering at the radio, then out the windshield, then back at me, in the same order, non-stop. It was easily the most surreal moment of my life, hearing myself not half an hour before being force-fed back to me. It was hard to grasp that the words had belonged to me, had been formed and emitted by my brain and then my mouth, had conceivably been my own in an amorous, amorphous packet of time, but had somehow been captured and spread like crop dust, insecticide, poison throughout the land.

"And with those three words that every man loves to say, Mr. Eliason Nye became, instead, Mr Derfy Burger. Fortunately, Derfy admiration runs rich in his veins."

My stupid voice came blasting through the speakers again.

"Wow. I have always been a fan of the Gerbroni brothers," I heard myself say.

"Hey! I didn't say that," I protested. Ding Dong shushed me.

"I dressed as Private Pickle for Halloween last year," my voice said again. The car practically shimmied sideways with the force of laughter that was released by my nobody compadres. I think TJ called me a "homo."

"Hey! I'm lying! I didn't say that either. I said Willy did that!"

"Heh-heh-heh," said Ding Dong.

"Oh little chieftain," said Snowshoe.

198

"Pickle man," said Little Dinger. The man on the radio persisted despite my pain.

"Most people are familiar with the names Fred and Larry Gerbroni, the intrepid brotherly duo who bought a small burger stand in California and stream-lined it into the global empire that we know today. In the span of five decades, the Gerbronis made their dream of fast, cheap food the most recognized brand in marketing history," the NPR guy said. "We have yet to see if their largest campaign will make history and whether Mr Derfy Burger will join those historical ranks. But either way, things will never be the same for the previously unknown man from Leadville."

"I didn't say any of that stuff, I swear," I protested.

"What, they just got a guy who sounds a lot like you to say it?" Little Ding asked, playing bongos on both of his cheeks, like he was trying to awaken himself from what could only have been the most hilarious dream he ever had.

"Well I said it, but not in that way," I tried to explain as Ding Dong navigated us through the snow that was quickly becoming blinding. "I said *Willy* dressed as Private Pickle, not me. I swear." Before I could defend my manhood any more, Terri Dolan took control of the airwaves.

"That was Bobby Dewhurst in Silverthorne, Colorado. Thank you Bobby," she said to a recording of the real-life Bobby, who was probably already jetting off somewhere to ruin someone else's life. Some sort of muted trumpet/sitar arrangement played NPR's eight note musical theme, which blended into the sound of a cash register and the bass line from that Deep Purple *{Pink Floyd—ed.}* tune about money being a drag and keep your hands off my bag. After a little bit of that nonsense you could hear Terri panting like a hyena waiting to set herself upon my kangaroo carcass, I just knew it.

"Hello, I'm Terri Dolan and you're listening to NPR," then that annoying eight note theme again. "In observance of Derfy Burger's big celebration, its crowning of its very own Mr Derfy Burger, we've invited on to the show a very special guest: the leading expert on consumer culture and the marketing techniques of mass hysteria,

William vonMorgansteen of Spawnee State University, coming live all the way from upstate New York. Are you with us Mr. vonMorgansteen?"

A long pause then an "I'm here" came out of the radio, a low voice scratchy and intermittent, like it was being broadcast from Pluto, reassembled on the moon and shipped down to earth in the back of a 1976 Chrysler.

"Having a Ph.D in consumerism, Mr. vonMorgansteen..." Terri began.

"Please call me Willy," he requested.

"Hey Snowshoe, it's your twin brother," Little Ding laughed, sticking just the tip of his tongue out of his mouth. Willy nodded but was listening too intently to say anything.

"Thank you," Terri resumed, then paused a full three seconds for effect. "Gosh, let's just jump right into things. What do you think of this Mr Derfy Burger campaign?" she asked, all coy and even-toned.

"They're going to murder me!" I cried. I had listened to NPR enough to know where open-ended questions like that led. She may as well have drawn and quartered me.

"I think it's absolutely appalling," came the obvious answer.

"Of course he does," Ding Dong replied, smiling. VonMorgansteen had that nasally, smarter-than-you kind of voice that probably got him beat up every day in school. But he was on the radio now, something special. I waited for him to torpedo me. And he did.

"The first button Derfy's is hitting is that of connection. Let's be frank, Terri. The last thing Derfy Burger needs is to feel that it can add to its legacy of being the world's favorite restaurant by plucking one simpleton out of how many millions to represent their every-man appeal, but that's what they've done. It's very catchy today to portray your business in a non-thinking, non-discerning, non-threatening way because that is how your average consumer responds to his environment. The idea behind it is to broaden your base and try to reach as many customers as possible, of course."

Terri said, "We all know 'You are entitled to a derfy day' has been Derfy Burger's traditional slogan for years. Out of vogue today?" she asked.

"We all are entitled to a derfy day today, Terri," and they chuckled good-naturedly and probably had attended the same damn ivy league college, full rides with books and meals on smarmy scholarships, bastards. "It's apropos that you bring that up first. It's interesting, in our aggressive culture today, that Derfy Burger is 'Gonna make you eat,' which they stated in a press release this morning has replaced their 'You are entitled to a derfy day' campaign, starting today."

"I didn't know that," Terri said, all full of baloney I'm sure because Terri worked at NPR and knew everything.

Willy vonM continued: "It's the truth. They announced it as a precursor I suppose to their bigger media event this afternoon, which until now has been cloaked in greatest secrecy. So what we have is Derfy Burger going from the passive aggressor offering you the chance to have a derfy day and now they have transmutated into the fine eatery that will do anything in its power to make you eat, to bring a touch of joy into your otherwise joyless day. They are going to 'make you eat' instead of just giving you the opportunity to have a derfy day, whether you take them up on it or not."

"What's this guy talking about?" I sniffed defensively, waiting for them to start grilling Eliason Nye. No one answered, Ding Dong merely shifted a little in his seat and pulled on that dang mustache of his with his teeth.

"But it really comes down to the mantra of today, does it not Willy: choices, choices and more choices?" Terri said.

"Well, of course, but you have to ask yourself, What kind of choices are they really giving me? I can have a heart-taunting slab of beef burger, a fat-laden piece of chicken, a fish sandwich composed of some sort of sea dweller that likely took its last tug of salt water sometime around the year 1972. Or I can load up on French fries, which pack a bigger wallop of sodium and fat than even their deep-fried sandwich monstrosities."

"So our choices have actually become more limited with the proliferation of these businesses giving us what we supposedly want?" Terri asked (and sort of said at the same time.)

"Indubitably," Ding Dong said aloud, nodding.

"Undoubtedly, Terri. In the past, a very distant past admittedly, you may have strolled downtown to your favorite restaurant or were dragged during family vacations as a child to some roadside diner, and even if it served the same kind of standard fare as everyone else, the atmosphere was different, the ingredients just a shade more varied, the recipes more regional. Whereas today we have fewer truly dynamic choices of where to eat because one, we don't have as many mom and pop restaurants anymore because they were driven out of business, not necessarily wholly and intentionally by Derfy Burger and all the other fast food joints but by, well, this is my second point—independent, small businesses have been killed by our inability to make a decision. Or our desire to not want to make a decision, perhaps. Ordering a Gerbroni burger, Supa Big, is a no-brainer because it takes no thought and adds nothing to our dining experience. It does however satisfy our need for a fatty, salty, sweet diet, the triumphant triumvirate of the twenty-first century marketer."

"And that bleeds over into all facets of our lives?" Terri guessed.

"Oh absolutely," answered vonMorgansteen. "It peppers our conditional responses to what we wear, what we drive, where we live, even with whom we choose to mate."

"Howso?" Terri asked in that ribbony, nonchalant tone of hers. Ding Dong responded by notching up the volume.

"Well, we're shopping in our name-brand jeans and eighty dollar t-shirts, cruising around in our SUVs, staying at chain hotels as we make our way across the country to be the next non-traditional family to settle in some of the U.S.'s current boom states: Texas, Arizona, Colorado, Utah, even Florida and South Carolina to some extent. We stop at DerfMart to pick up the same useless thing that our neighbor is buying, and we'll discard it just as quickly because there is not much craftsmanship, no care, no originality, made in China, no speck of difference about the product that we can latch onto and call our own, to covet almost, as bad and unbiblical as that sounds. There is no umbilical attached to us and it. Mass culture, especially ours, breeds familiarity and with that, mediocrity. I find it enthralling."

That was quite a mouthful, even for Terri .

"The marketing techniques of mass hysteria is another of your specialties," she said.

"I guess you could say that," he said with a chuckle ending abruptly, like he had raised a paper cup of water to his lips and drank sweetly. I was kind of beginning to like this cat. His voice was mellifluous and even-toned and damned soothing, like the world's greatest dad would speak. Hell, maybe he was drinking green herbal tea from a mug that said "World's Greatest Dad" on it. I could picture him in upstate New York, the sun dropping behind the bare trees in the west, a warm fire not far from his elbow, maybe his shirt sleeves scrunched halfway up his arms, his stockinged feet (which he unconsciously rubbed together for extra warmth, a habit he carried over from lying in bed, being a late Saturday morning riser) up on a cushioned wicker foot rest. The first dying autumn leaves gently peeked into his study window before twirling to the grass, a gray storm pushing in from the north was fat with snow. And there was Willy vM, being funny, being serious, being interesting to white and black folk alike in a clunky old car going up some mountain three thousand miles away. His wife was off somewhere having just picked up their twin girls from a private boarding school where all the rich kids always seem very interesting to the rest of us poor folk, particularly on film. Mother and daughters would be out shopping for vegetables for stew later that night. I was damn jealous. No doubt W.v.M. would have a little bit of neck hair that grew in just two days after getting a haircut, he'd fill out his shirt in the paunch department but was tacitly proud of it as a sign of age, without question he would be Jewish because he could actually string two cohesive thoughts together, and he would be the guy you always wanted to sit next to at dinner and then hang out with in the kitchen afterwards, either chatting about nothing, like family matters, or covering the big stuff, like the marketing techniques of mass hysteria.

"What about this Nye fellow in Colorado?" Terri asked. Oh boy. "Could he possibly know what he's in for?"

"Can we change the station now?" I whined. Ding Dong gently shushed me again.

"I would have to say a very emphatic 'no.' Unless this guy has some sort of degree in business communications, I'd say he's in for quite a ride, no matter how many hours of pop culture he's been subjected to in his lifetime. But even a degree or a working knowledge of the vast and tangled web of consumerism would not automatically grant him immunity from the incipient, jaw-clenchingly idiotic nature of the business, of selling and consuming."

"My notes say he works in a snowshoe factory," Terri said, without the benefit of the sound of shuffling papers to prove that she was actually looking at notes and not just making up off the top of her head the most absurd profession that she could think of for the delight of her audience.

"That's kind of quaint isn't it, so Colorado," he said with a bemused chuckle.

"All logic would say that this guy doesn't bring in a lot of money," Terri said, at which Mr. Mass Culture agreed, correctly, despite Snowshoe Willy's best efforts to provide me with all of my material wants. "And that he's probably not running around in eighty dollar t-shirts," at which he again, uncannily, guessed right. "A dream then, in Derfy Burger's quest to find an everyday person with whom your average American, particularly teenagers, can relate?" Terri asked.

"Truthfully, that's a tough one, and Derfy Burger must know that they are skating on thin ice here. This guy, if he's too poor or backwards, may tip the scales the other way and have no appeal to the teen audience, which we all know is the promised land for marketers. Fast food chains have already sucked in the infants with the cheap toys offered with every meal, and by snatching the youngsters they get the parents in tandem. Teens are the big market right now; their population has gotten Supa Big, so to speak, in one generation. But they still have to relate. They want a superstar but also an unknown entity to take to their hearts. Girls desire a male role model unto whom they can lavish and therefore unburden and hide their insecurities. Teenage boys, in typical fashion, don't go so deep—they're pretty dumb. They are just looking for someone to copy. But Derfy Burger is risking finding a real pinhead in that great haystack we call the United States of America."

I glanced over at Ding, about to ask for a translation, but he just put his finger to his lips and motioned to keep listening.

"I think we'll see with this Nye fellow your classic high school film plot: new kid in town taken for ugly duckling because he's unknown and maybe a little different; ugly duckling discovered by aloof, cool kid with an actual heart of gold—that's Derfy Burger; ugly duckling turns into swan with help of cool kid, maybe even outshines cool kid; swan suddenly lavished with unwarranted praise, fame, adulation; swan spurned by cool kid for various reasons, usually jealousy; swan drowns self after realizing that the life of ugly duckling was more pure, that he has lost his true identity but cannot go back to his old life," Willy prophesied.

Little Ding tapped me on the shoulder. "You better stay away from water."

Terri inquired, "But doesn't it seem particularly, what's the word I'm looking for, self-defeating, for Derfy Burger not to grab a movie star or sports hero, even a supermodel, to hawk its merchandise?"

"I will come back to the point, Terri, but let me first point out that it's interesting that you call Derfy's product 'merchandise.' With so many of our mass quantity food institutions, you sometimes forget that you are consuming an organic product and not something synthetic. No one buys a Detroit Drag Chicken Strip Sandwich to put up on the mantelpiece of course, but Derfy Burger has cleverly gotten us to buy their little trinkets and action figures in Daffy Derfy meals for only pennies more, but those pennies add up. Of course we'll toss out the merchandise, the little toys and what have you, but just having them lying around on the kitchen floor or in the bath tub or in the back seat of the car gives them a sort of replaceable omnipresence, a fleeting permanence, if you can forgive the poetic illogic, even in our hustle and hurried world."

"You're forgiven, Mr. vonMorgansteen," Terri cooed.

"Thanks Terri. Of course the production of the merchandise, the exporting of jobs overseas to third world countries, the man hours, the consumption of materials and resources both renewable and non-renewable is the hard influence of the Derfy network and brings in major bucks. But the soft influence—the toys, the Derfy character action figures, the image—that's where the big bang is, the big money, which ties neatly into D.W.D.P., Derfy World Dominance Productions—"

"The largest distributor of children's movies, cartoons and music, which also has several Derfy theme parks across the U.S., Asia and Africa as well," Terri interrupted, as if we didn't already know what D.W.D.P. was.

"Naturally," Willy resumed. "DWD Productions is a purchasing and possessing juggernaut itself. It practically sustains the toy industry and therefore the GNP in Taiwan and Micronesia, but don't get me started on that."

"Yes, I think we won't go there," Terri said breezily, not wanting to ruin her guest's day. "But back to my previous question of hiring someone famous: in the past, what seemed to work best was pitting one music star against another, say for the first and second most-popular sodas. Not such a grand idea anymore?"

"Good, this is the second point I wanted to make earlier. I'm glad you reminded me. Not only have recent studies found that our teens are dropping behind significantly in math, reading and science to countries as varied as Finland, the Democratic Republic of the Congo and Laos but our kids are shamefully lacking in the pop culture knowledge that is so necessary to get by in the world today. A recent study out of Oklahoma was a real eye-opener, at least for me. I'll bring up just two examples that really stuck with me, if I may. In the eleven to eighteen-year-old age bracket, fully ninety-four percent of American kids could not name a single member of the Beatles. Incredible. Worse yet, sixty-seven percent of them, even when given four choices including the correct one, chose Elvis Presley as a brand name of indoor carpeting. They thought Little Richard was a sex toy. I won't even tell you who, or what actually, they thought Liberace was. What's going on here?"

"That *is* shocking, mmm," Terri said.

"Terri, even though my brothers and I couldn't stand when our father would put on his doo-wop radio station in the car, we still knew all of the artists, we knew the songs, we even knew some of the members' names from decades before. It rounded us out, gave us cultural appreciation. The Fabulous Florals weren't our favorites but could we ever forget them or their couple of songs?"

Almost beyond believing, Terri started doing some sort of doo-woop thing, then sang, "Hey Freddy Freddy, maybe you live above a fish store, but this girl Patsy loves your pompadour." Her voice was kind of sexy actually.

"Doo-wahhhh," Willy vonM. warbled. "You know it Terri ."

"Oh gosh," she said, giggling as her singing partner softly laughed along with her.

"What the hell are these fools talking about?!" Little Ding erupted from the back seat. "Man, change the station."

I looked over at Teddy, who seemed to be a little misty-eyed. There was an embarrassed pause on the station. Radio Willy sounded regretful to end the reverie.

"To pick the thread back up, you can pitch pop stars to the kids, but the star can't have been off the Top 40 charts or absent from a blockbuster movie for over two to three weeks as kids today have really powerful pop amnesia."

"Is that so?" Terri said creamily. She was getting sexier every second, I swear. Radio Willy was trying to get his professionalism back and play it straight.

"Well, I think this is where I depart from the rest of the country because I can't fathom drinking a particular brand of soda just because some chesty, blonde pop singer is bouncing around in her concert with a big cardboard representation of it behind her. That, I don't fully comprehend. But my daughters are soda number one loyalists because of its flavor-of-the-month pop idol endorser, what's her name, Spicey Vinda Lou?"

I kind of liked Spicey Vinda Lou despite my own self—she was pretty sexy for a sixth grader and had a great voice, ten or twelve octave range at least.

Terri mock gasped. "Your own daughters have fallen into the media tiger pit? For shame," she said with the proper gravitas that all of her listeners loved her for.

"You know, the barber's son always needs a haircut, the doctor's niece is always sick," Mr. vonMorgansteen said, laughing shortly, undoubtedly taking another swig from his paper cup.

Terri laughed a little and continued. "I'm still having a problem getting past this point, really. Surely with our mass hysteria culture and infatuation with the famous, a movie star is a much more appealing promoter, a safer, saner endorser, than what could potentially be just some crazy man off the street?"

"Oh of course, but like I said, companies today want to appear casual and hip. How else could Ian Ashbey, the owner of Macrohard Byte and king of the computer world, have a subset in his workers' contracts demanding that they wear acid-washed blue jeans on every first and third Friday of the month for casual Fridays? It's how you come across, Terri. Baby boomers know that movie stars, and certainly athletes, don't stroll into a Derfy's on Santa Monica Boulevard and order a Bacon Hexaburger with Supa Fries. Besides, it's really about the kids anyway. With this Derfy Burger promotion, kids assume that, if you're lucky or put yourself in the right spot, you can become famous for doing absolutely nothing, no work involved, which today's kids cherish. Ask any kid on the street what he wants to be when he grows up and it's not to be a policeman or a fireman or the president of the United States, it's to be famous. Remarkably, they don't make the connection that the president *is* famous, the most famous person in the world. Kids just want to be good-looking and get on MTV and shake their little booties for the camera, and who can blame them? Of course you can always be the progeny, the lucky son or daughter of someone who is already famous, and you've hit the jackpot. Even if you do absolutely nothing, if you go out of your way *not* to be famous, you'll still become famous, because then you're the kid of so-and-so who didn't do anything despite the great leap forward you were given before you were even born. It's the way of the new generation."

"It can make us old people really lose hope for the future," Terri sighed.

"Shut up, old lady," TJ said. "As if you guys were any better."

"Well, it's because of people like us, Terri, people our age, that this has happened," vonM. said.

"That's right," TJ responded.

"Yes?" Terri asked.

"A twelve-year-old doesn't work for nor is the head of any advertising firm that I know of, at least the last time I checked none are. *We* are the sellers and promoters, Terri. We didn't start this ugly advertising thing, but we are the ones who brought it to another level. We seem to have no shame when it comes to selling and expecting others to buy, even when we think we're offering something useful, a product, a gift, when actually it's just to fill the aching void in our lives, of not knowing our neighbors, of hardly seeing our kids after a ten-hour work day, of losing touch with our spouses. More stuff feels good, for about thirty minutes, and then there's that emptiness. I call it buyer's grief, the realization that finally getting your hands on that great pair of shoes isn't half as interesting as watching your kid trying to catch a butterfly in the backyard with a net full of holes, like I did with my daughter last Saturday," and he chuckled softly. "Not that I'm any better than anyone else out there. So how can we blame kids for wanting, demanding, all of this stuff when it's grownups who have foisted it on them? We need to look in the mirror."

"I don't think I have the heart," Terri said, then drew a heavy breath that seemed to mix harmoniously with the static. "My supervisor will probably kill me for saying this, but just the very fact that we're covering this campaign is multiplying the problem perhaps?"

"Oh that's been bugging me too, Terri," radio Willy said without, I thought, remorse. "But it's news. Really, the thin line between news and advertising has been smeared for some time now, at least in this country. Celebrities are mere products of their own image, if that makes sense, and they make up ninety percent of the news today. But don't lose heart all of you unknowns out there—I foresee a not so distant future in which people will do anything they can to get onto television, and we'll gladly watch it, discuss it and elevate it to iconic pop status, even if it's just some guy eating a bowl of toenail clippings for a thousand dollars."

"Eewwww," Terri said.

"I know. I saw that on late night TV in England on a trip I took there some months back. I was giving a lecture on the effects of the monarchy's control on public advertising from the Battle of Hastings until today. Let's just say the Brits' academic interest in just about everything coupled with their royal control of public manners and private courtesies throughout the ages has made their advertisements almost palatable, as opposed to our more democratic approach. I found their penchant for self-mockery most endearing, in contradiction to our advertising approach which is very serious, often violent and certainly, well, stupid. Just watch a beer or truck commercial sometime."

"Unfortunately I see my boss flagging me down from just outside the studio, which either means I'm about to be fired or we're just about out of time. Let's hope it's the former," Terri cooed, just loving herself. "So Mr. Nye then—victim or villain in our world of the hard sell?"

Oh gawd, I gulped, preparing for the worst. It had been so fun not talking about me.

"Victim, obviously."

Hurrah!! My hero continued: "A victim in that he wandered in off the street and was catapulted into the limelight. A victim that, with a million dollars, a person's life is irrevocably changed, either for good or bad. A victim in that he will actually have to eat about a million Gerbroni burgers in the next year. A true modern-day victim when he is forgotten in say, a year, and doesn't understand what he's done to deserve our ambivalence. He's done nothing of course, we've just tired of him in our fast-paced, eat'em up spit'em out world."

"You've tired of him already I fear?" Terri asked, a real sweetheart.

"How could I? This is exciting, I will say that. To see what happens to Mr. Nye is one aspect. I mean, Derfy Burger has caused a stir on a global level, they've taken a gamble. For goodness sake, they could have just gone out and found a brick-layer and fashioned him into your everday person who loves a hot fudge sundae every now and then. But, the marketers at Derfy Burger went out on a limb with this billioneth-served gag. What Mr. Nye does with his victim/villain status is one of the few non-scripted scenarios in his control. I think it's where the true drama lies. I saw the guy on TV—unfortunately he seems pretty harmless."

"He saw you on TV, mate," Ding Dong said anxiously.

Terri asked what we had all been wondering. "Could he have been planted in that Derfy Burger? Perhaps he has known all along, Derfy Burger has known, and he has taken acting classes, singing lessons, cleaned himself up, gotten ready for the spotlight. Perhaps it's not a gamble at all."

"Oh he has definitely not cleaned himself up."

Hey!!

"You know, I've thought about that Terri, of Derfy Burger planting a spokesperson, but taking that gamble, of being found out, is a bigger gamble than ending up with some fruitcake as its spokesman. I think we learned our lesson in pop music in 1988, when the lip-synching golden boys from Jamaica climbed the billboard pop charts and went..." and at that point, the car panted into Eisenhower Tunnel and we were mercifully out of radio contact.

CHAPTER SIXTEEN

"The Collapse,
1:58 p.m."

"We need to get out of here."

"Okay. Where do you want to go?"

"I don't know, Dad, just back the car up and pull to the side."

Julia shrugged and frowned in reply. I told her "We can go walk through the cemetery. I'm kind of tired of going to the lake." She nodded slightly. "I think it's too cold anyway," I said. Although it had been the end of August, once the sun started tipping toward the west in Leadville the breeze took on a chill. "Where do you want to go?"

She frowned even deeper. "Out of Colorado."

"Oh," I said, just a little surprised. "You mean *out of here* out of here. Where?" Please don't say Texas, please don't say Texas, please don't say Texas, please don't say Texas.

"Maine," she said, brightening a little.

"Maine! What the heck for?"

Her shade returned, but not as heavily. "I don't know. Because it's the only state with one syllable."

Well I hadn't thought about it that way. Let's pack'er up then and hit the road. I shifted from one foot to the other, not wanting to tell her it was a silly idea.

"It just looks pretty, and I don't think anything ever happens there. It looks like people just haul around wooden crates of lobsters all day or something. I don't think people kill each other in Maine. It's like Bulgaria or something—people don't really do anything or make the news." She looked at me and smiled, blushing a little at her silly idea. "I know, it's a silly idea."

"No, no, it's not a silly idea. But they boil lobsters alive I'm pretty sure."

"I guess I don't like that so much." She walked over to the window and leaned, straight armed with palms flat on the sill, against the glass. She stood looking out over the softball field beneath my window, at the mountains and pale sunshine, for what seemed several lifetimes, her forehead smudged up against the glass. She did not bother to turn around when she spoke. "Remember when we went to that Edward Hopper exhibit in Denver last Christmas?"

I waited just a hair too many miliseconds after my initial five-second pause before saying "yah-uh," which was meant to charge from between my teeth as a good, solid "yeah!" and Julia knew I was full of baloney, lying. It was not a real lie though, it was a lie to keep me from looking like a complete imbecile. That kind of lie didn't count. She turned around, resting her hip against the sill and folding her arms. She really did look cute propped against the window in her beige sweater, arms folded carefully across her belly. Something in there, unaware of our machines and our instruments and our schedules and our pasts and our joys and disappointments and machinations, was growing into one of us. I didn't even know it.

"Remember we saw the old guy wearing that top hat with the purple umbrella?" she asked. I looked befuddled still, unfortunately. She sighed. "They served the really expensive vanilla cookies with the chocolate filling in the reception area for free."

The memories came rushing back to me in a flood. "Oh yes," I said triumphantly. "Oh yeah, he's the guy that did that painting of Elvis serving coffee to Marilyn Monroe and James Dean in that diner at night."

Julia rolled her eyes. "Remember you really liked the one painting of the guy in the tie standing at the old timey gas pump and closing down his station at night? It looked like it would be in Maine."

"Yep." I actually did remember. "Nobody around to bother him at all. Close up my shop and let me go to bed, nice and early, if you don't mind."

Julia rolled her eyes again and fiddled with her bottom lip. I asked her if she remembered that she ruined it for me by showing me another painting of the same guy really close-up in his chair on the side of the gas station, kind of looking like he was trying to hide. He was just relaxing in the morning sun, thinking about the day ahead but there above him was his wife's head sticking out of the window yelling at the poor guy. God. He looked like a mummy. He looked half-dead, all waxy, like he was either sleeping with his eyes open or he had just died nanoseconds before and the life was only half-extinguished from his eyes.

"He was just having a little sit-down and collecting his thoughts and the lady had to come out and start yelling at him."

Julia unfolded her arms and gave me the Nazi death stare. "He was probably out there sleeping when he should have been working."

"Yeah maybe."

"I think it was sunset anyway, not sunrise."

"Oh," I said, thinking to myself. "I always assumed it was sunrise in a painting when things are still dark and shady on one side. How can you tell?"

"I guess you can't," Julia said, looking at me funny, kind of lost, like she just realized all over again how much she loved me. She even came over and kissed me lightly on the lips. "How do you know it's not been light and things are just beginning to get dark on the other side?"

I had to think really hard about that one but skipped it anyway. "I like the one where the couple is sitting at the side of their house and the grass is all yellow and grown up high, like they live in the middle of a wheat field or something. Remember that one?" She told me she did, of course. "I guess that guy never heard of a lawn mower. What do you think that little dog hears off in the woods?" I asked her. She smiled at me and said nothing. She was making me nervous. "I don't know," I said, "I think his paintings are kind of scary. The people are always looking at something else. They're just really dark."

Julia kissed me on the lips again, then on the eyes and chin and my forehead. She was making me nervous as hell.

"I want to move there," she said. "I want to live in a little wooden clapboard house with wooden floors painted white and the windows looking out onto the woods."

"Not if it's like the woods in those paintings. They're too dark. I'd be afraid just to go out and get the mail."

"Then we'll live in a place where you can open the windows to the sea and the curtains can blow in and you can hear tugboats off in the distance. We'll live in an Andrew Wyeth painting instead of Edward Hopper, though we'd be moving from a rich palette of vibrant colors to all earthy browns."

I nodded and then remembered that I had no idea who Andrew Wyeth was and that I didn't understand a thing she just said. "I don't think I know him."

"Sure you do. You know that painting in between Mrs. Windass and Mrs. Barmby's class in school, the one of the girl crawling on the ground and looking up at the house on the hill?"

"Oh yeah, that's my favorite painting in the world." I gushed. I really did like it, no lie.

"That's Andrew Wyeth."

"She's like a blind girl lost out in the field or something. That's a great one. I could live there." I always got lost in her little world because the painting hung on the wall between math and language arts class. I always pretended that I was some stranger from out of town in the 1920s maybe, and I would happen by in my little jalopy and give her a lift to the house and she would be this ravishing, knockout beauty, which you cannot tell from the painting because you only see the back of her head, and we'd get married and she would be really kind and forgiving because she was blind.

"I bet you always pictured her as some gorgeous country girl, and you'd save her or something," Julia said.

I balked. "Please, I just really like that painting. It's really well-executed."

"Then we'll go to Maine," she said, brushing my cheek with her thumb and looking dead into my eyes, sad almost, but smiling tautly. "It would be a wonderful place to raise a child."

The hint sailed right over my head. "Okay," I said.

"Stop acting like a child. We can't turn around."

"Aw Dad," TJ said, falling back into his seat and slapping his knees. "Just back the car up."

"We can't turn around Ding, we're inside the tunnel. Be sensible now."

Eisenhower Tunnel was a engineering masterpiece: a hole through a mountain. It was about a mile long though, and saved weary travelers the travails of looping around Loveland Pass, which had drop-offs of several thousand feet and whose terrors were immeasurable on a wintry, snowy, dark day. For this I was thankful to Mr. Eisenhower, and on this day I was more grateful in that he afforded me a dose of silence from the outside buzz of the planet. I was beginning to get cold feet already—I had always rather enjoyed my anonymity, sort of, at least up to the point where Zica Dunga had pinched my tookus. And though the pinch still felt like a soldered burning mark on my flesh, the joy had been fleeting. I was back with Eliason Nye again.

"Looks like a little roadwork on the tunnel," Teddy said to me in a comforting way. I think he was sensing my panic. We had entered the tunnel at a pretty good clip, sandwiched between two pick-up trucks with non-Derfy guys at the wheels. I would have bequeathed my crown to any of them, with a small cut of the million of course. Inside the tunnel, the normal two lanes had been narrowed to one and a couple of workers in grimy yellow suits with reflective strips wrapping around the chest and back, everyman kind of workers, guys who would have made perfect Mr Derfy Burgers, were on mobile man-lifts changing light bulbs overhead. It was darker than usual in the tunnel as every other light was turned off for the men to replace, and the dark-light-dark-light-dark-light flashed by like intermittent dead and electric seconds of my suddenly weird and claustrophobic life. I could feel my pupils widening then clenching with each foot that we traveled, my heart beating to the same rhythm of the overhead light pattern. I suddenly wished that nothing had happened to me, that I was still in bed, wondering what would happen if I just lay there all day, if anyone would come looking for me, would anyone care, thinking how boring my life was. I was beginning to panic for sure.

"Speed up, Dad. We've got to get out of here," I heard TJ yap, but the words were strangled with the pit-pat-pit-pat of the wheels on the uneven pavement, the passenger-side tires falling with a clunk where the road and manhole covers did not quite meet, the lights whirring by and the fellow's brake lights in front of us tapping on and off as the constriction of lanes and confluence of cars began to turn us into one solid, moving mass in the tunnel, like a log bumping the sides of a chute, and we kept speeding up and going faster and nearing the truck in front, and the truck behind with its shiny chrome frown for a grille kept inching closer to us from behind and a man with a headlamp emerged from a tiny door in the left-side of the tunnel, as if this was the hollow of a giant, pregnant snake pushing him into the darkness with only a measly headlamp to guide him, and Ding Dong sped up so fast that the extinguished lights blurred into the lit ones so that my eyes saw only a streak of fluorescent, filthy green light on the other side of the windshield and we kept speeding up, faster and faster, faster and faster so it was with some alarm that I noticed the tunnel collapsing and caving in behind us, the headlights of cars fifty yards back being instantly snuffed out in plumes of dirt and smoke and diesel with millions of tons of mountain pulverizing the metal and wheels and passengers into dust yet I could hear nothing but a deafening rumble of blood in my ears, a whooshing and hollow roaring that felt like my head may implode as everything around us caved in and filled a gawking void with yet more darkness.

"Are you feeling alright," Ding Dong asked me. I stared at him wild-eyed, jerking my head to the back window, watching the collapsing ceiling gaining on us, unable to speak.

"I think you need to relax and concentrate on your breathing," Teddy instructed. He tapped on the brakes lightly and the stream of fluorescence broke a bit. "Look, there's the light at the end of the tunnel, so to speak," he said, tapping my shoulder and pointing through the windshield. I jerked around to the front and breathed heavily.

"Ding Dong, the tunnel's not falling down around us, is it?" I gasped.

"Lord I hope not," he said, quickly checking the rearview mirror. "You're in a bad way, aren't you?"

"The man's freaking," Little Ding squawked.

"Hush up," his father frowned, turning his head slightly to the back seat. "Are you alright then?" he said softly, turning to me again.

"I think I'm having a nervous breakdown, Ding," I gulped, my heart knocking so violently against my ribs I thought it may prick a bone and leak to death slowly. I yawned, wide-mouthed and stuttering, trying to pull in more oxygen. "Somebody help me," I moaned in that vacuous, drippy but panicked tone that people use in movies when they have been shot in the gut and find the last bit of strength to reach up from the ground, clutch their best friend's forearm and strain under the words, "Don't let me die, Billy, don't let me die."

"You'll have to do the song and dance for them for the rest of your life," Ding said sadly. "Already you're starting to despise what you've become."

"I don't know how to sing or dance, Teddy Ding Dong," I cried.

"I can help in that department," TJ said excitedly. "I've got all the right moves. You'll need a manager too—that's me."

"Hush up," his father commanded.

"I was just buying Willy three Gerbroni burgers. That's it," I said, the panic welling up, ready to spout like a geyser. I could feel it. "It was just chance. I'm just a normal guy, like you guys. I didn't do anything."

"Breathe," Ding Dong instructed, "breathe, relax. Look, we're almost out of the tunnel." And I tried to breathe, but it wasn't so easy when I was thinking about it, like blinking. I was seconds from just opening the door and flinging myself out, and just when I felt I could stand no more, we began to emerge from the tunnel and into the weak light of the snowstorm that bled slightly inside the exit. I tried to exhale the darkness of the hole as the static on the radio started to fill the car.

"I'm just a jerk off the street. You guys know that," I offered apologetically. "I don't deserve anything more than anybody else."

Ding Dong, to his credit, was doing all that he could to soothe me. "Getting a million dollars is pretty nice, but you may have to put this in the right light. Maybe this is all some sort of divine intervention from God to make you stop and think about your life, to make you a better person."

"It's going to take a lot more than God to make me a better person," I yelped as we banged fully out of the tunnel and into the snow-dusted light. The radio frequency began to recognize our antenna and salient words were forming out of the static. Somebody was talking about me, even on the other side of the tunnel, which felt half a world away from Silverthorne.

"No!" I shouted.

"All right," Little Ding said, smiling and grabbing my shoulder. "Back to life."

"We should turn around here," I told Teddy, as we neared the exit for Loveland ski area. "We can get off and drive under the road and go back where we came from, I think. Just, maybe we should take the pass back. The tunnel is a little dangerous. I think we can turn here."

He looked out the passenger-side window but did not move out of the fast lane. Sentences now were being emitted from the radio.

"…is a numbers game. It's patently absurd for Derfy Burger to claim that they know exactly who their billioneth-served customer is," said an unfamiliar voice, a younger guy, maybe one who was still studying to get his master's degree in the Patent Absurdity of Life. Terri's familiar voice chimed in as we beat right past the exit for Loveland.

"I imagine that Derfy Burger won't make those sweeping claims— I don't know. I'd assume that they picked a certain Derfy Burger in a scenic part of the country, probably low on crime in a fairly modern, smaller city and said, 'Okay, the sixty-third person in today will be Mr Derfy Burger' or Ms Derfy Burger if such had been the case."

"I've eaten at Derfy Burger probably four times a week and have for many, many years. I'm just a little miffed about their approach," the man spat out, like he was in some confrontational debate with the

Secretary of the Interior and he had thirty seconds to refute some pointless argument that no one cared about. "To have a true Mr Derfy Burger, per se, they should have held a sort of lottery where you received a ticket with each meal and then on an appointed day, say the Fourth of July, because you don't get much more American than Derfy Burger and the Fourth of July, you hold the big drawing. That would be the hugest day in history for any company ever on the face of the planet."

"A bit hyperbolic, aren't we?" Ding growled.

"Perhaps," Terri said sanguinely, though you could tell, after speaking with Willy vonMorgansteen, that this guy was minor league, "but it's too late now, isn't it? There already exists a Mr Derfy Burger." There was a moment of silence. "And reports are coming in that he somewhat improperly and promptly fled the scene. Could this be part of the act? Surely not. Derfy Burger spokesmen and local police—" but Ding Dong leaned over quickly and snapped the voice from existence—*our* existence at least.

"Hey!" Little Ding protested. His father shot him a nasty look.

"The man is giving me a headache with his squeaky little voice and his rhetoric. He must be as fat as a house, eating Derfy Burger four times a week. It's people like that…" but he did not finish his sentence and stared straight ahead, giving his mustache a tug with his teeth and lips.

"I guess we should turn around at the next exit," I suggested meekly. "I don't know."

"Come on Dad, put the radio back on," TJ pleaded. His father hitched up his shoulders and said nothing. "Dad, this is a big moment for our boy Eliason, for all of us," Little Ding persisted.

"This is not a big moment for us, son, or for anybody. It's a small moment made to look big," Ding Dong replied.

"Come on Dad, switch it on."

"Absolutely not."

"Hey Derfy Burger, help me out here. Tell my dad to switch on the radio."

"No way, dude. They're going to start getting mean about me."

"You're going to have to toughen up that skin, bro. You are Derfy's slave. Welcome to the ownership club, welcome to slavery and chains. I can tell you all about it."

"Leave the poor man alone, TJ. He's had a rough morning. Don't get political on us right now, not at this time."

"Here comes another exit," I told Teddy. "We can probably turn around."

"I'll leave him alone if he turns that radio on. Come on, pickle man. Help me out. Come on, I want to hear how your parents invited King Fred to your birthday party when you turned sixteen."

"That's enough TJ. Just let it rest now."

I watched as we passed the exit, Teddy not giving it a second glance.

"You don't know anything about this man, Theodore Junior."

"I didn't know you had become his little buddy. Funny how a million dollars suddenly makes a guy shine."

Teddy looked as if he might burst. We happened to be right at an exit so he pulled onto it and jammed the car to a stop in the middle of the road, not even bothering to pull to the side. Once more I flossed my teeth with the windshield. I was too scared to face Teddy but on the edge of my vision I saw him shift his body slowly to face TJ. He was seething.

"If you ever speak to me like that again—" but he was not able to finish, he just growled a little. "I'm not one of your friends who you can insult at any time. I'm your father."

I was still too petrified to face either of them but I was pretty sure that TJ had his head down, concentrating on his lap. Teddy slowly turned forward again, backed up the car about ten feet on the exit road, slipped onto the shoulder and merged slowly back onto the highway as if every move he had executed had been perfectly legal. I guessed we weren't turning around. After three more exits slipped by, after about ten minutes, I sat there glumly and heard TJ speak.

"I'm sorry Dad. It's just been a crazy day." His voice was a little shaky.

"It's okay son. You know your dad always loves you, no matter what."

"I know Dad."

It was kind of sweet in a way. We all sat quietly, especially Willy, who had not opened his mouth in what must have been ages for him. I watched another exit pass by. Then another. It was too quiet in the car.

"I never had a Derfy birthday party," I said for no particular reason. "Especially when I was sixteen." Teddy nodded at me seriously but I heard TJ snicker to himself. "I might have been pretty uncool when I was sixteen but I wasn't *that* uncool. Besides, Peter Potato scared the hell out of me when I was a kid."

TJ made another quick snicker sound. "But you said on the radio that you dressed like Private Pickle for Halloween."

"Man, I swear to god I didn't say that. I said that *Willy* dressed like him. I was just kind of making fun." I turned to look at Willy but he appeared kind of ashen. I was getting a little worried about him.

"That's pretty weird that they did that to your voice," TJ admitted. "Made you say something you really didn't say."

"It makes you wonder what else they're going to do to you," Teddy said, almost sadly.

"I just want my million dollars and for them to leave me alone."

"I doubt that will happen, mate," Teddy said, sounding very, very sad, almost like he cared about me. Maybe he did, somehow.

I watched another exit zoom by, then another and another, and I didn't really care anymore that we were not taking them. I was getting almost comfortable with my poverty and anonymity again.

"Yeah, Peter Potato is kind of weird," TJ said from out of nowhere. "Hey, pickle man, can you turn the radio on again? I'm curious what they're saying about you now."

"No way. They're probably digging up things from my teen years that I wanted to keep hidden and now the whole world knows about them."

"What, like you dressed as King Fred for your own birthday party when you were sixteen? Not Private Pickle. I knew it," TJ said slapping his forehead, doing his little snicker snort. "Where did you find the boots?"

"I don't even remember my sixteenth birthday. It's kind of sad."

"I do," Teddy said. "Hull City versus Man City with my dad. Abysmal. Soggy pitch. Soggy bap at halftime."

I didn't know what the hell he was talking about but TJ laughed a little to himself. Just the way he laughed, to himself almost—I knew he really loved Teddy Bell.

"Come on pickle man, turn on the radio," TJ said, sliding forward to the front seat and leaning over it. I shook my head violently. He reached out his hand to turn the knob but Ding Dong slapped it down.

"Let the man have a little peace," he said.

"Come on Dad, we're missing lots of good stuff. Come on, burger man. Just for like ten seconds," he insisted, snickering. More exits flew by as we got deeper and deeper into a trouble we did not yet know about. I was playfully slapping TJ's hand away, helping out Ding Dong, keeping TJ away from the radio. TJ was snickering away and I was feeling more and more comfortable about surviving this trip. "Come on, just click it on for like ten seconds. That's all."

CLICK.

"Hey!" I heard TJ say in surprise, about to turn to him and tell him that maybe I would let him cut a couple of places in line at my autograph signing in Denver, but what I saw made the blood rush out of my brain.

From out of his day bag Willy had taken the gun he had offered me earlier, which before had looked like a pea-shooter but now loomed as large as one of those silver monsters that Doc Holliday was always pulling out of his holster before he became too weak from gonorrhea {tuberculosis—ed.} to hold anything, and Willy had the muzzle directed at Ding Dong's right temple.

"You had better stop this car, ass-munch," Willy directed.

CHAPTER SEVENTEEN

"The Bell Cracks,
2:15 p.m."

"I can't do that. I don't know what will happen after that, if we wait too long."

"But, I can't…. Can't you just wait a little while longer?"

"Eliason, baby, I can't. We need to go now. Come on, I really need your help."

"Are you sure there's no other way? Can we just—"

"No, we can't talk about it any more. I'm already, I get a headache just talking about it. I said on Sunday…Baby, it's already Wednesday and I'm leaving tomorrow. I have to leave tomorrow, early, whether you're coming or not."

I said nothing and listened to the wind outside my apartment windows pushing the panes of glass against the frames. I said nothing. Then I heard the door close quietly.

"Would you like to open the door and throw yourselves out then?"

"Like I said, just slow the car at the next exit, stop and let us out, Mr. Bell."

"He's gone barmy," I heard Ding Dong say coolly, evenly, almost like he was watching a scene on television. I could see his temple throbbing beneath the muzzle of the gun. His adam's apple looked stuck halfway between his collar and his chin.

"You better quit pointing that thing at my dad!" TJ shouted. He grabbed Willy's arm with both hands and jerked madly.

"Little Ding, no!" Teddy cried, the gun knocking the soft flesh of his neck just below his earring, then the headrest, then close to his throat as Willy straightened his arm. "He'll shoot me! Let him go, let him go!"

"I won't let some damn fool shoot my dad!" TJ shouted. I could see his fingers tighten on Willy's forearm like a bear's teeth into a flopping salmon, the folds of Willy's jacket bunching up between his fingers and oozing out the sides.

"Theodore, no!"

"Make him take the gun away, Dad."

"He's going to accidentally shoot me."

"No, Dad!"

"Junior, please." Ding Dong's voice was no longer calm, panic was riding the edges of it. Willy looked scared as hell, his cheeks and forehead blanched with tiny red dots in some sort of rash. TJ shook his head and pursed his lips, tightening his grip. Jesus, Willy.

"Bear, maybe you should put the gun down," I said, trying somehow to sound calm, but my voice sounded like it had been poorly recorded on a melted cassette and played through a recorder with dying, leaking batteries left out in the rain for two years.

"Cannot do that little chief, cannot put the gun down. Now just reach out and grab that steering wheel."

"Don't do it, son," Ding Dong said to me. I followed his advice.

"Eliason, we did not ask to get into this. Now we are simply requesting to get out of it."

"Get out of what?" I begged.

"Whatever two kidnappers—one employing a false beard and the other, a gangster rapper—whatever they are up to, I want no part of it," Willy said, somewhat cryptically. "I am sorry Mr. Bell, but I will have to shoot you if you do not stop the car and let Mr Derfy Burger and me out."

This was serious. Willy was calling me by my new professional name.

225

"I can't do that," Ding Dong returned. Willy breathed in deeply, exasperated. He again directed me to grab the wheel. Ding Dong strongly advised against it, keeping his eyes on the road the whole time. I turned to plead with Willy, who appeared relaxed suddenly, more at ease than I had ever seen him. It was bizarre. Awkwardly, because Little Ding still had both hands anchored onto his arm, Willy took the gun from Ding's temple and motioned with it to the steering wheel by stiffly rotating his wrist, then rested the muzzle on Ding's skull again.

"I knew it Dad, I knew it. I told you not to pick these fools up. They're killers, just like I said. I knew it."

I could almost hear Willy's eyebrows peak in shock. "We?"

"I told you Dad. Nobody hitchhikes anymore unless they're going to kill somebody. I knew it. Nobody's killing my dad, especially a couple of damn fools like you."

"But we're not—" I began to say but Willy hushed me angrily.

"Just grab that steering wheel and ease us over to the side of the road little chief, and these two gentlemen will see that nobody gets hurt."

Then a hollow whirring sound met my left ear, an insect sound. Buzz-buzz.

"Answer that phone and you are a dead man," Willy said to Little Ding. God, TJ's phone was ringing.

"Don't you threaten my son," Teddy said so menacingly I felt the latte splash up from my stomach into my chest, and most likely cause permanent scarring in my right aorta. I heaved for a breath and the obvious conclusion hit me: Willy was going to get us killed, all of us. And it occurred to me that I didn't know him all the hell that well. Maybe he *was* a murderer, a crazy kind of murderer, a small town, Leadville, very clever to have fooled everyone for such a long time with his passive-aggressive soft psychoanalytical doo-da, llama loving kind of murderer. I forgot to tell you that Willy once owned a llama but it ran away. He loved that llama.

"Eliason, grab the steering wheel."

"I don't know if I should Willy." Buzz-buzz.

"Grab the wheel, little chief."

I leaned over a little, dropping my left shoulder and easing toward Teddy like an iceberg into the ocean.

"Mr. Nye, if you try to grab this wheel I will run us off the road."

"Grab it, little chief."

My head felt like it was going to split. The latte now splashing my left aorta. I choked a little on the reflux. "I can't Willy, I can't. If I don't grab the wheel then you can't shoot Ding Dong. I don't want you to shoot Ding Dong." Buzz-buzz.

"Do not make me beg you to grab the wheel. Otherwise we shall all die."

"Jesus Willy."

"Little Ding, do you have your seatbelt on?" Teddy asked, his maddeningly cool voice having returned. I don't know if TJ nodded or not—I was too afraid to turn my head but I did hear the unscrunching of Willy's coat and then a snap. Willy seized his opportunity from TJ's released grip. I felt something hard against the back of my head, the unmistakable feel of a hard steel muzzle, the front-sight post digging into my cranium.

"Grab the wheel, little chief."

"Jesus, Snowshoe, don't shoot me!" I squealed. "Whose side are you on?!" Buzz-buzz. My hand involuntarily shot out to the wheel, but I did not grab it. I couldn't. I let it hover in mid-air, shaking. I felt the dent in my skull disappear and from the corner of my eye saw the muzzle return to Ding Dong's temple

"Dadgummit, Eliason, what have I told you about trusting everybody? Now look at us."

"You got into the car first, not me. I was perfectly content to sit in the Camaro. You didn't have to leave work today if you didn't want to."

"We have to see your mother."

"Well it won't matter if we're both dead!" Buzz-buzz.

"Now you two quiet down. It's no good arguing," Teddy scolded, ridiculously. "I'm afraid you two have become part of the plan anyway," then he looked almost thoughtful. "It wasn't supposed to be that way."

"What plan?" I cried.

"Yes, Mr. Bell, exactly what plan?" Willy asked, like he was James Bond or something. Buzz-buzz.

"A plan that I'm not wholly prepared to reveal yet, for your own good."

"I don't like that answer," Willy said, clutching his right wrist with the fingers of his left hand, like he had probably seen a million tough guys do in a million gangster movies. "Alas, I have never killed a man," he sighed.

"Don't you do it Snowshoe," TJ frothed, reaching for Willy's arm again.

"Don't TJ!" his father warned. Buzz-buzz.

"Willy, don't shoot Ding Dong," I pleaded.

"I'm afraid I may have to, little chief," he said sadly. "Sometimes the logic of violence is the only answer to an illogical situation."

"But you're a hippy!" I cried.

"Sometimes a situation can transform us into that which we do not usually seem." Buzz-buzz.

"I can take him, Dad," TJ said.

"Don't!"

"Grab the wheel little chief."

"Okay, Willy, okay, you psycho. Just don't shoot."

"Don't grab this wheel, burger man. If this car flips we all die." Buzz-buzz. "And this car will flip before any bullet enters my brain."

Buzz-buzz. Buzz-buzz. Buzz-buzz. We all sat suspended like bugs in amber while the car hurtled along.

"Stop this Monte Carlo or I'm going to have to shoot," Willy cried. Buzz-bUZZ. BuzZ-BUZZ. BUZZ—

"Yo this is TJ," I heard from the back seat. "Hey, what's happening? Really?"

From out of the corner of my eye I saw Willy's head snap left. I would have given my million derfy dollars just to see his expression. I noticed the gun move from Ding's temple.

"Don't point that gun at my son," Ding Dong warned. I saw the gun and Willy's hand slowly return to their previous resting places. It would have been comical in a TV show or some other funny situation in which someone was holding a loaded gun to someone else's head.

"No, not much going on here," Little Ding said into his phone, making his eyes big at us and putting a finger to his lips for us to stay quiet. "Yeah, what's that? Really? That's good. Yeah, yeah, just a second—hey Dad, Darryl's team lost so it looks like he can come here for Christmas. Hey D, let me call you back in a little while, okay? Cool, cool. Yeah, me to. Yeah I saw the Derfy Burger guy on tv too. I know, it's crazy. Okay. I'll talk to you." I heard a beep and there was silence. I turned to look at Willy, who still loosely had the gun trained on Ding Dong's temple, but his head was turned toward TJ, his white mustache mere white bristles above the gaping black hole of his shocked mouth.

"Darryl's my cousin. He plays football at college but his team lost for like the tenth straight week so they're already out of any bowl game," he shrugged, almost apologetically.

"Oh fooey," Willy popped unexpectedly, like a fart in a public space, and miraculously he moved the gun away from Ding Dong's head. I turned slowly, petrified with fright still, to see him looking down at his lap, at the once-again odd object called a gun nestled between his thighs. He looked completely deflated.

"Thank you, William," Teddy said, all cool, but I saw him loosen his shirt collar and voluntarily release his adam's apple with a heavy swallow. "You might have killed me."

"I did not wish to kill you, Ding Dong," he said, still looking down, like a punished child.

"Man, Snowshoe, you almost gave me a heart attack," Little Ding said, clutching his chest. I swear I felt that I was in some weird play where the director forgot to tell me what my lines were, or what the following scene would be, though the other three had rehearsed for months. Ding Dong breathed in deeply and cracked his neck.

"Why did you do that Willy?" he asked. "We were just driving."

"Perhaps it is none of my business after all," Willy said, his voice a little constricted as he bent over with a grunt to return the gun to the backpack at his feet, "but, what gives with the beard?"

And I thought to myself that it was a pretty premier question, seeing that the man was sporting a laughably fake beard, a man who I might add had just kidnapped a well-known celebrity as well as a small-town entrepreneur.

"If I told you I'd have to kill you," Teddy replied.

"Jesus!" I exclaimed, choking again on a soup of latte and gastric acids, coughing, eyes burning and tearing.

"It's just a joke, burger man," Teddy said quickly, "an expression."

Willy thumped me on the back as if I were choking on an ostrich egg then rubbed little circles between my shoulder blades saying affectionately "there, there little pup." TJ laughed with a liquid snicker and said I'd be alright, pickle man.

"I've had a rough morning," I apologized. "I'll be much better when I have my million dollars."

"That is right little chief," Willy said, touching his right nostril. "You get your million, we three shall take our extra hour. All is fine and fair in the peaceable kingdom."

TJ looked at him as if he were completely crackers.

"Sometimes you're pretty crazy, Snowshoe," TJ informed him. Willy beamed and started reciting, "You might live above a fish store but this girl Patsy loves your pompadour." We were all going mad. I took a deep breath and wondered if Willy even had filled the gun with bullets, if he knew how to shoot the dang thing, if it wasn't just something inside a plastic bubble that he had won with a quarter from a gumball machine in front of DerfMart. This is all too weird, I thought to myself, Willy being the weirdest of the weird, and that I needed to leave the car.

"I don't know if it was an unfortunate circumstance, or if you two were meant to put Little Ding and me on another path," Ding Dong said abruptly, to no one it seemed except himself. "I just don't know."

"You don't really have to say anything about the fake beard, or anything," I offered. I wanted no part of some mass murderer's raging rampage to kidnap and possibly disassemble global celebrities. The less Willy and I knew the better.

"It's really absurd, riding with Mr Derfy Burger," Ding Dong said with a shake of his head. I watched his big hoop earring swing back and forth, the mark just underneath and faintly visible still where Willy had pushed the open hole of the gun against his skin. "We should let the two of you go."

"Yes," I agreed.

"Why so absurd?" Willy asked. I slowly turned to him with an extreme look of hush-up on my face. He pulled his mouth into a circle. He sputtered despite himself, "Why so absurd to be riding with Mr Derfy Burger?"

"I just don't know if it's good or bad, if our chance acquaintance was meant to enhance or cock-up Little Ding's and my plans," he said, still more to himself than anyone else. "*Do* we have to get rid of you two?"

"No!" I said quickly.

"I will hazard that I could give you an outsider's perspective or possibly propose an exit strategy," Willy said. I snapped my head to him once more and offered a look, I hoped, of extreme agitation and annoyance. He rounded his mouth once more into an "o" and shrugged. "Are you okay, little chief? Your face is awfully red," he informed me.

"You're going to make the burgermeister break out in hives," Teddy said, somewhat medically, but also making fun a little bit, I thought.

"Uh-oh," Willy said, scrunching forward in his seat, embracing the headrest with both elbows and rubbing my shoulders. I pulled forward in repulsion.

"Man you look gay," TJ said, pulling back in repulsion.

Willy stopped and turned to Little Ding. "Affection between two friendly men should be something to be heralded, not spurned."

"Okay," TJ said sarcastically, tugging on the brim of his cap and grimacing at me. "Dad, I think you said too much already."

"I don't know, TJ. It must be a sign."

"There aren't signs anymore, Dad. Nobody believes in signs anymore."

"Nobody believes in anything anymore. It could be a sign from God though," Teddy told him. I knew TJ wanted to say "There is no God," and probably would have if someone other than his own father had said such a thing. Instead, he made a barely perceptible sound, almost a tisk, and a kind of agnostic shuffle with his spine against the seat and a push forward with his shoulder blades.

"It's a sign. Someone brought us together," Teddy insisted.

"The law of common convergence," I said, but everyone ignored me, except for Willy, who dismissed me with a bugling of unworded academic condescension.

"It could be dangerous territory we would be getting into," Teddy said, continuing his inner monologue that became an outer dialogue with the windshield. "Do you gentlemen mind if I get metaphysical on you?" he asked.

The only getting physical I wanted was out of the car but of course Willy nipped in with "Oh jolly no, as long as it does not hurt." I heard his butt scrunch to the front of his seat once more as my face turned crimson and my stomach bled fire again. This talk was going to get us into trouble, I sensed it, though usually I was about as perceptive as a roll of toilet paper. *[Shut up Willy.]*

"Dad, don't," TJ warned.

"It's not as easy as some people would like you to think, to kill a man," Teddy told us. My stomach suddenly pulled in on itself and felt stitched together with burlap thread, and refused to pull apart.

"Jiminy kristalnacht. Carry on, Theodore senior," Willy said, pulling further forward so his chest pressed against the back seat. If I just snapped back my left hand and released, like an ancient wheeled slingshot, my knuckles would tap nicely against his teeth, nose, face and, in the worst case, produce instant silence, in the best case, permanent silence.

"I believe that how you die often determines how you will live on through eternity," Teddy said.

"Interesting," Willy said. I could have killed him.

"A gentle death, if possible, allows you peace in the afterworld. A violent one—I hold a gun to you so that you're scared witless, you know you're going to die, then I shoot—and your soul screams forever. You will haunt us."

"Humph," Willy said. "Interesting still, perhaps melodramatic. Continue."

I could have killed him right there, violently, melodramatically.

"Perhaps it's what makes ghosts and evil spirits. If a man—actually more so a woman—dies a horrid, violent death then it must leave a physical imprimatur on the spiritual world. The anguish leaves behind a stamp or a trace of something, like a reassembling of elements. When you read about how some people die, how terrified they must have been, how they are—" but he could not finish. "It must leave a physical fear behind that floats around and alters the chemistry of our world in a way. It changes things."

"You're bringing me down, Dad," TJ frowned.

"What if I die on the operating table under anesthesia and I don't know I'm dead?! What if I assume I'm just still getting operated on? What releases my soul? Who's going to tell me on the other side that I'm dead?"

"St. Peter?" Willy said not very helpfully.

"I remember reading about a bloke years ago who was driving down the highway in Dallas and he got smashed by a 747 when it crashed on landing. The people on the plane knew they were going to die and that's terrifying, but the bloke in the car? You're just driving along and listening to the radio, thinking about what you're going to do that night, thinking about where you're going to go for lunch then bang, a very big sudden bang and you don't exist anymore. Does he even know it? Does he know he's dead?" Ding Dong glanced over at me. I was feeling sleepy again. I shrugged nervously at him.

"I do not know Theodore, I always thought you simply died," Willy said, not much more helpfully. "You simply pass from the physically well-formed to, well, the non-physically not-well-formed." He twisted his mustache and looked disturbed. "Your body returns to the earth, nourishes the soil, and your thoughts are cast out into the cosmos."

"You're not supposed to talk about it so much or you jinx yourself," Little Ding warned us, pulling down his cap a bit more on his brow and crossing his arms.

"We could pull over right now and kill you," Ding Dong said. I felt a certain heat start to cook my forehead, the sweat rising on the ridgeline of my brow, my stomach twisted up and ragged like an old, red oil cloth left-over in the Monte Carlo's trunk. My brain simply stopped working, trying to figure a way out of this mess that Willy had masterminded by not being a good, solid, hard-working American, because I never would have gotten into the Monte Carlo if I had been alone. No way. Pudenda seemed a million innocent miles away.

"Well Theodore, if that is what must be done, that you must commit homicide, then you must," Willy said sadly and shrugged. Now I turned cold. How could he? Willy had turned against me, obviously—they were going to kill me and split my million dollars three ways. I froze, hoping like one of a million times previously that I was invisible, that I was somewhere else, that I was somebody else, lost at sea, stranded on a mountain, trapped in a cave—at least I would have had a chance.

"We won't kill you of course," Teddy said. I felt my lungs processing oxygen again, cautiously. "But I just wonder, and I ask you Willy, because it seems that burgermeister is having trouble with his respiration, that if I were to kill you, and you had prior knowledge, would you kill me first?"

"Would it be a traditional method or a humane, state-subsidized, government-controlled execution?" Willy asked. I turned to look at Ding Dong, who looked at me blankly, then at Willy, who was certainly enjoying himself. I really wanted to kill him.

"Just the traditional western way: gunshot, stabbing, strangulation."

"Come on Dad," TJ said, furrowing deeper into his coat. "We don't know anything about these fools."

"Willy already had his chance to kill me."

"Yeah but he would have killed all of us, himself included. He's not stupid."

"Why, thank you Theodore Junior," Willy blushed.

Ding Dong turned to Willy, one hand still on the wheel. "Would you have killed me, Snowshoe Willy?"

Willy thought for a bit, rubbing just below his bottom lip where a soul patch would have been if Willy had had any soul. "I suppose in a far-flung battlefield, say you were a great Mongolian warrior and I, a defender of the ramparts of Vienna, why yes I would have been forced to kill you. If you were a first-line cavalry scout in a German Wehrmacht Panzer division and I, upon receiving orders from my commander at Stalingrad, were asked to extinguish—"

"I mean just now, William," Teddy thankfully interrupted. "Would you have shot me?" Willy appeared hurt by the interruption and merely shook his head.

"I don't know if I would have. I have read that to kill a man is not so easy."

"And that leads me to my next point: if you *knew* I was going to kill you, would you kill me first?" Willy said nothing so Teddy said, "There are lots of ways to be thinly involved in killing another man, no matter how large or small your impact. Willy, I know you love to philosophize so let's imagine I was driving in my car and you were driving another car and I accidentally crashed into you and killed you. If you had the chance would you try and kill me first?"

"I think if I knew you were going to kill me in a car crash I just would not drive my car that day."

Ding Dong chuckled. "I just wonder sometimes if, from the second you were born, the moment you emerged from your mother's womb, I just wonder that if a person who was meant to get into an accident and kill another person, if every decision that person ever made or every choice he ever had to live with or every thought he put into action, every—calculation of action—was directed at ending someone else's life." The cold vinyl of TJ's seat made a plastic crunch from his shifting body but he said nothing. "It's not freedom of choice, it's just some sort of continuum of existence. I'm beginning to think that we don't have any say-so in any kind of destiny."

I felt his eyeballs on me but I kept staring straight ahead. I just didn't want him to kill me before I got my million bucks, that's all. I didn't care for this conversation at all.

Willy thumbed his bottom lip then scratched his temple. "So Theodore, you would dispose of me if you were privy to some future information and knew that someday I might accidentally dispose of you?"

"Yes," Ding Dong said without hesitation.

"Then so it must be," Willy said morosely with a heavy heart-felt sigh.

"Well I'm not going to kill you, Snowshoe," Teddy said. "We're just talking."

"Yes, I know, but such are the vagaries of life," Willy said with yet another stony sigh. "Action breeds wealth, talk brings poverty, and so it goes for health and mortality, or that's what my stockbroker used to say."

"That's what I said—talking about death brings death."

"And action brings life and wealth!" Willy said, jutting that imperious finger in the air.

"Did you say you have a stockbroker?" TJ asked incredulously. "You rich or something?"

"I was possibly going to be," he said wistfully.

I thought of Tad and Ross, the Aspen snowshoe business dudes, standing outside of the Snowshoe Hut in their business suits, scratching their heads at the locked door, calling out Willy's name, delicately knocking on the window, accidentally dropping onto the sidewalk thousand dollar bills that bulged from their pant pockets.

"Little chief, you have not spoken in ages," Willy said, rapping me on the shoulder.

"I would prefer not to," I said curtly.

"Oh yes," he said and I knew he was tapping his nostril at TJ and even heard him try to say "His mother" as quietly as he could to him, but I still heard him. From the corner of my eye I saw TJ nod stiffly. I felt Ding Dong's eyes staring at me hard, and my own started to tear a little, not because I was sad but because I hated being stared at. I pretended to play with the window handle.

"I think I've said enough," Ding Dong said for my benefit. He slowly began to pull at his fake beard, drawing in his cheeks, sticking a bit of the fluffy stuff on the steering wheel. "Let's discuss something else."

"Let it be known, Theodore, before we move on to other fascinating subjects, that I would prefer to die an old man in my bed, no man having killed me and I having killed no man." Willy placed a reassuring paw on my shoulder. "And, I would certainly not kill your mother or father, Theodore, if that meant I would be able to premeditate your own demise and therefore ensure my own existence."

"That's quite alright, William. I already have."

Willy sounded confused. "How have you ordered your own demise in order that I may live?"

"Oh it's not that," Ding Dong said, letting the words hang in the air. I heard Willy squirm. TJ was silent. I could hear him breathing shallowly.

"It's that I killed my own mother and father already," Teddy said.

CHAPTER EIGHTEEN

"Javier Boeve,
a Real Revolutionist's Bollocks,
2:26 p.m."

If you spend enough time in a guy's car, at some point you'll always find out that either his only power drill is always under-charged and he has to borrow yours or that he is an ex-con or that he killed his parents. It's simply guaranteed. Travel with a woman long enough, any woman (under the age of forty-five I think), and you'll find out that she never loved men, never really desired a single man, and that all women secretly want to be lesbians, they're just not sure how to go about doing it. That's just a theory though, not a guarantee.

"You did *not* kill Grandmum and Grandpa," TJ said with a heave, as if he had heard such a thing a million times before and felt obligated to deny it, even though he knew his father would follow-up contrarily.

"I did," he said to me, gluing those painful brown eyes on me.

"Theodore, will you tell us about it?" Willy asked like some sort of stupid talk-show host. Teddy did not go into great detail but explained that he had met his wife, TJ's mother, in England while she was studying there on an exchange program, they fell in love, he moved back to the States with her and then his parents, both Brits who were tired of the "north England gales, the poor heating and their town's dreadful football team" arranged their paperwork and followed them to Colorado to a tiny town outside of Denver. Teddy opened his own little restaurant with a British theme, was quite successful, and his parents poured their hearts and energy into the place, almost treating it as their own. Then along came Derfy.

"Americans have a peculiar penchant for wanting the same thing over and over again," Teddy told us. "We had a nice place, cozy, cheap. But then Derfy Burger came to town, then DerfMart, and in their perfect little way they put all of us right out of business. Naturally, there were only nine or ten family-owned places right downtown, it was a small town not unlike your Leadville, but within a year we were all closed down. Doleful." He shook his head at the memory. "People will tell you all about free enterprise, but they haven't a clue. They'll tell you that you didn't work hard enough. They'll say you didn't offer anything different. They'll assume your service was poor. They'll say everything about Darwinism and supply and demand, about 're-inventing' yourself, about being in the wrong business, about accepting it and moving on because that's what the people want. And you know what—it's a bunch of bollocks." He was silent for a while. I could only accept that "bollocks" were bad things. He rolled a bit more of fake beard from his jowl and looked at it thoughtfully. "But what do you do when people *prefer* to drink from Styrofoam cups, when they *choose* to sit on plastic seats in an air-conditioned sort of sterile operating theatre of a place? What does it say about what they want, or the experience they're willing to forgo, in order to feel a comfortable...sameness? I still haven't figured out Americans after twenty years. We had a group of elderly ladies who would come in every Thursday morning for three straight years. Then one year we had to close for three weeks and take care of some issues back home. We came back but the ladies had moved on to Derfy's. They would go sit there on plastic seats bolted to the floor and drink bad coffee from cardboard cups. We never saw them again—well, occasionally in one-sies and two-sies we did but never all six of them at the same time again, just gathering in their horrid strip malls."

I closed my eyes. I had a certain image, yes, of abandoned strip malls bleached to a lemony white by the sun, the asphalt parking lot some prehistoric tar pit, ribbons of heat writhing through the air like a serpent woman with her arms porpoising above her head, her armpits as white as bone and her hair as black as charred wood. And I would walk barefoot from one end of the mall, say the eastern end, and I would get to the western edge and step off the warm cement that ran in front of the boarded-up doors and land on the sand dotted with thin blades of grass stretching to the horizon. And each blade would blow like a snake's tongue, whipping back and forth. The ground would be warm against the soles of my feet, enough to toast my whole body, and it would feel splendid after nine months of winter. Then I would peek around the westernmost corner. Behind the edifice would not be gathered a pile of metal trash cans or a loading dock or another strip mall. There would be nothing—nothing but sand and waving grass. There would be no rocky mountains or great lakes or death valleys or even trees or rocks or sage or highways, just sand with undulating, spearmint-green blades of grass, rolling and rolling and curving with the earth all the way to the Pacific. Then I would find that the strip mall I had been standing next to was not made of buildings at all, just false fronts that someone had propped up a hundred years ago on the side of a stranded and deserted, crumpled-up highway that led to a dead town with its clusters of wooden, broken homes, vines bleeding out the windows and trees nubbing through the living room roofs, the chalky, crumbling walls of the downtown café and drugstore and post office leaning on one another and helping each other kneel slowly to dust.

"You didn't kill Grandmum and Grandpa," TJ repeated. "You didn't kill anyone."

"And we wouldn't be killing anyone, Eliason, so just get it out of your head."

"I know, Julia, I know. It's just, something feels bad."

"Of course it feels bad, they *want* you to feel bad. I just need you there."

"*I* brought them here Little Ding, *I* said we could support them, *I* told my parents 'Come now or you may not see me for a long time. Come, you will have a grandchild one day. Come be with me and Janine, you'll love it here.'"

"Janine was my mom," TJ said softly. Willy nodded sympathetically, that damn beanie bobbing above his Farto! patch.

"And she was a fine woman," Ding Dong said, pulling back his cheeks so tightly I could almost see his molars poking the skin from inside his jaw, the tendons in his neck pulling and wriggling like taut rubber bands.

"And this is where you shall let us out of this car," I heard the voice in my brain saying, the muscles in my throat beginning to pull the cords of my larynx together and release them in a snap, pull them apart again, release with a pop, perhaps a push of air, with the wonder of syllables and words, but it was Willy's voice I heard in my ears.

"But your wife, Teddy?"

"She died visiting Dad in jail," TJ answered.

"And this is where you shall let us out of this car," I heard the voice in my head saying again, urgently.

"Oh sweet Mary," I heard Willy say.

"My old dear dad put so much time into our little café," Ding Dong said, ignoring TJ and picking up one of the other many loose threads that were dangling like some sort of floss from everybody's mouth except my own, which remained, I thought quite smartly, sealed tightly. "He was there more than I was. It had become his baby in a way and of course my mother wanted to be down there with him, to be with him, for all of us to be together. It was wonderful." He stopped speaking, the car slowing down just a little as his foot relaxed on the pedal, and I knew that he was there again, in his little café, all the Bells safe and happy, comfortable, the future long. "I suppose I wasn't completely surprised when he had a heart attack not long after *they* came to town." He spat the word "they" like grit from his mouth, "they" of course being Derfy's. "Our numbers immediately started going down. Of course Dad was the first to know. He had his second heart attack, the one that killed him, not long after we were forced to close for good. It was the stress wasn't it? They killed his baby. When Mum died it would have been from a broken heart wouldn't it? But nobody knows. Six months after Dad. Both my parents gone and my business gone in eight months. How does a normal man live with that?"

There was a long, long silence, only the sound of the tires rubbing against the highway in soft, wet, regular moans filling the car.

"And you were in jail?" Willy chanced. By this point I had again ceased entertaining any hope of our survival and allowed his suicidal intrusions.

"Ran right through Derfy Burger with my truck, didn't I? Decapitated King Fred," Ding answered without missing a breath, smiling.

"Oh!" said Willy.

"Just a statue near the ketchup dispensers though. Looked like there was blood everywhere. Damn near killed myself," he said, turning his head all the way around like an owl to display a two-inch scar above his left ear. It looked like a muddy river running through a clump of sagebrush. "Don't really know what did that. It's always been kind of dead there since, kind of numb," and he absent-mindedly stroked an index finger along the scar. "Anyway, the judge was this huge fat bastard. Said he wanted to make an example of me, not because of my color or because I was a 'foreigner' he said," and he stiffened his spine. "The judge said he was offended by my action and was 'gravely worried' about what the loss of Derfy Burger, if only for a short time, would do to the town's economy. The miserable bastard put me away for twenty years." Willy gasped and Ding shook his head, putting a finger to his scar again.

"Came out in the paper several months after the trial that the judge said on record that what upset him most was not being able to get his weekly Albaturkey Triple Decker sandwich." *{Editor's note: proclaimed "Official Sandwich of New Mexico, 1978."}*

"That is a good one, heavy on the mayo and cranberries," Willy noted. I turned and glared at him. He looked surprised. Ding Dong asked if we had ever heard of a man named Javier Boeve.

"Oh jolly good," Willy clapped. "Trivia! Javier Boeve, Javier Boeve," and he twiddled his lower lip. "Was he perhaps a second-string member of the 1977 Pittsburgh Pirates?"

"Hardly. He's a revolutionist, the dog's bollocks," Teddy answered.

"Hmmmm," said a perplexed Willy. "A revolutionist. And these 'bollocks' things you keep referring to, these 'dog's bollocks' things, are they good things?"

Teddy gave him a quick chuckle without turning. "Oh yes, at least they are for the dog."

"Hmmph. Is the Boeve to whom you are referring the 16th century underground Jugoslavian novelist-slash-member of the Baltic-Turkish Romantic writers' protest movement?"

I almost reached around and slapped him.

"The very one," said Ding, releasing the steering wheel to jut a Willy-like finger in the air, "in some weird, obscure universe perhaps. Let me help you out Willy," he said with a chuckle. "Javier Boeve was, in a roundabout way I suppose, the reason I was in jail. Javier Boeve is from a tiny village in France and he lived his whole life as a farmer, a complex man I'm guessing in a way that only a Frenchman can understand. It's hard for a Brit to relate, and impossible for a Yank. Derfy moved in not far from his village and within a week he had burned the place down. He told newspapers he could not abide the genetically-modified food, the air-conditioning, the little packets of bitter mustard. Brilliant. Direct action, no negotiating. The craziest part was that he got off lightly, with just a small fine. Luckily for him it was at the beginning of a time of strong French nationalism, when the government was officially banning most things American from their society. They even banned words such as 'le weekend' from the vocabulary."

"But we do not say 'le,' we say 'the,' silly," Willy said incredibly.

Teddy chuckled. "Not much later, another Derfy's in the region mysteriously burned to the ground, then another and another, though they were clever because no one was ever hurt. And they couldn't tie Boeve to any of them. But like all revolutionaries, Javier wanted to be jotted down in *some* history books so at the fourth Derfy's he was purposely photographed with lit torch held high, a pack of people behind him and looking like some sort of 'Liberty Leading the People.' He was always going to be caught for that one."

"A wonderful painting, 'Liberty Leading the People,'" Willy added. "Very creative composition, the 'v' technique really draws your eye all over the courageous scene. Someday you will be blessed to see it little chief, I'm quite sure of it."

"Well, with Boeve's mug all over the nationals, there was nothing for the government to do but to prosecute him. Naturally, the best course for a revolutionist to take is one through jail, not unlike an actor in a slump going through a very publicized rehab program. Naturally he became a hero and spent most of his time in jail writing a book and publishing his journals. Having said that, his jail was more like a country club for the stars. When his time was up he offered to remain behind bars to show that he 'couldn't be broken.' He wrote another book, had a small role in a film, started his own gardening show on tv, and got his culinary license, all while in the slammer. Only in France," Ding said with a smile my way. The anger in his eyes had seemed to completely disappear. I nodded at him and smiled back. Mine and Willy's chances of getting sliced into pieces seemed to be subsiding.

"Within two weeks of his forced expulsion from jail, another Derfy's burned, but it was happening with such occurrence and in so many parts of France, Boeve just sat back quietly as Derfy's decided it was best to vacate the country. As far as I know, the only Derfy's in the Republic of France is located inside the heavily-guarded gates of EuroDerfy, which is most-frequented I'm sure by vacationing Japanese, wealthy Germans and homesick Americans from Army bases just inside the German border."

"My brother went three years ago with his kids and was very disappointed," Willy said. "He was most upset that he had to use the euro outside the amusement park and that not a single hotel in France accepted the dollar. Can you imagine? We *are* the only superpower, have they not heard?"

"That's right William," Ding Dong grimaced at the windshield. "So, I only served ten of the twenty years but that didn't matter, did it? Little Ding was seven years old when I went in to the Buena Vista Correctional Facility in 1987. I missed him growing up. They destroyed my family twice."

There was an extremely long silence so I just concentrated on the sound of the tires peeling and unpeeling themselves from the road. The air pushed out of the heater vents gently. I could hear TJ breathing faintly from the back seat. Once again Willy's rear end munched the back seat as he shifted forward.

"Please, Theodore, only if it is not too painful to discuss, but what happened to TJ's mother?"

I noticed Ding Dong look into the rear view mirror at TJ, who I could tell from the corner of my eyes was staring out his window as if he was not listening. His was a tiny window up high, tall and narrow, like a prison cell's view to the sky from the back seat, a peculiar design from the Monte Carlo engineers.

"Well William, she was in a terrible accident on December 9, 1995," Ding Dong said in a very avuncular way, almost as if he meant to calm Willy, or was reading the first sentence of a fairy tale.

"Oh Teddy, no," Willy said, touching his shoulder. Ding drew in a deep breath and put a hand to his forehead.

"She was on her way back home to Colorado Springs after visiting me in Buena Vista. She had left TJ with a sitter. It was bloody freezing all over Colorado that night and snowing like mad. I wished she would have stayed in a hotel nearby but she wanted to get home of course." He glanced at TJ in the mirror again but he pretended to be concentrating on something outside his tiny rectangular window. "Nobody really knows for certain what happened. She stopped for petrol just in town, just outside the jail property and, well the cashier inside the store told police that she had seen a teenage boy pull up in a truck at one of the pumps." Ding stopped and seemed to be catching his breath. "He was messing around with a cigarette lighter near his gas cap. I can only guess that it was frozen somehow and he was trying to unfreeze it. I don't know."

I had half-turned in order to see Teddy and Willy and TJ, all of them.

"And his truck exploded," Willy said, twisting that mustache like a nervous madman. "Ronald Radford the Rocket," he breathed. "He was the top scorer on the Buena Vista Demons high school basketball team that year, a senior. Incredible long-range shot accuracy. He was a local hero that season. Buena Vista was knocked out of the play-offs in the first round without him when they were slated to go to state. There was a picture of all the players wearing black armbands during the game in his memory. It was all over the Leadville paper for two weeks, his tragedy. Burned another man very badly and killed a woman if my memory serves me correctly."

"Yes, William, killed a woman," Ding swallowed.

Everything in my body went cold: my blood, my brain, my heart, my feet, my stomach latte. Even the air from the vents seemed suddenly to have a chill to it. Willy did not make the connection at first.

"But your wife, was she in an accident driving—" Willy began, then paused. "Holy dog's bollocks—" And then total silence as if there was not a single soul in the car. "That woman was your wife, Theodore."

"Yes, William, that woman was our Janine."

I could see TJ squirm in his seat then resume being a statue. Snowshoe Willy could not find any words. I wished once again that I was an inhabitant of Pluto.

"And that is why Theodore Junior and I are taking Javier Boeve's lead and blowing up as many Derfy Burgers as we can today at the stroke of midnight."

Had Teddy not, about a thousand moments before, mentioned possibly going into some very dangerous territory? You can call me extra-perceptive but I think previously mentioned territory had been entered.

CHAPTER NINETEEN

"The Highly Technical High Tech Plan, 2:51 p.m."

"Dad, no," TJ pleaded. "They know too much already."

"Yes, they know too much. We either have to take them all the way or not at all," and he swerved off the highway onto an exit road that we were about to pass. I believe I squealed as two of our wheels lost touch with the ground and I knew we would plunge into the river running beside the highway. Ding Dong crossed over the river, pulled a hard right, and executed a wonderfully precise one-hundred and eighty degree rotation into an empty dirt lot hidden from the highway by a stand of tall, shivering trees, their south sides covered in bright green moss crawling up their trunks. Straight ahead was an old shack with a rusted tin roof and a decrepit water wheel leaning into the river, but it looked to have ceased turning centuries ago. Way up on a hill on the service road maybe half a mile away to our right sat the tiny wooden, rectangular silhouette of a house with a tinier rectangular silhouette of a truck on one side and another, largest rectangle of a barn slumping in a field behind. I knew the barn would have a huge, faded, flaking American flag painted on the door, I just knew it, and Julia would be leaning against it, waiting there for me, for some reason, to take me away. I knew that if I threw open the door and ran for it, dropping and crawling on hands and knees, feeling each rock and weed like a blind girl in a painting, I would never make it because Teddy would catch me in the car and drag me back into his world. Or I would drop dead of a heart-attack about fifty yards into my earnest sprint. I had not necessarily been vigilant in my high-altitude training for the next Olympics.

"Now that was quite a feat of skill," Willy said, removing his forehead from his own tiny window and bending his perpendicularity back toward the car's interior. Somewhere mashed between his girth and the side of the car lay a mashed, helpless laundry basket. He rearranged his beanie and breathed out. "Your exiting highways and entering dirt lots is almost southern hillbilly in its skidding sensibility," Snowshoe said. "So what is the plan, Stan?"

"I didn't want to miss the exit," Teddy explained, bending around and crooking an arm over the back of the seat to face Willy. "The plan is a simple one," he said eagerly, "and everything I ever needed to know I simply looked up on the internet. I had loads of free time in jail, and I wasn't going to very well be lifting weights or watching cable television all day was I? It was so easy, William, as you probably know, being a bit of a technophile." Willy nodded his head solemnly. "Everything was there: how to make homemade bombs, how to set them off, timing devices, where to get materials, where to buy Chinese throwing stars, where to get handcuffs and where to get keys to get out of handcuffs, how to build a small atomic missile from fertilizer and an old coffee percolator, masks and disguises, knives and guns and manuals. Some bloke in Scotland was even selling a cannon complete with 18th century fully-fitted cannon balls. I seriously looked into that one but the postal fees were a bit beyond my reach."

"I bought a llama off the internet," Willy said.

"See, it's all there," Teddy told me, then turned to Willy. "And it's not even difficult to find. Type in a word and a billion things come up. You can find anything about anyone or get anything you want in a matter of days, delivered right to your door. It's brilliant."

"And what did you get from the internet?" Willy asked courteously. I guess we had officially become part of The Plan whether I wanted to be or not.

"Everything Willy, everything," Teddy said excitedly. "I got all the materials for small homemade bombs and how to put them together, in weeks. Wonderful. I even managed to get everything smuggled into jail by a fellow I met on-line. Nice bloke, a courier."

"Friends in high places," Willy smiled, tapping his nostril. I was beginning to have an alternate-universe sensation in my extremities, a weird buzzing in my brain. I did not like where we were going.

"So my idea was—are you okay burgerman?" I suddenly heard Teddy ask. I must have been an interesting shade of blue-red-green-brown because he looked at me with a fair amount of concern. I swallowed and nodded.

"Okay, then," he said, looking out of the corners of his eyes at me and addressing Willy again. "With these brilliant timing devices they have now, you can set off multiple explosions simultaneously in various, far-flung locations. That's when I got my idea: take out three or four Derfy Burgers at the same time. People will get a real message, they'll know it wasn't just an accident but rather a statement."

"But Theodore, you could kill someone," Willy informed him, as if that really seemed to matter at this point.

"Oh no, the bombs will all go off at midnight tonight. Derfy Burger is locked up tight. The absolute latest we've ever seen anyone working was a little after eleven, cleaning up. No one will be hurt, guaranteed, except for the Derfy franchise we hope. Maybe they'll stop and think for a moment how they affect people's lives."

"So tonight at midnight we will be waiting for the big boom? Hmmph. Interesting," Willy said.

"Little Ding gave me the idea, sort of. He didn't really mean to."

"It was after a trip I took to New York," TJ interrupted. Willy perked up and Teddy swiveled around to face them, both of them almost surprised, as if they had forgotten he was there. "I told Dad how crazy it was that my watch kept switching time by itself when we went from one time zone to another, even on the plane. It was like my watch had its own brain."

Teddy nodded and stared at his son for a moment. "So I thought, my original plan was to set a small bomb in one Derfy's in each time zone. It wouldn't be big enough to knock out a city block of course but it would do enough damage to shut that particular Derfy Burger down, possibly for good. Well, all the driving and flying and coordinating was proving to be a bit pricey. Then I thought, maybe if we centralize and do it in a smaller area then there can be a sort of ground zero, a defining area that ripples out. Someone out there will carry on the torch and pass it on for someone else to pick up and it will spread."

Willy shifted in his seat. "I rather think that Americans have lost their ability to protest. Maybe they will not see the connection in all of the Derfy Burgers getting blown up."

"If they don't they're blind," Teddy said, sounding offended. "If everyone around us is so thick then we'll have to move, Little Ding and me. You can't be so daft, William?"

"I just hope you do not hurt anyone," Willy said, reddening a bit.

"I don't think so William," Ding said with a quick shake of his head. "Everything is in place in Silverthorne. Mr Derfy Burger's coronation gave us much more time than we needed. It almost threw a spanner in our plans." He gazed over at me with what I thought was menace. "Next we're on to Idaho Springs, just down the highway, then on to the suburbs of Denver. And when it's all been done, maybe we'll leave the country, at least until things settle down. Who knows? Damn, burgerman, you look like death itself."

I choked a little and said, "I think I have latte poisoning," and leaned my head against the headrest for a minute.

"So are you staying or going?" Teddy asked Willy and me. I started to reach for the door handle, to get out of that car as quickly as possible. I would have jumped through the closed window if not for Willy.

"Staying, naturally," he said. I slowly turned my head to him, poker-face style so as not to give the game away to Ding Dong, pulled back my lips and snarled at him with bared teeth, jumping into the back seat and ripping out his jugular, swinging it like a dog with a piece of old rope, his screams echoing through the valley.

"Maybe it's not so smart to be hauling around Mr Derfy Burger during your thing today," I said to Teddy. "I might attract a lot of attention."

"You might distract a lot of attention too," Ding Dong said, pulling the last piece of fake beard from his chin line and looking at it annoyed.

"But I won't use you like a pawn like that, Derfy Man. Besides, there's nothing around here, if you get out of the car. The two of you will freeze."

"Maybe we should just go up the road a little and you can find a gas station to drop us off at," I suggested.

"At which to drop us," Willy corrected me. I almost socked him.

"I know you must be a little out of sorts. Hell, I'd be uncomfortable if I were you."

"Well done, Theodore. Grammatically spotless."

Teddy looked at Willy but ignored him. "I'd be uncomfortable as hell in your situation. You can stay here if you want, and we'll leave, but it's cold out there."

"Dad! You already told them everything. We can't just leave them."

"We have to trust them TJ. It's all we have left. We can't force them to do something that they don't want. Right, Burger Man?"

I didn't know whether to nod or shake so I sat there doing absolutely nothing, wooden. I felt Willy's fingers on each side of my scalp, turning my head side to side.

"No, Ding Dong," he said, mimicking me, "you can't force us to go with you but there ain't nothing out here but sticks and snow. A city boy such as me will freeze." He forced my head into a couple of more shakes then patted my hair down flat.

"I think I just really need to not think about anything anymore," I said.

"Then you're staying," Ding said quietly, cranking up the Monte Carlo, which sounded more prone to remain sheltered its own private patch of dirt. "Just tell me when and where to drop you off, it that time comes."

He reversed, we passed over the river again and merged slowly onto the highway. We were all quiet for maybe ten minutes, just thinking to ourselves. Ding Dong was nutty as hell but who was I to step in and tell a grown man he was a total fruitcake. I had vaguely become Mr Derfy Burger, yes, but as long as I remained inside that car I was still just Eliason Nye, at least for a little while, because the outside world didn't exist in our tiny space at the moment. I just wanted Ding Dong to keep driving and driving and driving without ever stopping. The seat and sleep began to engulf me slowly. My vision began to blur and we unpeeled more silent miles of highway.

"Bloody hell!" Ding Dong said, jumping and straightening the rearview mirror.

"What is it Dad?!"

Ding Dong nodded to the mirror with a grimace. I turned around to look out the back window just in time to see three policemen wrapped up like wooly mammoths quickly closing in on us, their sirens screaming and revolving red and blue.

CHAPTER TWENTY

"Miss Portia Sagoo and Idaho Springs Too, 3.01 p.m."

"Bloody hell," Ding Dong repeated, his jaw clenched. "Everyone act very casual. This was all planned right? Right, Snowshoe Willy?" Willy nodded his pale face Teddy's way. "Right, Mr Derfy Burger?" I couldn't get any words past the lump in my throat and nodded gamely at Ding Dong. Little Ding crunched down in his seat and jammed his fists into his coat pockets. Just as I felt Ding Dong decelerate and start to pull over to the side of the road, two cops whizzed to our left; one stayed at the driver's side while the other pulled to the front. The last remained behind. The policeman in front pulled us along, motioning with a wave forward to continue apace. Then the one at our side lifted his black visor momentarily, gave us a big wink and salute, then stiffly lowered his visor again.

"What in the name?" Ding Dong asked.

"Dad, I could be wrong, but I think it's a police escort," Little Ding said with a short trumpet laugh, "like we're the president or something."

"I don't think so Little Ding. They probably think we're armed and extremely dangerous so don't do anything silly."

We continued forward for at least a mile with the policemen staying in their positions, every minute or so swapping places with each other like bees hopping from one flower to another.

"Well, it appears that we are not being pulled over," Ding Dong said, exhaling all of the tension in the car.

"I'm telling you Dad, it's a police escort. I've seen them on tv," Little Ding insisted.

"But who in the, why do we need a police escort?"

"Why do you think?" Little Ding said, crossing his arms. The car was silent.

"Burgerman," Willy said suddenly. "Of course. He is bigger than the president now, or even John Lennon."

"Holy Jesus," Ding Dong said, looking over at me like I was some sort of mystical figure. "I almost forgot, we're with royalty. But how long can they keep this up?"

"Until Idaho Springs," I burped, falling into my seat and pointing up out of the windshield. Above the highway, flapping in the breeze across four lanes, was a banner reading "Welcome to Idaho Springs, Ellison—Mr Derfy Burger!!"

TJ let out a hoot. "Check it out, *Ell*ison, pickle man. I don't know what you did in another life to deserve this but it must have been good." He clapped and slapped Willy in the arm. "Don't look so scared, Willy. We're home free now."

The sign looked professionally done with my name, though messed up, in huge red letters on a yellow background. A smiling caricature of King Fred was on the left side of the sign, my name crammed into the all-purpose space. It was a good thing for Derfy Burger that Nebuchadnezzar didn't step up to the counter—it never would have fit. Just as we drove beneath the sign, its right side ripped away from its post and slapped the hood of the car in the blustery wind. It almost knocked cop number two from his cycle as it lashed across the highway and twisted against the opposite pole.

"There you went," TJ commentated.

Now upon entering Idaho Springs, I could try to explain to you the depths of abnormality I thought the USA had reached: imagine the worst game show you've ever seen, the most horrible sitcom ever produced, the craziest true-life documentary ever committed to celluloid, put a slightly deranged but outwardly normal person such as me or yourself at the center, then shake it up like it was all in a snow globe (just to make sure it was super mixed-up) and then pretend like it was all very important. And you would have the next scene in Idaho Springs. On the left side of the highway squatted a high school football field, "Home of the Golddiggers" read a crude painted sign on a chain link fence that separated the highway from first downs and blocked punts. The high school band, in purple and gold, was spread across the snowy field and playing something that we could not hear because the windows were sealed tightly and the wind was blowing the notes the other way. On the south side of the highway where an old water wheel usually turned until freezing temperatures rendered it immobile under a chassis of ice, a giant hamburger revolved slowly.

"My, my, I think the hamburger is real," Willy said breathlessly, his nose smudged against the window. "Look at the size of those sesame seeds. And look at all the decorations. Eliason, you are bigger than Christmas."

I instantly felt like I had diarrhea. In the far end zone of the football field, up on a roughly hewn wooden platform with people in coats buzzing around them, two lucky youngsters, a quarterback and cheerleader perhaps, had been crowned for some sort of achievement. The royal couple looked distinctly chilly in their garb, but they also looked so damn happy and didn't even notice the car as we swept past; they would probably have joyous teen sex later that night in my honor. A horse and several dogs looked excited to be included in the events. Some goats, sheep, a couple of llamas and something else with dangerous-looking horns were set up in a petting tent with kids running amok. I saw booths set up and people selling caramel apples and hot cocoa and spiced cider and sticky popcorn balls and other Halloweeny things along with autumn carnival items. And the scene suddenly struck me with how sweet and quaint it all was. It looked completely spontaneous. The town probably had not had an autumn fair in a hundred years, and despite the wind threatening to tornado the whole scene away to Kansas, it was so specifically normal and beautiful. Families were bundled up and talking and patting each other on the back and breathing warmth into their hands and cupping their ears as more snowflakes from the west wound their way through the valley to the old mining town. The whole scene really did look like an etching from an old book of a place where you always wanted to live, of kids with fishing poles in the summer and sleds in the winter, a place with people whom you'd want as neighbors and city council members.

"Oh let them have caramel apples with a generous serving of seasonal goodness on the outside, coconut shavings for example, not just plain caramel," Willy said hopefully. "It looks just wonderful here," but the police kept shooing us through town. And then we reached the other side of Idaho Springs, maybe only half a mile down the highway.

The policemen kindly led us off the highway and into the parking lot of a Derfy Burger that had been completely renovated maybe three months earlier. At least twenty thousand people must have been milling about among the roller coaster rides going up and down and spinning with lights ducking in and out of the stiff steel skeleton, next to a huge slingshot-looking thing that launched little kids into the air and brought them back down with a boing, under a parachute drop upon which a fellow could lose his toupee, between puffy plastic slides full of air anchored down in the wind, and around some smug looking dude with honey bun earphones stuck to the side of his head in a disc jockey booth who was pumping out something loud and awful from speakers about the size of the Empire State Building. A neon red and yellow DerfiBird helicopter sat like a giant insect among ants in the parking lot. All the kids here seemed to be the owners of very bad complexions. We rolled to a stop in the middle of the crowd and a harried-looking man bundled over to the car. Ding Dong rolled down his window.

"You caught us a little off-guard," the man said. He was wearing a suit, and had a rock star earpiece stuck to his ear and a thin microphone cutting across his face to his mouth. He leaned through Ding Dong's window, across him (Ding had quickly reassembled his silly beard where it hung like moss from his cheeks) and held out his hand for me to shake. "You don't know how happy I am to see you. We were tracking you pretty well until you got to Eisenhower Tunnel and then the Colorado Department of Transportation wouldn't allow us to break into their closed-circuit TV monitors inside the tunnel. Oh don't worry, they will be made to pay for their wantonness. Then we lost you in the snow. What happened?"

"We thought it would be nice if he showed up at this Derfy Burger with friends, like a normal, everyday kind of guy would do," Ding Dong cut in.

The man quickly surveyed Ding Dong.

"We were going to give him a ride in our King Fred Burgermobile. It's a red and yellow humvee with hamburger hubcaps," he explained, "but better that you came with friends, Nye. Great idea. Less pretentious. Everybody loves a humble winner," he said with a business-like smile. He fake smiled past Ding Dong into the backseat, looking Little Ding up and down and held out his hand for Ding Dong to shake, his eyes still trained to the back seat. Perhaps he thought Willy was star material as well *[whatever Willy]*. He pulled his head out of the window but didn't seem to be looking at Ding Dong at all. "A fine afternoon to you. Name's Jerry Piper, marketing division of public affairs."

"Shaunessy McNutter, professional footballer, Sheffield Wednesday," Ding said, pulling back from the steering wheel and zealously pumping the man's hand. "This is my adopted nephew Nobby Styles-McNutter," and he motioned to the back seat. He was speaking with a strange accent, like this little cartoon Scottish guy in a kilt that used to do commercials for IckySticky scotch tape.

"Good afternoon Mr. McNutter, Mr. Styles-McNutter," the man said with a stretched smile, his head bobbing between window and headrest to get more personal views of Ding Dong and Little Ding.

Ding Dong glued on a smile of his own, saying, "And the nice, older white gentleman in the back seat was actually a woman two weeks ago, Miss Portia Sagoo. The operation in Trinidad—the city, not the country, in southern Colorado, the sex change capital of the world, do you know it?, a splendid town—anyway, the operation was a cracking success, to which you can bear testimony. We're taking her, sorry, him, to see his ex-husband in Soft Teat, Iowa. What are you called now, Portia?"

257

Snowshoe sort of squeaked at Ding, and turned a luminous pink. "I, I…"

"Oh no, I remember: Noel Lickbum. A pseudonym if I ever heard one, and a cracking good one at that," Ding said, winking at Mr. Piper. "He got it from English history. Very famous, Admiral Lickbum. You know him, I trust?" Ding asked, nodding at the man.

"I don't recall learning about an Admiral Lipbalm in my American history class," Jerry Piper said officially.

"Lickbum, man. And you wouldn't have, would you, because he's English. Jolly good, neither do I, remember a Lickbum that is. I'm Scottish, right? Don't know my English history too well neither, aye, Noel?"

"I, I…" stuttered Willy.

"Got to speak in voce alto with him, a bit hard of hearing," Ding Dong continued. "Footy accident in the terraces of Boothferry Park, grocery store end. Have to really yell at him. Aye Noel?"

By this time the man had trotted over to my door and opened it. Ding Dong had failed to notice, it seemed, that we were surrounded by thousands of people in the parking lot. Teenage girls were shrieking like I was a real-life member of Pro-Teen, and the crowd was closing in steadily. Jerry had his arms outspread as I lifted myself out of the car.

"Would've been a bigger crowd but the weather scared a lot of people away. Free pony rides up the street on the football field, too, at the country carnival," Jerry apologized. "But the people love you, Mr. Nye, love you." I was about to thank him, to correct him—it's Mr Derfy Burger thank you very much—when he tucked his head into the car. "You can come with us, Mr. McNutter, and your nephew too," then he shouted to the back seat, "For security purposes Mrs. Lip Balm, you'll need to stay in the car." Then he added as an afterthought, "Please report any suspicious behavior upon my return." He nodded quickly and slammed the door. I tapped on the window, held up three fingers and mouthed, "Three hamburgers?" Willy flipped me the bird. Piper promptly ignored the Bells completely and pulled me into the mass.

Once inside, I did the radio-TV-multi media gig, only the media people kept me longer this time, about two hours (probably because

Ding could not kidnap me this time). I did not see him or TJ the entire time I was being interviewed and was in the middle of "interacting live in the Private Pickle chat room" on the internet with some crippled kid in Buenos Aires when Jerry Piper tapped me on the shoulder and told me I was due at the Wadsworth Boulevard Derfy Burger in Wheat Ridge at seventeen-thirty hours, and "would you like to travel in the King Fred Burgermobile or experience a once-in-a-lifetime lift in the majestic DerfiBird?"

"Are there Gerbroni burgers in the majestic DerfiBird?" I asked.

"'Fraid not. Against FAA rules to have carrion in a non-winged flying means of transport," he informed me. Who knew?

"Oh," I said. "Maybe I can go with my friends."

"With Mr. McNutter?" he asked incredulously.

"With who?" I asked stupidly.

"With McNutter and Mr. Styles-McNutter and the other thingy," he clarified.

"Oh them," I said with a chuckle. "Of course. What other friends do I have?"

Piper glanced at the crowd of about eight million people now. "I don't know, sir. I may have to clear it through my chain of command, if you want to go with your friends."

"Where's your spunk, Piper? Are you not a self-made man?"

"I suppose it would be okay."

"I'll arrive like an everyday, normal kind of guy. Who goes to work in a helicopter or a private winged means of transport?"

"Not me, sir," Jerry said, almost looking for once like a normal person.

"Then I'll go with McNutter," I said. "Oh, I need real quick three Gerbroni burgers, a caramel-patchouli shake, some copasize fries and a box of those little cookies shaped like the French Friar." I had eaten about two hundred burgers during my interview, but I knew Willy would be famished.

"Sir, copasetic size, or 'copasize' fries are at Dippy Hippy Burger. We make our items supa-big. And Dippy Hippy has choco-patchouli shakes. We have only chocolate and other traditional flavors," Piper said under his breath.

"That's right, Piper," I said, like a boss would do.

"And sir, the handicapped kid in Argentina," he said, kind of in an official but admonishing way, "he's physically-challenged, not handicapped or impaired."

"God yes, Piper," I said, looking him up and down. "Hey, Jerry, do you know Leigh at the Silverthorne Derfy Burger?"

"Afraid not. Everyone behind the counter was an actor or model flown in from Los Angeles. They're on their way home already."

"Well Godspeed, Jerry. Godspeed."

I stood some distance from the car and signed about a billion autographs in the time Piper came back with Willy's bag o' goodstuff. He did the outspread arms Moses-thing for me while I threaded through the people. I did stop to sign a girl's chest with a marker. He said he would see me at seventeen thirty hours in Wheat Ridge. As I dropped into the car a gaggle of pubescent girls shrieked and bum-rushed me and Jerry. I regretfully pulled shut the door and handed Willy his food which he delicately ripped from my hand.

"They want into your knickers, they do," TJ said with some weird accent that I suspect, had I ever watched Public Broadcasting Service (PBS), would have been a wonderful rendition of some frocky man-about-town on Brideshead Revisited.

"They don't want me, at least they didn't an hour ago. They probably just want Willy's Gerbroni burgers."

"Oh, Gerbroni burgers," he said gleefully, diving into the bag.

"They don't want me. They want my fame and my burgers. But they don't want me," then I said something a little crazy, "and I don't want them."

"I'll take'em," TJ said.

"Save me a red-head," Willy said spearing five or six fries into his craw, his cheeks already puffy with bun and burger.

"Ding, we need to be in Wheat Ridge at seven-thirty," I said. The girls were rocking the car back and forth and would probably overturn it within minutes. Somehow the four of us were ignoring everything outside of the car, as if a thousand rabid girls physically moving the car, girls who had not yet passed fourteen summers and were smudging their foreheads and lips, hairless arms and budding nubs, sometimes entire rubbery bodies against the windows, was an everyday occurrence for us.

"They're barking," Teddy said. He had gone pirate for this adventure, sporting his straggly beard, an eye patch and some sort of red do-rag over his hair. "That's an adjective, William, for 'crazy' in traditional old English usage."

"Oh wonderful," Willy commented. "This one I will remember," he said, tapping the side of his nose with a finger draped in ketchup, which was transferred to his nostril.

"Willy, can I have some of your French Friar cookies? I feel my blood-sugar dropping," I asked. He managed to pry a hand from one of his burgers and pass me a single cookie, about the size of a quarter. "Here you go chieftain. In times of uncertainty, excitement or misery, food is your friend. Remember that and you will be a much happier man, like me."

"Thanks Portia," and I swallowed the cookie without tasting it.

"How are we going to get out of this one?" Ding asked, lowering his eye patch to give himself a more traditional two-eyed scan of the throbbing crowd surrounding the car.

"We just have to get to Boulder before the weekend."

"It's kind of far from here. Why do you have to go so far?"

"Because I want to go where no one knows me. Anyway, the doctors around here aren't as good as the ones in Boulder I think," Julia told me. She sighed and pursed her lips. "It's just all making me feel so crummy."

"Me too," I said. "I don't know what to feel anymore."

"Me neither baby, me neither," then she thought for a second then added, "but you should be feeling something."

It wasn't like I didn't feel anything; it was more like I couldn't feel anything.

"We're going to be alright," Julia told me.

CHAPTER TWENTY-ONE

"Look Before Entering....,
16.57 p.m. "

LOOK RIGHT BEFORE ENTERING HIGHWAY

Piper must have called in the National Guard because a bunch of dudes in Army-looking uniforms appeared from nowhere and began halving the crowd in front of the Monte Carlo. Ding Dong slowly rubbed the car's nose against people in the crowd as they dropped back in twos and threes, and finally we reached the edge of the parking lot. Unlike the parking lot, the street was practically without a soul as we emerged onto it with almost exhilarated relief. We passed over a raggedy Main Street with a few lonely-looking storefronts and found ourselves almost immediately merging onto the highway ramp, thus necessitating the sign to look right for cars on Main Street before hitting the highway.

LOOK RIGHT BEFORE ENTERING HIGHWAY

Now, do you think the wording on a highway sign could spark a philosophical debate in a car of four somewhat intelligent people who had just partaken in one of the world's weirdest mornings ever? If you answered "it shouldn't," then I bet you have never traveled with a guy with an English literature degree.

"Do you suppose," Willy began, snarfling his third burger in about two bites, "that the sign is directing us to look right, as opposed to looking left, before entering the highway, or is it advising us to look immediately before going, as in 'right before' entering the highway? Because I see that the burgerman is not following I shall use an example, por ejemplo: 'I brush my teeth *right before* going to bed."

I turned and stared at Willy in dumb amazement.

Ding Dong swiveled his head toward Willy's direction, letting the highway pull the car onto it more than Ding Dong directing it himself it seemed, and answered, "Perhaps it means 'look, right,' which I believe has no equivalent in American English. But you must add a comma and then finish the thought: 'Look, right, before entering the highway…make sure you know how to drive a bloody car.'"

"Oh, you might be on to something Theodore," Snowshoe said, snapping his fingers and wiping a brush line of ketchup from the bottom fringe of his mustache. "I reckon that the younger gen, an American teen particularly, would say, 'Look, like, before entering the highway, like, make sure you're all good and all.' Just for an example, though that example was a verbose example and might not fit on a highway sign."

"I think it must mean to look right, the opposite of left, before entering the highway," Little Ding offered. Snowshoe nodded.

"It would be mildly curious for the Colorado Department of Transportation to erect a sign telling us to look where we are going right before we go there because you do that anyway, right? Not to chisel the finest point on it, but you do not just stumble blindly into traffic and hope other people will avoid you, or that you will not hit someone else. That would be a ridiculous way to drive, and to extend the metaphor, of conducting your life."

"Um, Ding Dong," I quickly interrupted, "we have time to get to Wheat Ridge by seven thirty right? Jerry Piper said we needed to be at the Wadsworth Avenue Derfy Burger in Wheat Ridge by seven thirty for my next appearance. Do you know where Wadsworth Avenue is?"

"I do, dude," Willy said. "About twenty minutes ahead 'tis all, just wander lonely as a cloud straight up the highway," he giggled, looking self-satisfied. He shifted in his seat, the crumple of a burger wrapper cascading in my ears." 'Neither evil tongues, rash judgments, nor the sneers of selfish men, nor greetings where no kindness is, nor all the dreary intercourse of daily life, shall e'er prevail against us, or disturb our cheerful faith that all which we behold is full of blessings.'" *(That is Wordsworth, Willy, not Wadsworth, fool—ed.)*

"What the hell are you talking about?" Little Ding asked. Willy touched his nostril and winked. "What does intercourse have do to with anything right now?" Little Ding demanded.

"It's just a few lines from Tinturn Abbey," his father answered. Willy looked shocked and slightly dumbfounded at the man behind the wheel. "Wonderful stuff. Every English schoolboy has to learn a bit of poetry, doesn't he?" Ding explained. "From one William to another. Wonderful."

Willy blushed despite himself. "I do not take compliments very well," he said, grinning so wide and making that mustache dance like a happy caterpillar. I heard Little Ding start to speak, stop, then go ahead.

"I'm not a poet or anything, but do you guys think that the sign meant look 'right,' as in look good, look normal like you're *supposed* to look before entering the highway, like you don't want to go making people all nervous, looking like an idiot getting onto the highway, all zig-zagging and stuff. You know, look right—like 'Do these pants look right on me?'"

"Um, Willy, do you think we have enough time to make it to wherever that Derfy Burger is?" I asked.

Willy delicately placed two fingers to his lips, almost as if he was smoking without a cigarette, so as not to spout burger bits all over his lap as he spoke, his mouth two-thirds full of bread and meat.

"Not to ignore your theory, Theodore Junior, but Eliason," and he turned to me all dewy-eyed, "I cannot believe you are playing the game already."

I stared at Willy for clarity but he merely shrugged his shoulders.

"And what game am I playing exactly?"

"Oh Eliason," he said finitely, as if I had shot him through the spine with an arrow. He took an extra long drag on his shake through his red and yellow striped straw. "Think on it a while, chieftain."

I swiveled in my seat to face forward, my arms crossed, fingers scratching my ribs in annoyance. I just wanted my money, shut up and leave me alone already. The big green highway signs overhead pointed right (as in the opposite of left) to Denver and an odd exit that swung off to the left and under the westbound lanes of the highway led drivers to Golden and then Boulder.

"But do not think too long," Willy said urgently, then he tossed a super tragic, Hollywood riddled sigh my way. "Oh little buddy, how we become misled by the fruits of our non-labor."

"Okay," I said, watching one scene from my window peel itself away to be replaced by another scene and then another. Willy made a sound like a small animal being bitten by a slightly larger animal, then jumped over the back of the seat, cranked the wheel left and lunged us into the fast lane.

"What are you doing man!" Ding yelled.

"This exit," Willy howled, "this exit! This man has bigger fish to fry!" and we were almost sliced in two by the guard rail separating the turn-off from the rest of the highway as we jumped onto a two-lane state highway, slooped down a hill and bent a hard curve. Ding Dong slid into the first dirt area and allowed me to eat the windshield once more with a squeal of brakes.

"Willy, you do not, DO NOT, ever grab my steering wheel again! I'll kill you! Are you mad, man?!"

"Barking!" Willy barked.

Ding Dong angrily pulled the do-rag from his head and felt around for his fisherman's cap, squaring it on top of his skull. "What the hell are you doing!"

"This man," he cried, pointing a nubby finger at me, "has another agenda. He just needs help remembering what it is!"

"Well you had better begin helping me remember what it is!" Ding reared, yanking off his eye patch and tossing it on the seat between us. His old red eyeballs were back.

"Mama," Willy said softly.

"Your mama's not going to help you now," Ding growled.

"His mama," Willy said, jabbing me between the shoulder blade and spine. I instantly knew how it felt to have a spinal tap, thanks Willy.

"His mama's not going to help you either, William," Ding said, once more beginning the arduous task of pulling off his fake beard, his shoulders pulled up even higher in anger.

"His mama cannot even help herself," Willy said. The car became quiet, a self-conscious, embarrassing kind of quiet. I turned to glare at him.

"She's not a dang invalid, Snowshoe," I said. He looked at me sadly. "I mean, you make her sound like she's drooling all over herself or something. She's just got cancer."

"Hah, just cancer! Just cancer, he says," he said, tapping Ding Dong on the shoulder. "And Niagara is just a small cascade of water," then to finalize the matter he added my mother's official diagnosis as seen on endless medical charts in countless clinics in the greater Denver area: "His mother is in a bad way, a really really bad way."

"I thought she was really really *really* bad this morning," I mock corrected him. "She's making a recovery obviously."

"One should not be so glib about one's mother's health," he said.

"I think the burgerman man knows exactly how he feels," Teddy said, "and doesn't need to be told."

Willy was silent for a split second. "He has been invaded by the Derfy Industrial Complex. We have lost him already Theodore," he cried.

"Now you're making *me* sound like an invalid," I told him.

"Already he has forgotten about his mother, the prime reason we began this journey," Willy continued, as if I were not there, "and the boy's mother has not long to tread upon her own mortal path I must remind all within earshot."

"Gawd, just shut up Willy, please," I begged.

"And though young and old are not oft equally wise, it is oft young's innocence that—"

"Willy, please," I begged, "please. Please."

"Eliason, I only urge that we—"

"I know what you're urging."

"I am merely trying to save—"

"The burgerman needs no saving," Ding growled so forcefully that Willy instantly sewed up his lips and turned a little pale. "This man knows what he has to do."

"Oh only I wonder—" Willy began to wonder.

"I don't…" Teddy interrupted, notching up those red eyeballs one more level and beaming them toward Willy, "…wonder. This man knows what to do. Whether it is to stay or whether it is to go."

I turned to the Dong and he gave me a look, well, I wasn't sure how to read it. It was confident but halting, confidence in me, my character maybe, but trepidation in my decision-making. I held out my hand and he shook it seriously with the kind of nervous frown a dad gives his son who is leaving for a far-away college for the first time. I turned, pulled on the door handle and shouldered open the door.

"What?" I heard Willy ask in a kind of panic. "Where are you going, little chief? What do you mean, Theodore? You are not coming with?"

Willy looked about to cry. He tore me up sometimes, when he said things, dangling participles in his angst, like "coming with."

"William, I believe we're all on different agendas now. It's your chance to walk away now," and Teddy smiled weakly at both of us.

"But Theodore—" Willy began to insist.

"Out the door Willy," I interrupted, the door giving a metallic sort of crunch then whine like the opening jaws of some sort of future human-consuming space monster. The wind entered the car and moved around Willy's disused burger wrappers. "At least it's not snowing," I comforted him."

"But—" he insisted, though I interrupted him once again by shoving the seat forward and grabbing him by both lapels.

"Out!" I commanded, yanking upward.

"I must clean this mess," he said muffled, his mouth buried in his coat which I had hoisted up to his ears in my efforts to dislodge him. I heard Ding Dong chuckle.

"We'll get that William. TJ, why don't you slide up front."

Willy emerged from the car with a grunt, darting his hand back inside to grab his travel bag and then tugging unevenly on the bottom of his coat. He offered me a remonstrative look and a sigh.

"Time to move along, veteran plains drifter," I told him.

"My people were of the sedentary bent, I told you."

I watched TJ's head emerge from the car followed by his considerable bulk. I noticed for the first time that he was pretty tall and could be intimidating if necessary.

"My dad shouldn't have picked you two up," he said, directly at me with a scowl. "I know you'll probably go right to the cops."

"But you are our mates," Willy protested. I loved Willy sometimes: not our "friends" but our "mates." He put his hand up to TJ's chest and brushed back and forth delicately. It was an odd but endearing gesture. "I have an eye on Mr Derfy Burger. I will keep him directed on an honorable path. We will do the right thing."

"I know *you* will," he said at Willy, then scowled at me again. Just because a guy's got a million bucks doesn't make him all bad, does it? For a short while in the car I actually thought that TJ had started to like me, but I guess I was wrong.

Willy bent down with hands on knees and peered through the open door. "Theodore, are you sure you willn't accompany Eliason and me all the way to Boulder?"

And I'm not a gambling man or a frivolously generous one either, but I would have given half of my non-taxable earnings if Ding had said with disgust, "No way man, they kill their children there. Bad karma," but alas he didn't, he merely shook his head.

"Let's motor, chief," I said to Willy, because he liked when I spoke 1970s to him in times of emotional incertitude. Little Ding was standing in the wind with his arms crossed, waiting to get into the front seat, staring at the ground and mumbling to himself, "This is crazy. You guys are going straight to the cops, I know it."

What happened next was easily the most hilarious moment of a very unfunny day: Willy put his index finger under Little Ding's chin and lifted it upward, so that they could see eye to eye. I thought for a disgusted millisecond that Willy might try to kiss him.

"TJ, we are you mates and we *will* do the right thing." He then gave TJ the craziest bear hug you'd ever see between two unrelated men. Remember what I just said about the most hilarious moment of the day? Willy topped it by telling TJ in utter seriousness, "For you, may the plains be flat, the prairies fruitful, the rivers plentiful and the highways well-paved," and he held up three fingers in some weird Indian salute.

I swear to god Ding wiped away a tear as he tucked himself into the car. They began to roll away but after about fifteen yards, the car stopped. I was sure that they had had a change of heart and were going to shower bullets upon us. Little Ding rolled down his window and Willy powered over to him. I loped over as well.

"Keep this. Use it, don't lose it," TJ said, handing Willy a slip of paper with his cell phone number scribbled on it. Willy affectionately pawed his shoulder through the window.

"See you on the dark side, kid," I said. I'm such an idiot. He looked at me funny, rolled up his window, Teddy pulled the car into a U-turn and the Bells zoomed away.

Willy stood there silently, just watching the road where the Bells had disappeared, his back to me, travel bag down at his feet, hands on hips. Willy was a deep fellow so I, being of the shallower sort, *[Shut up Willy]* could only guess at one of the million thoughts on his mind and therefore took a stab at what must have been trying his soul.

"Willy, what exactly is 'assmeat?'"

"It simply fit the situation, which called for force, now shush," he said, without turning, and he began pacing the opposite way of the Bells' exit, walking toward Boulder. I estimated that we would arrive moccasin-style in approximately eleven days.

CHAPTER TWENTY-TWO

"The Metaphor of the Interdigitated Elk, 5:11 p.m."

Willy and I did not speak for about half an hour as we hitched through the canyon. We may as well have had our thumbs amputated for all the attention they were getting from friendly passing motorists. The wind had thankfully died down a little but the cold gusts off the river swirling over rocks and fallen trees on our right-hand side was making me shiver. The river was wide, at least thirty feet, and twisted alongside the road for ten miles. The road itself was dangerously curvy, tucking in and out of tunnels, and every here and there a pile of dirt kibble lay in the street as rocks that had dislodged themselves from the surrounding cliffs and smashed to bits on the surface. I knew at any moment a car would follow the laws of centripetal force, miss its curve and dash into Willy, poor fellow. I kept a safe couple of steps behind.

"Eliason, in not so many seconds I am going to have to attend to a call of the wild," Willy called over his shoulder, breaking into my thoughts of nothing. I skipped ahead to catch up and saw that he had his fist pressed into his sternum, the thumb digging into his right rib cage.

"Burger overload," he belched, looking around desperately. "Providence!" he exclaimed, quickening his pace to a shallow bend in the river about fifty yards ahead, where fairly sizeable boulders allowed white folk to easily cross to the other bank of wild brush and trees. "I am going in," he informed me at a trot now. From a distance I watched him stash his backpack behind a boulder, which he marked by scraping onto its face some sort of stick man playing a flute or something, then hug one rock after another until he had successfully forded the water, putting his toes down on terra firma with a full-body spin to face me across the river. Even from so many feet I could see his face flushed, his mouth panting but he gathered himself after a brief time and offered the heavens and me a sort of whoop-yelp-whee-whee with arms raised over his head. He was killing me. He scampered through some brush and ducked behind an abandoned wooden miner's shack not far from the water's edge. After about five minutes he came poking out again, his face still flushed.

"Hey Eliason, quit leaning against that rock formation and come check this out," he called to me across the water.

"I'm not coming to look at your turd," I called back.

"Don't be crude. Just come here. You simply have to see this."

"What is it?" I whined. "I thought I had deeper fish to fry."

"Bigger fish," he corrected, "now shut up and get over here."

I too hugged the series of precarious rocks, not as choreographed as Willy had, and pounced onto dry land with a triumphant smile.

"That was well done, little chief. You may have a future in the Indian business," Willy congratulated me, pulling me by the hand. I recoiled.

"Did you pack out?" I asked. He looked at me in confusion. "Jesus Willy, you've lived in Colorado for ever, you're an Indian for Christ sake and you don't know to put your stuff in a plastic bag and dispose of it properly?"

"That is just for camping, now silence," he demanded then added, after feeling my hand retracting into a fetal fist inside his own, "In case you are worried about hygiene, I swinkeled urine on my hands to clean them, which is the best method for on-site sterilization."

I snatched my hand away from his as we walked slowly ahead. Just behind the miner's shack lay a small meadow with a collection of stumps around its perimeter, another outer line of adult pines providing a welcoming calm away from the wind. What looked like the remains of a wagon, its rotted wood spearing skyward in every direction, sat in the middle, the rusted iron rim of a rotted wheel leaning against a nearby tree trunk. It was quiet and peaceful.

"I like it here," I whispered. "Can we stay?"

"You cannot even hear the road, just the gentle bubbling of old man river," Willy whispered back. I smiled at him. He motioned for me to follow him to the other side of the wagon. "Be careful over there," he pointed to the short distance, where I knew something fetid festered. We walked practically on tip-toes about fifteen feet away.

"I really like it here," I whispered. He nodded without turning then held up a palm to my chest, motioning to come to his side. He had his eyes trained to the bare grass. I followed his gaze.

"Are those bones?!" I whispered, aghast.

"A metaphor, for your new and exciting future," he whispered back.

There in the bare grass lay two sets of massive antlers, one pair much bigger than the other, along with two skulls and some scattered bones. When I bent down to look closer I could make out a spinal column, a thigh with a knobby knee joint attached, a shin bone with a hoof clinging to the bottom, and a mixed mass of skeleton that was in various states of disintegration. The bones had been bleached a luminous white and almost stripped clean, like an aspen limb floating in the currents of a lake and denuded to an ivory white by the waves.

"It appears that they died in a great intra-mammalian struggle," Willy whispered. "It seems they locked antlers and could not get undone and died side by side. I have never seen anything like it."

It was magnificent.

"It's kind of gross," I said quietly, noticing a tuft of fur that bristled with the leaves in a whisper of wind. Willy bent down on one knee beside me and the pile.

"You're not going to bless it or something are you?" I asked.

He looked disparagingly at me. "Do not be silly. The biologist in me wants to have a closer look. Look at the size of those molars, jiminy. The struggle of life and death occurred right here. It is beautiful."

"But they both died," I insisted.

"'Tis true, but they died nobly. They died fighting." I told him I was quite sure that they died trying to disentangle themselves. Willy disagreed: "You see how the smaller antlers jut up through the jawbone? Come closer and inspect, little chief. Do not be afraid to get a bit of dirt on your knee pads. There, you see? It is my hastily formed hypothesis that the littler fellow with his more dynamic and lower center of gravity speared from under the chin the bigger one, who died from traumatic brain injury or from extensive blood loss or even possibly from cleft and palette collapse, and the little guy dragged him a pretty good clip trying to break free but ultimately lay down in exhaustion to expire slowly, and I hope, peacefully," then he added thoughtfully, "I reckon.... Though his bones appear to be fairly twisted round and backwards, as if he struggled until he met his great antlered maker on his way to the elk Elysian Fields."

"You got all that from this pile of bones?" I asked doubtfully, ignoring two-thirds of what he said.

Willy nodded and pursed his lips and sighed, "He brought the bigger combatant down, which was probably more than an end for which he could have hoped." He stood with a grunt then picked his butt without any regard for my being right next to him, the result I was sure of using dried leaves and pine needles as a backside wiping device. "However, this is all creeping me out a little so let us repair to the road once more."

"But I like it here," I protested. "Can we stay just a bit longer?" but Willy was already shuffling through the meadow, glancing back momentarily to see if I was following. He disappeared behind the shack and I heard ouches and owws and dadgummits fading among the brush and through, what I would discover on the other side of the river as Willy rolled up his warm-up pant leg in grim heroism, a good-sized briar patch. I hugged the succession of boulders once again to reach the road-side of the river and looked back longingly at the peace and windlessness of the hidden meadow. Willy was staring at the road.

"I guess it was kind of creepy," I said. "I just wanted to, I don't know."

"Stay forever and enjoy the peace?" Willy said. "I understand, young chief in training. The good earth is the only sanctuary a poor man can afford."

"But I'm kind of a millionaire," I corrected him.

"Spiritually poor," he corrected me, bending down to gingerly roll up a pant leg. "Christ o' mighty, look at all these dadgum briars. Give us a hand, medicine man." I knelt beside his almost hairless shin.

"No, I do not shave my legs, and no more silly questions about my physiology," he told me. I pinched a single briar that was embedded in his few blond strands of hair like a fly in a spider's web and gave a hefty rip. Willy cried out.

"Leave it! I shall do it! Disperse." He pulled at another clump of hair, grimacing, then tenderly unfurled his warm-up pant leg down to his shoe. "I shall attend to these later," and he scooted to the clump of boulders by the water. "Little chief, dare I ask if you transported my travel bag to another place?"

"Jesus Willy, someone stole your bag?! You've got a gun in there."

He poked around for some time, mouthing things about the "vagaries of trust, the sacred bonds of leaving other people's stuff alone."

"But your little flute player dude is on those rocks," I informed him, shading my eyes and pointing to another cluster of boulders some thirty feet away. He looked to where I pointed and narrowed his eyes at the faintly white little flute player stick man scratched into the brown face.

"Gladly you have passed another test for which I have devised for you, young chief. A good Indian constantly takes mental snapshots of his immediate surroundings and if all appears uniform, breaks the stalks of nearby rushes, native grasses, etcetera to mark his whereabouts, for he may pass this land again after forty summers and need to identify his crossings. You have passed with high marks another test."

"You just forgot where you stuff was," I said. "Don't give me all that bull."

"Hush," he said, collecting his bag and shaking it to make sure of its contents. "It is all good," he told me, reaching inside and stirring things around like a lottery guy digging into his velvet bag to swish around the lucky ball with your number on it, pick it up, drop it, swish around some more and pull someone else's ball out. "My quick action is still here, ready to serve and to protect," he said, pulling out his pea-shooter and holding it aloft.

"Put that thing away," I fired. "You're going to accidentally shoot somebody."

He blushed and put the gun back inside. I stared at him, shaking my head, and told him to make sure the safety was on. He offered me a quizzical look.

"Oh Jesus, Willy, that thing has been on 'fire' this whole time? You don't even know that it's got a safety? You're going to kill somebody."

"Oh I am rather certain it has never held any bullets but one can never be certain. Do not fret needlessly young buck."

We began to pace the side of the road again. After about five minutes of watching Willy's thumb break the wind and listening to him identify certain igneous, cretaceous, subcutaneous and other prehistoric rock formations, I asked him what he had meant by saying that those old moose antlers were a metaphor for my life.

"Elk, little chief, not moose. I thought that mayhaps you had not been listening."

"I was listening, I just didn't care at that point."

"Interesting," Willy said.

"I mean, I cared, but, those bones were kind of freaking me out."

Willy ambled along. "Look at the wonderful weathering on that strata, equal parts wind strafing and water erosion. Very unusual for central Colorado. The metaphor, chieftain, pertains to you, the smaller elk, taking on the titan, Derfy Burger."

"But I'm not taking on Derfy Burger," I protested. "Ding Dong is. Why would I take on somebody who's going to give me a million bucks? And the little moose died anyway. I don't want to be the little moose."

"Elk," Willy corrected, hooking his arms behind his back, shaking his travel bag in thought with each step, pacing and stepping deliberately like a detective guy in a movie going over for the thousandth time the details in a murder case he just could not crack. "And could you take over on thumb duty, thank you very much. The idea is just the cotelydon in the embryo of a seed of an idea that I have not had time to fully water and fertilize, but the long and short of it is, perhaps you do not yet know that you are taking on Derfy Burger. I believe you may be the physical manifestation of Ding Dong's motives."

"Aren't the physical manifestations of Ding Dong his blowing up a bunch of Derfy Burgers today?"

"Okay, you are the spiritual manifestation of Ding Dong's motives. Little chief, the metaphor of the interdigitated elks is that you must not be ground down by the behemoth that we know as Derfy Burger, no matter how many promises they offer you, no matter what they ask of you, no matter the number of shiny coins and treaties they offer you. You must not let them kill what I know as the Great Spirit of Eliason Nye."

"The great spirit of Eliason Nye?" I asked doubtfully. I did not know about even the goodness of my spirit, the mediocrity of my spirit, nonetheless the greatness.

"It is a good spirit," he said nodding to himself, as if he needed convincing.

"I still think you're mixing me up with Ding Dong. You're mixing your metaphors," I insisted. Willy looked a little impressed, surprised that I knew what a metaphor was and how to mix them *[Get stuffed, Willy]*. I asked, "And what's going to happen when I'm not in Denver by seventeen thirty? Piper's going to kill me. Everyone's going to be waiting and I won't be there. I'm the worst Mr Derfy Burger ever."

Willy stopped. Just by his drooping frame I could tell he was exasperated. He looped his pack over one arm and turned to face me, waiting for me to catch up and putting both his paws on my shoulders. He sighed, looking down at my chest. "In not so many words, little chief, do not let the big elk drag you down." He turned heavily and started walking away, picking at his butt again.

My thumb must have been lucky because minutes later we were much further down the road in the back of a Land Rover, two frat boys with their backward baseball caps in the front seat, bikes on top of the cruiser after a weekend in the mountains. After not so many minutes and miles Willy pointed to the side of the road and thanked the boys, tugging me out of the Rover with such haste his pack became entangled in my feet.

"What the hell did you do that for?!" I yelled as their cloud of dust settled around us, watching like a cowboy (hands on hips, back slightly arched, toes pointed outward) as our best ride to Boulder sped away. "They were going all the way to Boulder."

"My bad," he said with no remorse.

"Well, how are we going to get there?"

"I don't know baby. Maybe you can borrow Willy's car."

"Maybe," I said, totally depressed. "What about Katy?" Katy was one of Julia's friends all the way from kindergarten. Her jeans were always too tight and she wore high heels every day, even in the snow, but I liked her anyway.

"Maybe," Julia sighed. "I asked her on Friday. She said she probably could take me but I haven't talked to her since. She told me to call on Wednesday so I guess I'll call her."

I knew what I needed to say: "Julia, I'll drive us even if it's in a donkey cart and I have to pull it half the way," but I said instead, "I don't even know what day it is."

"It's Tuesday, baby."

CHAPTER TWENTY-THREE

"Bacon Smalls Loves Howdy Boobs, 5:49 p.m. "

"I'm sorry, Eliason, I just could not take their 'music' anymore," Willy explained through the settling cloud of dust. "A bunch of whiney, probably upper-class white dudes shredding their adenoids and playing heavy metal-type music with an occasional bar or two of rapping? I'm sorry but my ability to ignore mediocrity gets less keen with each passing year. Ewww, jerky," he said, directing me to grab his satchel and floating over to a man selling jerky on the side of the road, leaving me to stand there looking stupid. The jerky seller was dressed in dirty overalls, long white beard, a ridiculously large and sweat-salted straw hat and looked about a billion years old. It is my own theory that anyone who has ever worn a straw hat, big, large or with flowers sticking out from the brim, as part of his/her daily wardrobe, as a serious item of dressage and not as part of some Halloween costume or just for gardening or something, is a total loon. He looked like an 1840s gold-rush miner, or a rendition of a gold-rush miner on the back of a cereal box, a pick-axe over one shoulder and a dewy-eyed burro by his knee, urging kids to use the map on the back of the box to find the treasure, a crummy little plastic thing, hidden inside the box.

"Hello sir, could I sample some of your habenero ostrich jerky?" I heard Willy asking after I grabbed his kit and sidled up to the two of them. The man grunted and held aloft in his even hand some weird-looking stuff.

"I don't usually give out samples of my ostrich jerky," he said in a broken chainsaw drawl. Willy took the piece deliberately and fingered it into his mouth like you see old farmers do with a plug of tobacco. He turned his back on the man and faced the river, his hands clasped behind his back. I continued to stand there stupidly, silently. After several minutes, Willy kindly faced me and the jerky man again.

"How about some peppered alligator?" he said, all ballsy. The man reached into a sealed plastic container in the bed of his truck and pulled out a wad of reptile. Willy took it from his palm like a pair of dice.

"I don't usually give out samples of my gator jerky," the man said. Willy turned his back again. I watched him in amazement. The man cocked a suspicious eyebrow at me. After some time, Willy turned again and ridiculously asked for antelope.

"I don't usually give out samples of my antelope," but he did ridiculously, to Willy, as he did with a pinch of venison, wild turkey and condor. Sometime between the caribou and rattlesnake, I, bored as hell standing there by myself, addressed the man. He had his ear pinned to a transistor radio with a white cracked plastic front that I swear he stole from my bedroom back in 1979.

"Been listening to the news all day?" I asked cool as hell.

"Nope. Got here at six-thirty this morning. Day started before then." He cocked another suspicious eyebrow my way. I shuffled my feet in the dirt. "Day's not all done yet neither."

Clever. "Anything interesting going on in the world?" I probed.

"Nope," he said, taking a quick look at Willy's back.

"No big story in the news today?"

"Nope," he said helpfully. This guy was a real barrel of laughing monkeys.

"Heard about that Derfy Burger guy?" I asked, hitching up my shoulders and kicking at more dirt.

"'Gettin' groovy, goin' trippy, feelin' derfy?'" the guy asked, recalling a slogan that Derfy's had used to great success during the years 1963-1967. I had seen the ads on the nostalgia channel between two terrible shows from the '60s that I accidentally began watching downstairs with Jimbo and Mrs. Baltusis one evening when Julia had parent-teacher conferences all night. I tried to push through the jerky man's lack of social skills.

"Guy won a million dollars for doing absolutely nothing," I said. Jerky man said nothing, he just looked tired. "Can you imagine that?"

"Nope," he mumbled, "lucky son of a bitch," and he eyed the river bank even more wearily as Willy the jerky machine was making his way over. "Million dollars'll ruin any regular guy's life."

Willy stopped in front of us. "I guess a little buffalo will suit me," Willy said with such entitlement it was baffling.

"I don't usually give out samples of my buffalo," the man reiterated to no effect at all.

"This will keep for three months?" Willy asked. The man shook his head and said, "two, max." Willy countered with a smile: "Wonderful. Gourmet." The jerky man stared back at him blankly. Willy turned to me.

"Four pounds of meat are needed to make one pound of jerky as twelve ounces of moisture are lost per pound in the drying process." At that, he offered his back again and rambled to the river bank.

"Your bud knows a lot about jerky," the man said with that damn eyebrow cocking all over the place.

"Believe me, it's new to me," I said.

He reached into a container and popped some meat into his craw.

I said, "So you think a million dollars would ruin a guy?" Gawd, I shouldn't have said anything because then the guy wouldn't stifle it. That's the problem with guys: at first they won't talk to you, then money or jerky comes up and they won't shut the hell up.

"Do I think a million dollars would ruin a guy? Hellyeah," he spat. "You got to kill some people, step over'em and knock'em down to make a million bucks. You can't just get it for nothing. You got to *make* a million so you know how to *spend* a million, you hear what I'm saying? A million dollars is evil. A man who makes over a million dollars is evil. There ain't enough good things in this world to spend a million dollars on so it'll make you evil. That's a guarantee, you know what I'm saying? You take a normal guy and he becomes really bad with a million dollars—really, really evil." I foolishly asked him why. "Because he don't know it's evil. You take some business typhoon, some hot shot big city guy and he knows it ain't right, sitting in an office one-hunerd and twenty hours a week, neglecting his kids and friends, probably hasn't made sexy with his wife for six years, but he'll do it, he'll sit in that office, because deep down he's evil, you know what I mean? He'll have a family just because he wants one, then he'll neglect them. He'll make friends just to use'em. He's designed to be evil so when he turns out to *be* evil, it ain't a surprise. But you take a normal guy like you or me and turn him bad? Oh feller, that's bad news, really bad. Because he had to go a lot further to get evil. He had to fight a lot of uncommon natural laws for what God gave him. It's like a priest fondling a child. You know what I mean?"

Yeah, I knew what it meant: this guy was completely nuts. Willy stumbled over, saturated in jerky I was sure. "Well hi, what are you two gentlemen discussing?"

"Nothing," the man said, eyebrows aloft again.

"You have some nice pemmican, sire," Willy said to the unsuspecting, still suspicious peddler. I cocked my own eyebrow at Willy's mentioning of a stranger's pemmican, and at calling him "sire." He put each finger tip to tip as he spoke.

"Africans called their jerky 'biltong' whilst Native Americans had several types of jerky, commonly mixed with berries and nuts. Yummy. The word 'jerky' is derived from the Spanish word 'charqui'—stressed on the second syllable of course." Of course. I noticed the man's eyes beginning to glaze over. "Do you use rib or sirloin cuts?" Willy asked.

"Maybe," the man replied. The poor fellow never could have suspected this kind of interrogation when he set up his tarp in the dark of morn eleven hours earlier.

"Loin or chuck?" Willy persisted rather rudely I thought.

"You know a lot about your jerky, fella," the man halfway growled. Snowshoe shrugged and pursed his lips so the man returned to his radio.

Pulling him to the side I whispered, "You have to buy *something* now that you ate half his stock."

"I am kind of full now," he whispered back. He looked a little green. "It is a little known jerky custom that if you ask for a sample of a seller's wares he must accept your offer, no matter how many samples you request."

"The guy's going to make jerky—sorry, char*qui*—out of us. Buy something," I demanded.

Willy cleared his throat. "Where is the beef?" The man hitched his thumb behind him, indicating the rear of his truck. Willy sounded brassy when he asked, "Do you have in your bountiful possession any papaya-sweetened Hawaiian?"

Jerkyman shook his head. "Teriyaki."

Willy hummed a little jerky tune to himself for several minutes. He was really busting the guy's balls. Pa-dee-pim-pum, a-pa-diddy-pom-pom. Some old country guy was singing through the radio about his girl being "so round, so firm, so fully-packed, yeah that's my gal. She can make my five o'clock shadow come round at one," or something weird like that, I swear to god. I noticed the jerky man staring hard at us.

"Ya'll renegades?" he asked from nowhere, cutting us with that stare.

"Pemmy-pum-pum, a-pom-pum. Renegades? Maybe," Willy said, crossing his arms and looking right through the jerky guy. I think the habenero pepper had fried Willy's brain. "Revolutionaries, perhaps. Have you ever heard of Javier Boeve?"

"Ya'll guys can't have my territory. I got a permit for this area, if you're sellers and what not."

"It is kosher. We are not sellers, just consumers," Willy assured him.

"Ya'll ain't renegades? Ya'll ain't here to steal my spot?"

"No way brother. We are just consumers."

"'Cause I already got to get here at six in the morning to beat some of the other guys, the riff-raff. I got a right to this area. I'm legal and ya'll ain't," he grumbled. This was Willy's fault, for agitating the poor fellow.

"We ain't, ahem, we are not sellers. We are just hitching to Boulder. His mama is not well," Willy said, nodding my way.

"You swear?" the man asked, both eyebrows cocked. He spat in the wind.

"Yes, she has been ill for some time."

"No, no," jerkyman said, putting his hands over his head in frustration. "I don't care about his ma, I mean I do care about his ma, but ya'll swear ya'll ain't sellers?"

"Scout's honor," Willy said, putting four fingers over his heart.

Jerky peddler turned to me, all fiery. "Why ain't you eaten any of my jerky, boy? You one of them vegan people?"

"No," I stuttered. "I just usually eat jerky in a wrapper, from the gas station or something, you know, just Derfy Jerky or something."

"Cow butts and lips and hoofs and tails!" he sneered, rearing back like a python. He looked so angry that Willy jumped in.

"It is criminal, I know. Hey friend, what is your name?"

"Bacon," he said shadily, looking over Willy's shoulder at the cars whizzing past, like he didn't care to divulge such top-secret information as his name. "Bacon Smalls."

I began to laugh but Willy elbowed me in the zyphoid process.

"Well I am called Arthur Lawrence Charlesworth and this here is my traveling companion Charles Arthur Lawrenceworth," Willy said, extending his hand. Bacon Smalls grumpily gave it a shake. "From where do you hail, Mr. Smalls?" The poor fellow looked at Willy like he had asked him something in Indo-Chinese. "Where are you from, sir?" Willy clarified.

"Oh," Bacon said, "well, I like to consider myself a Colorado native, but I was born in Monck's Corner, you know, in South Carolina. Moved out here from there about, oh let's see…" he said, looking to the sky like he was doing some pretty tricky higher arithmetic in his head, his lips counting over and over again for about five minutes until finally he said, "about three years ago."

I accidentally laughed aloud—a real native. He rolled an eyeball around in its socket at me. "What's your name again?"

"Um, what's my name again, Willy?" I stuttered.

"Arthur. Yours is Charles. I am Arthur, remember?" Willy said, widening his eyes at me.

"Boy don't know his own name? Ya'll trying to be funny?" Bacon asked, reaching into his front pants pocket slowly and pulling out a knife about the size of a saber-toothed tiger's fang. Willy watched him evenly. I could really kill Willy.

"I hate to reveal his family secret Mr. Smalls, seeing that we hardly know ye, but my friend here has just had a sex change operation. His former name was, erm, Betty Lichterbusch. He is not accustomed to his manly name yet. It takes some getting used to."

"Your name's Betty?" Bacon asked.

"I guess so," I said, glaring at Willy, a familiar knot tying up my vocal cords.

"I thought you looked kind of girlish," Bacon said, looking me up and down, tapping the knife's flat edge against his knee. It looked like the kind of knife, a big honker, whose end you could unscrew and there would be a little spinning compass on the end and enough room inside the hollow knife handle for some matches, some string, several topographical maps, a week's supply of food, and the body of a twenty-four year old white male if you hacked him up just right and packed him in real tightly.

"The operation was not a complete success," Willy said, keeping his eye on the blade. "He has a couple of more surgeries to go, poor fellow. A little more nipping where there was not much tucking to begin with," Willy said, gesturing to an area somewhat near my crotch. "And he is terrified of knives as a consequence."

"Well, ya'll are just lucky you didn't make fun of my name like most people do," Bacon warned, thumping the knife against his thigh, "but what can a guy named Betty say to a guy named Bacon?"

"Mr. Smalls, how can a genuine man ever make fun of a jerky pioneer such as yourself?" Willy said. Bacon looked at him skeptically.

"Well, that's probably true. You know, you know a lot about jerky for a regular guy," Bacon told him.

Willy inexplicably turned crimson. "We have a seller in Leadville. Great product, some of the best in the region."

I looked at him curiously. "We do?" I asked.

"You boys are from Leadville!" Bacon cut in excitedly, looking from Willy to me and back to Willy. "Are you kidding me? I love that town. Oh man, I love that town! Great people there, real nice and normal, like me," Bacon said, his fierce façade instantly melting away. "You must know the girl that sells jerky there then? Taffy Rogers? What a gal," he whistled through his teeth. "Great *product*? More like great legs. Hound dog she's good-lookin'. What great legs. We use the same distributor. Yep, she's real nice. Great legs."

"That is right, yes she has, hey Mr. Smalls, how 'bout a quarter pound of pepper beef," Willy said, still red in the face. He glanced quickly over at me. "Oh shoot, I must have left my wallet in Ding's car," he said, patting his butt, not too frantically I noticed. "Do you have any money, Eliason? Uh, Betty…Lichterbusch, Charles." Bacon was too busy fumbling around with plastic containers to notice anything odd about Willy while I tried to figure out why he looked so embarrassed. I fished out my wallet and told him I had exactly one dollar and fifty-three cents. Willy grabbed his bag from me and opened up his wallet.

"All I have is a twenty," he whispered, "but shush. Maybe he will not have change." He asked Bacon if a check was acceptable.

"No checks," he answered finally locating the pepper beef and siding next to Willy. "It's been real nice visiting with you fellows, seeing that you're not sellers and all and that you know Taffy," he said all gushy. "Yep, that gal in Leadville's mighty nice. Got a great pair of boobies that just jump up and say 'howdee!' I love'em."

"Boy she does," Willy murmured, blushing to a shiny crimson. "Boy she does."

"You get up to see her much? She's right up at the entrance to Climax Mine ain't she, with that little pink tent? I tell you, I'd be buying jerky every weekend if I lived closer to your parts, just to see her. You get to see her much?" He tucked the sealed plastic bag of jerky into Willy's hand.

Willy shrugged a little. "Occasionally. Mr. Smalls, you are a fine businessman. What do we owe you?"

"That's on the house of course. Any friend of Taffy's deserves the finest jerky in the land. What about you, pardner? You look a little slim around the gills," and from the same deep pocket that he produced his knife he dug out a length of stringy jerky with brownish fibers fringing its length. "Special batch right here," he said, flashing the knife through the air like some kind of French guy you would see in a movie about French guys from three centuries ago who always carried around swords and wore pointy shoes with heels, and he sawed the piece in half like an old piece of rope. Handing it to me he said, "I keep some right here," patting the pocket nestling next to his crotch, "right by my little boys. Keeps the meat warm and, kind of, what's the word I'm looking for?" he asked Willy.

"Pliable," Willy answered. Bacon said "uhhhhhh—"

"Buttery," Willy amended.

"Yep," Bacon said, fanning the designated strip at me then folding it into my hand. "Buttery." Indeed, it was warm and soft as tanned leather.

"Go ahead, Betty, tuck in," Willy grinned. I stood there effetely, handling the stuff like a small live animal, my gag-response beginning to kick in. Willy saved me, mercifully. "Mr. Smalls, you are a fine businessman, possibly one of the last trusty ones of our kind. Would you mind very much if we hitched from your spot?"

"Shoot no," Bacon beamed, "friends of Taffy. Eat up while you're waiting."

Willy and I dragged our bodies over to the road and stuck up our thumbs, though it seemed useless. My ears felt like they were about to fall off from the cold. Willy was being very pensive and after about five minutes I said, "Hey Bear?"

"Listening."

"How do you know so much about beef jerky?"

He looked to be blushing all over again and offered some clap-trap about knowledge being power and how good it is to be well-versed in as many subjects as possible, how it makes you more employable and simply better company at dinner parties.

"But beef jerky?" I asked, incredulous. Man, he was shining like a tomato.

"Hey Charles," Bacon called to us, "can you tell that gal in your crotch of the woods, Taffy, that Bacon Smalls sends his best. You must get to see her all the time, doggonnit."

Willy moved his hitching thumb to his side, as an a-okay to him, then moved it back again for a guy on a passing motorcycle. He hummed again, nervously—piddly-pa-pa-pum. We stood in silence about five minutes more, then a realization hit me.

"You dog," I said to Willy. He looked at me out of the side of his eyes. I quoted Bacon to him: "'If I lived closer to you I would be visiting her every weekend.' That's where you were disappearing to for an hour and a half every Saturday and Sunday last summer, leaving me alone during the busiest part of the day."

"I do not know the subject to which you are alluding in your crudest of manners."

"You were going to see howdy boobs, you dog."

Man, Willy looked to have had a maraschino cherry for a head, he was so red. "Jerky has been appreciated and consumed by our ancestors for hundreds of years. There is even mention of jerky in some ancient Egyptian Sanskrit."

"You dog."

"I was merely supporting a local artisan. She has fabulous honey-glazed trout."

"I bet she does," I grinned. "Willy, exactly how much were you spending on her?"

"I was not spending on her, but on jerky," he said, leveling his eyes at me and trying to sound condescending, but it was impossible. "Not much, about two hundred dollars."

"Two hundred dollars over the summer!" I shouted.

"No—a week," he peeped.

"A week?!" I shouted again.

"It is an addiction, Eliason—Betty—an addiction."

"What, going to see perky breasts every weekend? And it's Arthur. I can't believe you were—"

287

"It is the jerky, young buffalo slayer. The jerky is the addiction, not the wonderful, sun-tanned, smallish breasts of a mountain woman always dressed sans bra," he said, holding up a wedge of jerky and shaking it at me. I asked how he managed to eat two hundred dollar's worth of jerky every week.

"I did not," he said, looking slightly dyspeptic at the memory. "You may recall the 'buy a pair of snowshoes, get a half pound of jerky' promotion last September?"

"You said we were doing that because of the post-summer slow-down blues."

"Well," he said with a piffling little shrug my way. "You *did* notice a small spike in sales at the time and called it a brilliant marketing maneuver to help clear some inventory."

"I don't remember saying that."

"Eliason, I tried to eat all the jerky at first, but my iron count was astronomical. Plus, it was backing up the poop deck."

"Did you ever ask her out at least? Please tell me you did."

"That is not really my style, little chief."

"Jeez, Willy. You were spending eight hundred dollars a month on this chick and you didn't even ask her out?"

"I am shy," he said, thickly. "It is why I have a hard time looking for jobs as well." He hoisted his chin into the air, all uppity, like he had ever combed the classifieds for a job, for though I had only ever known Willy as the successful small-business entrepreneur that he is, I could not have known that Willy had held countless interesting, mind-expanding jobs after high school, before his incredible run in the snowshoeing industry. "She *is* ravishingly sexy though," Willy added to erase anyone's doubt.

Bacon paced over to us after a minute or two, pulling a couple of lawn chairs behind him in the dirt.

"Yep, she's sure nice," he said, propping open a chair into which Willy immediately dropped himself before the metal legs were completely straight. Bacon bent down to his knees with a groan louder than your grandpa bending over to tie his shoe from his rocker, grabbed the back leg firmly and wrenched the front leg forward, rocking Willy in the chair back and forth several times, a pile of pebbles and dirt scooping out of the ground and collecting along the edge of the metal connecting the two front legs, Bacon yelping in pain when his finger was pinched underneath, pulling it out and shaking it in the air, a couple more shifts against Willy's mass with his shoulder, and finally all the legs were straight. Bacon unbent himself with an ever louder groan, sucking on his finger and standing a good distance behind Willy.

"Now, you did not have to do that," Willy said with false, stern admonishment, looking over his shoulder at Bacon and putting his hands on his warm-up knees, patting them warmly then rubbing his kneecaps. "What a wonderful feeling to have a bit of a sit-down however. My knees were really crying out."

Bacon sauntered in front of us again, his finger wriggling out of his mouth. "You know, I got to ask you fellas in all honesty and what-not, why you didn't make fun of my name. You know, like most people say 'Bacon! Lemme guess, you were born in the morning while your mama was having breakfast. Bacon? Is your wife's name "and eggs?"' Har-har. Haven't heard that one a million times."

"We didn't make fun of you because you are a total loon, a dangerous loon with a big honkin' knife," I said to myself.

"We did not make fun of you, Mr. Smalls, because we are gentlemen," Willy said sternly. "And if my own dear Mum has taught me anything, it is this: never make fun of a man's name and never make fun of a man's dog. That advice has failed me never."

"I'll remember that for sure," Bacon said, sucking on that finger. "You're a smart feller, Charles, a real...real..." and he searched his lexicon for the proper and fitting adjective, "smart feller."

Willy smiled at Bacon, who went back to his jerky, thank you lord, after a customer pulled in and asked about his smoked ostrich. It was a business rich in unintended sexual innuendos, Bacon's jerky selling.

Pointing to the other lawn chair folded up and lying next to him in the dirt Willy said, "Grab a seat, little chief. Go on, take a load off," as if he had offered the same exhaustive courtesy that Bacon had shown him, doing me a big damn favor. He gave it a little nudge with his toe my way.

We sat all bundled up, hands buried in pockets, bodies as rigid and unrelenting as ice cubes, and watched the cars speeding past as the sunlight began to dwindle and more cars' headlamps started to illuminate the pockets of blackness with greater frequency. I hardly talked and just listened to Willy. "That's one hundred," Willy said at one point. "What time do you think it is?" he said at another. "Do motorcycles count as rides? If so, there goes ride number one-hundred and fifty exactly." After so many minutes the darkness began to settle around and in front of us though twilight was still resting atop the water behind us, its blue-light unimpeded by the hills and tunnels, dusting through the valley with the river. Bacon was quietly beginning to wrap up his gear. He came over again, sounding super sensitive.

"Man, it's getting a little dark isn't it? I'd like to give you boys a lift home but I don't live in Boulder you see." He spat somewhere through the twilight; I heard it hit the dirt with a sspudt. "Don't really like it there, too many smarty-pants type of people there. I live just a few miles away, the other way, right outside of Blackhawk."

"Good legalized gambling there, yes Mr. Smalls?" Willy asked.

"People getting rich every day. Everybody but me that is," Bacon said, "The wife only lets me play the nickel machines. Can't make nothing that way I tell her. She doesn't seem to mind not having nothing. Says she's happy. I don't know. Whoever knows what makes a woman happy." He didn't say more but stood behind us quietly, which was completely freaking me out because I couldn't see him. He probably wanted his chairs but it felt like a waitress hovering beside our table with the bill, making us leave before we wanted to so she could get another table of customers and up her tip count by a couple of more bucks. Bacon left us again for a long spell, preoccupied with a sudden steady stream of customers then with putting away tubs of jerky, disassembling the small tarp over his truck, bringing in his signs, spitting, scratching himself in rude places. Then almost magically he was at my right elbow.

"Holy heck Arthur, what have you done to Betty? It's all dark and all but, why are you crying Betty? Was the jerky too spicy for ya?"

"It is merely the wind, Mr. Smalls. Betty has very sensitive eyes."

"Well take my hanky."

"Oh dear," Willy gagged.

And a car fish-tailed into our area, kicking up a bit of dust, its tires practically coming to rest on our toes. Willy pulled up so quickly that he tumbled over backward in his chair with a heyarrrhhh. His feet were still skyward when I heard the car door crack open followed by the words "We didn't know if we'd ever find you. Hop in the back, gentlemen."

Oh god....

CHAPTER TWENTY-FOUR

"Saved by the Bells,
6:19 p.m."

"Do you think it is right?" Willy had asked me as we lounged in our lawn chairs by the roadside, my butt and hamstrings frozen to the metal edges right through my pants. Of course I had to ask him to clarify what was right or not because he had been talking non-stop and incessantly about things I can no longer recall, the overuse of cones, spheres and cubes in modern art, low-carb survival techniques of australopithecines, the life cycles of deciduous trees and conifers, for instance, counting cars one-hundred and eighty six, one-hundred and eighty seven, one-hundred and eighty eight....

"What Teddy Bell is doing naturally—is it right?"

"Of course it's not right," I said through my scarf, which had formed a sort of ice barrier through saliva sublimation between my mouth pressed against the material and the frigid air outside. Willy glanced over at me in surprise I think, that I was so quick with a definitive answer, and because I had not been talking at all since we sat down. I told him, "It's not right but what can you do if he's made his mind up? It's not really my place to interfere, just like it wasn't his place to make us stay in the car if we didn't want to."

"But you are Mr Derfy Burger," Willy said.

"So what. Why should I get in the guy's way if he thinks what he's doing is right, especially if he's a nut job? Anyway, it doesn't really have any effect on my life, does it?"

"But you are Mr Derfy Burger," he insisted. I shrugged as best as I could with my eight million layers of winter clothing. He was silent for the requisite number of moments in order for him to be able to sell the next item and also be able to appear, in my eyes at least, as self-righteous as possible. "What about the starving children of Africa? Do *they* concern you?"

"No," I said immediately, because I knew it would stifle him and he might not be able to muster enough gall to give me the requisite condescending glare. "So just shut the hell up about starving kids in Africa," I told him, and to really cut the thread of conversation completely I practiced the two-second pause rule and added afterward—two-second pause—"hippy."

I ignored Willy's puffings and hunched up my shoulders to try to keep some warmth inside my body from escaping to the cosmos, and scrunched my knees together, bouncing a little. My chair squeaked and creaked in the silence between Willy and me. I kind of felt bad for calling him a hippy and being a bit rough with him.

"Willy, I don't know if it's right. Who the hell knows what's right anymore? It's just that...Ding Dong feels like he has to do it, you know."

"I simply do not know if your average citizen would support his method. It is rather a Draconian approach to his problem."

"Well I kind of get the feeling that he doesn't care what anyone else thinks about his methods." I watched Willy watching the cars passing by, his lips quietly counting each one's passage: one-hundred-ninety-two, one-hundred-ninety-three. He sat there inside his thoughts in the spaces between fenders and bumpers.

"But to make such a statement, little chieftain, such an outward display of aggression, is he not asking for people to support him, or on the other hand to turn against him?"

"I guess so. I don't know."

"So he is forcing us to become concerned with everything that has happened to him, and consequently with anything that might happen to him in the future."

I felt the cold bite of the chair's metal licking the back of my legs, its arms my elbows, the back of it my shoulder blades. I didn't care at that point. I just wanted to be home in my bed, nice and warm.

"Man, I think he's just angry and wants to blow up some Derfy Burgers. It's like kicking a cat after your boss has yelled at you. You just do it out of anger or something. I don't think he's going to go running all over the place blabbing about what he did anyway."

"I would never kick a cat, nor a dog, nor any domesticated pet for that matter," Willy said, jutting a mittened finger in the air.

"I wouldn't either Willy, probably, but, sometimes you can get mad enough to do something you wouldn't normally do."

He sat there quietly again, thinking, then asked whether we should go to the police. I had thought about it many times between the moment Ding Dong stole me from the warm, million-dollar cradle of my Silverthorne Derfy Burger until the precise moment that Willy asked me whether we should go to the police, but I found that I didn't care anymore. I didn't care. In Ding's car I had convinced myself that at some point we should turn the two crooks in to the police, but that was when I was warm. I wasn't warm anymore and I didn't care anymore. Being cold has a funny way of making you not care about anything, except being warm again. I flippantly asked him what he thought. He piffed and piddled and did a little wiggle. The nylon straps of his chair squealed and threatened to rip themselves in half and splinter into oblivion. He said he didn't know. I told him it would not matter what we thought shortly after midnight, when the fireworks were set to go off, and it certainly would matter even less to me because I would soon be back in the arms of the Derfy Gestapo in the Wadsworth Derfy Burger. He then asked how deep I thought our involvement was.

"I'm no lawyer, Willy, but I suppose we're accomplices in a way."

"But we did not *do* anything," he whined, and you know when someone says "We didn't *do* anything" instead of just saying it plainly without any stress on any word, well then they are surely guilty. "All we did was get into his car. We merely requested a ride."

"Well, it's our choice now isn't it? Ding Dong said he was leaving it up to us whether we wanted to turn them in or not. The choice is still ours, isn't it?" I looked over at him but he was still staring straight ahead, too cold to move.

"The choice is like, totally ours. We don't have to listen to anyone else—not my parents, not anyone in town, nobody. *We're* the ones making the decision. Either way we'll be okay, I think. Won't we?"

I felt like diving into a hole and covering myself up, just resting there where no one would ever find me. "I don't know Julia. What do *you* think is best?"

"You know what I've probably decided to do but I need to know what you want, baby. Tell me what you want to do."

"*I'm* not turning them in," I answered. "No way. I just want people to leave me alone and I'll leave everyone else alone."

Willy stared across the road, in the distance, and languidly chewed on his jerky like a kid eating notebook paper in third grade.

"Ignorance of the law must count for something," he said. "Or should we just pretend that we did not know what they were doing? Yes, that is a better plan. Let us get our stories straight. Quick, chieftain, what kind of toothpaste did you use this morning?"

"What the hell are you talking about?" I snarfed through my scarf.

"We have to make our alibis watertight. There passed car number two hundred by the way. What toothpaste did you brush with this morning?"

"Dude, we only have to know that kind of stuff if we're gay and we want to live together in Europe and get married or something." He looked at me skeptically. I nodded several times to reassure him. I was also pretty sure that in my haste to avoid Dave the Drunk I had left my apartment without brushing my teeth at all. They were beginning to get that familiar rough, streaky feeling on the fronts and they felt all plaqued up with gook in between each tooth when I ran my tongue between them. My breath must have been something else. I continued watching about a million more cars go by, with people inside going about their business, pushing pedals and checking watches and thinking about the end of their days and journeys. I still didn't care. I told Willy that I personally thought Ding Dong was crazy for telling his plan to two total strangers and then leaving us, that we were bound to go straight to the police.

"But his father was always going to have a heart attack, was he not little chief?" Willy asked. "I do not know if you can blame Derfy's for all the tragedies that beset his family."

"Yeah, but they didn't help anything did they? Man, they put his whole family out of business. You can see Ding Dong's point in a way, can't you? You can see why a guy would get mad can't you?"

"Well, yes, but there is a difference between getting mad and taking things to the fringe of lunacy. What if he kills someone accidentally?"

"He's not going to kill anyone. He's got it all planned out."

"Fie to the well-laid plans of mice and men," Willy said, settling down deeper into his chair. "Perhaps Ding Dong will triumph after all, David versus Goliath, only to become king of the chosen people." Okay. "I just fear the collateral damage."

"By 'collateral damage' do you mean dead people?" I asked.

"In a former, more literal sense, yes."

"He's not going to kill anybody okay, so just quit worrying."

"So that my point may be known to future witnesses, do not go telling me that it is his choice to slaughter the innocent or not, you pragmatist," Willy said.

"Man, Willy, you're getting yourself all worked up over something that hasn't even happened. Just relax. All I know is I'm not going to tell anybody whether they can or can't do anything."

"Perhaps it is this laissez-faire approach that has landed us in such 'hot water.'"

"I think it is time for you to pipe down," I said and that immediately put the clamp right down on Willy. It was getting balls-unbearably freezing as the sun's last rays pulled themselves out of the canyon. I directed my empty thoughts to a sign across the river that said, "In case of flood, climb to safety." The sign depicted a stick-figure guy with an impossibly large, round head scrambling over some triangular-shaped boulders beneath him. The guy looked really panicky, although everything on the sign was made of the simplest, most rudimentary geometric shapes. Scrambling, fumbling, bumbling. I asked Willy if the river ever flooded. He didn't say anything. Now I was going to have to kiss his butt because I had been mean to him, and I usually preferred when he didn't speak at all, but I was bored as hell and cold and getting a little scared again about nothing I could pinpoint. I just felt nervous. "Hey silent warrior, what time do you think it is?"

I think he said through his scarf "It shall not work this time, chieftain," but who could make out any words filtered through that stupid muffler. I sighed, a nice big Hollywood one for him, which I never did but I was desperate.

"I'm going to go chill out with Bacon," I said. I saw Willy's head shift a little bit but he knew I was full of it and stayed motionless. I had to start thinking aloud now, which I also usually never did, but it was just to hear someone's voice. "Do you think it's seventeen thirty yet? It's got to be getting close. Yep, seventeen thirty's just around the bend and here I sit."

I heard all kinds of squeaking screws and bolts and nuts coming from the chair as Willy dissembled his gear, turning my way while tugging down his scarf and pulling up his hat so I could fully see his eyes.

"Chieftain, was that a subconscious linguistic slip?! Did you say seventeen thirty?"

"I don't know. I don't know, why?"

"There is a glacial difference between seven thirty and seventeen thirty, chieftain!"

I thought back to Idaho Springs. "I don't know. I'm pretty sure Jerry Piper said seventeen thirty but, it didn't make sense really. It just slipped out right now."

"Oh chieftain, how different would the result of Little Bighorn have been had General Custer collected his reserves at seventeen thirty, not seven thirty!"

"Willy, what the hell are you talking about? Be serious now."

"Oh I am serious as rain. That is military time for five thirty, of which we are well-past. Well well-past, not seven thirty. Derfy Incorporated must be scouring the Badlands for you. And I shall assume that they are none too happy about your second disappearance and absence."

"What the hell did he tell me military time for, I'm not some army wing nut. Dude Willy, Derfy's is going to kill me. They're going to strip me of my crown." I bolted right from the chair and began pacing next to the road, my hands crammed into my jacket pockets. I did several loops, Willy keeping his eyes warily on me like I was a honking poisonous spider in the corner of his bathroom that he just happened to notice while sitting down on his toilet with severe and time-consuming gastrointestinal distress. "I was going to be able to support all of us. Now they're going to take away my million dollars," I ranted.

"They will not, chieftain. *You* are Mr Derfy Burger."

"They will Willy. They'll find someone else. They destroy everybody's life. Look what they did to Ding Dong. You think they care about me?"

"Do not panic my boy. Sit, before you get hit by an errant car. Come here, sit. You are making me nervous. Come here now."

"We have to get to Wheat Ridge now before they take away my money!" I shouted, seized by a manic flash and running right up to the road. "I'm already late." Stepping into the road I began waving my arms over my head at an approaching car. "Stop! Stop!!"

"Chieftain, no!" Willy shouted, dislodging himself from the chair, which in a comic situation would have been hilarious because it remained glued to his body as he waddled himself my way, bent at the waist. "Sweet Jesus!"

A car, a big black car, a truck really that was impersonating a small eighteen-wheeler, not a truck at all but a beast that lumbered to get eight miles to the gallon, a sort of all-terrain army looking thing that was wider than it was tall rounded a corner and was heading straight at me as I stood in the middle of the road flagging my arms like a crazy maniac in a movie. The humvee thing swerved to the side where a sort of ramp that only a screenwriter could conjure up waited and the truck mounted it, went airborne and jumped right over me, taking my beanie with its muffler as I stood there paralyzed…or that is how I had pictured it in a snap second as a perfect Hollywood set-up. In real life, I stood there paralyzed and in retrospect, I realize that the car was nowhere near to hitting me and that I was more to the side of the road than in the middle of it but the guy honked anyway to mock me and Willy as we rolled around in the dirt after he gave a good wrench to my arm, which seemed to elongate and precede my body by several seconds, and smothered my scalp in the ground, the chair still wedged to his bottom and waving back and forth like a metronome above us.

"Get off me you big tub of goo," I exhaled, trying to gouge out his eyes. Willy was slightly heavier than I, and he was pushing the air right out of my lungs with his girth. His lack of balance had forced his face right against mine, the chair the highest part of our entanglement, and he could not upend himself into a more casual position.

"I shall, but only when you agree not to partake in such foolishly dramatic activities," he huffed, gulping for air, his chest moving up and down with labored breath against mine.

"We have to get to Wheat Ridge," I wheezed.

"There is nothing for it now, Eliason. We shall get there in good time," he wheezed, chomping at more air.

"You're sweating all over me. I can't breathe." He pulled in tighter. "I can feel your mustache on my cheek, you homo," I groaned.

"Promise me."

I found one last ounce of air and yelled "Yes, yes! I promise!" and he peeled his face from mine then slowly backed off me in reverse like the biggest, most awkward, reddest-cheeked snail with a mustache that you ever saw. I jumped up and dusted myself, angrily kicking some dirt at him.

"You crushed my vertebrae!" I cried. Willy silently wrenched the chair from his posterior, set it upright and lowered himself into it, pulling his hat down and scarf up again. He sat there breathing heavily and after half a minute pulled my empty chair a little closer to his, motioning for me to sit.

"No way you bully," I said. He gave me an accusatory scowl. "You didn't have to squash me," I scowled back.

He dusted off his arms and pointed to my chair again. I stood by it stubbornly, glancing back at Bacon, who had been putting his plastic tubs of pukey meat back in order and had missed the whole scene. Willy was just trying to save my life, and I knew it, but I had never wanted to be so close to another man, certainly not close enough to feel the bristles of his lady killer against my cheek. I was afraid that it might awaken some latent feelings that had lay dormant for much of my life *[Shut up Willy]* and I was at that time unwilling to address them. I sat down and put my head in my heads. Willy said nothing but I knew he was watching me. After several moments I felt his hand on my back, patting. I involuntarily jerked away but not so far that his hand lost contact and he continued patting absently.

"That million dollars was going to solve everything," I said on the cusp of tears. "Do you know that Willy?! Everything was going to be fixed. Now I'm back to nothing and Julia's going to leave me!" I could not stand to look him in the eye. "You don't know everything that's going on."

I felt Willy's hand stop patting, but he kept it on my back. He rubbed a couple of swirls on my coat then returned his hand to the armrest and sighed. I peeked over at him as he stared straight ahead. I could tell that he wanted to speak but he was not quite certain of how to arrange his words. He just stared straight ahead for how long, thirty seconds, ten minutes, thirty minutes then pulled down his scarf and looked at me, frowning, almost like he might cry himself.

"Little chieftain, you know that you are my only real friend in the world," he began. Was it a movie line or real time? I felt like bawling anyway. He stopped and inhaled. "My dear little chief, I know that Julia has traveled to Boulder to end the life that has been growing inside her."

I picked up my head and stared at him.

"'Tis true," he said softly.

And I just sat there staring at him, until he looked away, uncomfortable as hell. I might have spoken but I could not. I just sat there, facing him but not really looking at him. At some point I moved my body forward again to look at the panicked man fumbling over his rocks, until the sign became invisible in darkness, the headlights of passing cars illuminating his yellow background as they bent a curve then straightened out, bent another curve and disappeared around the next corner. I just sat there. And Willy just sat there. I knew Bacon must have been putting his things away and would come for his chairs soon. But I just sat there. And Willy just sat there and maybe fifty cars passed.

"It is not for me to judge you, Eliason," Willy said softly after maybe fifteen minutes had passed. I turned my head and stared at him again. Though my brain was empty, my feelings so flung far that I could not possibly have meant him any sort of malice, my eyes must have burned because he quickly looked away and breathed in heavily. Perhaps a thousand more cars passed.

"Do you have any gum, Willy?" I asked after some time.

He shook his head and we sat there silently again as more cars passed.

"How did you know?" I asked finally.

Willy took some seconds to collect himself before saying, almost nervously it seemed, "I have known for some time now, little chief, maybe two months. Or at least I have known from the time that Julia became certain." I stared at him with open mouth.

"Chieftain, she is as much my friend as yours." I could only turn away. "I suspect that she came to me because she thought that I might know what was going on in your head. I could only tell her that I did not know."

"You don't know anything," I lashed out, and he turned from me so hastily that I could have poked him with a burning rod and had the same effect. I knew that underneath his scarf his entire face must have been flushing red, that his stomach raw, his legs shaking. And I had never felt sorrier for anybody in my whole life. And I sat there in his anguish until I knew I wouldn't cry if I spoke.

"I couldn't go to anyone."

"You could have come to me little chieftain," he said without pause.

"Why would I go to you? What would you have said?"

"I would have said nothing. I would have just listened."

I heard Bacon fussing behind us, clearing his throat to get our attention but we ignored him.

"She kept coming to me and I kept chickening out," I said, and Willy had known the whole time. He had known for two months but he had kept it all in, waiting for me to say something but all I could talk about was my damn Uncle Matthew and other stupid stuff. "I guess she's done it then, a couple of days ago, Friday morning."

"Friday was only yesterday, little chief," Willy said. I did some quick calculating—could it be possible?

"God, it feels like five days ago, forever ago."

"'Tis true," Willy said softly.

I did not really feel like talking but someone else took over my speaking apparatus while I remained numb inside myself. "Are you sure you don't have any gum?" I asked. He shook his head again without even checking. I watched and listened to a car rumble by. "It seemed like a good solution two months ago, even last week," I said. "We're poor, Willy. How could we afford a kid?"

"Everyone becomes poor once they have a child, monetarily. No one can ever afford a kid."

"We just wanted to wait, until we both have really good jobs and are financially set."

"You can wait forever then. Chieftain, there is always going to be a better job out there and therefore always a better time to start a family." He wasn't helping anything at all. "Now you have a million dollars and you are right where you were three months ago."

I could have strangled him just for a piece of gum.

"I would give a million dollars to be in your situation, little chief, I mean before the whole Derfy Burger excitement, to be starting a family."

I had never pictured Willy as a married man, with children and dogs and dinner plates and summer vacations. Could he ever have wanted such things or did just the thought of them bring a certain romance to his imagination?

"You're only like forty or something Willy. It's not too late for you."

He didn't say anything, but I heard him swallow like he was forcing down a bit of dry toast, and his eyes got all squinty. I waited for him to say something but he never did.

"Do you think it's right, what we're doing, me and Julia?" I asked for no particular reason other than that I vaguely cared what Willy thought of me as a human being. Still he said nothing, he simply looked pained. "You think it's wrong then?"

I thought that he might never speak again. He jigsawed his pinky nail between his back teeth, fighting with some of Bacon's stringy jerky, and finally said, "Julia and I, not me and Julia," jigsawing a bit more. He looked at me briefly then stared straight ahead, sounding wooden, like he was reciting from an ancient Navajo text on sex education: "When the brave enters the squaw, sex has occurred. Life has begun. The first degree of the sacred circle has been drawn. Life has begun."

"Dude, you sound more like the Pope than Sitting Bull."

He shrugged. I asked if he really believed that baloney he just fed me.

He thought for a moment. "Spiritually, yes. Politically, no. Physically, maybe. It is what is written in the great book of the Havasu." I looked at him perplexed, and he added, "But you can fudge around with the syntax a little."

"So do you think it's wrong?"

"Who knows, little chief? It can be right or wrong for any particular person at any given second of his or her life. But it seems that the people who are the most certain that it is wrong are those who have never had to face it or will never have to, either through good planning or great luck. All I have ever been certain of is that some of the most sacred, concrete opinions that one holds usually turn to sand the instant that one finds oneself standing in quicksand. Having said that, however, I am glad my mamma did not do it."

"Why, was she going to?"

"Gosh, I do not think so, but she was very young when she had me." He stopped and was thinking to himself about what, I could never say and did not ask. "You should be happy that your own mama did not do it either. Where do you suppose you would be now?"

"Well I wouldn't very well know where I would be, would I? It's not like I'm super grateful to my parents for having me or something. I mean, it's nice here and everything but if I was never born, I wouldn't know any better would I?"

"But with whom would I be talking right now?"

"To yourself I suppose, and everyone would think you were a crazy nut."

"But I would never have gotten to know Eliason Nye. My life would be so different."

"Man, you probably would have met about a thousand other people. Maybe a girl. Your life would be a lot different, probably way better. Who knows?"

"Do not say such things, little chief."

"Oh don't start getting all Hollywood on me." He looked stung. I told him it was true, and that he knew it, logically. "It's like not having air-conditioning or something if you lived a thousand years ago. If you never had it, if some space alien from the future told you about it, you'd probably say 'Man that would be great, but it's not something I have is it? So go away.' All of these people I keep reading about telling me how wrong it is and that Julia and I are sinners or something, they can adopt our kid if Julia and I can't take care of it, if they want us to have it that bad. But they never will. They just talk."

"But there is nothing to adopt now, little chief."

"Well they wouldn't do it anyway would they, bunch of hypocrites. They say they would but they wouldn't, especially when they started feeling inconvenienced."

"Oh I must believe that some people would. I think you judge our kind too harshly."

"They're full of it, Willy. They just want to tell everyone what they can do with their lives so just shut up." I had read so much literature in the last three months I was sick of everyone on all sides. Willy looked hurt all over again. "I didn't mean you shut up, I meant everyone else who thinks they care or that it's somehow important to them, they can go to hell. What difference does it make to them?"

Willy pulled in a breath and discontinued his efforts to free the stubborn jerky from his molars. "Thank you for clarifying that it was I who need not shut up. Little chief," he sighed resolutely, "I think the only difference it would make is to Julia. I believe that you, as a man, can carry on as if only something slightly traumatic has happened, but to Julia, she will never be the same no matter how logical the solution seems right now. She may heal, a little bit, but there will always be a hole there that you can never fix."

I felt like he had kicked me in the head.

"I am not here to judge you, little chieftain, or to tell you what is right and wrong. I can only guess what may happen. I can only hope for the best."

It was then that I started to cry, whimpering almost, and felt the wind start to whip around me, bringing the first evening snowflakes with it from the west. It took only seconds for the warmth of the tears to turn cold and feel like little caterpillars tickling my cheeks and trickling into my scarf

"Holy heck Arthur, what have you done to Betty?" I heard Bacon ask. Almost magically he appeared at my right elbow. "It's dark and all but, why are you crying Betty? Was the jerky too spicy for ya?"

"It is merely the wind, Mr. Smalls. Betty has very sensitive eyes."

"Well take my hanky," Bacon said. It was too dark now to see but I heard the cloth unfolding with several crunches.

"Oh dear," Willy gagged.

And then came the Bells.

CHAPTER
TWENTY-FIVE

"Atop the Mesa,
6:36 p.m."

"To what twist of fate shall we attribute the pleasure of your company once more?" Willy asked in a state of high giddiness. We were both parked in the back seat of Teddy's car now, Willy replacing TJ's old place and I now in Willy's. It was a new and interesting perspective to see the back of the Bells' heads now. If at any point I needed to pull that gun, they were totally defenseless.

"The twist of a killer traffic jam on I-20," Teddy answered. "We had not made it very far up the road when everything came to a complete standstill. We heard on the radio that there was a roadblock set up to flush out this fellow," he said, nudging his head my way.

"Me?" I said meekly.

"Naturally. I guess you didn't arrive at the next Derfy's when you were meant to?"

I shook my head "no."

"And now everyone's getting nervous," Teddy said. "TJ and I thought it best to turn around so we took the next exit and came back, hoping that they didn't think to shut down this road." TJ was being very quiet as his father spoke.

"Just as I suspected little chief," Willy said kind of to himself, doing his television show detective thing again, thumbing his lower lip.

"Which exit did you utilize Theodore, so we can gauge how far the Derfy Mafioso have crawled our way."

Teddy could not recall but Little Ding tersely said he remembered seeing a sign for Buffalo Bill's grave. Willy clapped his palms together like an infant.

"Jolly right, did you see the buffaloes!? What majestic creatures. I often take that exit to sit and travel back in my mind to a time when game was bountiful and covered the plains with their numbers, the sound of hooves like distant thunder, the smell of—."

"Willy!" I interjected. He jumped several inches.

"Okay," he continued, adjusting his cap, "knowing the exit and its distance from Denver, well, I would say soon the Derfy crew will become wise and figure that we are not on the highway but in fact on this road. I would guess that the time shall soon come, and come very soon, when they seal the exit of this very road, for at the end a traveler can go either left to Boulder, straight to Golden or right to Denver."

"Do you mean right to Denver, as in immediately without going through the space in between, or they can turn right and will just be on the road to Denver?" TJ asked with a bit of a squawk, turning and laughing at Willy. I was relieved to see TJ back in spirits. I was still pretty sure that he didn't like me still.

"Oh well done, Theodore Junior," Willy said, again putting his hands together. "Perhaps they mean—"

"Don't start that silliness now. This is serious," Teddy growled. TJ immediately stopped laughing.

Willy cleared his throat and said, "Theodore, it is my humble opinion that you best 'put the pedal to the metal,'" and at that Ding Dong torpedoed out of the dirt lot and filed in behind an eco-friendly car with some kind of stream-lined, space age appendages over its back tires and what looked like two Q-tips bobbing just above the seats' headrests ahead of us.

"Oh Jesus, they must be close to a million years old. We'll never get out of here," Ding said, and to prove it, he almost killed us three times trying to pass on blind curves before he finally accepted our snail-like progress out of the canyon. "My god, it's not a school zone you bloody old man. At least pull to the side and let us be on our way," Teddy said, and the man pumped his brakes just to annoy him more, pump-pump. "I'll kill him. You're lucky you're an old geezer and I can't be rude to old geezers," he seethed. "You get eighty miles to the gallon not because you have a green car but because you drive so slowly you're practically going in reverse." Pump-pump. He took off his fisherman's cap and rubbed his head several times, slowly putting his cap back on.

"That is an interesting concept, Theodore," Willy said with a twist of his mustache. "Do you really suppose that if we drove in reverse everywhere we would use less petrol, as if we could fool our cars into thinking that we were not actually going anywhere, but perhaps back in time?" From my vantage I could see Ding's face, and Willy could not, which was probably fortunate because he looked murderous. Ding said nothing.

"Ding Dong, I think the worst thing is that I was supposed to be at that Derfy's in Wheat Ridge at five thirty, not seven thirty," I said.

"You're joking?" he said, looking at me in the rearview mirror. I shook my head.

"Bloody hell, no wonder they had the highway blocked off. They'll have the whole planet looking for you now."

"You can just drop us off again," I suggested. I had to admit that I was still a little frightened of both of them.

"I don't think that's a good plan Dad," TJ interjected. Ding nodded in agreement.

"No, really, you can drop us at a police station or something and just keep driving. Then everyone will know where I am." I received an even edgier silence than my previous idea. Suddenly the old geezer in front came to a complete stop.

"What the—!" Ding shouted, the car's tires offering a short squeal. He quickly rolled down the window and stuck out his head. "My god, there's a bloody mountain goat in the middle of the road! What kind of a god forsaken place—"

Willy excitedly jumped to the edge of his seat and stared out the window with a broad smile. Teddy just as quickly rolled up the window, popped open his door without a word, slammed it and began walking to the car ahead.

"I believe your Pop has gone barmy," Willy said to TJ.

"Maybe," he said sadly. "It's been a crazy day for him." He watched his father through the windshield and looked ready to cry.

"I imagine your plans have 'gone to pot' as well," Willy said sympathetically. TJ nodded at Willy.

"We decided that if we found you and Burger Man we'd take you to Boulder and knock out a Derfy's there. They've only got one that we know of," he shrugged, trying to sound nonchalant but he still sounded nervous to me.

"You are exactly right, Theodore Junior. Boulder is chock full of the hippy type and they do not look kindly upon these corporate who-do's. In fact there was a big hoo-hah several years ago when Boulder stymied a 900,000 square foot GigantaMegaDerfMart when they tried to move into town. But shortly after they turned down the GMDMart they had to relent to Derfy Inc. and ultimately allow a Derfy Burger. Oft times Derfy Inc. can resort to some strong-arm tactics but the good folks of Boulder held out as long as they could and proclaimed, 'Not in my backyard.' They have soul bro. Nimby," Willy finished.

"I hate those GMD commercials," TJ said. I silently agreed, except that I really, really hated GMD and its newest incessant ad campaign about "throwing in everything including the kitchen sink," a commercial which features a stoner-type dude with sticky-up hair, you know the kind of guy who looks like he has studied how to look disheveled, being led to the employee break room by a hapless, buttoned-up, bespectacled manager guy who points to the sink. You hear a ripping noise and next we see the stoner dude clutching a sack of goods in one hand and dragging the sink behind him through the parking lot with the other hand, bits of pipe and screws trailing behind him with each step. Willy the bastard dragged me into a damn GMD in Salida last winter and the commercial was on an endless loop on about fifty televisions with screens about the size of Zimbabwe in every section of the store. You might want to know why we were in a GMD, an hour from our home? Well, Willy had seen a coupon for a buy-twelve-get-one-free candle that smelled like freshly-baked apple pie, a bargain he could not pass up, which of course he purchased, but the candles were so big they barely fit into his backseat, and he's only burned about one-third of one of them because he's constantly hungry smelling it in his house. In fact, *he* smells like apple pie all the time now. But the thing that really gets me about GigantaMegaDerfMart is not the million televisions or the dollar bargain bins which are no bargain at all but pieces of junk, or the ability that GMD has of opening only one lane when the largest number of people are waiting in line to buy stuff. No, the worst thing about GigantaMegaDerfMart is the door to the snack/employee room, because it says "Team Members Only." Bastards. It doesn't say "Employees Only" or "Private" or "Sleeping, Drooling Employees Slowly Going Insane on 15-minute Break Inside"—it says "Team Members Only." I wanted to puke when I saw it. I suppose some rich CEO in the French Riviera considered the sign good for company morale, bastard, to be a member of a "TEAM," not just some schlump making minimum wage in a windowless, airless box that produces its own acid rain on humid days. Bastard. It was all I could talk about on the drive back home, so much so that Willy had to quiet me down and tell me to open my window for some non-freshly baked apple pie air.

"So you guys were just sitting there the whole time, not doing nothing?" I heard TJ ask Willy.

"We were conversating a little," Willy said with a serious wink my way, touching the side of his nose.

"'Conversating' about what?" TJ asked skeptically.

"Two scholars such as we?" Willy said sternly. "What did we *not* discuss should be the question."

"Okay, what did you *not* discuss?"

"We did not discuss the importance of having a good breakfast in order to start off your day right," Willy said, almost astonished by his wantonness. He absently stroked his belly.

"You guys didn't call anybody that whole time you were out there, not the cops or anybody?" TJ insisted.

"And how shall we have done that in the middle of a dirt lot, Theodore Junior?"

"Neither of you guys have cell phones?" he asked incredulously.

"The devil!" Willy spouted. "Those little creatures are rare where we come from, young pilgrim from the outlier of the technological age."

TJ shook his head in belief. At that point Ding Dong came back into view. The car in front of us began hedging forward cautiously.

"Damn goat," he said when he placed himself stolidly in the car, "and freezing out there," and with hardly a thought he goosed the engine, zipped to the right of the car ahead into a small turn-out and sped past, coming within feet of plunging us into the river before pulling left back onto the road and leaving the unsuspecting old couple to ponder the sudden appearance of a cranky old Monte Carlo shooting black acrid smoke at them. I felt my heart enlarge in my chest and tick about a thousand times in five seconds.

"Couldn't put up with that for much longer, could we?" he said satisfactorily. "What did I miss?"

"Nothing of consequence," Willy yawned and within ten minutes we finished our whipping through tunnels, hugging curves, sliding around bends, nipping around fallen rocks in the middle of the road and there looming ahead was the stoplight and our turn to Boulder.

"Hook a Louie at the intersection, Theodore," and though I fully expected a line four-deep of police cars, all with guns-drawn smokies at the ready to take us out, we passed through the light without notice.

"Eighteen miles to Boulder," Teddy said sounding relieved, reading aloud a sign on the side of the road. "Well that was easy."

"Too easy," TJ told him, sounding tense again, and before he could say more, the darkness inside the car was lit up by flashing red and blue lights. "I knew it!" he shouted. Ding Dong looked into the rearview mirror and pulled those tension shoulders up again. He wordlessly pointed to the glove box and TJ began riffing through a clear plastic bag of what appeared to be driver's licenses. Ding told him not to forget the insurance papers.

"Where do you want to be from, Dad?" TJ asked quickly, holding up the assortment of licenses in the flashing lights in order to read their fronts. Ding Dong told him to grab the one on top.

"Here's one from Wyoming," TJ said sounding nervous as hell. "At least it's close by. Okay, you are, I can't read it," and he squinted at the license, holding it close to his eyes, "Ambrose Lang—Lang something? You have a beard in this one though, Dad."

"Oh Ambrose Langley. A lovely run in 1909. If not for goal differential we wouldn't find ourselves in such a predicament still, the only club never to have been in the top flight," Ding said lazily, shaking his head. "Damn Hull City."

Willy asked "Whom? Who was running—" but Ding said "Never mind that now," and he began hastily assembling his silly beard, which was mangy and forlorn after so many applications and untanglings. Willy tapped him daintily on the shoulder.

"Maybe you should forgo the beard, Theodore. It is not very convincing. Perhaps you can tell the officer that you just shaved."

"I think that's a good idea William," Ding Dong said, slowly pulling over to the side of the road and turning off the engine. "Now don't do anything that you'll regret, please. We are all still in control of this situation if we work as a team. Are you in Burger Man?" he asked, turning fully to face me. I nodded, probably unconvincingly because he stared at me for about ten seconds then said, "Right. Okay Ding, give me the stuff. What's my name again?"

"Amley Lang something," he stuttered. "Angley. I'll just call you Uncle A or something. I don't know about him though, Dad," and I thought he wagged his head my way but could not be sure.

"Don't worry about such things now," his father reassured him and I turned my head just enough to see the cop ambling over and within seconds he was tapping on the window with the butt of his flashlight like cops always do. When Ding rolled down the window, he shined the flashlight one by one in each of our faces with that look of perplexed authority that cops have when they shine their flashlight in your eyes. I thought he would call me out for sure and I could get out of that damn car and be on my way but when Ding Dong asked what the problem was, the policeman merely nodded to the rear of the car—he was not a very chatty fellow and seemed distracted by the fake license. He said nothing, he only turned and headed back to his car.

"Okay then," Ding said to himself, cranked the engine, and pasted the gas pedal to the floorboard, spitting up gravel and dust just like a gangster in a movie.

"Theodore, do you think this is a good idea," Snowshoe called from my shoulder, the sudden g-force twisting him and gluing him to my arm. I gave my arm a sharp hook upwards, not yet ready to feel the familiar brush of his nose bristles on my skin again.

"Perhaps not a great idea, but a good one—the car isn't mine," he calmly informed us. "One of my mates in jail provided me with this little beauty. Young TJ and I didn't wish to use our own car in case something went awry and we had to make a break for it. Deception, gentlemen, deception. Hold tight," and he sped through a red light and hooked a right off the road onto a dirt track. "This looks acceptable," he said as if picking out a blueberry muffin in a coffee house and barely hesitated as he barged through a wooden gate barring drivers from a single-lane dirt road that snaked behind a newly-built subdivision and twisted up the side of a vast mesa. "I always wanted to do that," he smiled, re-enacting crashing through the wood fence by pulling forward against the steering wheel then smashing himself back into his seat, saying "crr-aaasshhhh." TJ flung himself backwards, hitching himself up a little to see out the back window. "I don't see the cop anywhere, Dad."

"Of course not. He's looking for Ambrose Langley, he is."

"And where'd that cop come from?!" TJ shouted at me.

"Junior, relax! Sit," Ding Dong ordered, pulling TJ down by the seat of his pants. He scowled and twisted around.

Willy said, "Perhaps I am not qualified to offer an opinion at this moment, but I feel a little nervous about this course of action. That police officer appeared rather gruff."

"Maybe we should have just turned ourselves in," I added tentatively, keeping my eyes on TJ as Ding Dong turned off the headlights to conceal ourselves in total darkness. I noticed the silhouette of the back of TJ's head turn into his profile then his face as he looked at me, but where his eyes should have been were only black depressions. "Maybe that cop was just doing some sort of routine check or something and would let us go," I said.

"I doubt it, burger man. You see, my mate in the cell next to mine, Johnny Shoes, set me up with his car. He's been out of jail for about two years, like me, but I think he probably slips into his old ways fairly easily."

"'Johnny Shoes'—a moniker no doubt," Willy educated us. "Wonderfully catchy. And for committing what crime was 'Mr. Shoes' in 'the big house?'"

"Grand theft auto," Ding replied as we hit a bump, in the dark, at a pretty high speed, all four tires losing communication with the earth so we almost sailed off the side of the mountain, "so not only would my license come up bad, the car would too. I think you understand," and we hit a dip that threatened to disembowel the entire chassis of the car.

"Mayhaps slowing down would be a phenomenal idea," Willy said, tapping Ding on his shoulder.

"I think I'll slow down now," Teddy said courteously, and after about ten minutes of picking our way along the course in total blackness we found ourselves atop the mesa. He pulled up right to the edge so that far below we could just make out the lights of the houses, orange street lamps, a bright pool of white light from a gas station, the faint whizzing blue and red lights of the police car. We all got out of the car although it was rather nippy so high up. Ding Dong and Little Ding went a short distance away and had a muffled conversation among themselves.

"A million stars," Snowshoe whispered, tilting his neck skyward. It was beautiful atop the mesa: flat and vast, so big we couldn't see the other edges, only the one which we were facing. It was like a giant, fat-stemmed mushroom that mysteriously sprouted out of the fields of Golden. To the east, a billion yellow lights of the suburbs of Denver spread out and sparkled silently below us; on the southern edge, small and colorful like children's toys, the skyscrapers of downtown Denver jutted out of the jumbled glittery mass. Scattered dots in the sky sailed without sound overhead and aimed themselves to and away from the airport way out in a vast emptiness of darkness. The stars overhead would soon be hiding behind a patchy clutch of clouds, the western storm stuffed with snow and following us all day, was roiling down from the mountains and getting ready to puff its way over the plains.

"This mesa feels very sacred," Snowshoe continued whispering. Then he said in a hushed tone, pointing to a smaller pocket of sparkling jewels to our right, "There is Boulder. There are your mother and Julia."

"Yeah," I said, squelching something in my throat. "Hey Snowshoe?"

"Listening."

"Ding Dong and TJ seem kind of suspicious about something."

Willy turned a little my way and looked concerned but he didn't say anything.

"I don't know what it is, it just seems like they seem nervous about something, especially TJ. He keeps looking at me like he expects me to confess something. You heard him yell at me."

"Oh I do not know, little chief."

"I think he thinks we went to the cops or something. I don't think he likes me anyway. He never did."

Willy crossed his arms and looked over at the dark shapes of the Bells in the distance. "Well, that is simply your low self-esteem surfacing once more. This seems hardly the time for a psychotherapy session, little chieftain."

"I'm not trying to psychoanalyze myself. I just thing we need to watch them closer."

"More closely," Willy corrected. "I shall keep my eagle eye trained upon them," he assured me, but I couldn't tell if he was making fun. "However, shush, because they are coming our way again."

Ding Dong gruffly ordered us back into the car and I shot a look Willy's way; he touched the side of his nose and narrowed his eyes at me.

"It's nice on top of this little mountain, but it looks as if the policeman's reinforcements are arriving below," Teddy informed us.

"Theodore, actually this is a mesa, an isolated, relatively flat-topped natural elevation more extensive than a butte but less so than a plateau. It is Spanish for 'table.'"

"Well who knew?" Ding chuckled. Willy touched the side of his nose at me again then asked how we would get off the mesa without running into the "smokies" down below.

"Well, my granddad always used to say 'if there's a way up the front, there's always a way down the back.'"

"I hope you're right Dad," TJ said nervous as hell. Willy quickly glanced at me and just as quickly touched the side of his nose my way and we jumped into the back seat after Ding Dong said "On your bikes then."

Fortunately a road did lead off the back side of the mesa, which we followed without headlights once more and after fifteen bumpy minutes we reached the bottom, our moods improving with each foot that we traveled undetected on the flattened, dirt road. TJ mocked Willy.

"A mesa is a relatively flat natural elevation—" but he stopped short as the white silhouette of a truck shifted into focus out of the dark. Ding Dong turned on the headlamps and gave the truck a nice bath of light, the bulking machine spread right across the road. It had bright red flames painted from tip to tail and the windows were all fogged.

"It appears that a cowboy may be inside 'gettin' lucky.' Dig the bumper sticker," Willy said. I forced my eyes to read "City boyz suck." I could only imagine the monster inside. TJ let out a little squeal and "Dad, don't!" when Ding Dong flashed his brights a couple of times. Nothing. He tooted the horn shortly. "Dad!" but still nothing. He tooted longer, rudely, which effected jerky silhouetted movement through the window.

"We're dead. Guys in trucks always have guns."

The driver-side door flew open and you know how cowboys look when they're angry—they grab the sides of their belt buckle with both hands and walk on the heels of their boots. He was tall and skinny and I could see that he was saying the "f" word and looked ornery enough to wrassle an ostrich to the mud. He was wearing just a white t-shirt despite the cold. Ding Dong instructed Willy and me to duck down below the seat.

"If this hillbilly is ever a witness, he'll throw everybody off if he swears he just saw two handsome black men in the car," Ding said. I immediately hit the deck and could hear Willy struggling to fold his flubby body in half, which I pointed out to him cruelly. He was grunting like a wounded camel and Ding Dong told him to try to breathe a little less asthmatically. Ding rolled down the window.

"I'm sorry sir, but—" he began, but the cowboy cut him short. By the sound of his voice and from his previous appearance, I'd say he was about nineteen. Ding could take him in a second.

"Just what do you think ya'll are doing?" he asked. I couldn't see him but he sounded like he was keeping his distance a couple of feet from the car.

"I'm sorry sir, but the only way out—"Ding started.

"Don't care, don't care. Ya'll know ya'll are trespassing? Ya'll know this is private property?" the boy who liked cows asked. He was starting to annoy me, as was Willy's travel bag, which he had flung over to my side of the floor to make room for himself and was poking me in the scrotum. "What were ya'll doing up there?"

"Actually, I was just showing my boy here where he was conceived." Teddy was speaking in some sort of weird accent that I suppose he thought sounded southern American. Little Ding leaned across his father and said, "Howdy."

The cowboy was silent for a moment. "Ya'll trying to be funny?" he asked. He reminded me a little of Bacon Smalls.

"I kid you not. Now we'd like to be on our way, we're fixing to go on a fishing trip tomorrow, but your truck is in the road," Ding said, pointing through the windshield. The cowboy asked him why they didn't go down the other way.

"We wanted to see this side of the mesa naturally," Ding told him.

"The what?"

"This isolated, relatively flat-topped natural elevation more extensive than a butte but less so than a plateau. It's Spanish for 'table.'"

There was a long moment of silence. "Oh." Then I heard a girl's voice calling from the truck. "Uh, just a second," he said, then yelled, "What!?" He paused and yelled "What?!" again. At that point, from my vantage on the floor, I could see the top of the mesa where tiny flashing blue and red lights appeared to be heading down the back exit. I nudged Willy, who was conducting a major battle keeping compact. He squeaked upon seeing the lights.

"What!?" the cowboy yelled again. I could hear the girl's shrill voice cutting through the wind but couldn't make out what she was saying. "Ya'll wait right here," and I heard his boots on the dirt as Ding rolled up the window.

"I am dying. My knees are exploding," Willy wheezed, involuntarily unpacking himself like an origami rose. Ding Dong pushed down on Willy's skull and told him it would be more difficult to fold his body up again.

"My belly," Willy groaned. He sounded funny all contorted, so it sounded like he said "mah bellah."

"Mama, mah bellah feels funnah," I simpered. "Ah got da biggest bellah in Mississipuh." Willy tried to sock me in the kisser but he could barely unfold his fat arm so it was more like a love tap. It still kind of hurt though, the bastard, where he scratched me with a bit of fingernail.

"Ding, did you notice the headlights coming down the hill?" I struggled to say, all folded up as well, glaring at Willy.

"Yes. Now you two keep down, he's coming back." He rolled the window down again.

"Howdy," the cowboy said. The Bells did not say anything. "Uh, my girl wanted you two to know that we were just making out. We weren't doing it or nothing."

The Bells still said nothing. I could hear boots shuffling in the dirt.

"She wanted me to apologize if I was rude, too."

Still the Bells said nothing.

"Goddam it's cold," he said with a nervous laugh. Still the Bells offered only silence. They were really busting the guy's balls. "Uh, when you fellows were up there, was it romantic and sexy and all?"

then he quickly added, "I mean, not for you two, but for a guy and his girl?"

Ding Dong smacked his lips and said, "Like Dolly Parton in a push-up bra."

I could actually *hear* the cowboy smile. Little Ding said, "Feller, I was conceived up there. That's how romantic sexy it is."

I heard the cowboy slap his hands and then rub them together like someone anticipating something good.

"Hey, you fellows are awful nice," he said. The car lights were about halfway down now, disappearing periodically behind the switchbacks. "Ya'll just wait. I'll back up and you fellows go on by," then he said in aside, "Maybe I'll work on making a baby up there myself."

"Well god bless and good luck," Ding said, and I heard the cowboy say thanks as he turned to go. Ding Dong beckoned him back. "There were two white men up there, a younger and an older one. Keep an eye out for them. I think they're of the wrong sort, if you know what I mean. They're still up there. If you see any cops come by tell them there was improper man love happening on the mesa."

"You know, I think I saw those guys on a motorcycle, wearing them leather biker hats and mustaches?" cowboy said in surprise. Ding nodded his head vigorously. "Hell yeah I'll tell the cops, if I don't kick their ass myself," and I heard his boots scampering off. Ding put the car into drive, finally, gave the truck a last friendly toot as we passed by and we zoomed away. Willy began the difficult process of disentangling himself with a series of whimpers, begging for mercy and pleading for a quick and painless demise.

"Craig is going to hear about this," he huffed my way then explained to the Bells. "He is my weekend tai chi instructor. I am, however, about as limber as a paint stirrer, even after three sessions. You know, Eliason, I always suspected that Craig was not a fully-trained tai chi master. Mine eyes have seen the glory of his diploma on the wall, and it always appeared rather counterfeit, homemade."

"Smoky told me Craig made it on his computer—wanted to try out his new printer," I said, grimacing as I untucked my right knee from behind my left ear and settled into the backseat again. "He's got another one hanging in the bathroom saying he's got a PhD in female anatomy from Smoky Mountain University or something. It's pretty real looking."

"That huckster," Willy chuckled. "What a charlatan. Well I will certainly be getting my twelve dollars and seventy five cents back. I really thought I had been loosening up lately, dadgummit. Oh the power of the mind."

"Do you think we lost the cops, Ding?" I asked.

"I daresay we have," he answered then looked at Willy in the rearview mirror. "He seemed to come from out of nowhere, didn't he, that policeman?"

"Scared the dickens out of me," Willy told him, lifting his Farto! cap from his head and fake mopping his brow in relief.

"Almost like he had been informed," Teddy said to him.

"Almost," Willy said and shifted a little in his seat. "Well I am quite certain that Derfy's has been scanning the entire area for the burgerman. He is already late to his next 'gig.' I am surprised that they have not sent the Derfy Chopper out for us."

"It's the majestic DerfiBird," I told him. "They wanted me to fly in it to Wheat Ridge." I heard TJ blow some air out of his mouth to show his disgust.

"I just don't know where that policeman came from," Teddy said, tugging on that earring loop, rubbing it between his thumb and pointer finger like he was shining an old penny. "He didn't seem to recognize the burgerman, so he wasn't acting on a tip from Derfy's but instead from a concerned citizen." He stared at Willy in the rearview mirror, completely ignoring me.

"Well Theodore, you do not think," and he looked over at me with huge eyes then back to the front seat, "you do not think that we tattled on you?"

"How can a man know anymore?" Teddy said as be bottomed out in a huge pothole with the sound of metal scraping dirt. We crept along in silence for some minutes. Willy glanced over at me. He nodded at his travel bag then, with hands in his lap, made a representation of a gun with his fingers. I shook my head vigorously—not that again.

"You have fleas in your ears, burgerman?" Ding asked me.

"No Ding, I was just—" but I couldn't even come up with a good lie and just motioned a limp shrug at him. He had been looking at me in the mirror. We rode in silence again.

"Look at those dumb cows," TJ said after a while, staring out of his side window. A herd of about twenty were nudged right up against a barb-wire fence that skirted the dirt road, their spotted hides fading in and out of the darkness like ghosts. "Future burgers."

Finally we reached the end of the dirt strip and arrived at a main road that rose and fell in a series of hills on both the right and left sides of the road. A car rushed downhill as we reached the edge, then its headlights climbed a long hill then faded out of sight over it. Ding gently pushed on the brake, as if he didn't know where to go, or more aptly, what to do with us. We all sat there dumbly.

"This is the main road to Boulder. We are simply about five miles further down from the mesa. You would want to go right, Theodore," Willy said softly, as if he had already been walked to the gallows and was offering some final thoughts about his life and the state of the republic. Ding hesitated momentarily, turned right and we rolled slowly downhill, struggled up the next hill and then began rolling with speed down the next hill. There were no streetlights or any signs of life other than a railroad track that wound in darkness through the open valley to our left and disappeared miles away into the Rocky Mountains. It was lonely as hell. And then it started: a thumping noise. An unsteady, revolving thumping noise that began as a low murmur then grew in volume as the car gained velocity going downhill. Then the noise became a steady thump, almost non-stop, getting louder and louder and the car began to shudder.

"What is it Dad?" TJ said urgently. "What is happening?!"

"It is the majestic DerfiBird!" Willy cried, tucking his head into hands and crouching down into his seat. Indeed, the sound was not unlike a helicopter about to land on the roof. "Execute an evasive action, Theodore!" Willy called out. If I had not been scared as hell and about to be crushed from above by a manic burger helicopter it probably would have been the funniest thing I ever heard. I noticed that Ding Dong was struggling with the steering wheel, vibrating and shaking, like a man in a life or death battle with a python.

And at that moment I heard a deadly popping sound and the car shimmied on its own left then right, Ding scarcely ahold of the wheel now, but he managed to veer the Monte Carlo Beast over to the shoulder, manhandling it to the bottom of the hill and pulling off the main road onto yet another dirt road with a violent gladiatorial sound of metal on earth. We came to rest next to a small wooden house, boarded up for some time, a barbed wire fence stretching to our right with an old tree leaning painfully into it and across the road. There were no cows, no lights, no life. I imagined that the whole area had been farmland about fifty years before, before progress had turned it into nothing. Ding Dong heaved a big sigh and cut the lights and the engine. All was pitch black.

"Flat tire," he said with a crack of his knuckles. We all sat there silently. After a minute or two TJ asked his father if he would turn the car on again, for the heat. His father said nothing, his hands still cemented to the steering wheel. I could smell sweat. Then he began shaking as violently as the car had.

"Dad, Dad! What's wrong, you look ill. Dad!"

Teddy turned to him. He released his hands from the wheel and slowly peeled off his fisherman's cap, his hands shaking noticeably. "Theodore Junior, do you realize how many explosives we have in the trunk of this car? We could have been blown sky high."

TJ looked at him, not in surprise but in shock. "Dad, you've been driving a hundred miles an hour over those potholes on these crappy dirt roads. *That* should have killed us!"

"I know son, I know. I just thought of it, just now." He slowly put his cap back on. "We never would have finished the job. We've got to do it, son," and he leaned forward to the dashboard, twisted a knob and the overhead light came on in the car. Willy squinted a hundred times like a bunny rabbit surprised in the middle of the night by an incandescent bulb over its cage. Teddy fumbled around with his hand under the front seat, then came back up with the biggest honking silver pistol I had ever seen outside of a movie and he pointed it steadily between Willy's eyes. The thing made Willy's gun look like a paper clip.

"God bless America and the Second Amendment. Don't go for yours, William, just get out of the car. You too, burger man, and don't do anything foolish. Little Ding, wait right here," and we stepped out into the frigid night.

CHAPTER TWENTY-SIX

"The Shot, 7:50 p.m."

My legs were warm and wobbly when I got out of the car. Ding asked TJ to take the keys out of the ignition and give them to him. The wind was not as strong as on top of the mesa but it was still cold as hell. Ding Senior loped around to the back of the car, used the key to unlatch the trunk and opened it with one hand, the other hand carelessly waving the pistol back and forth with each task. I was trying to duck out of the way of its muzzle with each pass but Willy simply stood there stoically.

"Theodore, I am afraid that I am petrified of being locked in a trunk. I would prefer that you kill me now rather than unceremoniously stuffing me in there, driving me halfway across the country and then burying me in an unmarked grave."

He was scared as hell, I could tell, but Ding Dong only laughed like a crazy man. He was shifting things around in the trunk, unable to see with no light, half-mindedly training the gun on Willy.

"It does not have to end this way, does it?"

"What way would you like it to end?"

"I don't know, just another way I suppose."

"Well baby, we have to decide something. We're running out of time."

"I just think that a little more time would be okay, Julia, that's all. I just wish we had more time."

"Doesn't everybody?"

"Just start pulling the stuff out, and watch this baby," Ding said to me, motioning to a blinking light and a little lump in the dark of the trunk, then explained, "It's highly explosive so try not to bump it with the spare tire or the jack," then he said more to himself than anybody, "though I guess they *would* have exploded on that patchy road. Maybe they're faulty."

"They appear to be functional," Willy said. "I see the light blinking."

"You be quiet," Ding Dong said. Willy took a small step back and stared at me but the darkness was too deep to read his expression.

"Right Nye," he continued all business-like, "find the stuff you need to change the tire and get to work. A man should put in some honest work for a million dollars."

It felt like an hour had passed before I located the damn jack, then I had to lift up some floppy, mildewed carpet and a bit of decayed board that would have smelled really bad if you were shot and placed on top of it to die slowly. It felt like another hour by the time I found the little donut spare tire. I probably would have had an easier time just running alongside the car, holding it up by the axle, all the way to Boulder. Willy did his best to help me occasionally but I knew just by his truncated movements that he was scared as hell, or had to go to the bathroom.

"Oh drat, I spilled antifreeze all over my hands," I heard Willy say, his hands aloft as if they were on fire, when I was at some point between slicing my hand with the crowbar and wedging my finger in a lug nut hole while trying to dislodge the tire from its berth. "Theodore, one should really replace the caps on such containers immediately after use." Ding Dong, however, had gone over to Little Ding's window and was leaning inside it, discussing something in muffled tones, his hand and the gun resting on top of the car roof but still trained our way.

"Do you think he is determined to kill us?" Willy whispered to me hurriedly.

"I don't know," I whispered back, my mind a blur. "I think he might, Willy. God, how did we end up here?"

"We did not do anything little chief, as you know, but I suspect he thinks we called the police. He also seems to think it was I, so maybe you have a chance. But he could be bluffing."

"I'd hate to call his bluff and lose," I whispered. "Man, my stomach is killing me." Willy nodded thoughtfully, smoothing his mustache. I said to him, "And what do you mean 'I have a chance.' We're in this together and we're getting out together."

I could tell just how he positioned his feet on the earth that Willy was genuinely moved. I even saw his shoulders rise up, his chest get puffy, his body ready for action.

"You could crack him over the skull with that crowbar, but make sure your strike is true little chief, right across the corpus collosum."

"I don't know where that is. Maybe you should do it. Don't you have practice with tomahawks or something?"

"I suppose I could," he said, unwinding his arm like a batter at home plate.

"A whole lot less whispering, a whole lot more tire changing," we heard Ding call back to us, making me jump and hit the back of my head on the open trunk.

"The man has ears like a hawk," Willy whispered right against my earlobe.

"It's like a bad movie, Willy. A bad, bad movie. What should we do?"

"Just do not lose hope, little tomahawk."

"He's going to kill us," I said, and felt like throwing up everything I had ever eaten in my entire life. Willy was silent for only a second; generally he would have stood there, thinking for about ten minutes, like he was in deep thought even if he wasn't, but there was no time for that now.

"Little chief, I do not have much to live for," he began in whispers, and suddenly I knew the situation was irretrievably hopeless, because Willy had ended his sentence with a dangling participle and didn't even attempt to undangle it. This was bad. "I have had a fair life. I would have preferred to have been married, had several children, visited Madagascar at least once to see their Bromdignagian grasshoppers, and maybe learned how to play a wind instrument, but when the nitty gets gritty, you let me take the gritty little chief."

If I had not been so scared I would have laughed outright at Willy, standing there in that damn Farto! cap. I suddenly had a sense of very bad foreboding. Ding Dong emerged from the car with a rag and delicately handed it to Willy to wipe his hands, smiling at him.

"You've not even removed the tire, burger man!" he exploded. He zeroed the pistol in on me now and growled for me to speed it up. "I don't know about you burger man. Hurry up!" he barked when I turned briefly to say something about the tire being stuck, but there was a bowling bowl where my Adam's apple was supposed be. Willy looked at me, astonished, then at Ding Dong.

"This might take just a little while, Theodore," Willy said. "The man is a bit frail," and he started talking about a million words a minute. I knew he was trying to distract Ding Dong from his anger, maybe even to deflect it back to himself. It appeared that Ding Dong now thought *I* was the culprit. Bi-polarity is not pretty, even in the seemingly outward-appearing normal. I finally got the tire out and hustled over to the side of the car, cranking it up (not as easy with TJ's butt still sitting in the front seat) then one lug nut, two lug nut, three lug nut, four. Well, the fourth actually did not come off, which is typical. The last lug nut never wants to come off even in the best of situations, and particularly won't budge when a guy has a gun to your head and you're pulling your own nuts trying to get the last damn lug nut off. I mean, if I knew beforehand that I was going to go through all of this trouble, I would have just told Ding Dong to shoot me and take a taxi to Boulder, but I had already loosened the other three lug nuts and owed it to Willy, who may be able to escape in an uncommon fit of derring-do, to finish the job. Willy was still motoring on non-stop about anything that came to mind.

"Almost done," I huffed after about five minutes, "though my hands—"

"Just finish up there, burgermeister. No time for small talk," Ding interrupted stiffly. Oh man, I was a dead man. Here he was enduring Willy's endless babbling about nothing, but he was dead curt with me. Ding Dong sidled over to me then leaned down to my level, nudging his shoulder against the tire. The car rocked slightly and I wished that it would fall on him, or me, or at least Willy because he was giving me a headache.

"I just keep turning over in my mind why that policeman pulled us over. I simply don't understand—I was doing the proper speed limit, following all the road rules, not attracting any suspicion and yet he still pulled me over." He searched my face with those cold dead eyes of his and pulled on that freaking mustache with his tongue and teeth. He looked downright sinister. It was dark, and his eyes looked like two cannon holes in the sides of an old brown, algae-eaten, sunken ship. I knew he was glaring at me. "There must be a reason."

"Could be a million things, Ding Dong," I gulped, though I was getting a little angry because I was sweating under my clothes and knew I would get a cold if I were to live long enough to get one.

He made a weird rattling noise with his larynx and pulled the gun up to my temple. "Why don't you tell me one of those million things and I'll decide if it seems reasonable."

My Adam's apple was no longer like a bowling ball, it was a damn bowling *alley*. My mouth was full of sand and honey and molasses and tar and cotton and sap and grape jam and the mucus of an eighty-year-old man dying of emphysema and countless other unmentionable sticky things. I couldn't possibly speak.

"I said, Tell me something burger man. Go on then. Were you afraid of losing a million bucks?"

I managed to unstuck my peanut butter tongue from the roof of my mouth. "Maybe the cop knew Mr Derfy Burger was in the car."

"Perhaps," and he steadied himself, cupping his chin in his hand, "but wouldn't he have said something when he came to the car like 'Bloody hell, I can't believe this is happening to me. It's Mr Derfy Burger!' It's not every day that you get to meet a man who won a million dollars and would do anything to get to it, including betray his own friends and acquaintances." He stood up and towered over me.

"Ding, I, I…" I said, adhesively. Nothing else would come out. I couldn't pull my eyes away from his, as scared as I was. I felt like I was gazing up at a complete stranger, like I had never spoken to him before.

"You know mate, I told you before that it was your choice to go to the police or not, but then I decided that jail was not a happy time for me. I don't want to return, ever. I don't want to be found out, I don't want to eat food that's shite, I don't want to look out a little window with bars on it, I don't want my son to…" but he stopped short. "So I retract my statement. I'm sorry it happened this way, but sometimes life is like that. It's too big now, Nye. It's not too big for me and Little Ding to handle, but it's gotten too big for one single person," and he patted the top of my head, "to send awry. Why did you have to go to the police, Nye, why?"

"Ding…" and the lump now moved to my tongue. I couldn't say anything at all. He knelt back down and stared at me.

"It seemed that higher forces were moving us along, but you had to defy them. Why?"

"I didn't Ding, I don't know how to—" but he tapped the muzzle against my temple. Every nerve, cell, tendon, hair follicle, fluid, everything, in my body seemed to jump erratically in alarm then pull back in fright. I couldn't defend myself; how could he expect me to? The wind whistled between us and I could faintly hear Little Ding singing in the front seat, his finger snapping a couple of times to the beat. Ding Dong's face was so close to mine that I could smell his breath, which was of nothing and struck me as odd, absurd—shouldn't it smell rotten and nervous, steely, or like a creek in a heat wave? I felt the hard circle of the muzzle denting my temple.

"I thought I could trust you, you damn fool," and he spat out the "f" in "fool" so hard I thought I might see it hit the ground, sailing an inch or two in the wind, but too weighty to take flight. "Now we have to do something I never wanted. Damn you Nye," he said, putting an arm around my shoulder and hugging me closely. "Damn you."

I don't know what took over me, the tension maybe, his weird arm around me, my mother, Julia, but I shouted, "Do you want me to finish this damn tire or not!?" I was going to die like a man, angry and obstinate and changing a tire. There was a wet silence and my words echoed between my ears. Then there was wind. Then there was Willy.

"It was I," said his soft voice from the darkness. He emerged from the rear of the car and pottered stiff-kneed over to us, like a mummy. Ding Dong swiveled his face to him. "My conscience got to me, Theodore." He had his hands crammed in his pockets and looked so achingly vulnerable. "The little chief and I stopped for jerky and I used the gentleman's cellular phone. You saw him. We were sitting in his lawn chairs," and I thought to myself that if Ding Dong had ever happened to stop at Bacon's tent any time in a very bizarre past life, he would have known that there was no way the man owned a cell phone. He probably didn't even have a rotary phone. "His name was Bacon."

"The man's name was Bacon," Ding asked, unbelieving.

"Bacon Smalls," Willy answered. "An intriguing fellow," he said, unzipping the neck of his jacket and plunging his hand inside, trying to find a pocket.

Ding Dong popped to his feet and started jumping around like he had sat on a hot stove, training the gun on Willy and shouting "Ay-ay-ay!" Snowshoe pulled a baggy from his chest and innocently said, "Teriyaki beef."

"Christ man, I thought you were going for your gun! I almost did you in, man!" Ding shouted. Willy apologized and said he would be smarter next time, poking his hands back into his pockets.

"There won't be a next time!" Ding Dong shouted, more annoyed than angered. "You betrayed me."

Willy took half a pace backward and cleared his throat. "Ding Dong, Theodore, I am sorry that I turned you in, but I believe that what you are doing is not right. Even young Ding does not like it."

Ding Dong took some hesitant steps forward and pressed the muzzle against Willy's throat. "Why are you bringing my son into this?" he growled.

"He is scared," Willy gulped, those damn hands in his big puffy black jacket. He could just as easily have been standing in a freezing parking lot before a Saturday afternoon college football game, knocking back some beers and wieners with Ding Dong, waiting for the game to start so they could drink more beer and get thrown out of the stadium for hurling plastic beer cups at the referees. It could have been that way if Snowshoe wasn't a fruitcake and Ding Dong wasn't a psycho and there wasn't a loaded gun and a lifetime of cultural differences between them.

"My son is not scared," Ding hissed.

"Theodore Junior is scared. He told me in the DerfMart in Frisco. He loves his dad and does not wish to let you down."

"He loved his mother too, and his gram and gramps," Ding said, peering through the back window at TJ, who had turned the overhead light on and seemed to be fidgeting with the radio, oblivious to what was happening. I silently, at last, loosened the last lug nut, shimmied off the tire and eased it quietly to the ground.

"Wait a minute—he told you of our plans all the way back in Frisco?!"

"Oh, yes Theodore. We were simply smelling different laundry detergents in the laundry detergent aisle and he 'spilled the beans.' It was like he could not hold it in any longer."

"You're being serious with me? You knew all about our plans even before we went into that first Derfy Burger? And you pretended not to know this entire time?"

Willy stood silently, just staring at Ding Dong for what felt like hours. I scampered on all fours like a frightened monkey over to the donut tire lying on the ground and pulled it over to the naked axle.

"Theodore, he does not really know what to think. He just wants you to be proud of him. He wants to believe in what you are doing, and he does in an unselfish, child-like way, but he is scared. He does not want his papa going to jail again. He is very afraid of accidentally killing someone."

"We have it all planned to the second."

"Plans do not always work as they should. Did you plan on being here at this time?"

Ding Dong stared at him. "They tore my family apart."

"Eliason tried to convince me not to tell the police, but I felt that I must. I am no longer as young and idealistic as he. So you can see, I am completely at fault here, not the little chief." He glanced over at me, hesitated, then said, "Theodore, some folks might go as far as to describe what you are doing as morally reprehensible."

I knew Ding Dong was staring at me but I was too afraid to look up and over at him. For a second I thought about being a hero and clocking Ding Dong in the head with the tire, but then decided against it. I could hear Little Ding whistling to something on the radio now. He hadn't turned around to see what was going on the entire time. I screwed up the courage to sneak a peek at them and miraculously I saw that Ding Dong had relaxed and lowered the gun, his eyes on the ground. Though it was dark I could see Willy's chest heave under a concealed sigh. His face was turned my way, and I could tell he wanted to touch the side of his nose, to show me that everything was going to be okay, but he was afraid of what such movement might provoke from Ding. I heard the wind pushing into my ears, heard Little Ding whistle badly to part of another song on the radio, and saw Ding lift the hand without the gun to pat Willy's puffy chest, then bundle up the top of Willy's coat, zippered all the way to his throat, in a tight fist. He brought the pistol up, between Willy's chin and throat, so that his brains would be blown skyward into the moaning wind.

"Morally reprehensible is the man who turns his back on his friends," Ding said in a peculiar, unemotional tone. "Morally reprehensible are those who cry for the sun in the dead of winter, and when it does show itself, cry louder because it offers only light and no warmth. Then they turn to the moon. Morally cursed are those who stuff themselves with rubbish, watch it, eat it, listen to it. Morally reprehensible are those who do nothing even when there is so much to do. Damned are the scared who do nothing. And hated are the ones who preach, like me Willy, like me," and he grabbed the back of Willy's jacket and spun him around, nudging him forward, now the gun aimed heavenward at the base of Willy's skull. "Dangerous are the ones who do nothing. Come along now William."

"You can't take him," I said, still kneeling, holding the donut tire in one hand, my knees dimpling the dirt.

"You just finish with your job," he told me, taking the gun from Willy to point it my way, then putting it back against Willy's head. They shuffled off into the darkness toward the old house. Their shoes on the loose gravel sounded far away, military-crisp and cold. Soon they hit soft dirt and it was like they no longer existed—silence. I could hear Willy speaking rapidly, jawing on about something, but they were too far away for me to understand any words. They were just noises riding on the wind. I knew Willy was nervous and scattered and clawing for his life.

"Hey, where's my dad? Where's Snowshoe Willy?" I heard a voice above me. TJ had rolled down his window and had his head stuck out in the cold. "What are they doing?"

I ignored him and started forcing the donut tire on, twisting the lug nuts and turning madly. If I finished in time I could run over and help Willy.

"I can kind of see them over there. What are they doing?" I heard TJ say but I was too busy sweating and twisting and cursing.

"Hey man, that's looking good," he said, craning his neck around to see the tire. "I didn't think you had it in you burger man. Good job." He laughed, more a taunt than a laugh. "You know, my dad didn't really think either of you had called the cops but I convinced him that you did, burger man. You did, didn't you? You got to get that million dollars."

I stopped and stared hard at him. "No I did not call the cops."

"You didn't?"

"You really think that idiot jerky guy had a cell phone?"

"Really? And you guys don't have cell phones?"

"Of course we don't have cell phones," I said, getting angrier.

"Everybody's got cell phones."

"Well we don't."

"That's crazy man. You guys got internet, or just a post office? You got a post office?" he asked, but I gave him a good, cold stony silence.

"You mountain cave people need to catch up with the times," he said and leaned out his window, resting his stomach on the sill, rocking heavily up and down, his arms dangling toward the ground. "You think this jack is strong enough to hold me?"

"You're going to break it. Are you crazy?" I said, jumping away from the car.

"You're a little on edge burger man."

"Wouldn't you be if some crazy guy had a gun to your head for the last hour." I really wanted to jump up and pop him in the mouth but that would not help Willy.

"My dad's not crazy, burger man," he replied coolly. "Everybody else is crazy, including you." He waited for me to say something but I did not. "If you say my dad's crazy again I'll kill you," but it was missing the malice that had saturated his father's words. "You got that?" He looked at me and I looked back without saying anything.

"You know what your problem is burger man—you've had everything given to you your whole life, and now you're about to get more."

I didn't say anything and crawled back over to the tire. "Just let me finish so I can go help Willy."

"I'm sure you got everything you wanted, never had to worry about nothing, went to schools where everybody is perfect, got a new car, or even a big white truck for your sixteenth birthday, went fishing with your dad every weekend while mine sat in jail."

I steadied the tire on the car and searched for the lug nuts in the dirt with an open hand.

"Must've been real nice burger man. Now you can buy both your parents new houses. Hell, you can buy them fifty houses, one for each state."

I found one lug nut, blew the dirt off it, twisted it on, and proceeded with the next three, silently.

"Of course your dad can get a job as some corporate executive at Derfy Burger now and your family can have a billion dollars and your kids can have a trillion dollars and your grandchildren can have a bajillion dollars and never have to work. Think of me sometime burger man. Can you find it in your heart while you're out playing golf with daddy."

I slowly pulled myself up with the tire iron in my hand. Little Ding pulled up short and leaned his elbows on the sill.

"Go ahead and say something else about my dad," I seethed. All those years of holding it in, never talking about him, were about to come spilling out. "Go ahead."

"What's your problem, psychoman?" he said, taking his elbows off the sill, his eyes wide with fear, but it was too late. I hit him so hard with the tire iron that blood from his nose sprayed the dashboard, then I hit him in the brow, on the cheek, a groan, across the back of the head until he no longer moved, silence except for the radio. I collected myself and breathed in steadily.

"You got a damned crazy look in your eye, kid," Little Ding said, his hands up slightly at his face for protection. "What the hell are you doing?"

"My dad died when I was ten and if you say one more thing about him I'll crack open your head with this," I said, waving the tire iron at him, but the wash of anger had already passed, just like that. Little Ding had pulled himself wholly inside the car for safety but he probably knew I could never hit him.

"Your dad's dead, man?"

"Yeah he's dead. You got anything else to say?" I said through my teeth.

"No man," he said, keeping one sideways eye on the tire iron and then turned inside the car, pretending to be playing with the radio. "Maybe you should finish with the tire so we can get out of here," he said from the side of his mouth. I stood shaking, staring at him, the tire iron hanging limply in my hand then I walked slowly to the tire, panting like I had run up a hill, lowering myself again.

"Hey burger man, what are my dad and Snowshoe doing?" I heard TJ's voice, now apologetic, almost meek, ask.

"I don't know, having tea or something," I said. All of the fear and dread of traveling and death had finally caught up to me and I felt simply sapped. I finished with the last lug nut, tightening it as best as I could. Suddenly there was yelling by the old house.

"That's my dad," Little Ding said, leaning halfway out of the window again. "What's he yelling about, burgerman?"

I turned to face the source of the noise, the silhouette of the house a slight shade lighter than the darkness of a hill behind it. Along the back edge of the house I could just register Ding's figure, slightly taller and thinner than Willy's. He was gesticulating wildly at Willy's darkened shape and shouting something, but the wind carried all the sense of it away.

"Let me turn this rubbish off," Little Ding said annoyed, shifting into the car, snapping off the radio, then leaning out the window again. "What's my dad yelling about?"

"I can't tell," I said edging a little closer to the sound, straining my eyes, and a split second later, it happened, like a dream. There was a flash of light and a split second later a loud pop, like a firecracker, and the burst of light was just enough to illuminate Willy's black shape crumpling to the ground. The sound of the shot reverberated off the sandstone hills then crept away down the valley. A farm dog, closer than I expected any humans to live, barked twice at the sound and his voice too filtered away to nothing in the wind. I was frozen, squinting into the new darkness, a blue streak of persistent vision squiggling its way across the blackness of night when I blinked. And I heard Ding Dong laughing, distinctly and loudly.

And I remembered Willy, the first time I met Willy: I had been freshly transplanted to Boulder, maybe five months before, and living with my mother in a small, stuffy apartment behind a junior high school with a torn-up football field and a dead soccer field. The summer of 1995 had been a hot, dry one, but the trees offered relief and my favorite restaurant with the beautiful Czech waitresses and best pancakes this side of Poughkeepsie—you know the place, Marie's, just across the street from the hospital, was calling. Friends had been hard to come by and I had been throwing the Frisbee by myself, humming it high in the air and running after it, which sounds like great fun, but is not fun at all after about two and a half minutes. I was panting in the shade of a tree when Jeff and his two kids came to my rescue. That would be Jeff

Worster, as in older brother of Willy, tall and good-looking and athletic and probably slightly more successful with the opposite sex than his younger sibling, through no genetic fault of his own. He had been playing soccer or polo or bocce or something European with his little kids when he decided out of sheer boredom or kindness to offer to toss with me. He was good. Nice fellow too I thought. Good looking kids. Then Uncle Willy showed up in his warm-up pants and all hell broke loose. Despite outwardly appearing to be one of the most unfit people on the planet, which I remind Willy of on a weekly basis, he was extraordinarily gifted at frisbee disc control and could do some crazy acrobatic stuff with the clever piece of furnace-hardened plastic, including catching it behind his head and spinning it on his index finger. And you know what else Willy could do that I failed to mention? Walk on his hands. No lie. He learned this incredibly difficult stunt when in ninth grade he lost the love of his young years, Mikki Horswill, to a boy from another junior high who could sprint on fingertips, allegedly, though Willy always doubted the veracity of the stories. Willy learned the trick by the eleventh grade but she had moved on.... Anyway, at one point Willy was moving about on his hands, shoes up where normally his mustache is, and Larry lofted him the frisbee to catch with his feet which of course was misjudged and sliced right down between Willy's legs and nicked the underside of his god-given, unprotected goods with a reverse circular saw-like rotation that, as any man would know and judging by Willy's reaction, was rather painful. He came to rest with a puff of dry dust in the yellow grass, unable to right himself for at least fifteen minutes. It had to be the funniest thing I had ever seen, at least up to that point, in my entire life. Shortly thereafter, after a hearty breakfast of pancakes, Czechoslavakian kolache and chocolate milk, he offered me a job. I moved to Leadville shortly thereafter and for the first time in my life a person started calling me "little chief" and "El Nye rump shaka" and "snowshoe guru." I never would have believed it could happen.

And there lay Willy on the ground in the whispering wind. And Ding Dong stood over him laughing. Little Ding fell out of the window into a heap on the gravel, picked himself up in one movement and sprinted down the drive, screaming, "Dad, Dad! You didn't have to shoot Snowshoe! Dad!" The car, jarred by the action, split itself away from the jack and landed on the ground with a scrape of metal and a hushed thud.

In a flash of mental acuity I thought I should jump in the car and limp away with its little donut tire, getting out of there, of saving my own life because it's what Willy would have wanted (or this is the lying drivel that athletes always employ when a teammate dies from an overdose during the season: "Johnny would have wanted us to finish the season, go to the playoffs and win the championship because, well, that's what we want to do and well, we'll pretend that's what he would have wanted us to do when really it is just what we were always going to do.") Instead, I opened the door and grabbed Willy's pistol from his bag and sprinted after TJ, toward Ding Dong.

"I'm coming."

"You're coming now?"

"I think so. I just need to make sure it's okay with Willy."

Julia looked at me like I had slapped her. "You know what, just stay here. Just stay here."

"Are you angry? Didn't I say I would go."

"Just stay. It's okay. Really. Stay."

"You don't sound okay."

"I'm leaving in like, two days. I'm sure Willy needs you here. Just stay and make your snowshoes, okay Eliason?"

CHAPTER
TWENTY-SEVEN

"All Lights Out and a Ding Dong Daddy Good-Bye, 8:18 p.m."

As I ran I knew I would have to choose a movie scene, quickly, before I confronted the two Bells, because I had never fired a gun in my life. The guy in a pin-striped suit, hurtling sideways, parallel with the floor or even sliding across a well-placed table cleared of dishes and other pointy objects, sailing unblinking through the air with fingers clicking the triggers of two handguns like mini cannons was a good one...but I had only one gun. There was the cowboy outlaw with longish leather coat, honking big shotgun in hand, his mouth eating a cigar in the shadows of his hat, walking slowly, bravely, deliberately, the outlaw hiding behind a swinging door but gittin' his nerves ready to burst out onto the dirt street...but I was running and didn't have a shotgun and was never really sure how a shotgun worked—sure, I had seen plenty of scattered red and green casings on the ground during hunting season but never really worked out how they got bullets and gunpowder and stuff inside those little cardboard tubes. There was the space-age gunman who could spray off about a billion bits of shrapnel and laser and other intergalactic bits of anti-matter from his stainless steel blaster and manage to destroy entire aluminum walls of spaceship but only come within a mere centimeter of the bad guy's nose while continuing to miss him and destroy more interior walls...but we weren't on a spaceship a million years in the future. What else? Should I be the miserable soldier in every 20th century war movie who never seems to hit anything especially when his buddies are running around crazily, stepping on land mines, taking ordinance in their foxholes, getting one in the breadbasket from an unseen machine gun somewhere...but this was man-on-man, mano on mano, not a global fight for mankind's very existence, for democracy and capitalism. There was always the brooding, non-verbal henchman who served as a bodyguard for a guy with a foreign accent who hid behind pillars, not privy to the Big Plan but always managing to get taken out by the good guy silently or, given the chance to use his Russian-made bullet-sprayer, had a dead-eye for taking out windows, fish tanks, pillars that his buddies were hiding behind, while somehow only grazing the good guy before calmly accepting a stray bullet to his own forehead. There was always the hapless female who, upon confronting her personal abusive baddie, her hand shaking with nerves, finally squeezes the trigger only to find, to the killer's surprised glee, that she has forgotten all about the darn safety switch.... There's always the gun which fires perfectly, until the bad guy comes within the crosshairs...and jams.... There's the gun on the ground, inches out of the good guy's reach, inches away from the bad guy's reach so they have to wrestle for it.... Of course there's always the gun at the fingertips of the good guy, bloodied and on the ground and possibly dying, who reaches out for it, his salvation, only for the mean bad guy to kick it away with a snort.... I couldn't think of any movie in which there was a gun with no bullets in it at all....

"Ding Dong!" I screamed as I arrived, finally, maybe ten feet from him. I guess I was squeezing the trigger about a million times, thinking that I was the guy in the movie that was never made, the one with the gun that had no bullets. And damn if that pistol didn't go off and remarkably, shatter a window not far from Ding's shoulder. I watched the broken glass in horror and listened to it patter in the dirt.

"Jesus Christ, Nye!" Teddy shouted, ducking about a half a second after the shot, his body shimmying sideways out of the way of the glass toward Willy. He looked to be instinctively shielding Willy's lumpen mass from the shards. "Nye!"

That is when I felt a sharp pain at the base of my skull, quick and snappy, a sort of internal crunching sound, then a sudden white light which dispersed into a million fruit flies, buzzing circles of black, scattering in and out among themselves, white on the edges, until they too dispersed into total blackness and then nothing. Damn if I wasn't dead I thought as I lay there, who knows for how long, hours? And then I was awake, fully aware of where I was and what had happened but too scared to move. For a second, a mere flash, I sort of wished that I was dead. I needed just to lie there until the Bells went away. But the air was too cold, and I could sense them breathing around me, over me, and I knew that Ding Dong and TJ were on both sides of me.

"They always slap people in the movies and the person wakes up," I heard TJ whisper. "Or they pour cold water on them. That always works too."

There was only silence but I could hear Ding Dong breathing. "He has a pulse, so we just need to give him some time," and I became aware of Ding's hand clutching onto my wrist. They had killed Willy and they were going to wait for me to wake up so they could kill me like a man or torture me or keep me as a hostage. I tried not to breathe.

"He almost looks like he's trying not to breathe," TJ said and my whole body stiffened. "What was that? Is he dying Dad?" His father did not answer. "I swear I didn't mean to hit him so hard. He was going to kill you Dad. He tried to shoot you."

"I know son," Teddy answered calmly. "And no, he's not going to die. I just hope you didn't paralyze the poor bastard. A two-by-four to the back of the head can be pretty bad."

"It was just laying there Dad. I didn't think, I thought—"

"It's okay son. He would have killed me, whether he meant to or not."

"Gentlemen, I believe I have recovered enough strength to make a fair and pointed diagnosis," I heard a third voice say, as close as the

Bells' but I was still too afraid to unpeel my eyelids. "The first course of action taught in first responder class, driven into our brains by rote repetition in case of such an emergency, is to loosen the three b's: belt, boots, blouse. Gentlemen, we are in muscle memory mode now. Chop-chop. Let us roll."

"But he's just wearing shoes, not boots," TJ said, almost frantically, scampering to my lower region. "I don't think he's wearing a blouse under all that coat. Anyway, he's a guy—I don't think he'd be wearing a blouse. That just leaves belt."

"A blouse in this instance denotes a loose-fitting shirt," the voice said. "We shall skip to step eight, assuming that we have checked for responsiveness, blood, burns, fracture, shock, etcetera. On to step eight: elevation of the feet," and I felt an abrupt tugging at the far end of my body.

"Easy, TJ. I think it best not to move him," Teddy said urgently. "What if he's broken his neck."

"Swiftly, gentlemen, move the victim onto his side in case of regurgitation. We do not wish for him to asphyxiate on his own vomit. We need a volunteer to clear his passageway with a good sweep of the finger from back of the mouth to front. Theodore Junior, all fingers on deck."

"I don't know William, I think it best not to move him," Ding Dong said.

"A point well-taken Theodore," the oddly familiar voice of Willy said. "Perhaps a slightly moistened cloth will do wonders for the—"

"I'm okay," I croaked and Willy jumped back like I had jabbed him with a cactus needle. I heard him, comically, scuffling in the dirt while he tried to collect himself. TJ let out a little yelp but Ding Dong remained hovering over me as I slowly opened my eyes. His mouth was close to my ear, as if he had been unfailingly checking my vital signs for hours, days. "Just don't put your fingers in my mouth," I said.

"Nye, can you wiggle your toes?"

I'm okay, Ding, really," I said, slowly pushing myself up on my elbows, "just kind of whoozy," and the million fruit flies came back with a blood rush of pain inside my entire skull. I felt like puking.

"Whoa there young warrior, remaining supine is what the medicine man has ordered," Willy said, pushing firmly down on my chest with an open palm. "You shall get the bends if you come up for air so quickly. Just ease it back down."

"You're not dead," I asked him stupidly.

"Not yet, little chief, not yet."

"But Ding Dong shot you. We saw it."

"Shot above him," Teddy said, wanting to laugh I thought but refraining.

"Yes, shot above me. It seemed the confluence of stress, exertion and yes, fear, all mixed up with the sudden shot of Theodore's pistol hurtled me into a fainting spell," Willy explained. "The trait, like hemophilia in the royals, runs in my family. My brother Larry tends to faint after getting off ferris wheels."

"What's he saying Ding?" I moaned.

"No one knows, burgerman. Just rest but don't sleep, okay?"

"Are you going to kill us?" I asked sleepily. There were no stars above, only a layer of low, gray clouds, lighter than the darkness around us.

"No burgerman, not at all. Now rest," and I closed my eyes without sleeping and listened to the three of them talking quietly among themselves, making quiet movements almost as if they were busily collecting all of our stuff after a perfect camping trip, and I had such a rush of happiness, of safety, of warmth despite the cold. I lay still and wished the feeling would last for much longer than I knew it would. I had no idea how many minutes had passed when Ding Dong urged me to sit up, and I needed three tries before the fruit flies went away and the pain did not sicken me.

"Not so hard next time, Little Ding," Teddy said.

"I didn't mean to, Dad, I swear," he answered. Ding asked if I could stand, then he and Willy hoisted me up by both armpits and they began to drag me along in the dirt toward the car. The cold came back. Time was running forward again.

"I only meant to scare you, Nye," Teddy explained. "I knew, obviously, that Snowshoe Willy was lying when he said that he had called the police. He's the worst liar I've ever met."

343

"Well thank you Theodore," Willy puffed on my right, struggling a little for breath. "I could not sell a nut to a squirrel either, unless it was an unnaturally good nut."

Ding Dong chuckled and explained. "I knew he had not called the police—he was trying to protect you—but I had to be certain that you didn't go to the police either. I thought if I pretended that I shot Willy and you came to his defense—which you did Nye, credit to you son, well done—I guess it wouldn't prove anything really, only that you more than likely had some integrity and stood by your friends. Good stuff Nye."

"I thought you shot Willy," I answered. I wanted to tell him I was more scared than brave at that point but I thought it an unnecessary and mood-dampening detail.

"Well I didn't expect our man to faint did I?" Ding laughed. Willy chuckled embarrassedly. "And where did you learn how to fire a pistol like that? Well done again," Ding laughed. I shrugged.

"I think you can walk on your own now," Ding advised, and sure enough I had strength enough to traverse the distance to the Monte Carlo. My head throbbed a little still, but was mostly delicate to the touch. Ding Dong gushed over my finishing the job of changing the tire, rapping the rim twice with a knuckle. He almost tripped over the crowbar, which had become wedged between the tire and earth after the car fell off the jack. He tugged on it with no effect. "Don't know how you managed that one Nye."

"That was my fault," TJ said. "I'll move the car," he said hastily. He had been silent after I had awakened and now seemed eager to do something useful other than brain me. His father told him to turn on the car and the lights so we could find all the various pieces of equipment.

"Go forward just a little, I think the jack is also under the tire," he directed to TJ through the window. "No, you have to back up a little. That's it. Is it in reverse now? Do you have it in reverse?" The car began to slowly back up. "Okay, that's good. Can you fetch the other pieces, William? How are things back there, burgerman?"

"I think I'll be okay," I said with a yawn, popping my ears, carefully probing the back of my neck with my pointer finger. "You know, I think the hood of my coat cushioned things a little. Hey Ding Dong, can you come look at this for just a second?"

He asked what was wrong, was I bleeding, hurrying to the back of the car beside me.

"Well, the headlights are on but we've got nothing in the back," I said.

"You're right," he said, telling Little Ding to push on the brakes, but there was only darkness. "You're as right as you've ever been, burgerman. Nothing."

"If such is the case," Willy began, "then any policeman worthy of his badge would have 'pulled us over' within seconds of seeing our folly. In fact, he would be downright hostile that we would even attempt to drive such a moving violation on his roadway. There is your answer, Theodore, as to our prior misdemeanor."

"Damn Johnny Shoes," Teddy said, approaching the trunk, asking me to get the keys from the ignition. "That bugger loaned me a bum auto."

I got the keys from TJ, who asked how my head was, and returned to the back of the car, hesitating as I passed them to Ding Dong.

"Don't be frightened Nye. You and Willy are in the clear. You're not going inside," and he opened the trunk to return the jack, stopping momentarily to study the blinking lights of his tiny bombs. He bent over and looked almost to be polishing the bulb encasings with his thumb. He stood, stopped for a second, lowered the trunk enough to peer at TJ through the back window, then delicately sealed the lid. "I understand if you're still a little nervous Nye."

"The after-effects of shock," Willy said, putting an arm around my waist. "Let me guide you into the car. Come then, great tamer of Appaloosa," and I wasn't sure if it was my muddled brains or simply Willy who was making no sense. TJ took over driving duties for his father, who thanked him softly, and wondered aloud how we would get all the way into Boulder with no backlights.

"Slowly," Teddy recommended.

"I can take us a safer and less traveled, yet more cursory way. I like to follow this route upon, when visiting my brother, I have discovered that I need to acclimate myself to the big city at a slower rate," Willy explained. "We shall be traversing the old roads of Boulder county proper, those routes that once connected farmers and ranchers and other tillers of the soil but are now mainly unused by, perhaps even unknown to, the speeding, traveling masses ferrying their offspring to ballet classes, kung fu lessons and after-school algebra courses." Once again Willy had allowed me to quaff his verbal tonic of near-death, sleep, administered by his incessant babbling, and I rested my head against the seat. I think it was an involuntary snort that alerted him and effected a brisk slap to my cheek from his doctorly hand.

"No no, chieftain," he said to my cursings. "Those who have been concussed must not sleep, or even to doze. If you begin to feel drowsy again, please give me a signal upon which I shall administer another smart report." I cursed him again.

"You're sure we're on the right road, Snowshoe?" TJ asked, glancing into the rearview mirror. William assured him with a "Quite sure" and TJ admitted that he had not seen another car since we had turned on to this road. I rolled my head to the side and looked out Ding Dong's window upon black open meadows that must have sung with frogs in summer and grabbed snowdrifts within their dead grass shoots in winter, down dips and over hiccup hills, across a narrow stone bridge, through vast stretches of darkened road and field to half a sky of stars not yet hidden by the advancing wall of clouds. We drove directly west, straight to the mountains but not into them, skirting the Foothills, upon which we entered a snow shower softly falling. After several minutes it became a sort of blizzard and rendered visibility almost nil.

"This is good," Willy told us. "No one will be out driving in this. Theodore Junior, do you see the red light atop the tower in the distance, the one which looks almost like a chimney? That is the former insane asylum and lies just blocks from my brother's home, a premier place to 'drop off' the young chieftain and me."

"He lives down the street from a loony house?" TJ asked. "That's crazy."

"Well, it is not 'loony house' anymore. I believe it is a recycling center now. My my, we have not seen such a snowfall in the Foothills since the great white-out of '77. Splendid."

We passed the darkened and rather beautiful insane asylum/ recycling center that nested right up against the mountain, then coursed through a neighborhood of grand, old trees and big lawns and house lights dimmed behind the thick veils of falling snow, and rolled to a slow stop at Larry's curb. His house was dark, the lawn already completely white except for large dark freckles where elm and oak branches shielded the ground from snow.

"That's a nice house," TJ said.

"He is a lawyer," Willy admitted almost shamefully. "Theodore Junior, if you continue forward you will meet Broadway, the main thoroughfare of town, although you are 'taking a gamble' by driving on it with no lights. Upon your decision, turn right and perhaps two miles later you will meet Foothills Parkway. Turn left and after several stoplights you will find yourself facing Boulder's only Derfy Burger."

"Thank you William," Ding Dong said, letting himself out of the car and propping the seat forward. I emerged, then Willy with his backpack, and we faced Teddy Bell.

"We'll come see you in Leadville, Snowshoe," TJ called from the driver's seat. "Burger man, sorry about your head. Send us a postcard from China or something."

"William," Ding Dong said, extending his hand. They shook and Willy gave him a giant panda hug.

"Burger man, all the best to your mum. Send us a postcard from China," he grinned.

"Or something," I said, shaking his hand. He lowered himself into the car, closed the door quietly and lowered the window. But he didn't say anything and they rolled away without sound, almost as if they did not exist, never existed, the snow muffling the tires on the pavement, the headlights blunted in the fog of snow. I watched him slowly roll up the window. It was the last time we would ever see them.

"Did that feel like a proper good-bye?" Willy fretted.

"Yes, you didn't say anything. That's the best way," I told him.

"Really? I always fancied a long, dramatic speech in such a situation, though I have never really been in such a situation."

"It's okay, Willy, really. You did great," and I expected him to be sopping up freezing, solidifying, icy tears from his cheeks but he was dry-eyed. We looked at the tracks of the Monte Carlo, which were already disappearing under the snow. I asked, "Willy, how far is the hospital from here?"

"Goodness yes! I am sorry Eliason, I was lost in my own revery. It is a walkable distance. Shall we?"

"Do you want to visit your brother or anything?"

"Would you like to be alone on this portion of your journey, chieftain? I understand if you need some Eliason-time before seeing your mum."

"No, I just thought you might want to see your brother, or at least tell him that you're here."

"Oh, we shall have plenty of time for 'catching up.' It was only several months ago, you may recall, that I visited Jeffrey and we were participants on a microbrewery tour of Fort Collins. Sadly, much of the day is lost to drunken amnesia; however, I do recall that we went to a Pakistani teahouse the following day with my niece and nephew and my wonderful sister-in-law. I had some very interesting tea with floating tapioca balls in it. It was strange that—"

"Willy, I think you left your laundry basket in the car."

"Oh shoot!" he said, trotting forward several steps, his hand out in the air, nose pointed downward at the fading tire tracks like a snorting bloodhound about to track an escaped liquor store robber once the sheriff unleashed him. "As well as my peanut butter cluster bars!"

"Maybe Jeff has some," I reasoned, trying to console him. He walked several steps in the disappearing tire tracks, his head and shoulders drooping, then he turned toward me.

"Jeffrey does not eat processed sugar," and he stopped for a second, thinking, and pulled up his waistband with a dramatic flourish. "But chieftain, what is a laundry basket and a packet of peanut butter-flavored sweets compared to your imminent loss? Forgive me. Follow me, great warrior chief," he said, turning again and bending his Farto! cap into the snow. He kind of reminded me of pictures I saw, maybe in my fifth grade US history book, of a broken line of Indian ladies hunched under buffalo skins, walking into a bare, white, snowy horizon, I guess to their reservation, so they could die.

"Just one moment, chieftain," he said, turning and holding a hand up to my chest too late, so that I bumped into him. He dusted snow from the top of my cap, took a sideways step and began swinging his backpack by its strap in wide arcs. He let it fly high and it landed with a clumsy somersault into Jeff's lawn, unrolling in its wake a strip of dirty snow and leaves that clung to the top of the pack. I asked what the hell he was doing.

"Unnecessary baggage," he said, now paternally dusting off my shoulders. I asked if he meant it as some sort of crummy metaphor. He stopped, looked surprised, then tried to claim it as his own.

"Touche, little chief," and he turned to follow the tire tracks.

"Dude, you've got a gun in there. Some little kid might find it."

"Guns do not kill people, little chief," he said with a careless wave, without turning. I ran back and tossed it into some bushes and caught back up to Willy, who seemed not to have noticed that I had gone. I do not recall what we talked about during most of that walk, only that I was becoming nervous as hell with each step closer to the hospital. What if my mother had already died? And Julia was somewhere here in Boulder, but I had no clue where. What would she say had she known I was here? Any other person would have pretended like I didn't exist, or maybe even kick me where it hurts, or hire some Italian to beat me with an aluminum baseball bat or strangle me from behind with a length of fishing line, but not Julia; she would forgive me. She forgave everybody. I felt like crying, just a little, but all the liquid in my body was frozen.

"Not to intrude upon your world, Eliason, not that it is wholly my business, but I was just wondering about Julia, your thoughts."

"What thoughts exactly?" I said abruptly, shivering, because by then we had been walking for over ten minutes, my nose and lips were turning numb and I was getting that familiar freezing sensation of not caring about anything again.

"It is of no importance, just never you mind," he said quickly, as if he had made a mistake for asking.

I kicked at a half-submerged stick in the snow. "I'm just cold Willy," I said, kicking at another larger branch. "I wasn't really thinking about anything?"

Willy folded his mittens over his belly, walking squarely. "I was merely wondering how you would resume communication with Julia. I know she has taken up temporary residence, a weekend accommodation, with some sort of female friend here but how will you speak with her again?"

"I don't know. We didn't make really concrete plans. *She* wanted to make some kind of plan but I didn't listen. She must really hate me Willy. She has to hate me." I kicked at another branch, sending it into flight. Already the older, more brittle limbs were littering the street, cracking and crashing to the ground under the weight of the snow. "You hate me, I can tell. *I* hate me."

Willy slowed his pace, and kicked at a branch but missed. He was not always the most athletic sort, which I always liked to cruelly remind him.

"It is easy for a man to hate himself in retrospect, chieftain. This you shall learn. After the passage of some time we as men can explain away any infraction that we have ever committed, can rationalize our wrong-doings or blame others, unfortunately. I believe our man Theodore Bell is a fine example of such self-delusion. When you, my friend, begin to hate yourself 'in the moment' instead of days or years later, then you shall have reached feminine enlightenment, for only a woman begins immediately to hate herself for something she has done, or more presciently for what a man has done to her." He kicked at another branch but completely whiffed.

"I'm not sure, but I don't think you're making me feel better."

"'Tis not my job to make you feel better, and for this I apologize, but I can tell you this with complete surety: your Julia could never, ever, ever hate you. She is a rare person." He kicked at another branch, finally connecting. "Yes!" he shouted, which echoed through the empty streets. He glanced at me sheepishly. "The world could use more people like your Julia." We walked for some time, both of us kicking at sticks. "By your silence I shall infer that you agree with me, that Julia is a rare gem?"

"Of course Willy, what do you think?"

"It is only that sometimes I do not know with you, silent shaman. Mayhaps you should express your feelings more than just occasionally."

"Maybe," I said, wiping a flake from the tip of my nose. Again we walked in silence and I was seriously beginning to wonder if the damn hospital even existed.

"Pensive warrior, have I ever told you about my buddy Lee Potphil?"

"I don't know if I have the strength Willy."

"Lee Potphil was the second smartest student in high school," Willy began anyway, "salutitorian, very serious, taciturn, buttoned-up and bookish. Some said he was too droll to be good company, but we went back to pre-kindergarten, playground heroes," he said, touching the side of his nose my way. "Even back then I knew he would excel at the computer arts and it was no surprise to this man when he was offered one of the grandest jobs in Denver upon our graduation. When we lost touch with one another it was sad but not unexpected. Oh I had heard various rumors that he was working for the Central Intelligence Agency or even the Federal Bureau of Investigations but back in those Cold War days who could ever know."

I began to drift off into a vaporous fog.

"So it was with some shock that I witnessed his return to Leadville in the late 1980s, where he went into hiding for many years, living on the fringes of what little society we have in our little town. For years he did not speak to anyone, poking through trash cans, his hair caked with filth, shunning all humanity until the day he came into the shop. It was just shortly before you arrived now that I think on it. Anyway, Lee told me that I was still his only friend and he just wanted to talk to somebody, which was exciting yet sobering because everyone in town could only speculate what had happened to the man. Some said drugs, others said drink, and some claimed he was a government experiment gone bad. But the truth will always out and he related, after the coaxing effects of an armful of beers, that indeed he had been working for some underground government bureau that he was still afraid to reveal; however, that is not important. Lee had become a wealthy man doing what I could only assume was important work. He said that he 'had had it all': a fully furnished loft with hardwood floors and a view of the Capitol from his bathroom window, a chauffeur, an endless supply of young intern floozies, hand-tailored suits, nightlife, parties. He said he barely had time to walk his golden retriever, to clear his head. The man had the 'whole shebang.' And after not so many years he was finally promoted to the top job of wherever it was that he had worked but was too scared to tell me, the youngest person ever to hold such a position. He was your age now that I think on it, but this tale is not meant to belittle you, to make you seem like an underachiever. For the tragedy cometh," and he paused, sucking in and choking on the frigid air. "I may need an Uncle Matthew moment after this."

"No," I said sternly.

"Okay then, if one has to be so adamant about things, but like all tragic tales, this one has an unhappy ending. Would you like to hear it?" I looked at him sternly and he quickly proceeded. "The tip-top security building where he worked had the most advanced security system in the world at the time, he said. We are not talking about retinal scanners or fingerprint readers or voice detectors. No Eliason, those had already been hacked by the Russians." I did not even try to stifle a yawn. "I have still never heard of such a thing, but the place he worked had something called a Laugh Activated Prompting System, or as Lee called it, 'LAPS.' It seems that an American scientist had discovered in an unrelated experiment that our laughter is the most distinct characteristic about us, more so than fingerprints or dental records, maybe even DNA. By your not-so-stifled yawning I sense that I need to make this long story short. Chieftain, the most brilliant mind in the country at the time, Lee Philpot, could never get into the building where he worked because he could not laugh."

I gave him the most skeptical look I think one human has ever given to another.

"This is one-hundred percent true, little chief. This is not a fairy tale. I am not saying that Lee was completely humorless or without comedic sense, but after getting through three other security doors of inferior rank with ease, he was always stymied at that last door. He told me that when he approached the fourth door of the building, spoke his name into the sensor and was prompted with an automated joke from a speaker, he simply never found any of them funny. He said that computers are inherently unfunny, like Germans he said. He said the timing was all off, that you need a facial expression to appreciate the nuances of a knock-knock joke. Sure, he tried to fake-laugh his way in but the computer was designed to detect courtesy laughs. He told me that he tried everything, from reading a comic book at the speaker to tickling himself to making up his own jokes, but nothing worked. And the more that nothing worked, the more humorless he became, believing that indeed he was not a good-natured fellow. The computer, which is never wrong, convinced him of that. And nothing he did could get him through that door. Everyone in the department knew what a great mind was his and they did everything they could to bypass the system, but it was hard-wired in and impossible to change. And that was that," Willy said with a humph and a shrug.

"What do you mean, 'that was that?' What the hell Willy?"

He looked at me in surprise. "Well the rest is pretty self-explanatory is it not? He was offered a job in one of the departments that required him to enter only three doors, but they were all one door short of his capabilities and he knew it. He fell into a depression, lost almost all of his money and status and floozy supply, and returned to his hometown to go into hiding." Willy stopped walking and shook his head slowly side to side. "And today, Eliason, you know that man as—" and he hesitated, waiting for me to fill in the blank. I stared at him blankly. He pursed his lips at me. "Today you know that man as—"

"You?" I asked.

"Little chief, how could it be me when you know how ham-fisted I am with a computer?! Besides, I have been telling the story in third person, have I not?"

"Oh yeah, ummm," I said.

"You know that man as—"

"Uhhmmm—"

Willy sighed. "I know him as Lee Potphil, but you and the rest of Leadville know him as—" and he waited again, motioning with a roll of his hand to fill in the blank but I could not accommodate him. He sighed big Hollywood at me. "You know him as Laughing Lee."

I stopped and stared at him. "Really? Laughing Lee, the homeless guy in town?"

"Yes, Laughing Lee, but he lives in an old abandoned miner's shack up on East 5th street so technically he is not homeless."

"He doesn't have a car," I said. "Does that count?" Willy told me not to be silly. "Lee used to be smart?" I asked incredulously.

"And still he is, and deeply misunderstood."

"But all I ever see him doing is laughing and talking to himself. Or is that just part of his nutty, homeless mystique?"

"Please, Eliason, we are talking about my friend. It is these stereotypes of yours and the rest of town that undermine him and his feelings of worth."

"Well what are we supposed to think about him? Everyone probably wouldn't think he was crazy if he wasn't always laughing to himself about nothing. And I didn't know he was your friend until about two seconds ago."

"Maybe you shall see him with different eyes now."

I shrugged and after about ten steps of walking I asked Willy why the hell he had told me the story of Lee Potphil. "Do I need to laugh more or something? I haven't really had a ton of stuff to laugh about lately."

"It was, chieftain, merely a story."

"A story with a happy ending would not have been unappreciated."

"Eliason, simply, do not ever feel that you are trapped by your circumstances. Do not let the bone machine pound you into meal. Do not be impeded by door number three when you are truly a fourth-door man. Your life is completely different now and I fear a little for you. My friend, do not forget to laugh or cry at times, otherwise you will become Lee Philpot, laughing at things that are not even there."

I was suddenly morbidly depressed.

"Willy?"

"Listening," he said, I think anticipating something profound.

"How much further is the hospital? I'm really, really cold."

"Oh," he said disappointedly, "just around the next corner."

We came to the corner, a huge open park on our left-hand side. The hazy silhouette of a person shifted in and out of focus in the snow some distance away near a swing set, a smaller shape of a dog bouncing in front, the only two souls alive apparently other than Willy's and mine. Willy pointed to the large parking structure of the hospital, telling me that my trail of tears was near end, or something like that, that the main entrance was in the front so we needed to walk just another fifty yards, then he stopped dead, as if he had spotted a mother bear and her cubs just ahead. Once more he put a hand up to my chest, told me not to move, and wandered across the street, all the while twisting that mustache. He was intently studying a small, one-story office building that had the unmistakable square, beige-green ugliness of being built in 1950, and served as various guises of doctors' and dentists' offices ever since. Yellow police tape ribboned the exterior, wrapped around a couple of trees and over orange cones placed in the parking lot. All of the windows in front had been broken, the scorched black marks of a fire meandered up the brickwork above each window. Large swathes of singed ivy dangled and swayed lightly in the breeze over the panes. The main door was completely missing, a gapingly large, jagged hole in its place with a criss-cross of police tape attached from the top to bottom corners. Judging by the broken brick and wood, a bomb must have ripped it apart. The damage looked to have been caused recently, though it was muted and softened and rendered less horrific by the snow. Next to a police car a solitary policeman stood in the distance with head bowed in the snow.

"What is it Willy?" I asked, after I noiselessly crossed the street and stood next to him. "What happened?" He seemed not to have heard me, he made no response, and when I turned to look at him his face was filled with near-total fear and panic. He swayed a little, his mouth wide open, staring. "Willy, what is it?" I asked. Nothing. "Willy!" and I shook him violently. "What happened?!" Nothing, and I slapped him hard, twice. It felt great. He looked at me, shocked, his mouth still open, and I was about to take defensive measures against his retaliation, but he returned his eyes to the building and stood there with arms limply at this side.

"Willy, what it is?" I said gently, shaking his shoulder. "Willy?"

"I do not know how to tell you little chief. That is the—that was—that is the abortion clinic where your Julia would have been."

CHAPTER TWENTY-EIGHT

"Jesus the Janitor, 10.15 p.m. "

I pictured Julia in a white t-shirt, just a simple white t-shirt, sometime in May, in my apartment in the afternoon sunlight, so bright that she looked like an apparition, hazy and white and luminous.

"Why do you love me?" she asked.

"Hunh?"

"Why do you love me? Why do you love me more than anyone else?" Of course only a woman could ask a question like that, just to freak a guy out. I needed something poetic. I needed a proper reply, but a man never thinks of asking such a question, ever, and therefore has never really worked out a proper reply to such a question. I thought for a couple of seconds and I tried, I really tried.

"Because, I guess, because I never get sick of you." It was the truest thing I've ever said, probably, because women always want the truth, even though they never want the truth. She turned her back and continued being luminous and clean and hazy.

"Someone in the hospital will know what happened," and he peeled away from me without even checking to see if I was there and sped to the front of the hospital. The doors were all locked. "This cannot be," he said to no one, and seemed about to panic. He briskly looped around the opposite side and practically walked into the sliding glass doors of the emergency exit. I followed behind him, feeling lost. The lobby was completely vacant, silent only for the whirring of unseen machines. An older nurse was propped up behind the reception desk, her head dropped and studying something unseen. She did not notice our arrival.

"My dear woman, what in heaven's name has happened across the street?" he bellowed, sidling up to the desk. She looked absolutely appalled and gave Willy such a deathly look that I hung back a little. "I demand immediate answers," Willy persisted.

The nurse, who was probably about the same age as Willy, her hair up in a bun, a solidly built lady but by no means unattractive, stared at Willy then returned her attention to her paperwork.

"Am I speaking to the wind? What violence has been visited upon the clinic next door? Good woman, I am addressing you."

My mouth went dry. The woman said nothing, busting Willy's balls worse than Ding Dong busted the cowboy's. I stood by, trying not to be noticed. She looked like she had worked for five years, straight.

"I will have you thrown out of this hospital if you continue with your barbaric rantings," the nurse said calmly and sternly. Dang, she was kind of sexy when she spoke and Willy immediately melted. She was exactly his type.

"It is merely, well my friend and I wish to know the details of what has transpired at the family resource clinic, what sort of violence—," Willy sputtered, "my dear woman. Forgive me."

The nurse leaned on the counter and steered her cleavage Willy's way. I thought he might faint. She pointed at a little placard taped to the corner.

"You might have noticed that you are way past visitor's hours," she told him. Willy squinted at the print.

"I am afraid I misplaced my bifocals hour ago. Could you be kind enough to tell us—"

"Eight-thirty," she said, "and it is now ten-fifteen. If you have an emergency you may remain. If not, please exit the premises pronto."

Willy was taken aback. He had always been called quite a charmer by the womenfolk *[Yeah right Willy]* but he was making no time with this lady.

"It is merely," he said, looking desperately my way. "Do you know who this man is?"

She glanced disinterestedly my way and returned to Willy. "You probably wouldn't know that I'm seventeen and a half hours into an eighteen hour shift and that the furthest thing I am from knowing right now is who this young man is. Or caring."

"I'm here to see if my mom is okay," I said. She looked over at me but without expression. "I got a call yesterday, from a nurse here. She said my mother's not doing very well."

"You do know it's totally past visiting hours. I can't let you see her?" she reiterated.

"Yes, but could you maybe tell me if she's even here? That's all I want to know."

She relented, asked my mother's name, clicked some keys on the computer and said room 218, but that I still was not allowed to visit.

"She's okay then?" I asked.

"I can't tell just from looking at the computer, but she's probably doing pretty rad," she said, and for a second, just a flash, I saw a look of sympathy. "But I can't break the rules for anyone, and it's totally past visiting hours. No matter who he says you are," and she gave a slight shrug Willy's way. His mouth was wide open and he was staring.

"I'm going to go sit down for a minute, Tricky," I told him and moved like a zombie over to a red, stiff chair with stiff wooden arms and stiff seat cushions.

"Okay, little chief, go 'take a load off,'" Willy said, patting me on the arm without taking his eyes off the nurse. "But what about the family resource center?" he asked the nurse again.

"The abortion clinic? It was fire-bombed yesterday by some right-to-life whackos, or that's what they told us. Normally I might let the young man sneak back to check on his mother but not today. Security is way tight."

I hated when people, anyone, called me "young man." She spoke almost as if I was not there, already a ghost. And she also spoke as if she had three illiterate teenage boys at home who lived in the year 1988. I didn't like her very much.

"That is simply terrible," Willy said, steadying himself against the counter with one hand and holding his brow with the other. "We might have known somebody who was in there." I suddenly wanted to spring out of my chair and pop Willy.

"Oh man, that's sucky," she said.

"Do you have any information on, you know—" and he sort of cupped his mouth with his hands away from me so I couldn't hear the word but I heard it clearly anyway, "casualties?"

"Tons of them," the nurse bellowed.

Willy glanced at me, mortified, and he scrambled over the top of the counter, as if he was going to climb over it and paste his hand to the woman's mouth, to do anything to quiet her. Instead he knocked over a mug of pens and pencils that sprayed all over the counter. The woman was oddly unmoved.

"First off, they shot a doctor dead right through a window," she said, collecting a handful of the pencils and arranging them in the mug. "Then the sickos set off a bomb at the entrance."

I heard the panic in Willy's voice. "But no one was harmed, right, other than the unfortunate doctor?"

The nurse made a snort of disbelief and disgust. "You don't read the papers much do you? Looked at the news lately? They killed something like six girls in there."

"Oh no," Willy howled. "his girlfriend was in there! Oh little chief!"

I heard the squeaking of white nurse's shoes on the linoleum, then silenced by carpet, saw freckles above the nurse's bosom like continents of a map, her powder-blue scrubs, her glasses perched atop her head, her firm demeanor all towering over me. I thought she might simply squash me and I cowered slightly. Suddenly I just wanted to be reached around and hugged by her. She dropped down in the seat next to me, gracefully, and put her arms around me.

"You keep that chin up, young man," she said, and suddenly I loved that she called me young man. I loved how she smelled of disinfectant and something else, some kind of sanitizer or microbacteria-killing hand soap that only doctors were allowed to use. "I can find out if your main squeeze was in there."

I had no idea what the hell she was talking about and merely sunk my head onto her warm roundedness and felt her bare arm on my cheek. She started to hum some sort of extremely soothing lullaby, as she had probably done for thousands of expiring patients as the effects of their hemlock or oliander tea slowly took effect. And incredibly I fell asleep.

When I awoke, who knows after how long, I still felt the wonder of something so round, so firm, so fully packed and I began to unseal my eyelids, yawning contentedly, stretching, about to re-wrap my arms around the nurse…when I noticed with some alarm that she had grown a bristly white mustache. I sprang up and almost sprained my neck.

"Sweet Jesus!" I cried, jumping out of the chair and twisting around on the spot as if I was doing some sort of freaky new dance at an alternative nightclub, or was covered in red army ants, swatting at spots, swirling around, doing anything to wash the Willyness off me.

"I declare that I am not riddled with smallpox, young Cochise," Willy bridled.

"What the hell are you getting at?" I cried. "Were you stroking my cheek?"

"I was serving merely as a replacement lap for Nurse Betty. Despite your twisted oedipal wishes, I was not stroking your cheek."

"Betty who?" I asked, still in a lather, in defensive mode.

"Nurse Betty, the gentle lady upon whom you fell asleep and drooled copiously."

"Oh her," and I sat down heavily, drunkenly almost, crumpling in the chair. "Did you find out anything about the abortion clinic? Was it just a bad dream?"

He did not say anything, which put me more ill at ease than anything that had happened all day. I still felt groggy and wondered aloud why I kept falling asleep.

"Nurse Betty intimated that your black-out may have a causal relationship with getting knocked in the head with a cord of wood. She said it was okay to let you nap, though I have to admit some concern for you little chief. Taking into account the accumulation of events over the last three months I would hazard to say that you are hauling around a load with a stress factor of about two-thousand."

"I guess that's pretty bad?" I asked.

Willy nodded stoically. I absently rubbed the back of my head. It was tender and raised up still. For the first time I noticed an annoying buzzing in my brain that was not internal but instead a short Hispanic guy with curly dark hair who was vacuuming the carpet in front of us. The sound was like a million hungry locusts feeding on my brain. I lifted my feet for the man when he bumped the vacuum against my shoe, then Willy lifted his. The man thankfully turned off the crumb-sucking beast.

"Gracias amigo," Willy said.

"You're welcome, amigo," the man said, taking the seat next to me and sighing heavily, folding his hands in his lap. The three of us sat in silence, awkwardly, and I desperately tried to think if I knew the guy from somewhere. "You've been asleep since I started. I tried to wait for you to wake up by I thought you might sleep there all night. But it's okay." He stared off in the distance comfortably, like we were old friends. "I want to get home before midnight tonight, but I don't know if the buses are running with all this snow. I'd like to get home to my family."

"Of course, good man, of course, who would not?" Willy said. "The long and short of it is, our friend has had a along day."

"Yeah me too," he said, winding the vacuum cord lengthwise around his arm from hand to elbow. "This is my third job today, but who wants to hear about that, especially on Halloween? What you done today?"

I turned to weakly smile at him even though I didn't feel like it, but he seemed nice and smelled like cologne and deserved at least the smallest courtesy smile.

"I have six kids. Hey," he said in surprise but kind of matter-of-factly, "aren't you that guy from tv, the pizza guy?"

"Kind of, yeah, but burger, not pizza," I said, almost forgetting that a million years ago I was that guy on tv, Mr Derfy Burger.

"That's crazy," he said, laughing softly to himself. "Wait until I tell my wife. She loves you. I didn't know it was you until you smiled. You look kind of different than on tv."

I smiled weakly at him again and the three of us sat in silence. He offered me some chocolate. It tasted like no chocolate I had ever eaten.

"This must be made with traditional cocoa butter, not some sort of replacement lipids or soy licithen. Yumsers," Willy said after tasting a small square then breaking off half of the poor man's bar and cramming it into his mouth.

"It's imported from Mexico. What a shame what happened at the building next door. I usually clean there too but not any more I guess. Crazy people. Who would do such a thing?" the man asked. My stomach did the porpoise flip then turned in on itself and knotted tightly. I gazed at him: he was handsome in a boyish way, black mustache, curly dark hair. A patch on his shirt said "Jesus." How crazy is that? I wondered. Was he supposed to be some metaphorical figure or symbol or "literary device" that Willy was always bringing up in real-life situations. Was he supposed to save me or something, to set me on the path of righteousness?

"Little chief, we must determine if Julia was in that building. Nurse Maggie said that she would do whatever she could to help us. We spoke while you were sleeping."

"You knew somebody in there?" Jesus asked in surprise. "Oh no, my friend. If something like that happened to one of my daughters—" and he trailed off, lost in his own thought, then said, "I'd find whoever did it and kill him myself. I would." I always thought Jesus preached about turning the other cheek, etcetera, but maybe that was old Testament stuff. I knew Jesus, this Jesus, would create some hurting because he was a father, a real father. You could tell just by looking at him, even if he was a little guy, he would mess somebody up who messed with his family. He looked like he was born a father. "I keep an eye on my daughters all the time. They are beautiful girls, all of them, except Lupita. Not so much. She's the smart one. She has big dreams. That's why I work so much, for all of them, but especially Lupita's nursing school. It's okay. What else would a man work for?"

"Social justice for one," Willy said, "but with six children you—"

"I did all that when I was young," Jesus interrupted. "Marching, protesting for equal pay, fighting for equality. But at some point you have to leave it alone. I got old and tired and tired of telling people what they should think. Family is all that matters."

Willy looked impressed, offered Jesus his hand to shake and said, "Touche, Jesus," but he pronounced it "hey-seuss" with this kind of accent like he was in a taco commercial. Then he turned to me. "Somehow we have to find out about your mother too."

"Your mother was in that building too?" Jesus asked in shock.

"No, his girlfriend," Willy explained. Jesus raised his eyebrows. "His mother is in the hospital here. She is quite ill."

Jesus looked at me, his mustache twitching slightly. "You're having a bad day." And you know you're having a bad day when a guy named Jesus with three jobs and six kids tells you you're having a bad day. Nurse Maggie entered from some back hallway, her shoes squeaking on the linoleum.

"William, we're leaving when my shift is over. I called the morgue. You said you can identify the girl? She's probably all burned up and a pretty crispy critter if it's her."

Willy looked at me in horror and popped out of his seat. Jesus looked as if he had eaten some bad cilantro. I pretended like I didn't hear anything.

"Oh crap, I didn't think he was awake," she said, fixing me with her eyes. "I didn't think you were awake. Shoot. Crap. Willy, you can call him when we get there." Willy sheepishly told her that neither of us had cell phones. She and Jesus both looked incredulous.

"That's mega-whacky," she said, turned her back on us and disappeared through another door. Jesus told us to wait a minute, called someone on his cell phone, spoke in Spanish about a billion words in twenty seconds then hung up.

"My wife said to tell pizza man hello," he smiled. "Everyone is home and safe," then he tucked the phone into my hand like St. Francis giving a dove to a peasant. "You take my cell phone and use it.

Whenever you're done just leave it at the front desk. But take as long as you need."

I knew that once he had offered the thing to me he would never take it back, even if I begged him to keep it, or insisted that I would accidentally spill maple syrup all over it or would unintentionally call Taiwan for three days without knowing it or would leave it on a bus somewhere. Nope, he would never take it back. That's just what people from other countries do, particularly ones with people named Jesus.

"We could not possibly 'put you out' like that," Willy said but Jesus was already up, collecting the vacuum and about to disappear through one of the countless doors through which Nurse Betty kept vaporizing. He looked around the room cautiously then said, "This is my brother's shirt by the way. I'm not Jesus, I'm Cesar, but it's okay. Don't tell anyone. He's a mechanic if you ever need someone to look at your car," then a door opened automatically and swallowed him up.

"I wonder if Jesus makes house calls," Willy wondered aloud. "The Camaro could use a pair of miracle hands," and he stared off in space. "Young plains drifter, if things do not 'work out' for us now with Jesus *and* Caesar on our side, they never will."

I sat there in my own thoughts, listening to the bubbling and gurbling of a huge fish tank across the lobby. Willy shifted his weight and engulfed almost entirely my arm rest.

"Do not fret, young Eliason. Our Julia is okay."

"Do you think so?"

"I know so," and he touched the side of his nose. I watched movement in the fish tank, the plastic sea grass waving up and down, the sliding colors of fish from corner to corner.

"Willy, you don't think Ding Dong and Little Ding blew up the clinic do you?"

Willy looked surprised. "Gosh Eliason, why would they do that?"

"I don't know. They just seem kind of reckless and crazy, blowing up stuff all over the place."

"Of course they did not. Their 'beef' is with Derfy Burger, not random family practice clinics," Willy said, looking troubled.

"Besides, the incident at the clinic happened yesterday. They were miles away."

"It's not so far away for them to have done it and driven up to the mountains. It's only like a hundred miles. And they've probably got all kinds of remote-controlled timers that they can set off from another planet."

"Gosh, Eliason. I never considered such a scenario." He combed his mustache with a thumb then shook his head. "Eliason, in no way did the Bells have anything to do with the murders next door. It is a mere coincidence."

"Okay. It's just, it's too much stuff for one day," I said.

"It is too much 'stuff' for one *year*," he said, sliding down into his chair, spreading out his feet and folding his hands over his belly. I watched the colors slipping around in the fish tank. One buzzing machine somewhere in the lobby turned itself off and seconds later another turned itself on with a clank-clank-clank and then a constant whir.

"Are you hungry at all, Willy?"

"A skosh," he said. "There must be a snack machine somewhere on site."

"Yeah," I said. I thought I might just reach into the aquarium and swallow a fish whole. I listened to the burbling of the little generator in the water making bubbles and I felt soothed almost. Hell no was I going to fall asleep again but my head started to droop.

"Hey dude, do you have any quarters," Willy asked, "for the snack machine?"

I reached into my pocket, pulled out my wallet and dumped eleven cents and some lint into his open palm. He chuckled lightly to himself and asked, "Do you think the machine has change for a million dollar bill?"

"God, don't remind me," I groaned. I asked him what time it was. He said it was exactly the nineteenth minute of the eleventh hour of the day. Sometimes I could just slap him. I said, "Willy, maybe I'm just crazy but I've been thinking about something."

"Listening," he said, allowing more of his girth to swallow my arm rest.

"I mean, I don't know much about technology and stuff (Willy nodded his head vigorously, smirked and was about to say something smart but I cut him off) but I was wondering about when Ding Dong said Little Ding's watches and clocks and stuff kept changing time on their own. Well, tonight the clocks change—"

"William!" a voice boomed from the empty space of an opened door. Willy jumped to his feet so quickly his Farto! cap fell of his head. "We're leaving now! I'm off my shift mega-early. Come on!" Nurse Betty ordered. She had a white pleather purse hooked around her elbow, a tan coat cinched at the waist and a lime-green scarf on her head so she looked just like someone hanging out in the suburban kitchen of a 1960s sitcom. But she looked good. Willy stealthily grabbed his cap, stuffed it into his coat pocket and tried to straighten his hair. He looked at me almost haplessly. I knew he was in love.

"We got a new kid on this shift," Nurse Betty said to me, pulling Willy by the arm. "She's a little more chilled out with the rules." She stopped and stared at me, hard. She was going to say something to me, anything, to scold me or comfort me, but she didn't and pulled Willy toward the automatic door. "There's some pretty gnarly mints on the counter if you want," she said over her shoulder to me. The door slid open and they passed through it, stopping at the curb, sheltering at the overhang where Willy turned and peered at me through the door. But it slid closed. I watched them walk through the darkened parking lot where he stopped to gaze up at the snow and search for something in his pockets. Nurse Betty found his cap hanging out of his pocket and put it almost tenderly onto his head, then pulled him once more into the darkness.

CHAPTER
TWENTY-NINE

"The Only Pattern is Disarray,
11.45 p.m. "

It felt strange to sit there all alone. All by myself. I stared at Jesus-Cesar's phone in my lap as if it were an object left in a Nebraska cornfield, accidentally dropped by hastily departing aliens being shot at my Nebraskans. I just sat there all by myself and watched the snow come down outside the window. I tried not to wonder about what would happen in my near future, or what had happened in my immediate past—it was an odd state of amber-like, disconnected, slow-moving, dripping minutes that felt like near bliss, like a runner's high, except in reverse, sitting down doing nothing. A heater turned on close by and warmed my knees. I thought about sitting there forever. Then I thought about sneaking back to room 218 to check on my mother but a little Hispanic nurse came through one of the doors and stood behind the counter where Nurse Betty had terrorized Willy and me. She smiled. She was cute as hell. Surely she would let me go back and see my mother, I mean, she was cute as hell and had to be nice too. She was a nurse for chrissakes. Jesus' phone began to move like a nervous gerbil in my lap. I scooped it out like spilt liquid from my lap and dropped it on the carpet in shock. It began to play a song with some accordian and mariachis and some other south of the border stuff thrown in. I stared at the thing on the floor and heard the nurse giggle politely. I watched it squirm and play music on the floor.

"You should answer it," she suggested. I picked it up and started mushing buttons and, I'm quite sure, hung up on the person. She walked over and held out her hand and hit a button, squinting at the screen. "It was Miss Betty," she said, punched a number and began speaking into the phone, nodding and saying things like "yes, yes, of course," and "she's *his* mom?" and "if you think it's okay," then she hung up.

"If you ever need to call the person who just called you, hit this green button," she said, explaining it slowly, as if I was the new kid in kindergarten trying to open a new box of crayons. "This is my dad's phone so I had to show him how to use everything. My name's Lupita," she said, offering her hand.

"You're Lupita?" I said, just a little too shocked. Man, if she was the not-so-much pretty daughter then I had to meet her five sisters, or at least introduce Willy.

"Do you know me?" she asked, surprised.

"No, it's just your dad, he said, well I thought you were still in nursing school or something."

"I am kind of, I guess. I'm interning. Everyone says I should be working at a job where I can make money so I can pay off nursing school but, I don't think I want to be a waitress or something to pay for school when I can do this and know how it feels to be a nurse, whether I like it or not." I told her that I hoped she liked being a nurse and she nodded. "It's nice to help other people and all that jazz. Ask me in five years after I've cleaned out about a million bedpans and we'll see if I feel the same way. I've got tons of friends who went to college and owe a lot more than me but they've got business degrees, which is kind of helpful I guess. But they're all getting stuck in a rut or some kind of pattern of just making money—that's their only goal, is to make tons of money."

I nodded. She looked a lot like Julia actually, when she frowned or looked thoughtful. She asked how I liked her dad, and I told her he tried to vacuum my shoes. She laughed to herself. "Talk about a guy who works way too much," she said. "But he's my dad."

"Yeah," I said, "he's real nice. I like him."

"Oh, Miss Betty, when she called, she said she changed her mind and I can let you go back and see your mom. She's usually really strict so she must like you." I asked Lupita if she knew my mother. "Oh yeah. She's been in here for three days now I guess. Yeah, three days. She is always so nice when I check on her. Veronica?"

I was pretty chuffed that she knew my mother just like that, by name. "She must be a real pain in the neck if you know her by name."

"Not at all. I like her a lot. She's always in really high spirits. She's got a really nice sense of humor and does these really crazy, perfect impersonations of people."

"My mom?" I asked, disbelieving.

"Yeah," she said. "She's always got something real interesting to say. She doesn't talk just to talk. Or she's cracking jokes."

"My mom?" I asked, still in disbelief.

"Yes, your mom. Why are you so surprised? There's been about a hundred people coming to see her. She says they're her students trying to get better grades but I can tell they all really like her a lot. A couple of girls were crying when they left yesterday."

"Are you sure?" I repeated in disbelief.

"Why do you act so surprised? She's really great."

And I felt like the worst son ever.

"Eliason, I feel kind of obligated to tell you, she was sort of okay when she first came in but when I left yesterday she looked—not so great. She didn't talk at all. That kind of worries me. I'm not sure how she is right now, not to scare you or anything, just to prepare you."

"Oh," I said, and suddenly I felt completely unprepared to face my mother. I didn't want to see her that way. I certainly didn't want to think about her having a sense of humor. My mother was the kind of person who found her funny bone only when it was way too late, when things had gotten beyond saving. "Umm, how did you know my name just now?"

It was her turn to look incredulous. "You're joking right?" she asked. "Everyone knows your name. It was all I saw on tv today. Papa told me when I saw him in the break room just now, that you were sitting out in the lobby, which I thought was about the weirdest thing I ever heard—what in the world is Mr Derfy Burger doing here?! I didn't believe him at first. I think he told me so that I wouldn't have a heart attack when I saw you. I was going to call the Derfy Hotline, and then Papa told me you were here to see your mother and that she was pretty sick. I thought that was kind of nice, you know, coming to visit your mother even now that you're famous but I didn't know your mother was Veronica until Miss Betty called. I thought when I came through the doors there'd be a million people running around and cameras everywhere. It was pretty weird to see you just sitting all by yourself. Hasn't anyone called the Derfy Hotline?"

"I'm not sure I know what the Derfy Hotline is," I admitted nervously, pretty sure that I didn't *want* to know what the Derfy Hotline was.

"You're kidding again, aren't you?" she asked. I shook my head. "You're telling me you don't know what's going on in China right now, the contest or game show or whatever it is, 'Who Wants to Marry Mr Derfy Burger?' and all that? There's about a billion Chinese women going crazy looking for you. There's riots everywhere. Somebody burned down the American Embassy somewhere, Shanghai I think, but they said on tv that it was an accident. All of these women are trying to get visas so they can come here and find you but the Chinese government put some kind of emergency ban on all flights to the US for the next month. So they're going even crazier. Just before I came into work I heard one guy saying this is what could finally bring the Communist government down in China. You don't know about any of that?" I shook my head and she asked, "Haven't you been watching the news at all? Derfy Burger is offering five thousand dollars to the first person who finds you and calls the Derfy Hotline. Wasn't this all part of the whole promo thing?"

"Um, I don't think so. I don't even know anymore. Maybe," I said, because at that point who the hell knew. Maybe Ding Dong was part of the promo. Maybe Bacon Smalls was part of the promo. Maybe Howdy Boobs was part of the promo. Maybe Willy was part of the promo. Maybe every decision I made that day was part of the promo. Maybe every decision I had made my whole life was part of the promo. "They're only giving five thousand dollars to find me?"

"Yeah, cheapos," Lupita shrugged. "But five grand is five grand."

"Yeah," I said. Then there was complete silence, except for the gurgling of the fish tank. I told Lupita she should call the Derfy Hotline, to get the money.

"I was going to at first," she said. "but now—you wouldn't really get to see your mother. It's kind of nice and quiet in here after all the craziness on tv today. My brain hurts from watching it all day.'

"Yeah, mine too," I said, and she laughed softly. I told her the fish tank was a pretty nice addition to the lobby, and she remembered she had to feed them. She got up and dropped little papery red and white and orange bits of food into the water. I watched the slippery colors dart to the surface and gobble them up. I asked Lupita, "Do you think I should go back and see my mom pretty soon?"

"Yeah, pretty soon," she said, "but she's probably sleeping." I asked her if I should wait until the morning. "No! Not that long."

"I'm kind of scared to see her," I admitted.

"I understand. If you need, I can go with you whenever you're ready," she said, and I thought that she was about the nicest person I ever met. She told me she had to make some "rounds" and started to walk away, then turned. "She's had someone with her for the last couple of days, so don't worry about her being alone. We're not supposed to do it but we like your mother so much we kind of bent the rules."

"Oh," I said, trying not to sound surprised anymore. "That must be, um—" and I couldn't think of the blonde woman's name, the one with breast cancer, but her face came rushing back to my memory, and that turtleneck, like it was only yesterday and not five years ago. "That's good."

"You seem like a good person, Eliason. Don't get depressed by everything. Everything changes," she said, and I thought again that she was about the nicest person a guy could ever meet, and I didn't have the heart to tell her that she was wrong, that I wasn't a good person, and that she was right, that nothing gold can stay. I sat there for a while, thinking about how I needed to see my mother, but I couldn't move. I had thought about this moment many times in my past, the day that I would have no more living relatives. I thought I would be a much older man, however, when it happened. I never expected my mother to die so young. I admit, when I was a teen, feeling rebellious and disillusioned and angry at my mom for something, not buying orange juice or something, I had always thought how this moment, if it came, would make me such a sympathetic character, that it might happen in school (getting called over the intercom, going to the principal's office, listening into the phone) and I could have a little freak-out session in front of everybody, then I'd be an outlaw almost, the orphan boy, the kid who yanked off the make-out record from the record player at prom and slapped on an Iron Maiden or Joy Division album because I didn't care, I didn't have parents anymore, the brooding kid in school who had no parents anymore, the kid who drew stuff on his notebook in class instead of turning in his homework, I might dress in black to heighten the effect, the kid who the girls liked because he was dangerous and had no parents and lived in an abandoned house with no running water but could still quote from an assortment of fine literary works, how when I finally got my license I would buy a motorcycle and be the dangerous kid with no parents who rode a motorcycle, the kid with no relatives, no ties, nothing to keep him from doing wrong if he chose that path because there was no one to disappoint, no long distance calls from mom to grandma to break the news of what Eliason had done, whatever it was that I had done wrong, from impregnating some girl in junior high five years my junior to illegally downloading all of Rod Stewart's 1980s songs to accidentally burning down the American Embassy in Shanghai. I knew this day would come, and if it didn't come in junior high then I prayed that it would come when I was an older guy, probably with a family of my own, and I'd come home late from work one night and my wife would say, "Eliason, sit down for a second," and I'd instantly know that my mother had died, and I'd put my head on her shoulder without crying and she'd ask if we should tell the kids and I'd say something really adult like, "It's late, let them sleep. No need to wake them unnecessarily. I'll do it in the morning," and later I'd lie awake for a while with my eyes wide open while my wife slept then I too would fall asleep. At my lowest point I would think about becoming an evangelical maybe, and talk about Jesus (the carpenter one, not the hospital janitor one) to total strangers but then I'd realize that I couldn't take seriously a religion that wasn't at least twenty years older than I was, then I'd decide to have a little ice cream or something to make me feel better. And I thought that if this day came when I was in my twenties, then it would be oddly liberating. I wouldn't be a nervous kid and I wouldn't be an older man, worrying about funeral expenses and boxing up "earthly possessions" or figuring out where the hell to bury my mother, whether a religious person should read something next to her dirt and spray water over it—I'd just be a twenty-something dude without any parents, relatives, blood line, nothing. I'd probably go to the cemetery in some beat up shoes, stand over her grave for a minute or two, not really feel anything then wonder "What the hell do I do now?" and maybe pour some malt liquor beer over her headstone then walk away, thinking "What the hell do I do know?" But I knew, somehow, that it would be oddly liberating, not to have anything or anyone, that I could simply hop a plane to Egypt if I felt the hell like it or I could buy a condo in Aspen if the fancy struck me or I could take tango lessons though I was hopeless at dancing, because who the hell did I care to disappoint or impress anymore? Who was around to say, "Puh, tango, are you kidding, your father always had two left feet just like you" or "Egypt? But I haven't seen you in three years!" I'm not saying that I would go to Egypt before seeing my mother, or that I hated visiting my mother, but the point is, I wouldn't even have to consider it. I could just go without even thinking. I would have no ties to anything. I could do whatever I wanted. I could bend down and drink from the chocolate stream if I damn well felt like it. But I was in my twenties when the day came, and I didn't feel any of this. I just wanted to sit in a chair and not move at all. I prayed that the little mariachi-playing, quivering gerbil would remain still in my lap. Then, without thought, I held it to close to my nose so I could see the green button, pushed it and held the gerbil up to my ear. It rang twice then Nurse Betty yelled something from the receiver like "Cesar, como estas mi ahhhhhhh-migo?"

"Uhm, this isn't Cesar, it's Eliason," I said into the gerbil, scared as hell of Miss Betty.

"Who in the heck is this?!"

"It's Eliason—the guy in the emergency room," I sputtered.

There was a long pause in which I thought I heard Willy mumbling something in the background. "Veronica's kid? What in the hey is your name?"

"Eliason," I said, about to cry. "Uhm, could I maybe speak to Willy, please?"

"Yep, but we're not at the morgue yet, if that's what you want. This snow is totally crazy everywhere. Here's Willy," and there was quite a long pause as the phone was passed through the air between them. I could tell by the muffled brushings into the receiver that Willy was having trouble handling the little device with his mittens because at first I heard him say, hushed almost, "Little chief, what—oh shoot," and I heard the sound of the phone hitting something somewhat solid, the floor perhaps, then the clomping sound of boots slap-shooting the thing from one foot to the other like a hockey puck, more swishing, then ten minutes must have passed when I finally heard, "Little chieftain, what gives?"

"It's not important, I was just kind of thinking about something," I began.

"Firstly, how is your mother's condition?" he asked.

"I haven't gone back to see her yet," and he began to make noises of outrage so I quickly interrupted: "Willy, I was thinking about something, with Ding Dong and Little Ding." I could tell from the silence that he looked conspiratorially at Nurse Betty, then he said, "Just a sec—oh shoot," followed by another thud and more slap-shooting for about twenty minutes.

"I have switched ears for more privacy, little chief," he whispered, and I knew he was bending away from Nurse Betty, probably leaning his head and ear against the door. "What are your concerns for—eh, Darryl and John?" he asked.

"Who?" I asked. "No, Ding Dong and TJ—the Bells."

"Yes, that is right—" then he said heavily with exaggerated emphasis, "Darryl and John. You know?"

It took me a second then I said, "Oh yeah, them," then I took a dramatic two-second pause. "I think *Darryl* and *John* are going to blow themselves up."

A rush of air. Thud. Slap-shooting. Rustle-rustle-rustle. Thud. Rustle-rustle.

"Little chief, what do you mean?" Willy asked, all out of breath, finally.

"I was just kind of thinking about when TJ said his watch kept changing all by itself every time he went from one time zone to another, and I thought since the clocks change tonight it might screw them up. Their little timers will change all by themselves."

"Sweet Elysian, Eliason!" Willy said. "They shall blow themselves up unawares!"

"What should we do?" I asked, calmly. There was a long muffled pause and I could just make out Willy and Nurse Betty mumbling something to each other, then I heard Willy say "No, Betty, Eliason and I use the phrase 'to blow oneself up' allegorically, meaning to endanger oneself. His friends are out, erm, driving in this dangerous storm and I said, 'They shall blow themselves up' to denote that they may, erm, get into a crash or endanger themselves needlessly." I heard Nurse Betty's voice but couldn't understand her, then Willy said, "No, it is akin to one married spouse saying to the other 'Would you like to do the laundry tonight?' if their children are within earshot, and they actually are referring to, you know, love-making." I heard more muffled sounds from Nurse Betty and Willy said, "Oh yes, it is quite useful when one is engaging in the art of subterfuge," then quickly "not that Eliason and I are trying to deceive you about anything, or something, or someone."

"Willy, are you going to be going close to the Derfy Burger or anything? Maybe you can warn them," I shouted into the phone.

"No need to bark, young chief. I cannot simply drive up and say 'Gentlemen, you are about to blow yourselves up! Make haste!'" then there was another long, long pause in which, though I could make out no words, only the combined murmurs of their voices, I knew Willy was explaining his outburst again. "Young chieftain who feels the northern winds, I require a minute or so to think," and there was static and silence after Willy hung up.

I sat there looking at the gerbil, waiting for it to wiggle, but it didn't. Lupita had disappeared into some broom closet or break room somewhere and the colors in the fishbowl were gone, sated I supposed, where they reposed in their tiny plastic castle or hid behind the scuba diver with the treasure chest whose lid opened and closed every couple of seconds with the liberation of a bubble or two. I sat and thought about Ding Dong and TJ. I did some math in my head and figured that since we gained an hour, if anything, the Bells would have an extra hour to fool around with their stuff, but what if, at midnight, as they were waiting for the ka-boom at the Boulder Derfy Burger and nothing happened, I don't know, what if Ding Dong, in his desperation to make a personal statement, touched the blue and green wires together like he was hot-wiring a car or something in a movie and accidentally blew everything up. I wasn't a pyrotechnics expert but, it could happen, couldn't it? And I knew in the paper they always told us to change our clocks at two a.m., but maybe computers and watches and non-human things didn't need that two hour idiot cushion, that they could change at midnight back into the previous day at least for an hour without confusing themselves like humans did. I searched for a clock on the wall—almost midnight, incredibly. It was like we were in some action movie in which a guy, sitting in his car, discovered that it had been booby-trapped so that if he left his seat it would blow up, but it would also blow up if he didn't move his tush in six hours, and this allowed the pyrotechnicians just enough time to get there, sweat over things for five hours and fifty minutes until, gosh darn it, they figured out the system but it would take them about nine minutes and fifty-eight seconds to disarm it, maybe or maybe not, if everything went exactly right, and if they, most importantly, didn't touch the blue and green wires together or accidentally let drop a bead of sweat onto the ultra-sensitive ignition pad.... And it was almost midnight. I pressed the green button on the gerbil.

"Como estas, ahhhhhh-migo," Nurse Betty bellowed. After some seconds of silence she said, "This isn't Cesar, is it? Is this Veronica's kid again?" In a way it was wonderful to have a fourth identity: not Eliason, not little chieftain, not Mr Derfy Burger. I was now Victoria's kid, which was okay. I asked if I could speak to Willy again.

"It would be totally cool if you said hi or something."

I didn't really know how to react so I said, "Uhh, hi," then after what was becoming a bit of a tradition with the phone, a long long silence, I asked, "Could I speak to Willy?"

"Why didn't you just say so?" then the phone relayed once more the empty space between their two bodies, then I heard the static electricity swish of Willy's mittens.

"Chieftain, I simply cannot devise a method of communication with John and Paul."

"I thought it was Darryl and John," I said.

"Darryl and John Paul," he quickly amended. "Do you have an idea?"

"Didn't TJ give you his number when they were driving away that very first time? Didn't he write it on a little piece of paper?"

"You are a right old stick, chieftain!" he cried, and I won't describe what felt like the next twenty minutes of Willy removing his mittens, searching every pocket in his coat, cursing under the sound of old hamburger wrappers crunching in his pockets, etcetera, before he finally found the paper, gave me the number and told me to give him "a callback" after I contacted them. I put the number into the gerbil and pressed the green button. It rang and rang and rang and just when I was about to hang up I heard a click and a tentative voice say "This is Nobby."

"TJ, it's the burger man, Eliason."

"Jeez man, I didn't know who it was," TJ said, the line filled with so much static I could barely make out his words. "Man, what's going on?"

"Hey man, I think you need to be careful with your timer stuff. The clocks change tonight and I wasn't sure if it would mess your timers up." He said he couldn't really understand what I was saying. "We change our clocks tonight," I shouted into the receiver. "I don't know if your timers or whatever change by themselves, but they might get messed up." There was the traditional static and silence. I thought I could hear him and his father discussing something. Then he said, loud and clear as if he was sitting right next to me, "Man, we're just waiting. What about the clocks? Hey, how's your mother?"

"She's fine, Little Ding, listen, the clocks change tonight, you know, daylight savings or whatever, so I don't know if that's going to mess up your timers or whatever."

He cursed. "Dad, the clocks change tonight! Is that going to mess with the timing devices? What time is it, burger man?!"

"It's just about midnight I think. You don't have any left over things in the trunk do you, you know, explosive things?" I asked looking nervously around the empty room.

"Yeah man, 'cause we didn't go to as many Derfy's as we had planned," he said hurriedly. He cursed again. "Dad, do you thinks the clocks changing is—" and the line went dead, just silence. I sat there, open-mouthed, staring at the gerbil. I tried calling back three or four times but got no answer. It was exactly midnight according to the gerbil. I couldn't just sit there so I jumped up and paced the carpet, back and forth, forth and back, back and forth. I tried to call several more times but received no answer. Suddenly it began to wiggle and play mariachis.

"Ding!" I shouted into it.

"On the contrary, it is Snowshoe Willy. Nurse Betty is waiting for me in the morgue. Chief, what happened?" he shouted.

"I got ahold of them but when I told them about the clocks, the phone just went dead, right in the middle of talking to TJ. I keep calling but no one answers."

"Oh dear. Little chief, I have to go, but keep trying. Or I shall try with my phone."

"Maybe TJ just hung up because he had to concentrate on the stuff, right? That's what you would do, isn't it?"

"We shall see. Just keep trying to call them, little chief."

"He's probably too busy to answer now. That's probably why they don't answer."

"Do not panic, little chief. Do not bother with phoning them. That shall be my department. You just go see your mother. Promise me."

"I promise Willy. Okay bye," and I hung up and put the gerbil on the counter at the front desk. I stood there and stared off into the distance for some time. I couldn't put it off anymore: it was time to go to room 218.

CHAPTER THIRTY

"Mom,
12:04 a.m."

It was too easy to find room 218—210 then 212, 214, 216 then 218. I wished in a way that I had to decipher some cryptic sanskrit code to find the room, then shine moonlight through a prism on the hilt of my sword that would point to a hole in the floor where I'd have to assemble a scaffold of bones and climb through a window just big enough for my head high up in the wall that I would tumble through and land in a heaped pile of dust into my mother's room, and she wouldn't be sick at all but instead was the wealthy Queen of Jordan, my mother, and I had spent twenty-four years on a long journey to discover who I really was, and she told me all this as she rested atop a pile of gold coins with a gleam in her eye, a life-sized portrait of my deceased father wearing a tunic in a jewel-encrusted frame behind her.

I pushed on the door to room 218 but my stomach did so many flips that I had to reverse step and visit the latrine. I stayed there for some time doing my business, splashing water on my face, thinking, pulling hundreds of paper towels from the dispenser, and twisting my nerves into a taut twisted twined helix of shiny, unfeeling fortitude. I crossed the noiseless hallway and again pushed on door 218, gently. I peeked around the edge of the door. And there lay my mother.

I fully expected her to be hooked up to a hundred machines with tubes coming out of metal parts and going into her human parts, of pumps whooshing up and down like frogs on toadstools, of a blipping television screen threatening constantly to flat-line with a screaming unattended bleep, the stench of sticky disinfected human sickness thickening the air, my mother's pale-blue and bruised body scattered on top of the bedsheets. But the room smelled faintly of vanilla. And balloons and cards were plastered everywhere. And it was still and quiet. And my mother lay there under the sheets as if she was a little kid sleeping. She looked thinner, certainly, but not sick. I walked softly over to her, to not awaken her, and stared at her, which felt weird, not quite like looking at a statue because you know that a statue will never pop open its eyes and shout "What the hell are you looking at?!" And I knew that after a couple of seconds she would feel my presence, open her eyes, take her hand from underneath the sheets and croak "My son, dear, I've been waiting," just like in the movies…but she didn't. And I stood there wondering how long I should stare at her, waiting for something to happen. I read a card or two. I read the ingredients on the bottle of some hand sanitizer hanging upside-down on the wall. I thought about bending down at the tiny sink and taking a swig of water because I was dead thirsty. I looked at my mother a little more. They didn't show this part in the movies; okay, sometimes they would have that weird stop-action sequence where a visitor or two would be sitting in chairs, then they'd magically be leaning against a window sill, then they'd be propped up next to the person's bed, then someone else would come in and stand next to the bed, then the original person would magically return in a chair sloping over the patient in vigilance, all in the attempts of the director to denote the passage of hours and days, maybe even weeks. But what about the mind-numbing spaces in between? I bent down closer to make sure that she was indeed breathing. She was, rhythmically, shallowly. Out of the back of her left hand, held firmly and what looked painfully by white tape, snaked an i.v. tube into a sack of clear liquid hanging high in the air like a fern next to her bed. The tv remote control rested up against her thumb knuckle as if it were part of her life-prolonging equipment. Obviously the blonde minx with the turtleneck wasn't there. I stood there longer and started getting nervous as hell for no particular reason and lowered myself into a chair with no armrests by the door. From my vantage I could still see the lump of my mother's form between the spaces of the hand bumpers that ran along the borders of the bed. Most importantly I could see her nose and chin and their rhythmic rise and fall. I felt I could simply drop my head on my chest and wait for my mother to awaken in the morning. I knew that I should talk to her as I sat there, to tell her of all the mistakes I had made and the regrets that I had, all the things I should have told her years ago, apologized for not being a better son, you know all the Hollywood Hallmark stuff, but it wasn't my style, to talk to nothing but air vapor. When I was a kid I didn't even have an imaginary friend to talk to, and if any little kid was ripe to have some weird little ghost as a friend to confer with on life's major decisions (asking Shelly to the junior high dance) and to credit for minor bad choices (burning a whole the size of a basketball in the hallway carpet), I was the ripest kid of all. So I wasn't going to sit there and talk to my mother and pretend like she was listening, for my own benefit. And I'm pretty sure I fell asleep. At some point I heard a rustle in the room and I saw the curtain that divided the room into two almost imperceptibly ripple with movement. I froze. It was King Fred! Or Ding Dong. Or Willy. Or the minx. A hand slowly moved the curtain aside and there stood Julia, but she was wearing some crazy kind of white wig and a nurse's uniform. "Hey baby, what took you so long?" But I knew it was just a dream sequence that should have gone on longer and had more symbolism but I woke with a jump. Julia had looked old in that damn wig, and also like she was trying to hide or disguise herself. It had been a pretty real kind of dream for lasting only a few seconds. I sat there and waited for the dream fog to dissipate.

"Ma, are you awake?" I asked, standing and putting a hand on the bed bumper. She had no reaction. She looked like my mother still, not sick or anything but oddly not there, physically I mean, not psychologically, like my mother always used to accuse me of being when she started jawing on about some loco student of hers or some psychology review she had just read. There seemed to be no presence in her body. It was hard to explain. I thought for a second that she had died, then I heard movement on the other side of the curtain. I had seen enough horror movies to recognize a person dreaming while awake, to know that the most prudent course to take (at least to every member of the audience who wasn't half brain-dead) was to rip open that door, make a break for it, never look back, to definitely, certainly, never, ever go look behind the curtain, but I found my feet taking me there anyway. There was a little table on this side of my mother's bed, a kidney-shaped thing with a built-in seat like you'd see in an ice cream shop or from kindergarten, and a short can of grape something, juice or soda, sat on the table with a bendy straw leaning out of it. I thought about taking a sip because I was thirsty as hell, but didn't want to get cancer. It was a horrible thing to think but it's what I thought anyway. Then I heard a kind of whimper from the other side of the curtain, a sleepy-dreamy whimper, not a painful whimper. I was afraid, yes, to look on the other side of the curtain, to see the monster in the other bed who probably had something way worse than my mother, some old lady in a purple nightgown with a tracheotomy and a cigarette hanging out of the hole in her throat. Or there was just the little kid's nightmare monster there, big, hairy, ugly and evil with blood on its black claws and yellow fangs. I stood at that curtain for about a million years, I shouldn't, I shouldn't, what about a person's privacy, what about the monster, but I started to move the curtain aside very slowly, slowly because the little metal ball bearings riding inside the metal rod would sound like a thousand pellets of ice against a window if I moved too quickly. I peeked just beyond the sheet and saw a pair of shoes sticking out of some blue jeans on top of the blanket, as if the person had slept in her clothes and was going to make a break for it, Alcatraz style, sliding right through the vent grill next to the sink or out the window as soon as the lady in the bed next to her stopped jabbering about the psychosexual social rituals of the Incas and fell the hell asleep. Actually, upon more inspection, I noticed one of her shoes was off, untied and laying on the blanket. They were pretty stylish sneakers, not an old lady's kind of shoe. I thought they looked like the shoes that the blonde minx would wear. I peeked a little further and noticed the lady was lying on her side, her knees pulled up slightly in a half-fetal position. She had pretty slim, nice legs underneath her jeans for an old lady, I was sure. I pulled the curtain a little further and saw a kind of cute, fuzzy white sweater, mohair or something, pulled just over the top of her jeans. She was certainly a snappy dresser for a sick, old lady and I knew I would ruin everything by looking too far, to discover her shriveled old face. I knew that it must be the sassy blonde from years ago, just settling down for a ten-minute kip to energize the old battery before maintaining her non-stop vigil by my mother's side. Didn't Lupita tell me that the minx had been staying with my mother for a few days? I scrunched my eyes, leaving them only half-open, and pushed the curtain an inch or two, peered around and looked at the chin, the nose, the eyes, forehead and hair.

And there lay Julia.

I stood there with the edge of the curtain balled up in my left hand and swayed just a little. It had been a long day and I knew I was having another dream sequence in which she would open her eyes, ask me something weird and then disappear. I took a halting step forward, fell back on accident and knocked the kidney-shaped desk. Julia slowly opened her eyes with a tiny yawn, her delicate brown cheek resting on the pillow. It was about the prettiest thing I had ever seen. She looked right at me as if she had been expecting me the whole time.

"Hey baby, what're you doing?" she asked.

I stood there stupidly, looking at a ghost. "Just standing here." Nothing else came to me.

She looked at me curiously, rolled over and sat up, putting a finger to her lips to signal silence and patted the mattress beside her for me to sit down. I stood there, cemented to the spot. She patted the mattress again, beckoning like a person with food to a scared coyote. I moved forward tentatively, staring at her.

"Why are you looking at me like that?" she whispered with an uncertain smile. I still didn't have words and finally mastered the distance to the bed. I circled over her, riding a warm air current like a hawk until I floated up over her, circling right above her, up and up right through the ceiling and through the roof and out of the room, arcing up and up and up and up and up away. Julia sprang up and moved her feet to the floor grabbing me around the waist.

"Baby, sit down. You look like you're about to faint," she whispered urgently. She pulled me to the mattress and kept her arms around me. I waited for the moment when I would wake up and realize I wasn't just dreaming but hoping, asleep. "Maybe you should lay down," she said and I plopped down onto the bed like a block. I felt her hand guiding my head down to the pillow, then she shimmied down the mattress and pulled my legs up onto the blanket. I closed my eyes and tried to swallow but couldn't. I suddenly remembered that this was how my father's father died, when I was just a little kid: he forgot how to swallow, probably in a bed just like this one, in some hospital somewhere on the east coast, in the middle of the day when his brain forgot to tell him how to swallow, and he drowned from the inside out. I remember thinking as a little kid how crazy it was that someone, an old person who had been swallowing his whole life, could simply forget how to swallow. It had scared the hell out of me and for a while as a kid I would stare at my throat in the mirror at least once a day, swallowing, trying to teach it how to swallow on its own for when the day came that I would forget how to swallow.

"Baby, do you need a nurse?" Julia asked, worried, feeling my forehead. I shook my head slowly, staring straight ahead. I felt a tear collecting itself in the far corner of my left eye and escape with gay liberation. Julia stared at me but I could not move my eyes her way, afraid that she would evaporate. She wiped away the wet and lay down next to me, burying her nose in my shoulder. We lay there for some time, maybe half an hour until she said, "How have you been, baby?"

"Okay," I croaked. She asked if I was sure. I told her "I think so."

"I talked to your mother a lot," she whispered. I asked her what about.

"Oh lots of stuff, mainly you, when you were a kid." I did not want to talk, especially about me. I just hoped the one single solitary episode was not brought up when I tried on a pair of her underwear because it looked so soft and lacy and clean, and had since become legend in my mother's circle of Tupperware friends and probably countless Psychology 101 lecture halls across North America. "She told me all kinds of crazy things. Do you remember at all climbing on the roof of your house at night and pointing out different constellations and trying to throw rocks through them?" I didn't remember that at all. "And you were always trying to save baby birds." I did remember that. "And how you almost burned the house down playing with a bottle of her hair spray and a cigarette lighter when she was taking a bath." I kind of remembered that but had tried to block it out. "All she talked about was you, the whole time."

"That must have gotten pretty boring," I thought to myself.

"We saw you on tv. We knew you were coming."

I startled and rolled over. "You saw me on tv?"

"Yeah. Pretty weird. Your mother watched all day. She even watched the satellite feed from Tibet that didn't have sound to it. We saw you went from Silverthorne to Idaho Springs and then disappeared so we thought that maybe you were on your way here. We assumed you were coming but we couldn't really figure out why you kept disappearing. What were you doing?"

"I'll explain all of that later."

"It's totally, totally weird, Eliason, all that stuff that happened."

"Tell me about it."

"They're going to give you a billion dollars, for sure?"

"No, just a million."

We lay there thinking about a million dollars; at least that was what I thought we were thinking about. I was thinking about Julia being alive again and I was so damn grateful.

"We knew you were coming," she repeated. I asked why they were so certain, and told her that I wouldn't have been too convinced if I had been the two of them.

"Eliason, baby, I know you think you're the worst person in the world, but I know who you really are inside, better than you do. I knew you'd get down here somehow."

It made me feel a little sick inside, all the nice things she said. "Willy drove me."

She nodded and said, "That's what I figured. I told your mother it'd be a miracle if that junky old Camaro made it."

"It didn't. We got a ride from someone," but I couldn't tell her about the Bells, at least not yet, and she didn't probe.

"What about the Aspen guys?"

"You remember about them?" I asked.

"Of course. Why not?"

"I just thought you'd be kind of distracted with everything else going on." She always surprised me, old Julia. I said, "I don't know what's going to happen. I guess they'll get there and see we're closed and take their money somewhere else."

"That would be pretty dumb." She turned her head toward the curtain, as if she was looking through it at my mother. "When did you get here? Did you talk to your mother?"

"She was sleeping," I said. "I haven't been here very long. I think she might be," and I tried to pick better words, "she's kind of, I think actually she might be sort of dead already."

"Jesus!" Julia propped herself up in a flash but I held her by the arm. She looked at me in what appeared to be anger almost, surprise.

"Can we just let her sleep?" I asked.

"Of course we cannot just let her sleep," and she began to get up.

"I just want to lay here with you for a while and not think about anything. She's probably just sleeping."

She looked at me, started to make a movement out of the bed, then halted. "Eliason, don't you at least want to see her?"

"I saw her. She looked almost like she was smiling. I kind of want to remember her like that, if I have to."

She stared at me, pretended like she was going to lie down again then rappelled over me and vaulted to the floor. "Whoever heard of such a thing, letting your mother just lie there, are you crazy?" and she pulled the curtain aside, touched my mother's arm and leaned down close to her for some seconds. "Jesus Eliason," and she turned to me, "don't scare me like that again." She came back over to the bed. "Don't joke like that again. Don't talk about your mother like that. You can't say that she's 'sort of dead.' You have to say to people that she passed or went to a better place or something like that, when that time comes. Have a little respect for your mom."

I did. I *did* want to always remember my mother lying there like a little girl, before the world killed off everything that she cared about. And I looked around the room at all the balloons and flowers and cards and of all the people who obviously cared about her, and I thought that I might have misjudged my mother for a long time.

Julia made me move over and lay back down on the bedside closest to my mother. She lay there for so long that I thought she might have fallen asleep. I touched the back of her hand and she opened her eyes.

"I should have come with you, on Thursday," I said.

"It's okay, baby. I got over that a long time ago," she said. She fidgeted for a bit and said, "I didn't do it."

"Do what?" I asked stupidly.

She lay still then gazed over at my mother and then turned to me. "I didn't go to the clinic at all. I decided not to have the abortion."

Then I said the one worst possible word I could have said: "Why?" and realized it was the worst possible thing I could have said, other than "Why not," so I quickly added, "I mean, it's okay, that's good. Why not?"

She touched my hand and said, "I thought you would be mad or go crazy."

"No," I said, and felt like a real idiot, that I would make Julia feel that way, that she could mistake my weakness or immaturity or fear for being mad, or worse, for madness.

"When did you change your mind?" she asked.

"About the second that you left Leadville."

"Wow," she said, lost in a thought. "Even before all the Derfy Burger stuff?" she asked. I nodded. She said, "You know, I had kind of mentally taken you out of the process right when I left. I got madder and madder the closer we got to Boulder and thought you were a stupid boy, and Katie was getting me all riled up too. You know she had an abortion a couple of years ago, after she met that guy from Durango? Remember he just packed up and left and we never saw him again and nobody knew why, that jerk with the beard? Dirk?" I did remember him—I thought he was kind of nice. "Anyway, she said it wasn't a big deal and you didn't deserve an opinion about what I did at that point, whether I did it or not. You waited too long, baby." She stalled. "Why weren't you there for me, Eliason?" and she began to cry, almost despite herself, self-consciously it seemed, gently so as not to awaken my mother. I wanted the mattress to swallow me whole and I held her right up against me. Maybe some day, way in the future, I would be able to tell her why I wasn't there, if I could think up something believable. But right then, I didn't know why I had not been there for her. But she cried for about only half a minute.

"I promised myself I wouldn't cry, but people are always promising themselves that they won't cry when it's the thing they know they'll end up doing anyway, isn't it?"

"I guess," I said. "There's nothing wrong with crying." I touched her belly and rubbed it just a little. It was firm and maybe just starting to get bumpy but nothing that was noticeable. I would never have guessed if I already had not known what was going on in there. "I was pretty sure you were in there, in the clinic."

"It's terrible isn't it? I would have been if not for your mother, if Nurse Betty hadn't called me. She got ahold of me on the way down here. She said she called your apartment but the guy who answered the phone sounded a little weird or drunk or something—not very reliable. She said she called the shop and left a message but she didn't know if you'd get it. Baby, it's really time for you to get a mobile phone. The only reason she called me was because I was on the emergency contact list so she called me and said your mom was not doing so great. I thought it was more important to see her so I got Katie to drop me off first thing. I didn't know the clinic was right across the street. That was kind of lucky. I had an appointment for Friday morning so I had most of Thursday to spend with your mother. That was pretty lucky." She stifled a yawn. "Your mom was really surprised and happy to see me but I could tell she felt pretty cruddy and was putting on a good face for me—not much sleep for both of us."

"So why didn't you go to your appointment?"

She took a long time to answer. She sighed heavily, a real sigh, not a Hollywood sigh. "I don't know. We'd been talking for a long, long time, just about all kinds of things, a lot about you and me and life and stuff, and at one point she reached out and held my hand and didn't let go. I don't know baby, I don't know why then, I just knew that I couldn't destroy something that we had created."

My throat and chest and brain all knotted up then fluttered as I lie there. She rolled over and kissed me lightly on the cheek.

"I wouldn't say that she talked me out of doing it, not at all. She said she's too much of a psychologist to say something that she knew sounded like an order instead of advice." She laughed softly to herself. "She said advice is really just a more subtle demand anyway. She laughed at that."

I lay there still with a knotted throat and nodded a little. Julia knew I wasn't capable of speech yet.

"So in a way, she talked me out of doing it, or at least waiting for a little longer. But by then I had decided not to do it. I would have been in that clinic otherwise, Eliason. We heard the explosion even here in the room. She saved my life. And our baby."

And I think it was really the first time I thought physically, mentally, everything, about being a father, that it was going to happen, that we were going to have a baby. For a moment I felt absolute terror. And then I got runner's high again, lying down without running. I felt oddly peaceful and content and kind of warm. I hoped it would last more than a few minutes. My mother had saved Julia's life, indeed, and our baby's life, twice in a way.

"I don't know how to tell you what else," Julia said. "I mean, it's kind of, I think you'll think it's kind of a big deal, what else she told me."

I shook my head. "I don't want to know."

"I don't know. I think you should."

"I'm adopted."

"What?"

"You're going to tell me I'm adopted or something."

"No, actually. Why do you think that?"

I shrugged. "I don't. It just seems like something else you might tell me right now."

"It's a couple of things, actually."

"A couple of things?!" Oh great. I could handle one thing, but a couple of things? "What is it?" I asked, not really wanting to.

"Um, you were supposed to have a twin," she said, then added abruptly, "There were lots of problems and your twin died before the two of you were even delivered, kind of."

"What do you mean, 'kind of.' How does someone just kind of die?"

She looked at me sarcastically I think. "Well, there were complications in the womb I guess and the doctors told your mother that if she went full-term she had a ninety percent chance of losing both of you."

"Okay, well that didn't happen," I said.

She inhaled. "Yeah, I suppose. That was good."

I lay there and waited but she said nothing else. "Why'd you tell me that? Is that it?" I asked.

She was listless. "No." She seemed unwilling to go further and glanced at my mother.

"What is it? What else?" I asked.

"They told your mother that one of the twin's chances of survival would be a lot better if there was only one baby. So that's what she did."

"What?" I asked stupidly.

She looked at me incredulously. "She chose you, Eliason. The doctors had to, you know, kill the other baby and deliver it stillborn, which worked in a way, I guess, because you survived."

"Jesus," I said. I watched a balloon come to life and start weaving back and forth in front of the heating vent. "Why are you telling me this right now?" I grabbed my skull with both hands and squeezed. "Why did she do it?"

"She had to, Eliason."

I watched the balloon bob up and down. "Why did she pick me though?"

"Are you asking a rhetorical question or do you want the truth?" she asked. I looked at her, not knowing that there was a "truth" part of it. I thought the truth part had already come.

"You were stronger, that's what the doctors told her, because you were kind of," and she stopped, glancing at me, "you were kind of killing off your twin somehow, I don't know how exactly. Something of yours was wrapped around something else and you had been kind of killing off the other baby over time by taking all the nutrients or something, not that you could help it."

I lay there and didn't say a word.

"You were stronger and had a better chance of making it. It's just part of nature. Baby, it made sense to choose one of you."

"Why are you telling me this?"

"Because your mother thought it was important that you know."

"Jesus, I'm a murderer."

"Don't be silly."

"I'm a murderer," I said miserably.

"I knew I shouldn't have said anything. I knew you'd feel guilty but your mom said I had to. Eliason, don't be silly. You weren't even born yet."

"I could have had a brother," I said, thinking of all the possibilities of having a brother: playing ball, spitting, throwing stones off bridges at floating paper cups, running away from home, coming back. I could hardly stand it.

"Actually, the twin was a girl," Julia said, and I knew that the second she said it she knew she had made a mistake because I jumped like a shock of electricity. She immediately rolled over and held me tightly, apologizing over and over and over.

"A girl? I killed my own sister? I killed my own sister!"

"It's not that way at all, Eliason. You had nothing to do with it."

"I had everything to do with it—I was strangling her and taking all her nutrients and vitamins and whatever just so I could be stronger! I had everything to do with it."

"You were just a fetus, you didn't even know."

I lay there silently, staring straight ahead. Julia started muttering how she knew she shouldn't have said anything, how she knew I would react this way, that I would feel guilty.

"Well wouldn't you if you had killed your own sister? I should have a sister right now."

"You do," she said and I jumped again. She released me and pulled back a little, staring hard at me. "Why don't you sleep for a little?"

"I can't sleep Julia. What do you mean I have a sister?" She shook her head. I said, "Like I have a sister in my heart or something? Like her soul is with me? You know I don't believe that kind of rubbish."

She shook her head again. "It's too much right now, baby. Why don't you sleep?"

I lay there and closed my eyes. "You know I can't really believe in that spiritual stuff if you're trying to make me feel better. I don't have some twin soul out there watching over me, finding my lost keys and stuff. I don't believe that stuff."

"You could believe it," she said. "It's not impossible."

"I've never really *felt* anything though."

"Well, you couldn't really feel it if you didn't know about it first, could you?"

It didn't seem to make sense to me. I kept my eyes closed. If you're supposed to feel something, you're not supposed to know about it, or you don't have to know about it first, right? That's the whole point of *feeling* it instead of knowing it. "I don't get it."

"Sleep, baby."

"I can't, Julia." I kept my eyes closed. My bones felt sore lodged behind my muscles and poking against the inside of my skin. The tendons in my neck felt made of rope. My eyeballs felt blistered. Julia heaved a major sigh my way. I asked why she was sighing. She halfway rolled my way and I felt her staring at me.

"You have a real life sister out there."

I didn't move at all. I didn't even open my eyes.

"God Eliason, it's too much right now. Your mom's making me say it."

I continued to lie there with my eyes closed, not moving. Julia put her arm across my chest and breathed in heavily. Everything in my body was immobile and unresponsive.

"Okay, but…okay, your mom told me to tell you and that's the only reason I'm saying anything. She didn't feel like she could do it. But when you talk to her, maybe you can, then you can decide if, I don't know what. I don't know where to start…I guess she met this guy when she was in college. It wasn't a big deal she said. They thought they were in love but she said it was the sixties—everybody was in love. Your mother got pregnant and the guy got drafted to Vietnam about a month later. He was killed like two weeks after he got there, before the child was even born. So your mother gave the baby up for adoption. She didn't think she was ready to be a mother."

Jesus Christy Christ. Jesus Chris Christ. Jesus Cesar Christ. No big deal.

"My god, Julia. Did my father know about all of this?" I heard a creaky voice from my throat asking.

"Yeah. She told him pretty early on when they started going out and getting serious. It was an open-record adoption so she told him the girl could show up on their doorstep at any time. She didn't want to surprise him if she just turned up one day. She said your dad was pretty cool with it at all."

I thought to myself how my dad had been about the mellowest dude ever.

"Your mom never talked to her daughter and she said she kept in pretty good touch with the adopted couple for a while but she hasn't heard from them in a really long time, like eighteen years now. They just kind of lost touch. Your mom thought it might be healthier for everyone to just get on with their lives."

I kept my eyes closed and did a little mental math. "She's pretty old then?"

"She turns thirty-six next month your mom said."

"She's way older than me."

"Of course. I mean, your mother had to get over a lot of stuff and then meet your father and then be sure about everything with him and then she said she had trouble getting pregnant, so it took your parents a long time to have you."

"You mean 'us,' the two of us," I said miserably, thinking of my twin.

Julia said sharply, "Yeah, and you can imagine what your mother went through making a decision like that so don't go telling me you're a murderer. I won't listen to it. Your mother said she always felt like she had been made to pay some kind of price with your twin, for giving up your sister." She pulled her arms tightly around herself and sobbed. I pulled on her arms and tried to untie her.

"Why are you crying?" I whispered.

"Because your mother had to go through so much, way more than one person should ever have to, all by herself. She didn't have anyone. She never talked about your father did she?"

I thought for a few seconds. "No, actually." Then I thought a little more. It was true; she never had. "Why?"

"She didn't want to keep hurting you by talking about him. That's what she said, so she had to keep it all in."

I had never thought much about it. I whispered, "I just sort of thought that she had gotten over it real quick and it wasn't such a big deal, like she was trying to be strong or something. I thought she was just bitter about it all."

Julia put her fingers on her closed eyelids. "She said she never really knew what to do. Even after studying all that stupid psychology she said she didn't know the best way to help her own son so she didn't say anything. It was the worst thing to do." She turned her puffy red eyes my way and waited for me to say something. Usually I would have just sat there and said something like "Hmmph."

"I don't know. I never really put that much thought into it. It just happened."

Julia rubbed her eyes hard. "Your mother said you began to pull away from her when you got older, because you had gotten over the grief of losing your dad but that you never really forgave her for looking like she didn't care about him dying."

"That's just her psychology books talking," I said gently. I opened my eyes and glanced at her. She wasn't as tightly wrapped around herself, but she had her arms crossed over her chest, her eyes closed. I watched her for a while. She sighed and put her arms down by her side.

"Maybe she's right," I admitted.

"I think she might have been, baby. And that's okay."

"Yeah," I said softly, turning to look at my mother. I thought I saw her stir but knew my eyes were just fooling me. "Did she say she ever regretted what she did?"

"Giving up your sister, or the other time?"

"Both I guess."

Julia lay there, sifting through her thoughts for a second. "She certainly would have wanted both of you to live, of course. But she said she trusted what the doctors said and she definitely never regretted choosing you over your twin. She's very proud of the way you turned out, Eliason. She says you're a humble, caring, gentle person. And she's right. She said you're going to be the best Mr Derfy Burger they ever could have hoped for." She grabbed my hand and squeezed it. She sighed lightly. "She said she regrets giving up your sister in a way, you know, not ever talking to her or seeing how she turned out, but you can't go back and do it over she said. She knew it was the best thing to do, but she always wondered what could have been. Or that she deprived you in a way, or kind of lied to you by never telling you about her. All your life your mother worried that you thought you would be alone if something ever happened to her. And now you find out you were not alone, that you have family out there."

"Kind of took a long time to find out," I said. The balloon floating just below the ceiling lost its vibrating life as I heard the heat turn off with a low creak. "Do you think I should try to find her?"

"You've got a lot of things going on. Leave it for a while, baby. Let it soak in a little. She might not be ready to be known as the sister of the most famous person on the planet."

"Yeah," I said. I think she was trying to be funny but I was too drained to laugh. "I've got to go call Willy and tell him you're okay. Stay here and try to sleep." I got up slowly, like the oldest man on the oldest planet in the oldest part of the universe. I flipped the blanket over

Julia and took off her other shoe. She closed her eyes and immediately fell asleep. In the lobby I spoke to Willy briefly on Jesus-Cesar's phone. He insisted on hearing Julia's voice but I told him that she and my mother were both sleeping. Lupita was nowhere around so I returned to the room and closed the door quietly behind me. I knew just by looking at my mother, before I even pulled up short, felt my heart bump against my sternum, and walked up next to her bed to stand over her, that she was no longer in her body. Her chest did not rise and fall. Her body was merely a broken down human machine that I was looking at now, beyond repair or resuscitation. I stared at the scar on her chin and thought about how long ago it had happened, a person's whole lifetime ago, though hers was shorter than other's. It didn't seem fair. For some reason that I can't even tell you about now, I thought about a friend of mine from high school, Henry, who was hit by a car our senior year and died. His life had been so short and I had wondered at the time if his eternity would be a little longer than an old person's. It didn't make sense of course, but it made sense when I was standing over his casket that cool spring day, watching a hummingbird darting in and out of his Henry's flowers. I had wanted it to make sense for Henry at that moment because he had been a really nice, quiet guy. And it made sense somehow now. I wasn't sure what released my mother's soul when it was supposed to go, why she was dead now but she had not been thirty minutes before, why she floating up above me, released by her physical tether to reality, or was she sucked into the center of the earth, pulled in by gravity? Both made sense, and both made no sense. I was not happy and I was not sad, I was just standing over her and reached out a hand, because I couldn't quite believe that she was dead, that she wasn't just sleeping, that she wasn't in there anymore, and I brushed her cheek with the back of my hand. I reached across her body and unlatched her little gold wristwatch, turned the hands back an hour and put it in my pocket, then I gently lifted the sheet and put her arm underneath, gently so as not to rip out the I.V. held by the tape, pulling the sheet up to her chin. She looked so much like she was sleeping that I readjusted her pillow for her. And I stood over her as I had done when she was still alive. And I just stood there, imprinting her face on my mind. The door opened quietly behind me and Lupita peeked in. She asked how my mother was in a whisper.

"She's okay. Just sleeping," I whispered back.

"Okay, I won't disturb her then. I'll be up front if you need anything. Goodnight, Eliason."

"Thanks Lupita," I said and she sealed the door silently. I was thankful that she had not cleared anything from the room—my mother had believed in reincarnation and I looked at a styrofoam cup on the table, a withered rose, another balloon that was beginning to sag to the floor, and thought I should hoard them away, in case she accidentally slipped into one of them. I stepped lightly over to the other bed, quietly so I wouldn't disturb my mother's heavy journey into the ether, if she was still lingering, and I lay down next to Julia, taking her head into the crook of my arm where she nestled in closer.

"How are you baby?" she mumbled, but I knew she was more asleep than awake and would not remember this moment in the morning.

"I don't know," I whispered and turned my head to watch my mother, to see if I would notice anything leaving her. I lay there awake waiting for the dull gray light of morning that never arrived. The hospital started making morning noises before the light came, indistinct clankings of metal, spoons and forks, squeaks of wheels, murmured voices, though these were fewer because it was Sunday. Julia awoke, stretched, and began to get out of the bed to check on my mother, her stockinged feet softly patting the floor.

"We need to just go," I told her as she put on her shoes.

"What do you mean?" she asked, straightening and standing. "What time is it?"

"We just need to go," I repeated. I stood up, took her by the arm, stood between her and my mother and began to shepherd her by the bed. She stopped still then stared into my eyes without even looking at my mother.

"She's passed away? Oh Eliason," she said, grabbing my hand, turning to look at my mother. "When?"

"Sometime during the night. Can we just go now?" I asked.

"Yes," she whispered. "We'll tell someone at the front desk. Oh baby. Are you okay?"

"Yeah. It's okay," I said. I pulled my mother's watch from my pocket. It was exactly 6:43 a.m.

CHAPTER THIRTY-ONE

"The Liberated Bells and the Derfy Cage, August 2001"

Julia and I were on the train somewhere just north of Barcelona when I got a call from Willy. I had been doing the EuroTasticDerfy Tour for over a year, dipped down into northern Africa for the AfridelikaDerfy Tour within-a-tour for about four months, and was back up in Europe doing a tour-within-a-tour of a tour-tour. Needless to say my brains were scrambled but we had spent a wonderful day in the north of Spain.

Willy had kept me current on the trial of the guy who blew up the abortion clinic, but I was only about half-listening when he phoned because I had a hell of a sunburn and putting the phone right next to my face made my ear feel like a shriveled, wrinkly, just-out-of-the-oven ShrinkiDink. Willy had told me a while before that the man who blew up the clinic had tried pleading insanity at first, I think, but that didn't work. Then he had tried claiming self-defense for the unborn, but that hadn't worked either, or something. Willy had told me about this part when I was somewhere on the train between Prague and Zakopane and I was a little hung-over on Czech beer so the details were a little hazy. Then there had been the problem of how many people exactly the guy had killed: there was the doctor, a receptionist at the front desk and five girls at the clinic, so that was seven. But what about the unborn? Four of the girls were at various stages of pregnancy (one of the girls was not pregnant at all—she was only fourteen and was at the clinic because she was nervous that she might have gotten pregnant from kissing). Although the guy was a hero to the right-to-lifers, they had to concede by their definition that he had killed eleven people. There had even been an argument for some weeks, after the receptionist's husband had even been forced to testify that his wife might have been pregnant because they had "made whoopy" just four days prior to her murder, that the guy might have killed twelve people, but the defense did not follow up on that one.

"Yes, globe-trotting chief, I said 'the defense,'" Willy said, waiting for noises of shock from my end of the phone but I had been looking at something out the train window, an old Spanish church or a cloud or something. "It appears the defense has decided to use the old conservative Iron Skillet Approach: if one thing sticks then everything must stick, so keep the pan but scrape the mercy out of it until it looks clean. He may have killed seven of the already-born but he was in fact saving the lives of four, possibly five, of the unborn." There was silence as I thought about how warm the sun had felt on my face, so soothing. I think Willy had been expecting me to say something but I had forgotten what he had been talking about. "Pensive warrior, do you know what the newspapers are calling the murderer? The BK Assassin. That stands for the 'Baby Killer Assassin.' Eliason, is this big news in Europe at all? I was in the drug store yesterday and 180 Eleanor (she was on the drugstore bowling team in the city league and was known town-wide for her consistent 180-185 score) asked me where we would be if Mary, the mother of Jesus, had had an abortion. Had I had more time I would have mentioned where we might be had Frau Schicklgruber had an abortion as well. But I was only buying cough syrup and did not wish to get into a religio-philosopho-historical debate with the fine elderly dame."

A roly-poly little Spanish lady rolling a cart of drinks and potato chips and chocolate bars through the aisle of the train stopped at me and looked perplexed. After a couple of seconds she smiled, fumbled excitedly with a packet of napkins on her cart, then held out a pen and the napkin for an autograph. She offered me a free bag of prawn-flavored potato chips in thanks. She just kept smiling and nodding at me a million times so I did the same to her. I reached into my pants pocket and gave her some kind of note, five-thousand pesos or something and she started cooing and smiling even more, giving me another bag of chips with a picture of a red pepper on the front. I'd give those to Julia. Money didn't really mean much anymore, in the sense that I had so much of it and that the denominations of different countries from kroners to pounds to zlotys meant nothing to me so I was tossing them around like flyers for a new nightclub. I became aware of the sound of Willy's voice again like the annoying background buzz of Dave's tinnitus.

"However, and this is where the media are having 'a field day'—the pro-choice proclaimers have been forced to stick to their old definition, that the unborn are truly not born and cannot be counted as a life. Thus, little chief—are you listening?" I heard Willy say from somewhere. I began nervously watching a little kid with sticky-up hair and a lollipop staring at me—I knew he was going to start going bonkers suddenly and start shouting something about Senyor Hamburguese de Derfy or something like some other kid had done two days earlier on the train from Lisbon to Oviedo, almost causing a rail-line riot. When Derfy's got over this idea of making me travel the world like a commoner my life would get much easier. I had already asked Jerry Piper what had happened to the DerfiBird chopper but he only shushed me and said air space was at a premium in Europe. Willy continued, "So, the BK Assassin would be 'put away in the slammer' for 4,800 years if convicted of killing eleven people as opposed to seven people, not an insignificant number because he would only get 2,100 years, give or take a couple hundred years, if convicted of killing seven. The pro-choice people would like to see the bigger number given to him. As I have been arguing for weeks at the coffee shop, naturally, he is quite unlikely to see the end of either tenure."

"That's pretty crazy," I said, keeping an eye on the lollipop kid.

"You my friend may be somewhat gratified to know, in a telephone poll with an error margin of only plus or minus two points, that the BK

Assassin has become 'slightly more interesting' to the average American housewife this week than Mr Derfy Burger by 63 percent to 38 percent. Global chieftain, you have been out of the country for too long to hold our attentions."

"That's good I guess," I told him.

"If it makes you feel better, your numbers had 'skyrocketed' several weeks ago when Burger Kween leaked to the press that the BK Assassin was actually an agent working for Derfy Burger aiming to smear the BK image. That Burger Kween, who prefer their shortened nomenclature of BK because it is much hipper with the tween crowd, shares the very two same letters as the BK Assassin was just too coincidental to company executives, or to their shareholders more pointedly, or to their lawyers more exactly. It has become the conspiracy theory of the moment. Has it ensnared our Euro comrades as it has the American public?"

"I don't think so," I told him. "But I can't really understand what anybody around me is saying and I can't really read the newspapers. I kind of doubt that some guy killing a doctor in Colorado is much of a big deal here. They think everyone in America walks around with guns killing each other anyway."

"Shocking! I hope you are 'cleaning up' or image, burger man," Willy said.

"Kind of, I guess. A couple of months ago we made a surprise two-day excursion into Pakistan for a 'turn in your Kalishnikov, get a free bag of fries' campaign but it didn't turn out too well. Piper accidentally told me that it was really just a media stunt to boost Derfy's falling numbers in Pakistan. Man, Julia caught wind of that one and really went off on him. That's why we were there for just two days. We were supposed to be there for a week but we went to Afghanistan for the rest of the time instead. They didn't seem as angry but they still didn't seem to like me too much. I mean, they were polite and everything and kept giving me tea all the time, but they just didn't seem too crazy about us being there. We did spend one night in Saudi Arabia—very nice, Willy. Man, the hotel was huge."

"Listen to you, little chief, reeling off countries like some sort of amateur cartographer. Color me impressed."

"I know, dude. I've been trying to study up on Uzbekistan, Khazakstan and a bunch of other 'stan countries but they all kind of sound and look the same after a while. Julia is trying to teach me mnemonics or something to help learn them but it's not working very well. She's using it or something with Veronica to teach her a bunch of foreign phrases I think."

"At a year and a half?! She is a natural-born genius. Has young Veronica learned to say 'Uncle Willy' yet?"

"No, but it really sounds like she babbles the same way in Russian, Serbian, Polish and Ukrainian."

"Naturally—they are all from the Slavic family, are they not? Young Julia is going to be a child of the world. That is tremendous. And how is your Julia?"

"She's okay. Man, she really had to fight the Derfy machine when we got here. They tried to say that Veronica had to eat just Derfy baby food because it would look bad if she was always eating fruits and vegetables and stuff in pictures but Julia said no way. They're both eating only natural stuff here in Europe. She said it wasn't such a big deal in the States since you can't really find any natural food anymore but it became a real issue with her here."

"She is rock solid, your Julia." There was a moment of silence, which I sensed as Willy giving me a three-second dramatic pause. I was right.

"Chieftain, recall when I told you that the police had found pieces of the Bells' Monte Carlo strewn all over the Boulder Derfy's parking lot? But they never found any bodies?"

"Yeah, but you said the police really botched the investigation, didn't they, because they assumed the car was tied to the abortion guy somehow and they never checked *inside* the car, or at least what was left of it? Didn't they have the car put through some kind of compactor and turned into scrap metal or something?"

"Yes, it is true. You remember it well," Willy said, which was surprising because he had told me all about it when Julia and I were on the train between Grenoble and Dijon and those insane Frenchies almost derailed the train when they found out that Mr Derfy Burger was on board. We were in Javier Boeve country and barely made it out alive. I could have killed Piper for that move. Willy said, "Well, somehow, someone in the FBI connected the car at the Boulder Derfy's with the damaged restaurants in Silverthorne and Idaho Springs. That was a real genius move, that one. It took them only a year to figure out that all three were connected."

"But no one was killed, right? Did they just find out that somebody was killed in one of the Derfy's or something?"

"Not exactly, but they decided to re-investigate the case. They had a little trouble unpacking the Monte Carlo since it was about the size of a soda can and they said that their findings were inconclusive, but they thought they detected some drops of blood on one portion of the soda can—sorry, the car. Therefore, someone could have been inside the car when it blew up. They did admit, however, that it could have just been ketchup."

"So Teddy and TJ were definitely in the car then, like you always thought?" I asked. I had held out hope that somehow, for some reason, they had not been in the car.

"It appeared to be so. I had read about the FBI investigation maybe six months ago but I refrained from telling you about it. I thought it would be a little depressing for you."

"Yeah, it is. Dang," I said. The little kid with the lollipop had gotten up and disappeared through a door that kept sliding open and slapping shut at every slight curve of the train tracks. Julia and Veronica had been in the dining car for a long time having lunch, and I was beginning to fear that we were going to get separated when the little kid revealed my identity to the benighted, as yet still-peaceful travelers and I would have to leap seats and people and luggage like a runner in Pamplona at the horn's edge of an angry bull.

"But little chief, here is the news that mayhaps should have been revealed first, to shield you from jumping to enormously erroneous conclusions. I received a postcard this morning from a far-flung land."

He said nothing else. I thought he was giving me the four-second pause this time.

"Was it from those two Japanese chicks looking for Smoky or something?" I asked. I heard a swallow, a sigh, then what sounded like the bristly wiping of latte foam from a white-blond mustache.

"Just a sec, chief, I spilled a little 'cino on my sweat top," then I heard the hard sound of a phone bouncing on a tabletop, the shuffling of sweatpants across a cold, vast room, the creak of the bathroom tap, the sound of old pipes rattling into action, water running, some murmured cursing, then the sound of bells above the front door tinkling as a customer walked in, conversation, the distinct sound of Marty the Mailman laughing, more conversation, the bells tinkling again, silence, more silence, the soft pat-pat-pat of moccasins across the floor, the flush of the toilet, more silence, the hum of one of the leather-stretching machines, Willy himself humming a little tune then a short, sharp note of surprise. "Hello?" said his hesitant voice into the phone.

"It's Eliason, Willy," I said, rather patiently.

"Goodness, how long have you been on the other end?" he asked. I told him "not long. You were telling me about some kind of postcard."

"Goodness yes, chieftain. Let us gather our thoughts. The postcard—oh yes, the postcard. It was from Australia." Silence again. I heard the front door bells tinkle.

"Willy, I'll kill you if you put the phone down again," I said in a rush.

"Indeed," Willy said. "It is merely the wind. Eliason, the strange and rather momentous news is that the postcard reads—" and I detected again the sound of phone against tabletop and sweatpant shuffling. Willy returned in a slightly shorter passage of time as before and read somewhat breathlessly, "The postcard reads: Dear Willy and Little Chieftain, all is well here. Stop. Opened a new restaurant. Stop. Best wishes. Stop. Miss Portia Sagoo and Shaunessy McNutter. Stop. " Silence.

"What does that mean?" I asked.

"Do you not recall these names?"

"I don't think so. I mean, why did they keep writing 'stop' all the time?"

"Never you mind that. It is merely an old habit from my years of temping at a Morse Code agency. Do you not recall those names?"

"Umm, I don't think so."

"You do not recall these unusual pseudonyms as those utilized by Teddy Bell upon meeting your very own Jerry Piper, in the parking lot in Idaho Springs? Actually, he called me 'Miss Portia Sagoo' but that is a mere syntactic detail."

"Yeah, I kind of remember that," I said, but it felt like a million years ago.

"You know what that means then?"

The train was getting really near to Barcelona and I had still not seen Julia or our daughter. I was getting that nervous feeling that only getting on and off trains in a strange land can give a normal person.

"Could there really be two people somewhere out there with those names? That's weird. What are the chances of them knowing each other though?" I said dumbly. The kid with the sticky-up hair was back but seemed to be distracted by some other kid with an ice cream cone. I was safe until Barcelona.

"On top of your geographical skills you have really honed your edges of sarcasm, chieftain," Willy said, though I didn't know what he was implying. "What this means is that Teddy and TJ Bell are alive, well and living 'Down Under.'" The train began its slow slide into the Barcelona train station.

"Willy, I've got to go. I have to find Julia and Veronica. That's incredible, really. Wow, man, that's really cool."

"Little chief, one more thing. Another lady came out, this time in International Falls, Minnesota, saying she is your sister."

"That makes four in three months, doesn't it?"

"Well, one of those ladies was claiming to be your aunt, but it is very much the same thing, is it not—sister, aunt, niece?"

"Kind of but not really. Did they give her name?"

"Yes, but it is not the one in your mother's documents."

"Okay. Keep a head's up if she's ever the real one. If not, we'll just wait until we're all ready, if ever."

"You bet, chieftain. As well, I have just about 'wrapped up' your memoirs. Very exciting."

I was silent. "My what's?"

"Writing your memoirs of course. Your life simply had to be documented."

"Jeez Willy, you didn't talk all about my troubles in science class and stuff did you?"

"I suppose your memoir, in actuality, is just one day in your life. I had a bear of a time keeping my authorial presence from creeping on to every page."

I looked for the ice cream kid again and yawned. I watched the sooty buildings leading into the Barcelona train station and wondered who lived inside them.

"'Tis true, chieftain. In my efforts to retain your 'voice,' to keep your spirit, I was less than intermittently 'dumbing down' every page, cleansing your vocabulary of multi-syllabic words. It was rather difficult, chieftain."

I hadn't really been listening to Willy. "Did you make a bunch of stuff up, dude?"

"Had to, I was not present in many scenes. But believe you me, I made you a more than sympathetic character. Dare I say, you might even come across as the type of person that a music video channel presenter would follow with a camera and make interesting to his/her viewers."

"Good job, Willy."

Willy cleared his throat. "I received a letter from Jesus-Cesar thanking you for the anonymous lump sum of money to pay for Lupita's nursing school. It did not take them long to figure out from whom it came. Despite your natural inclinations, little chieftain, you are a real sweetheart."

"Shut up," I said. I had wanted the money to be a secret, just because it makes it nicer that way. "Don't mention it in my memoirs. Hey, I'll give you a call from Morocco, in a couple of days." I hung up and sprinted through the aisles to find Veronica sleeping in Julia's lap in the dining car.

"The Bells are alive," I shouted.

"What?!"

I lay in bed that night and thought about Teddy and TJ. They had accomplished what they wanted, in a small way. They had knocked out two Derfy Burgers and made a mess of the parking lot in a third. They would never take Derfy down, Teddy knew that. They did not start an anti-Derfy crusade as in France. No one took Teddy's lead and started an anti-Derfy campaign, which was pretty depressing. But they were living free. All was well, as Teddy had written. Nobody knew who they were or where they were, except for Willy, Julia and me. I smiled a little to myself. Suddenly there was a loud rap at the door and Jerry Piper yelled loudly, obnoxiously from the other side that we were getting up at six sharp to leave for Madrid, two days in Madrid, one in Valencia then a long flight to New Zealand.

"I'll kill him if he wakes up Veronica," I whispered.

"She's okay," Julia said half-asleep next to me.

"Julia, isn't New Zealand pretty close to Australia?" I asked quietly.

"Yes," she lisped sleepily, "right next door."

"Hmmph," I said.

"I love you, baby," she said, almost fully asleep now. She rolled over and breathed rhythmically, peacefully. Veronica lay in her Derfy crib and slept. I lay there myself in the dark with my eyes open and listened to the Spanish radio on its lowest volume. I thought of the Bells, and smiled to myself again, nervously. New Zealand beckoned.

EPILOGUE

"The Hills and Ghosts of the Ebro, August 2001"

Julia had impetuously jumped off the train with Veronica in her arms, squealing delightedly. I informed her through the window, anxiously, that this little village of five houses and six horses was definitely not Madrid.

"I know but look how sunny and bright it is. And they sell beer. Buy us a couple please please please. I'll wait here with Veronica."

"But the train only stays here for like, two minutes. It'll leave without us."

"You know the trains in Spain never run on time. Let's just stay here for a day or two and get away from stupid Piper-head and the Derfy beast."

I jumped to the platform and Julia grabbed me by the arm as I whisked by her.

"Look at the nice couple sitting at the table," she said, glancing at a couple sitting in the shade of the building. The woman's hat was on the table. He was trying to flag down a waitress just inside the doorway.

"They look hot as hell," I said.

"She's beautiful. Look at her. She's almost glowing. She's like an angel."

"I guess," I said. The woman was staring off into the distance, kind of lost, I thought. I scooted into the little building and kept an eye on the train. The waitress came in abruptly behind me, grabbed two beers and brought them to the couple. I swear I heard her say "stupid American" under her breath as she came back in, said something else in Spanish and a little man behind the bar poured two glasses of clear liquid into two short glasses. The waitress grabbed them and went back outside. I leaned on the bar and peered through the open door at the train. I watched Julia swinging Veronica in her arms. She was singing some nursery rhyme she had learned in Belgrade about a little girl named Tanja chasing her little red ball down by the river or something while Veronica giggled crazily. The man gave me the beers finally and I gave him something like a ten-thousand peso bill, I don't know. He looked surprised when I motioned for him to keep the change and he cried "Viva America!!"

"Here's your beer. Ice cold," I said happily to Julia. The train was still at the platform. Julia was staring at the couple and looking somewhat troubled. I asked if she was okay.

"Yeah, it's just, I don't know," she said, peering at the man and woman. I gazed at them and noticed the woman staring at the tabletop. A cloud rolled in over the fields. I exhaled with relief at the shaded respite from the overbearing sun. I told Julia I loved her. She removed her stare from the couple and smiled at me faintly.

"You know baby, the day you finally admitted to yourself that you were in love with me was the day you started losing something that a man should never lose when he falls in love with a woman."

"I can't guess…."

The End